Praise for Cryssa

SEVERED KNOT

"Bleakly impossible choices face the protagonists ... brutal aftermath of civil war. Stark but involving tale of early colonial exploitation strongly centres on an indomitable Scottish hero."

Historical Novel Society
2018 New Novel Award

"A richly atmospheric seventeenth century voyage through war, slavery, courage and hope. Mairead and Iain capture your heart and hold you hostage long past the final chapter. Unputdownable."

Elizabeth St. John
Author of *The Lydiard Chronicles*

TRAITOR'S KNOT

"This exceptional historical novel is a gripping tale of love and jealousy rife with unexpected twists and poignant moments that whisks readers on an unforgettable journey into the past."

Historical Novel Society

"Cryssa Bazos has crafted a complex, entertaining and multi-faceted story in which secrets and intrigue abound and in which the stakes are continually raised."

Romantic Historical Reviews

"A gripping tale of courage, love, and enduring commitment, a story that is well-imagined and executed with grace and mastery."

Readers' Favorite

"*Traitor's Knot* by Cryssa Bazos is a historical novel that will blow your socks off and leave you eagerly awaiting more from this talented author who so effortlessly paints a picture of the past with such emotion that it will stay in your mind for days to come."

Books of All Kinds

"This is a wonderful novel - richly detailed . . . Cryssa Bazos is equally at home writing battle scenes as writing romance, and the pace keeps the reader turning the pages."

Deborah Swift, author *Pleasing Mister Pepys*

Severed Knot

CRYSSA BAZOS

Also by Cryssa Bazos

Traitor's Knot

For Jay Stewart
In Memoriam

Severed Knot

———◆———

Chapter 1

———◆———

Tothill Fields, Westminster
January 1652

The Ayrshire lad lay mouldering in a corner for days before their English captors thought fit to drag him out. This proved to be the only way to get past their gaolers: a bloated body seeping blood and foam.

Iain Johnstone watched as the door shut, heard the bolt slide into place. The meagre light from the corridor extinguished. One hundred twenty-four days a prisoner of war. Deep in his marrow, he feared that he'd never see Scotland again.

His world was confined to a stone cell filled with his broken countrymen, a plague of rats, and the fetid stench of shite; his only nourishment a cup of thin ale and a few ounces of bread each day. This the reward for following Charles the Second into England to regain his lost throne. Fortune never favoured the invaders—unless they were Oliver Cromwell. If Iain's mouth wasn't parched and filled with sores, he'd spit on the ground.

"A pox on the damned curs," Iain muttered to himself, and not for the first time. He leaned against a gnarled post, his muscles stiffened by the cold. His torn, hodden-grey cloak provided little

1

warmth. Though a couple of braziers were positioned at either end of the cell, there never seemed to be enough coals to heat the room beyond a few feet. Iain alternated between stamping his feet and pacing a short loop until exhaustion defeated him. Those who rested on the stone floor succumbed the fastest to gaol fever, their battle-worn bodies claimed by damp and misery.

Once a battalion of proud men, they had been driven to London like a herd of cattle. Now each and every one of them waited for the cull. Daily their numbers shrank. In this cell alone, one hundred beaten men had dwindled down to fifty. Bouts of wheezing coughs and streams of bloody spittle eventually settled into deafening silence. With every loss, Iain found it harder to call out the names of the newly dead, but he forced himself to do it. He hoped when death finally claimed him, someone would be there to announce that Iain Locharbaidh Johnstone was on his way to join his ancestors.

A racking cough seized him, and he doubled over, chest burning while he gasped for breath. Damn it, his bones would *not* be buried in this shitten land. They belonged in the hills of his forefathers and buried beside his wife, not dumped into the common fields of his enemy. No worse fate for a Scotsman.

A hand touched his shoulder. David Glencross leaned closer. "All right?"

"Aye," Iain said with effort, grateful for his brother-in-law's concern.

Glencross snorted. "You look like something the hound tossed up."

Iain scratched his tangled beard. "Mind yourself—you look far worse."

Glencross looked gaunt, his copper hair lank, his face pinched. "It would have been better if they'd killed us on the field," he said in a low voice. "Better than rotting in this hole."

2

There had been a time when Iain would have knocked Glencross out for the defeatist suggestion, but the bugger was right. Iain had been thinking the same thing.

Powick—the pass to Worcester. The name tasted like dirt in his mouth.

Iain and his men had held that bloody meadow against Cromwell's Ironsides for the better part of the day. The fighting had been thick around them, with each man determined not to give up his square foot of ground, but there was only so much they could do against an enemy surging like maggots over a carcass. Iain's helmet had taken the brunt of an enemy sword, and when he'd regained consciousness, he'd found himself heaped inside a prisoner van.

The wind whistled through a crack in the thin daub, carrying the scent of river mud. Iain clung to that breath of air. For one moment, he was home on the Middle Shires. Then a moan yanked him back to reality.

McCaul, Iain's oldest friend, lay two feet away, gripped by gaol fever. Once dark and bluff as a mountain, the man was now shrivelled, his ribs showing through his ripped tunic. Massive fists curled into claws, and he lay still. Too still. A yellow pallor tinged his sunken cheeks.

Iain had dodged those fists on more than one occasion. The two men had scrapped together since before they were breeched, but that didn't keep them from having each other's back.

"McCaul?" Iain's voice was painful and raw. He dropped to his haunches and nudged the man. No response. "Alan?"

Glencross caught Iain's eye and shook his head.

"McCaul, you'd better get up," Iain said. "I've bet Glencross that you'll beat him for the next scrap of bread, and I mean to collect, right." He waited for a response. Nothing. "Get up, man. I'm beginning to think you're favouring the lad for this wager. We've been mates longer."

McCaul's lips began to move. Iain bent closer and heard him murmur the words from an old song that spoke to the hope of returning . . .

"Home," McCaul whispered. The dying man's words were a fist driven into Iain's stomach. How was he to honour his friend's last request?

Damn.

Iain rubbed his forehead with the heel of his hand. "We'll go together, right." The lie filled his mouth like bile.

McCaul tugged on the necklace he always wore. Even this movement was too much for him.

"What about that?" Iain asked.

"Take . . . with you."

Iain laughed—a derisive, mocking bark. How could he? But McCaul's sunken eyes wouldn't allow him to turn away. "Promise," McCaul whispered.

One moment of peace. McCaul deserved at least that. "Aye." Iain bent over McCaul and lifted the chain over his head. He clenched it in his hand and the silver links bit into his skin. "Who should I give it to?"

Silence.

"Alan?" There would be no further response. McCaul's chest no longer rose or fell.

Iain bowed his head and turned away. *Another severed link.* McCaul had been the strongest man he knew, his mettle like tempered iron. For years, Iain had thought him indestructible. If McCaul had been felled by this damned ordeal . . .

Iain reached across, his hand no longer steady. Tenderly, he shut McCaul's eyes.

"He was a good man," Glencross said in a low tone.

"Aye," Iain replied thickly. The back of his throat felt like he had swallowed a fistful of burrs.

They stayed there for a moment, nurturing their silence, before Iain rose. A few had gathered around, but most paid no attention to them. Just another Scotsman who managed to go home, even if home was now in the heavens and not the shires.

Iain lifted his voice so that it carried to the far reaches of the room. He'd honour his friend's Highland roots. "Alan McCaul Vic Achan Vic Coull has passed from this earth. May he nae be forgotten."

He repeated it three times, and by the last, his voice cracked. He cleared his throat and stared past the heads of his countrymen.

Iain no longer feared that he'd never see Scotland again. He knew with absolute certainty that he wouldn't.

The door swung open, and a gaoler appeared at the entrance. They've finally come, Iain thought. He and Glencross had covered McCaul as best they could, but a full day had passed and no one had arrived to carry the body away. Iain worried McCaul would be like the Ayrshire lad. That wasn't going to happen to Alan McCaul. Not if Iain Locharbaidh Johnstone had something to say about it.

"Hey!" He pushed his way past the other prisoners to reach the gaoler. "There's a brave man that's gone to his Maker. Fetch a man of God to give him a proper blessing—preferably a Presbyterian one."

The gaoler looked past Iain to where McCaul lay. "Brave man? Looks like a bloody Scot to me. One less won't worry me none." He shrugged. "I'll get to it when I do."

The man was about to turn away when Iain grabbed him by the throat. The gaoler stretched on his toes to avoid having his windpipe crushed.

"I told you to bring a man of God," Iain snarled in his face. "I'll nae ask again, ye shitten bastard. Get someone now, or there'll be *two* bodies that'll need a blessing." The gaoler's face turned purple, and he spluttered a cry for help.

Two guards rushed in and pulled Iain off the gaoler. Before he could shake them off, they grabbed his arms and pinned them behind his back. Iain roared, but their hold tightened until he thought his shoulders would pop.

"Enough," a voice called out. "Gaoler, cease."

A lean, dark-haired man strode into the room, a sharp contrast to the grubbiness of the guards. His crisp, cream brocade coat showed off the duskiness of his skin. *A bloody Welshman by the look of him.*

"I have no time for this indulgence," the man said. "I've asked you to bring me a prisoner by the name of Captain Iain Johnstone."

The guards pulled Iain forward. "Your man," said the gaoler.

"Iain Locharbaidh Johnstone?"

The hairs on the back of Iain's nape lifted. This man knew his byname, even pronounced it correctly as Lockarbee. "Aye? What do you fockin' want?"

The Welshman ignored the question and turned to the gaoler. "Where is that private room you promised?"

"Aye, my lord. This way." He adjusted his cap and motioned for two soldiers to grab Iain.

They pushed him through the door and hurried him down a narrow corridor to a small room. A cracked window overlooked bleak, marshy fields. Iain squinted against the flood of sunlight. As his eyes adjusted, his attention locked on several earthen mounds. They stood out like fresh scabs. Iain couldn't tear his gaze away. That was where he would end up. Bitterness choked him. *Southron bastards.*

"A moment alone," the Welshman said to the gaoler, but the man made no attempt to leave. "Was there something in my order you didn't understand?"

"My fee." The gaoler struck out his grubby hand, bold-faced.

The Welshman smiled, but Iain wasn't fooled. He hadn't missed the flatness in the man's black eyes. "Send a boy to fetch it from Chief Justice Blackmore. 'Tis upon his business that I'm here."

The gaoler's eyes widened. "Pardon, my lord. I wasn't aware." He was already at the door. "Knock when you're ready."

The door clanged shut behind him.

Iain drew himself to his full height. He refused to show weakness before this one. "Who are you?"

"Nathaniel Lewis, barrister of Lincoln's Inn at your service." He selected a stool and, before he sat down, dusted the seat with kid-leather gloves. Motioning to another stool, he said, "Take your ease, Scotsman."

Iain's curiosity overcame his desire to defy the man. "I don't know you. What's your business with me?"

"You're Captain Johnstone from Colonel Montgomery's regiment?"

"Aye."

"Formerly a moss-trooper?"

"Formerly?" Iain's brow lifted. "What are you, the law concerned with a bit of horse trading and border reiving? Here's a bit of fiddler's news for you—fighting for the King is an even greater crime, they say. Crusade elsewhere."

"And Lord Johnstone, the Earl of Hartfell, is your kinsman?"

"Aye," Iain said warily. The lord of his house had been held as a hostage for the good behaviour of the Johnstones for a few years now. *A family trait, this being imprisoned.* "He couldn't have sent you."

"Indeed, he didn't. I'm here as a favour for a mutual acquaintance—a friend, you could say," Lewis said, toying with a heavy onyx ring on his finger. "I was asked to facilitate arrangements for your release."

Iain remained silent. Foppish barristers did not walk into Tothill Fields and offer an enemy soldier a pass to freedom. This man smelled of privilege and ease, not the sort to get his hands dirty or risk stretching his own neck.

"No response?" Lewis said. "I see you're overwhelmed."

Iain leaned back in his chair and rubbed his sore shoulder as his mind whirled. He didn't know anyone in England. The Southroners he knew had either died at Worcester or were rotting in one of the other cells. "Who is it—this *friend* who sent you here?"

"I am not a lackey to be *sent* anywhere, Captain Johnstone," Lewis replied, his tone flat. "I choose my assignments with care."

"A man deserves to know who he'll owe his life to. Give me a name, Welshman."

"James Hart," Lewis said. "In this case, he's repaying you for saving *his* life. I believe that shall make you both even."

Iain scratched his beard and gave a grudging smile. *Damn that wily Southroner.* Hart should have been hanged a long time ago for highway robbery—instead, he had been rewarded with a commission from the King. *Of course the bugger managed to escape from Worcester.* "Where's the devil now?"

"Safely in The Hague with his family. He highly recommends the change."

Iain snorted and folded his arms across his chest. "I care only for Scotland."

A ghost of a smile touched Lewis's mouth, putting Iain on his guard. "I had hoped you might say that."

Iain's eyes narrowed. "Aye? Why is that?"

"What have you heard about matters in Scotland?"

Iain clenched his jaw and didn't reply. He hadn't been able to escape the talk of the guards. The bastards had taken great joy in gossiping about their bloody invasion and occupation. A copy of *Mercurius Politicus* had spread through the bridewell with the latest grim news. "Naught but English propaganda. I wipe my arse on it."

"I wish it were only talk. The English have occupied most of the south, including Dumfries and the border lands. Your home is there, is it not?"

"Aye," Iain gritted out.

CRYSSA BAZOS

"With most of the Scottish army taking their leisure *here*," Lewis continued, "Cromwell's commander, General Monck, has started to make inroads into the Highlands. There *were* four strategic strongholds that stood between him and a complete occupation of Scotland: Dumbarton, Bass Rock, Brodick Castle and Dunnottar. Now there are three. Dumbarton fell a fortnight ago. It's only a matter of time before the others are lost too. The Highlands are teetering on disaster."

Hot rage coursed through Iain, making him want to roar and smash something. He clamped it down and dug his heels into the dirt floor. "You're a bloody-mouthed rogue. Offer me freedom, then tell me that I won't have a home to return to."

"You can still serve your country."

"Aye? How do you see that?"

"In the Highlands. There are many from the south who have taken refuge there. They could use your leadership. The King relies on all his remaining allies. He will not forget those who help him."

Iain snorted. Will-o'-the-wisp promises. He was past caring a flea for that cursed Stuart King. The man was a cat—he'd land on his feet. The same could not be said for himself . . . or Scotland. "To the Highlands, you say?" Iain's attention drifted to the window and the rows of bare mounds. He had no home, no wife, and no son to leave his name. Highlanders were a strange breed, but at least they'd have a common enemy to fight. Anything to drive the caw-handed Southroners from their shores. "Aye," he said with a curt nod. "I'm your man."

The barrister smiled, a calculating expression that made Iain wary. "One more detail. You'll be carrying dispatches for the Marquis of Argyll."

"You're working with that worm?" Iain's brow rose.

"He is key to the resistance."

"'Tis a poor day when we have to rely on Argyll to save Scotland." Iain snorted. "Was that Hart's idea?"

"Hardly. It was entirely mine. Why waste an opportunity to achieve more with the same stone throw?"

"A right fool cause, putting your faith in Argyll. The worm will save his own skin first, damn the rest. The Campbells always do."

"King Charles works with whom he can. These are desperate times."

Iain studied Lewis carefully. There was something about his manner that still didn't sit well with him. He didn't entirely trust him, and yet Hart obviously relied on the man. Iain hadn't seen anything yet to suggest a reason. "Aye, they are desperate," he said. "My men and I are moss-troopers, and our forefathers reivers. We spit in the shifting wind. When do we leave?"

There was a heavy silence before he answered, "You've misunderstood my offer. There's no *we*, only *you*."

Iain stared at him blankly, not entirely comprehending. "My men are included in your pass, right?"

"Unfortunately, they are not."

Iain leaned forward, hands braced on his knees. "I have nine men left in my troop, and the rest are dead. I'll nae leave without them. Crawl back into your hole and find a few more passes."

Lewis shook his head. "Impossible. Getting even *one* required a great deal of creativity."

Iain jumped to his feet and began to pace. His gaze pulled to the barrow mounds visible through the grimy window. Thoughts of his wife and her grave on the crest of a hill flashed in his brain. Glencross was her brother—the pair had been as close as twins. Damned if he was going to sever his last tie to Innis and leave her brother behind. And abandoning his men like a cowardly toad? Impossible. Iain would deserve to be planted in the English ground if he turned his back on them. "No deal," he growled. "They are my men and have been loyal to me and my house long before this Stuart King drew his first breath. They come, or I stay."

10

"You would turn your back on your country?" Lewis's brow lifted.

"Don't talk to me about duty, you slimy Welsh bastard," Iain said. "I know the meaning of the word better than you. These men are kin, and I'll nae leave them here. We stand or fall together. You want your sodding dispatches sent, my men must come."

"We all must make difficult decisions," Lewis said.

"I've made mine." Iain reclaimed his seat and folded his arms across his chest.

Lewis's expression hardened. "I don't have time for this."

"You seem like a resourceful scoundrel. Get a few more passes. I can wait. I have all the time to piss on, right."

The barrister's gaze raked Iain from the top of his tangled blond hair to the holes in his boots. "You're flushed and sweating. Your hands are trembling. I give you a month, no more. And those men will be dead anyway. Time is certainly not your friend."

"And that worm Argyll needs your papers." Iain's laugh turned into a painful cough, leaving him to gasp for breath. When he regained the power of speech, he said, "Time is not *your* friend if you want those dispatches to reach Scotland."

"There's any number of men who can carry my dispatches," Lewis replied evenly. "This bridewell is full of candidates. I'm doing *you* the favour."

Iain couldn't argue with that. He might be stubborn, but no one ever accused him of being daft—nor of being a faithless bastard. He folded his arms across his chest.

Lewis drew a folded piece of paper from his coat and held it up. "One pass. Only one." The barrister's tone remained casual, as though he didn't care. But he did—Iain read it in the way the barrister's fingers gripped the paper and the hardness of his tone.

Iain frowned, tugging his beard. What had the man said? He wasn't a lackey to be sent anywhere. This man had his pride and cared for appearances. Why else would he appear here in this stinking hole dressed in spotless cream brocade? To prove something.

"Aye, there are others who would play messenger and kiss your muddy boots for the privilege, but then you'd have to explain to Hart how you failed." Iain let that soak in for a moment. "He's not one to ever let you forget it. I wager that would sting."

Lewis took a few moments to answer. His expression remained stony, but there was a telltale tic in his jaw. "I'll see what I can do, but I make no promises." He rose to leave and paused at the door. "You may have to reconsider your position, Iain Locharbaidh Johnstone."

"Go to hell."

Lewis carefully put on his gloves and gave a curt nod. "I may very well see you there."

When Iain returned to the cell, his men swarmed him.

"What did they want?" Killean Ross asked him. The youngest officer in the troop, Killean was a wiry young man whose father had ridden with Iain at the start of the war. Iain had agreed to keep a special eye on the son. *Failed there too.*

"Convinced the damned buggers to let us go, did ye?" another man, Masterton the Younger, said with a short bark of laughter. An old grizzled man, Masterton still answered to the Younger, long after his even more grizzled sire had been laid to rest. As usual, Masterton drilled close to the bone. Nothing slipped past that one.

"Aye, they were taken by my wit," Iain said wryly.

Glencross elbowed his way to reach Iain. "You've returned," he said with a relieved grin. "I feared you were headed for the rack."

"These Southroners have more sophisticated forms of torture," Iain answered. Needing some space to take stock of his bleak future, he wended his way back to the corner he claimed as his own.

Another man, Dunsmore, blocked his way. "What did they want with you?" Dunsmore wasn't one of his moss-troopers, but the man seemed determined to latch on to them. He had made no attempt to hide the fact that he was kin to a rival house of the Johnstones, the Maxwells—and a misbegotten whelp, if rumour could be credited. Iain couldn't decide what was worse—a Southroner or a Maxwell. Both seemed to be cut from the same cloth. "Out with it. We deserve to know."

"Piss off, Dunsmore. I owe *you* nothing." Iain tried to push past him, but the man planted himself before Iain like a rough-hewn troll.

"You were singled out by a whip-ma-denty toad, and I'm guessing it weren't for his amusement. Spit it out," he growled.

Normally, Iain would have knocked out the man's teeth and let him spit *them* out, but there was no point of fighting each other when their enemy stood on the other side of the door, even if it was a half-Maxwell begging for it. Here in the bridewell, old grudges were put aside. Even so, Iain wasn't yet ready to lay down and die. He squared his shoulders and crowded the bystart. "Back off, Dunsmore. You don't question my authority, right." Masterton and Killean moved in behind Dunsmore while Glencross stood beside Iain.

Sensing the mood darkening around him, Dunsmore backed down. "These lads deserve to know any news."

"Scotland is burning, and we're here. That's your news," Iain muttered, stepping away. He finally reached his corner and sank to the ground with his shoulder to the wall. Absently, he traced the hatch marks he had been scraping into the daub.

Glencross sat down beside him and tipped his head against the wall. He didn't say anything, only waited for Iain to work through his anger. Glencross knew when to give him space. Finally, Iain sighed and said, "They wanted me to take dispatches to Argyll."

"Aye, that worm?"

Iain grinned suddenly. For a moment, it felt good. "I told them to shove it. Needed my lads to go along. You're too amusing to be left behind."

Glencross snorted and then broke into a ragged cough.

Iain heard the rattling looseness in Glencross's chest. "When did that start?"

"What, this?" Glencross asked, swiping away the spittle with the back of his hand. "Nay, 'tis naught." His grin was brittle, and he turned away to continue coughing.

Iain didn't reply. McCaul had started that way. With the poor rations and the dampness, he had gone downhill within a fortnight. It might have been better if Iain had negotiated for one additional pass instead of ten.

"You should've gone," Glencross said finally.

"Shut up and get some rest," Iain said.

Glencross nodded and curled up on the ground.

Iain leaned his head against the post and closed his eyes. He shut his ears to the men moaning around him and allowed himself to think of his home in Dumfries. There'd be snow on the hills, and the sheep would be eating their way through the winter fodder. He pictured the dry-stacked wall that marked the boundaries of his land. Moss and lichen filled the cracks between the stones. Iain tried to remember the bracing scent of the winter fields and the path leading to the little grassy knoll in the kirkyard. At the base of the largest pine tree, a pile of rocks were stacked one above the other to form a cairn, marking where his wife and stillborn son lay.

If Iain died—*when* he died—that was where he needed to be buried. He hadn't been there for Innis in life, but he had meant to be there for her in death. But a common grave in the marshes was more like to be his resting place. Far from home.

A sound nipped at the edge of Iain's sleep, foreign to the usual snoring and coughing of men or creaking of a rickety building. It came from a distance, muffled yet urgent.

Iain propped himself on his elbow and canted his head. Silence— then pounding boots. He pushed himself upright, giving a warning shout to his men a moment before the door was flung open and a troop of soldiers charged inside with torches and cudgels.

"Get up—get moving," one of the guards bellowed.

The Southroners swarmed the room, kicking men to their feet, beating them if they didn't rise fast enough.

Iain didn't know what awaited them, only that he wasn't going without a fight. His men gathered around him, their expressions intense and focused. They were braced for a round.

"Always ready, lads," Iain called out to them, the Johnstone rally cry.

"Aye, ready," they answered back.

Roaring, they charged in unison at the advancing guards. Iain picked out one of the men who had pinned him earlier and drove his fist into his stomach. The guard doubled over, but before Iain could deliver a punishing uppercut, another guard swung a cudgel at his head. Iain dodged the swing but lost his balance. He stumbled backwards and couldn't recover quickly enough to fend off two more guards who rushed at him. Another cudgel swung, and this time he took it on the shoulder—pain ripped through his arm. He could barely lift his arm to fend off another swing. Just as he fell, he saw Glencross take a hit to the head before being dragged away.

Two guards yanked Iain to his feet, one grabbing him by McCaul's necklace. The links snapped, and the piece fell with a clang to the stone floor. *McCaul!* In vain, Iain tried to retrieve it, but the guards were already hauling him away to the door. No matter how hard he tried to buck them off, they only twisted his arms harder until he had to bite back a cry of pain.

"You will behave, Scotch scum," one man snarled in his ear.

Once outside in the darkness, a bitter wind slapped Iain's face. Flaming rushlight cut across his vision, and he flinched from the bright flash. The flare of smoke from the torches was acrid and stung his eyes. Men were being herded across the fields in all directions.

What the fockin' hell is going on? Were they being herded for execution? Iain dug deep to brace himself for what was to come.

Musket shots sounded. Iain flinched, hating himself for the weakness. He searched for Glencross and the others, thought he saw them ahead, but then a group of soldiers crossed his path.

In the distance, a man was calling out numbers. "One hundred five . . . one ten . . . one nineteen . . ." Someone slapped Iain on the back of the head and called, "One twenty. Last one for the *Jane Marie.*"

They herded Iain to a caravan of wagons where Glencross and the others were being held with muskets and staves. When Iain reached them, his captors pushed him to the ground. Iain heaved himself up and whirled around to face the guards only to find a sharp end of a pike levelled at his face.

"I'll not hesitate to spear you, Scotch devil," the pikeman said, jabbing the point at him.

"Then do it, ye bastard," Iain ground out. He held the man's wavering gaze and spat at his feet. The bugger didn't have the stones to do it. The pikeman's face darkened, and his nostrils flared. He drew back his pike and threatened to skewer Iain when another man, wearing his authority through his swagger, clamped a hand on the pikeman's forearm. "Give it over," he said. "We'll be shot of them soon enough."

"Good riddance," the pikeman muttered, glaring at Iain.

A loose collection of men inspected the gathered prisoners. They were dressed in the Monmouth caps and jackets normally worn by sailors, and they had the unsavoury look of the docks about them.

The pikeman jabbed Iain's back. "Get moving," he said and forced him into one of the wagons. "The tide won't be waiting long."

Inside, over thirty men were crammed in tight. Iain found himself beside Glencross and Killean. One of the tars secured the wagon door, and they were cast in darkness save for weak rushlight that flickered through the side grates.

Iain shouldered someone to reach the barred window and craned his head to see what was happening. The lieutenant of the guards was speaking with another man who seemed to be the leader of this ill-hadden group of men. After a brief discussion, both men nodded and shook hands. Coin changed hands, and the lieutenant whistled to his men.

"What's happening?" Glencross asked. But he knew the answer. They all knew the answer. The bloody English had just sold them.

White-hot fury burst through Iain's brain. He drove his fist into the side of the wagon. "Bastard Southroners." The wagon started moving. Iain gripped the wooden bars and pulled with all his might, but they didn't budge. "Misbegotten whoresons! Where are you taking us? Where the *hell* are we going?"

The wagon passed the pikeman. He looked up and gave Iain a mock salute before answering, "Barbados, mate. And good riddance to you all."

Chapter 2

———◆———

An Gallbhaile; Munster, Ireland

Mairead O' Coneill's violin called out to her. The only time she found
to play was in the predawn, when her uncle's family still lay abed. She
anticipated the taste of that charmed hour, alone and intimate with
her music.

Pressed between her two sleeping cousins, Mairead edged her
way down the length of the bed, careful not to wake the other
women. Ciara remained curled on her side, with a lily-white hand
tucked under her cheek, while Bronagh snored.

Mairead held her breath as she eased from the bed. She couldn't
bear Bronagh's questions if she were caught sneaking out of the
room. It was even too early in the morning for Ciara to defend
Mairead from Bronagh's shrewish tongue. Golden Ciara made
everything bearable, but even so, Mairead didn't share her early
morning indulgence with her; this was for herself alone.

She crept across the floor to grab her shoes and woollen cloak
from the chair. Not bothering to pin her hair, she left the light brown
curls to hang down her back. Mousy brown, Bronagh called it. No
matter, Mairead thought with a toss of her head. Ronan thought it
grand.

Mairead hurried downstairs, past the sleeping servants in the kitchen, to slip outside. *Freedom!* The predawn air smelled spicy and fresh. She dashed down the garden path towards the barn. The building loomed in the dim light, flanked by a stand of crooked firs. The glen of An Gallbhaile stretched before her like a gently sloping bowl. In the distance, the Galtee Mountains filled the horizon, growing more distinct with the lightening sky, as though they were being shaped before her eyes.

Inside the barn, the earthy warmth of cows and horses enveloped Mairead as her eyes grew accustomed to the darkness. A small opening in the hayloft gave all the light she needed. By now, the sky was beginning to turn slate grey.

She hurried to the far corner of the barn where a small trunk nestled beside the oat bin. Mairead knelt in the straw and withdrew from the trunk a bundle wrapped in a pony blanket. Eagerly, she parted the woollen covering, revealing the gleaming curves of her violin. It had been her cousin Diarmuid, with his winning smiles and conspiratorial winks, who had suggested she hide it in there.

Mairead's father had never held with the instrument, and she never expected Uncle Mulriane to be more accommodating. As it was neither a harp nor a lyre, it offended her father, and he refused to hear her play it. *Ireland is overrun with enough foreigners as it is*, he often railed, and he wasn't about to violate *his* ears too. This had been a matter of principle.

She had only come to own the violin through the ill fortune of a Scottish minstrel. The man had arrived from Italy and, after being in Galway six months, struggled to settle his credit in her father's store. Having nothing else, he offered to trade his violin. Despite his prejudice, Mairead's father wasn't a foolish man. Better to collect a little than nothing, so he accepted the man's offer and immediately passed the instrument to his only daughter. Mairead suspected that the minstrel's offer to teach her how to play was made so he would not entirely be parted from the instrument. Their lessons lasted a season, and in that time the dear violin had rooted itself deep in Mairead's heart. That had been the spring of her eighteenth year; three months before the devil himself, Oliver Cromwell, arrived in Ireland with his English horde. Two very long years ago.

Mairead ran a hand down the violin's smooth wood. The patina of wear only enhanced its beauty, and its shape fit neatly in her trim hands. There was something about the violin that Mairead craved, some quality of its notes that bound her to it. She daren't say out loud, lest she forever scandalise her Mulriane relatives, but it had a soul, and it spoke to her.

The cows started stirring. Not much time left.

When the air was bright and crisp, she had a desire to test her violin's voice against the fir-scented mountain air. She left the barn and hurried to the edge of a small copse, far enough away that no one would hear. She tucked the violin under her chin and raised the bow to the strings. *Thrum.*

Mairead never knew what song would come out each morning. If Bronagh had been particularly trying, Mairead played a fierce, uncompromising medley, and her bow quivered in retribution. Or after the first time—the only time—Ronan MacCarthaigh had made love to her in the barn loft, a soft melody poured out of her fingers, playful and brimming with the wonder of first love.

But today, the melody that came out of her was melancholy. She closed her eyes and revelled in its heart-tugging tones, so low and clear. Leaning into the tune, she thought of her mother lying cold in her grave and her father and brothers, still back in Galway, besieged by the English. If the town were forced to capitulate, would the English show mercy, or would they take their revenge and slaughter without remorse?

The fear, the ache of uncertainty directed how her fingers moved across the fingerboard, and she threw herself into the lament. The melody changed and introduced lower notes that played against the higher, unlocking gnawing fears, ones she dared not examine too openly for fear of what they meant.

Mairead's lover, Ronan, hadn't come around to see her after their initial tryst in the loft. One day turned into another until an entire fortnight had passed, leaving Mairead anxious. Theirs had been an impassioned courtship and Ronan most persuasive. Had he been called away to attend his father's business, unable to send word, or was he loathe to publicly declare himself until after the fear of invasion had been averted?

Mairead's excuses for Ronan's absence began to wear thin each passing day, leaving a mounting fear. Something must have happened to him. And during these troubled days, *something* might be very dire indeed.

The melody turned bittersweet, and her eyes pricked with tears.

The sun's rays arched across the sky, painting the clouds in soft hues of red and rose. Mairead's breath puffed out in the air in a silver mist. The cock crowed, hard and tinny. As she gave the violin a last caress with her bow and the final note trembled in the crisp air, a string snapped.

The song finished on a discordant note.

Mairead tucked her violin back in its hiding place, troubled by the ruined string. How she was to replace it, being indefinitely here in the country, she didn't know. Under normal circumstances, she could have sent word to her father for one.

At the thought of her father and brothers, a lump settled in her throat. She hadn't seen them for nearly a year, not since Mairead's oldest brother had brought her down from Galway to stay with Uncle Mulriane's family—to keep her safe from the invading English, who were besieging one port town after another. Cromwell and his lieutenants were determined to eradicate all Royalist support in Ireland for the exiled King Charles.

You'll be safe in the country, her father had assured her before she left. He had cupped her face and pressed a kiss on her forehead. The scent of pipe tobacco had lingered on his fingers and burrowed into her memory. Mairead had a sudden longing for home.

As she rose to her feet, the barn door swung open. Mairead spun around, and her heart skipped a beat when she saw who it was.

Ronan stood at the door holding his horse's bridle, his travelling cloak swept rakishly to one side. When he saw her, he blinked his amazement. "Mairead?"

Mairead held herself in check, locking her limbs so she wouldn't fling herself into his arms. He had stayed away for over a fortnight, and she wasn't prepared to reveal herself as either needy or desperate. "Ronan MacCarthaigh, what are you about, and at this hour?" She tried to sound nonchalant, as though she didn't care how he answered. Except she did. Her happiness hinged on it. Meanwhile, she drank in the sight of his chiselled features and thick, black hair, as beautiful as a raven's wing.

A strange look passed over Ronan's face before he removed his cap. "I've come to meet Diarmuid."

Oh. He hadn't come for *her*. Ronan avoided her eyes and instead made a pretence of looking around the place, as though he suspected Diarmuid of hiding in one of the cattle stalls.

"It must be fairly important, I suppose, to bring you out so early. The sun isn't even up," Mairead said. She found it hard to keep her voice steady, even though her heart was trembling in hurt and confusion.

As though to name her a liar, the sun slanted through the open doorway, lighting the straw scattered on the ground between them. At one time, Mairead might have edged forward, so casually, to step into the pool of sunlight to solicit a compliment from Ronan. Instead, she remained in the shadows.

22

"'Tis a matter of great import." Ronan glanced back at the door. His tone was distant, devoid of the honeyed warmth that had wooed her so thoroughly.

Mairead finally noticed the flintlock pistols tucked in his belt. A coldness washed over her, but she approached him boldly. "Why do you have those?"

"Never mind—best you don't know."

But Mairead thought she did. A man did not arm himself these days without deadly intent. She had overheard enough debates between Ronan and Diarmuid about the English invaders and how best to drive them away. "You're joining the Tóraidhe," she said flatly, desperately hoping she was wrong.

Ronan's expression hardened. "We follow Edmund O' Dwyer. We'll strike at those English devils and teach them Munster is not theirs for the taking. Every man who claims to love Ireland has a duty to fight these bastards. What kind of patriot would I be if I did not join the fray?" His black eyes shone with passion, though not for her.

Mairead drew closer. "I'll not think less of you if you were to stay here." She reached up to touch his cheek, but he drew away. Mairead dropped her hand. "Your da needs you, Ronan," she said more sharply than she intended. "Uncle Mulriane won't permit Diarmuid to go—"

"Pity's sake, Mairead. Your uncle knows. We go with his blessing."

A cold thought seeped through Mairead. She hugged herself tightly and said in a low voice, "When were you going to tell me?"

Ronan raked his tapered fingers through his glossy black hair and gave her a small smile. "I'm telling you now, sure."

Normally, Ronan's smiles weakened Mairead's knees, but this time she only felt unease. "You weren't planning on it, were you, Ronan? Had I not been here, you would have left without a farewell." A million excuses flitted through her brain, a million reasons why Ronan would have stolen away to battle the English without coming for one last kiss. Mairead discarded them all. "Do you love me, Ronan?" He hadn't once said it, not even during his wooing, not even after his having.

Ronan scuffed his feet against the straw and wouldn't meet her direct gaze. "Sure, I care about you, Mairead. But I . . . daren't bind you to me, not now, not with the uncertainty of this war."

Mairead's heart gave a sick lurch, and she could barely breathe. *But I gave myself to you. Is that not binding enough?*

Ronan's eyes darted to the door, and he straightened his shoulders. "I have to go." Before he left the barn, he added, "Be well, Mairead." With that, he shut the door behind him.

Mairead could not move. She stared at the spot where Ronan had been. Everything she had felt so sure about had crumbled to dirt. Ronan didn't love her. All those warm looks, catching her behind the barn and showering her with affection, had been for what—a quick toss? A passing fancy? Easily forgotten.

Mairead sank to the ground and covered her face. She had been so proud for having attracted Ronan's attention. Bronagh had always been sweet on him and preened whenever he was in the room. And Ciara—even she had a pretty blush whenever Ronan came by, no doubt half wishing that her father had betrothed her to Ronan instead of their cousin's son. Meanwhile, Mairead had hugged her clandestine love to her breast, the sweetness intensifying the longer that she and Ronan had kept their secret.

Such a fool.

Mairead squeezed her eyes shut. She couldn't cry; no tears would come, only a bleak despair. She drew her knees tightly to her chest, drawing herself into a ball over the shame and humiliation. Mairead had given him what was most precious to her, believing they would be together.

What was wrong with her that she hadn't seen his true nature? She had been fooled by his easy manner. His teasing smiles had disarmed her, and his touch had melted her natural caution. He had listened to her as though she were the only one in the world. How had she allowed herself to be flattered like a vacant twit?

One of the cows started lowing, a plaintive call. Soon a few more joined the chorus. Mairead rose, swaying slightly. She had to leave before the dairymaid came. She couldn't bear to see anyone, to exchange banal greetings when her heart lay shattered.

Mairead slipped out of the postern gate just as the barn door swung open. She hurried down the path, far from the dairymaid who was calling to each dumb beast by name.

A slight drizzle soaked the fields. The low clouds pressed down, thickening the air with a fine mist. Instead of heading back to the manor, Mairead followed the pathway towards the copse—there she could be alone. When she neared the tree line, she checked her stride. Ahead in the distance and farther into the woods, she spied Ronan. His back was to her, and he stood a little strangely. Then he shifted, and Mairead could see that he was not alone. A trim figure, fully cloaked, stood close to him, sheltered by his tall frame. A *feminine* form.

Right before Mairead's horrified eyes, Ronan drew this woman into his arms, and they exchanged a heated kiss. Mairead's stomach gave a painful lurch. As she watched, transfixed, the woman's hood slipped from her head, revealing a golden tumble of curls.

Ciara.

Mairead stumbled back, her hand pressed against her mouth. *How could she?* Ciara was already betrothed! How long had *this* been going on?

Tears flooded her eyes. Mairead whirled around and dashed back the way she had come. Scalding tears fell unchecked down her cheeks as she ran. When she reached the rear of the barn, she leaned against it to keep from sinking to the ground.

Ronan and Ciara! How *could* he? A wave of hysteria fuelled by rage flooded Mairead. *Faithless, inconstant wretches!* They deserved each other.

25

Mairead should have known—everyone loved Ciara. Even the sun vied for her attention. Ciara, with the sweetness of honey. Her family all worshipped her, even Bronagh. Pampered and sheltered, Ciara never had a moment of doubt or worry, while the rest of the world prayed for salvation.

Until now.

Ronan was leaving to join the Tóraidhe. Let Ciara worry for her precious love, worry that he'd never return to her. Let her taste the misery that shredded Mairead's soul.

Mairead turned towards the copse, the image of the two lovers seared in her mind. "I curse you," she spat the words into the chill air. "I curse you both."

In the days that followed, Mairead grew as taut as a string stretched to its limit. She took pains to avoid Ciara, which, like the barn cat, only made her cousin seek her out more. In the end, Mairead had to plead illness just to be left alone. Even then, she was sick at heart. Mairead had always looked upon Ciara as a sister.

A fortnight later, Uncle Mulriane received word that a band of Tóraidhe had been captured by the English. No word if Ronan and Diarmuid were safe or if they even reached the Tóraidhe camp. The household's mood now sank to the level of Mairead's despair.

The parlour clock continued its unrelenting movement through frozen time. The women were silent, each buried in their tasks, carefully skirting any mention of the Tóraidhe. Even Bronagh held her tongue. Mairead worked at the spinning wheel, giving only half a mind to the repetitive whorl of the flywheel and the wool that passed between her fingers. Across from her, Ciara sat carding while Bronagh and Aunt Fianna worked at their needlepoint.

Mairead stole glances at Ciara, who barely contained her worry while her embroidery lay discarded on her lap. Her cousin's normally rosy cheeks were pale, and she kept glancing towards the window. Mairead chewed on her bottom lip in thought. Ciara likely didn't know about Mairead and Ronan. How could she blame Ciara for being swept away by the man's charms? She had not been immune to them either. A deep sadness spread through her bones. She preferred the comfort of anger.

"Mairead!"

Aunt Fianna's voice cut through her misery. "What have you done to the wool?"

Mairead looked down at the bobbin and cringed. Instead of smooth yarn neatly wrapped around the bobbin, the threads were uneven and lumpy. She had never seen such a tangled mess. "Forgive me." Suddenly, Mairead's misery choked her, and she wanted to disappear, preferably through the floor.

Uncle Mulriane entered the room. "What's this?" He glanced down at the tangled weave. "Is this how they spin in Galway?" He softened his words with a wink.

"It's ruined," Fianna said, her voice rising to an agitated quiver. "Even if she tried to re-spin it, the threads will always be stubby. I've told you so many times, Mairead, keep your mind on your duties and not flit away to God knows where—"

Uncle Mulriane gripped his wife's shoulders and looked down at her, stern yet gentle. "Fianna, love. Everything will be fine."

Her aunt opened her mouth to reply, then snapped it shut. She closed her eyes and nodded.

"Mairead," her uncle said. "Play us a tune on the harp; that's a good lass. Bronagh can take your place at the spindle."

"What?" Bronagh dropped her needlework and glared.

"Hush, daughter. Mairead, the harp."

He's right. Maybe this will help. Mairead brought the instrument out of its corner and settled herself on a stool. She leaned the harp back until it rested against her shoulder. But her mind was blank. Mairead searched inward. Nothing. She ran her fingers across the strings, idly seeking for a chord of inspiration, but the notes sounded false.

Foolish girl for mooning over a faithless man.

Mairead refocused, preparing to launch into a melody—any tune. It didn't matter what she played; eventually, her heart would join in.

Something captured Uncle Mulriane's attention. He stiffened, then crossed to the window. The colour drained from his face, and he drew back. "The devil."

"What is it?" Aunt Fianna asked.

"English," he spat and tore from the window. "Stay here." He strode out of the parlour, calling for his servants, with Aunt Fianna chasing after him.

Mairead darted for the window and crowded beside Ciara and Bronagh for a view. Like a red ribbon unravelling across the winter fields, an English squadron descended on the estate. They fanned out and poured into the forecourt.

An officer cut a path through his men and stopped his horse a few feet away. He wore a buff coat with a red sash across his chest. "Brian Mulriane," he called out loudly. "Present yourself."

Uncle Mulriane strode out to meet him, supported by the men of his household and a sword belted to his waist. It was a poor showing against the English, but her uncle faced them proudly, with his hand resting on the hilt of his sword. Mairead cracked open the window to hear what was being said.

"What do you want?"

Instead of answering, the officer looked around at the main house and the outbuildings. He turned to one of his men. "Search all the buildings and gather everyone out here."

"Aye, Captain."

Aunt Fianna shrieked as the soldiers burst into their home. Ciara grabbed Mairead's arm while Bronagh ran to her mother. Mairead found herself being ushered from the house with Ciara clinging to her.

Outside, Uncle Mulriane argued with the captain. "Get off my land."

"Yours no longer," the captain said, dismounting from his horse. "I claim this land on behalf of the English Commonwealth."

Uncle Mulriane advanced in a rage. "You have no right."

"I wasn't asking." The captain turned to his men. "Torch the barn."

Mairead gasped. They wouldn't . . .

Rushes were set alight, and the soldiers swooped down on the barn with their burning torches. The lust of destruction seized them, and they were whooping and hollering as the first flames licked the dry straw.

Mairead watched in horror as the realisation slammed her. *My violin!* "No!" She broke away from the others and dashed towards the barn.

"Mairead! Stop!" Ciara tried to snatch at her arm, but Mairead slipped free.

Without rational thought, Mairead ran as fast as she could. Twenty horsemen stood between her and her treasure. She pushed past a dismounted soldier and avoided his attempt to pull her back. There was still time. She plunged into the burning barn.

Thick curls of smoke stung her eyes. Mairead covered her nose, and, taking a deep breath, she darted past the flames. A sob escaped her when she saw that the orange flames had spread to the chest. Before she could reach it, a soldier grabbed her from behind and lifted her off her feet. As though she were naught but a sack of grain, he hauled her out of the barn.

"Release me!" she shrieked, twisting and squirming to free herself. "I have to get my treasure!" She continued screaming, but he didn't understand Gaelic. "My violin! I have to save it," she tried again in English.

But he remained unmoved. Instead, he tightened his grip, and his arms dug into her stomach. She wanted to throw up. Mairead cried as the distance widened between her and the violin. The flames enveloped the chest, consuming it with savagery. Lost. Her violin was gone. Writhing under the flames.

The soldier strode through a circle of horsemen and dumped Mairead on the ground beside her cousins and her aunt. The kitchen girls and stable hands were all herded together.

"We don't treat with dogs and damned Tory sympathisers," the captain shouted to be heard. "Any man or woman" —his attention settled on Ciara—"caught treating with Tories will have their land confiscated."

Mairead struggled to understand his words; his accent was different from the English settlers who had once visited her father's store, but there was no mistaking that he knew about the Tóraidhe.

The captain motioned to one of his men, who handed him a pair of sacks. With a grim laugh, he spilled their contents to the ground. Two bloody heads rolled out, one blond and the other black. As black as a raven's wing.

Mairead recoiled and collided against Ciara. Her scream twisted in her throat. Aunt Fianna staggered towards the blond head and began to mewl, a deep, gurgling sound borne out of disbelief that turned into mindless rage. She dropped to her knees. *"Diarmuid!"*

Uncle Mulriane bellowed. He drew his sword and lunged for the captain, blade swinging in a deadly arc. The man scrambled back, drawing his sword to block the attack. Uncle Mulriane smashed against the other's blade over and over again, giving no quarter. The Englishman missed his footing, and his blade dropped. Uncle knocked his blade aside and quickly drove his point into the man's unprotected side. The soldier's cry cut through the other soldiers' shock and forced them to action. Before Mairead could shout a warning, they rushed upon Uncle Mulriane, smothering him. In a blink, they had dispatched his sword and had driven him to his knees.

Uncle Mulriane drew his shoulders back just before the Englishman's blade sliced into the back of his neck. The veins in Uncle Mulriane's throat stood out like cords as he collapsed. The captain pulled out his dripping sword and kicked Uncle Mulriane into the dirt.

"Brian!" Aunt Fianna shrieked and tried to rush to his side. A soldier blocked her way, but Fianna started clawing at him, her face twisted in rage and grief.

A silver gleam flashed in the sun, and Mairead gasped a warning, "Aunt Fi—"

Too late. The captain's blade buried in Fianna's stomach. Her eyes widened, and her mouth formed a silent scream. Blood poured out, staining her aunt's linen apron. She faced her daughters for one brief moment, then crumpled to the ground.

Bronagh started shrieking, an endless wail of disbelief and terror. Someone delivered a backhanded slap, and she flew sideways before hitting the ground.

Mairead pulled Ciara back when she tried to fly to her mother and held her tightly in her arms. They needed to keep their wits. Now more than ever.

The captain surveyed the estate. "Round up everyone still standing. There's profit to be made. Traders are offering good coin for Barbados labour."

Chapter 3

————◆————

Weak light filtered through the checkerboard pattern of an overhead grate. The ship creaked and swayed and occasionally gave a shuddering groan. The rise and fall of the waves churned Iain's stomach into a roiling mess.

Sweat and vomit of beaten men added to the noxious fumes of the slaver's hold. Iain shifted on the hard wooden plank, and the heavy shackles chafed his ankles. The irons barely gave him enough freedom to shuffle to one of the overflowing piss buckets.

A hot rush of bile flooded his mouth, and he fumbled to reach the bucket. As it tipped, he snatched the handle in time. He gagged and tossed up the remainder of his stomach. After the heaving stopped, he wiped his mouth with the back of his hand and moaned. A tremor shuddered through his body, and he sagged against the bunk.

Put me out of my misery.

Three levels of planks ran the length of the hold forming crude bunks for the prisoners. With barely enough clearance to sit upright, Iain was forced to either hunch forward or lie prone. Fate had turned out to be a greedy Southron captain, playing the averages—packing them in like herring and not giving a shit if he lost half his stock to sickness. The captain saved on their rations and prepared to earn a fistful of gold unites in Barbados with those that didn't die.

Barbados. Call it hell and be done with it, Iain thought. *Indentured, my arse.* The English claimed there were papers, but there were no shitten papers. They all had been pressed into slavery—Barbadoed. Iain had heard stories of those sent down to the West Indies. The ones that had survived the fields had a broken back and weak spirit— many had never been heard of again.

Iain had fought to survive all his life—as natural as breathing. But now a bone-weary heaviness smothered him, and he barely had the will to lift his head. He was no longer a man—only a slab of meat on a shelf.

Glencross's racking cough broke through Iain's self-pity, and he glanced over at his brother-in-law lying beside him. Glencross had turned a sickly shade of yellow, and his cheeks were flushed. A chill prickled Iain's skin. His brother-in-law worsened by the day. Glencross continued to cough, sounding more gravelly by the moment. The spasm intensified, and he bent over, gasping for breath until he finally spat out a glutinous hunk of yellow phlegm. He leaned over the edge of the bunk. His breath rattled in his chest.

Iain struggled to sit up and brought out the half cup of water he had been saving. Time meant nothing in the hold, and he didn't know if the next cup would come in an hour or a day. He swung his shackled legs over the ledge and found firm footing on the floor. Using the edge as support, he sidled over to Glencross. "Here, drink this," he told him.

Glencross tried to push the cup away, though his hands shook. "Keep your rations."

"And drink this shite myself?" Iain snorted. Though it tasted like the inside of rotted fish barrels, it was still water, and Glencross needed it more than he did. "Just a little, right." Iain lifted Glencross's head and trickled water into his parched mouth. Despite his protest, Glencross didn't turn away.

"Thank you," he whispered before curling on his side.

Thank you? That bit. It had been Iain who had convinced Glencross and the rest of his moss-troopers to support the King, to do their part, and all that, when Glencross would have been just as happy to have stayed home to mind his father's lands. They had no business invading England. What had he wanted to prove, agreeing to that madness? He had simply been driven by rage and a need to forget his grief.

What if Glencross didn't make it? His fever worsened, and sweat beaded on his forehead. He needed fresh air. The noxious vapours were killing him—killing them all.

Glencross didn't deserve to die a slave. None of them did. And Iain had thought their situation was untenable imprisoned in Tothill Fields. He snorted at the thought. Better to die a prisoner than a slave. He'd still have the pride of a man.

The ship shuddered, and Iain gritted his teeth to master his swimming head. He climbed onto his ledge and leaned against the hold's wall. If he kept still, this plague in his stomach would settle, but that was a torment of a different nature. Every time he shut his eyes, the image of his home haunted him. He couldn't bear to see the large cottage with its sloping view of the misty glen. He forced back thoughts of his land, flushed with the heather that spread across the hills; turned a deaf ear to the memory of bleating sheep. As soon as the troops disbanded, he'd intended to return. But that had turned into spring, then summer's end. Another turn of the wheel and lambing blurred into harvest. And still he was naught but an occasional visitor to his land, to his home, and to his wife.

The hatch creaked open, and a pair of sailors climbed down the ladder, both carrying two buckets, one filled with hunks of hardtack and the other with water. The mood in the hold changed. Prisoners shrugged off their lethargy and fumbled for their tin cups. Dunsmore, as usual, was the first to position himself.

Hounds lining up for scraps. Iain's lip curled. *Licking the hand that holds us down.* A fine one to talk, he thought, as he held out his own cup. Weak as he was, he'd not scorn anything he could get.

When the sailors reached Glencross, that contentious bastard Dunsmore edged in. "He'll be dead soon," he said with a meaningful nod to Glencross. "Your food's wasted on him. Give me his share."

The sailor shoved him aside. "Piss off. Each sod gets two pieces o' hardtack, and I don't give a damn what he does with it."

But the other sailor who ladled water didn't have the same outlook. He only gave Glencross half a ration.

Iain blocked his way. "You shorted him."

"He'll take what I gives him," the sailor said. "Be glad he got any at all."

Iain's knuckles itched to connect with the man's weak jaw, to knock a quarter cup more water out of him. The sailor must have noticed his mutinous expression and said, "You looking to argue with me? I might forget to fill your cup too."

Iain forced his fists down, reminding himself that Glencross would be the one to suffer from his rebellion. "No argument," he ground out sullenly. The sailor snorted, then sloshed a portion of water in his cup. Giving a final backwards glance, he moved down along the line. When Iain lifted his gaze, he met Dunsmore's mocking smirk. The man might as well have called him out as a weak coward. Iain clenched his teeth and turned away.

The hatch slammed shut, returning them to semidarkness. A movement caught Iain's attention. Dunsmore shifted closer to Glencross, his hand creeping towards the lad's hardtack.

"Touch that," Iain growled at Dunsmore, "and I'll break your fingers."

Dunsmore didn't withdraw his hand. "Waste your time on a dead man. Gowkit arse."

Iain got to his feet, finally feeling the surge of his blood. "Call me that again." *Do it.*

"Gowkit—"

Moving as quickly as his shackles would allow, Iain put a shoulder into the man. Dunsmore jerked away, then swung his fist. Iain seized the man's wrist in midair, twisting it down and behind his back. He tightened his hold until Dunsmore grunted in pain.

"I don't know how things are done in the Maxwell camp," Iain ground out, "but the Johnstones stand by their kin." With a quick snap, Iain pulled back one of Dunsmore's fingers and felt the satisfying crunch of bone.

The man howled in pain. "Ye *bastard.*"

Iain pushed Dunsmore into the piss-drenched straw and loomed over him. "Steal from one of mine again—take what doesn't belong to you—and I'll break more than your fingers." He spat on the ground and left Dunsmore to flounder with his shackles.

Iain returned to his place beside Glencross and handed his brother-in-law the piece of hardtack. "Eat up before another dog tries to piss on it."

Mairead could not purge Ronan's glassy eyes from her mind, not even through the long march to Cork. They were herded like cattle with the compassion of wolves. Mairead trudged behind Ciara and Bronagh while ten other Mulriane servants, both women and men, brought in the rear.

Rough hemp ropes were looped tight around Mairead's neck, sawing into her tender skin. The rope was tethered to the saddle of one of her captors, and she had no choice but to keep moving. She no longer saw the column of English soldiers on horseback. The red of their coats swam before her eyes and became Ronan's and Diarmuid's life blood. The steady thumping of the horse hooves became the refrain of heads rolling from a bag, over and over again until Mairead wanted to smother her ears. But she couldn't. The English had lashed her hands together.

Mairead stumbled and fell into the hardened mud. Her captor continued riding while she choked and dragged along the ground. She gasped for air as she struggled to find her feet. Black spots darkened her vision. The buzzing in her head turned discordant, piercing, at the same frequency as a pair of strings vibrating the highest note. The soldier finally stopped, and she lay stunned on the ground, her skirt torn and her elbows and arms scraped raw.

The soldier yanked her to her feet and pushed her forward. "Get a move on," he barked. When he climbed back atop his horse, he set a faster pace. Mairead spent all her energy to keep up.

Get a move on. The words echoed in her head.

When she was a child, her brother Niall had forever been yelling at her, "Get a move on, daft lass. I have better things to do than mind your ways." He had always had the responsibility of Mairead since their mother died—either that or eat a mouthful of fist and broken teeth dished out by their eldest brother. Which made things worse for Mairead as Niall's patience for an unwelcome task was never his strength.

Mairead could still feel Niall pulling her through the Galway market, squeezing her through the thick crowds.

"Get a move on," Niall barked, his voice suddenly harsh and strange. His face shimmered into the face of an English soldier. "Move *now*," the man repeated in his foul tongue.

Mairead cried out and fell again. Stones dug into her knees. She had braced her fall with her tied hands, and her wrists throbbed.

"Get her up," the English commander barked to one of his men. "No lagging behind."

Mairead tried to stand, but her skirts were twisted around her legs, and she kept floundering. A pair of hands gripped her arms, and all of a sudden something in Mairead ignited. "Release me," she yelled before hitting his jaw with her tied hands.

A burly man stopped trying to get her up and instead pinned her, crushing her with his weight. "Keep fighting, love." Rancid breath hissed between his thin lips.

Mairead tried to push him off, but she only amused him more. A rush of cold wind touched her bare legs as her skirts were hiked up. The brute's cold hands began to grope her knee and inner thigh. Mairead shrieked in his face. "Don't *touch* me."

Ciara was crying, pleading with them to stop.

"Soldier, get off her," the commander barked, reining in beside them.

Mairead's tormenter gave a short laugh. "Sorry, Captain," he said, rolling to his feet. "I was only trying to get her to stop." He grabbed her tether and yanked her to her feet.

The captain raised his voice so all his men could hear. "Hands off the maids. Anyone found with their fingers in the honeypot will see them cut off." With a flick of his reins, he wheeled his horse around and continued towards the front. "We'll get three pounds a head for the sluts, but a clean five if the daughters of the manor haven't been broken."

His words confused Mairead—she was no longer a maid. *Oh, Ronan.* A wave of sadness nearly crushed her, but she marshalled her thoughts—one small mercy if they thought she was still innocent.

Small mercy? They were going to *sell* them and ship them to Barbados. Mairead had heard the nightmarish stories of press gangs stealing people and spiriting them down to that heathenish place. This couldn't be happening to her.

The soldier ushered Mairead with short, jerky movements. "Irish bitch." He pushed her to take her place between Bronagh and Ciara before he remounted his horse. He yanked her tether for emphasis. "Fall again and I'll let you drag till you choke."

Another hour—or was it two? Mairead lost track of time. She almost welcomed the pebbles that dug into her thin-soled boots. She couldn't afford to slip into oblivion, not again.

Her attention drifted to her cousins. Ciara moved as though in a trance. She stared ahead with glassy eyes while Bronagh whined through the long trek, swearing vengeance.

Mairead became alarmed for Bronagh. Though she spoke in Irish, there was no mistaking the flavour of her words, and the English soldiers were growing more sullen by the moment.

"Bronagh," Mairead hissed. "Still your tongue."

"I am a Mulriane and will not remain meek and silent. I will curse them with my last breath."

"Do it in your head," Mairead said. "They'll spill your blood if you don't shut—" The soldier yanked the rope again and cut her off.

Bronagh's words chafed at Mairead like a dirty sliver of wood in a wound. They nipped and niggled, but Mairead couldn't understand what bothered her. Then Mairead realised what Bronagh had said. *I will curse them with my last breath.*

Mairead's breath locked in her chest as the enormity of what she had done crushed her. *Blessed Mother!* Mairead had cursed Ciara and Ronan! Wished her cousin to have a taste of misery and loss. *My God! This is my fault.* She had wrought all of this for the sake of her wounded vanity. At that moment, Ciara's liquid gaze sought hers as though she were somehow drawn by Mairead's guilty thoughts. When her cousin gave her a lost and trembling smile, the guilt nearly choked her.

Mairead stumbled along, consumed by her dark thoughts, until the soldier yanked her tether again. Her body reacted by hurrying along, but her heart wanted nothing more than for the rope to tighten and end her misery. I can't bear this, she thought in agony. A voice in her head slapped that thought down. *Survive.* Ciara would not survive this ordeal alone, and Bronagh was no use to her. This was on Mairead to make sure Ciara survived. She'd give her life to make sure of it.

They arrived in Cork the next afternoon, and Mairead was a hollow shell, weak from hunger and exhaustion. She had only been given a hard crust of black bread and a few scoops of water from a river when they last stopped to water the horses. Her legs wobbled, and she kept stumbling. Tears stung her eyes. How could she ever have thought Ronan's betrayal an unbearable tragedy?

Cork was flush with English troops guarding their prized gateway to Ireland. In the harbour, four ships with the English flag bobbed in their moorings while a fifth, a two-masted vessel, sailed into the harbour, her sails bleach white against a grey sky.

As they progressed through the narrow streets, Mairead saw townspeople watch their procession with expressions of loathing directed at the soldiers. Little value and empty gestures; none moved a toe forward to rescue her or the others.

She had to get word to her father—he had to know what had befallen her. If he found out, surely he'd secure her release.

An idea flitted through Mairead's head. She lifted her voice and spoke out in Irish to the people they passed. "I am Mairead O' Coneill, daughter of Liam O' Coneill of Galway. Tell him what has happened to his daughter." She managed to repeat it twice before one of the English guards threatened her with a beating if she didn't shut up. She hoped it was enough.

They passed a shop displaying goods in the window, and a sharp pain filled Mairead's chest. The shop reminded her of her father's, even down to the stacks of finished leather. A pair of men filling the doorway could have been two of her brothers, lean and coiled for action. They had sent her to Uncle Mulriane's home for safety. The irony left a bitter taste in her mouth. Mairead tried to blink away the tears. Several escaped and rolled down her cheeks.

When the procession reached the other side of the harbour, the captain led them to a blacksmith's shop, where they finally stopped. Bronagh and Ciara collapsed to the ground, as did many of the others. Though Mairead's ankle still throbbed, she remained on her feet. If she gave in now, she'd never get up. She'd find herself dragged by the horse over cobbles and dung.

The blacksmith's shop proved to be large shed tucked behind a spacious courtyard. Inside, the fire raged, and from her position outside, it seemed to Mairead as though a bright red eye glared at her. The captain entered with one of his seconds to speak with the blacksmith. She caught a few of the soldiers looking at them speculatively, but when Mairead caught their gaze, they quickly turned away.

The blacksmith, a brawny man with thick cords for arms, stomped into the courtyard with the English captain. To Mairead's mind, he could have snapped the captain in half with little effort. Instead of throwing these men out of his shop, he smiled and accepted the copper coins the captain passed to him. The coins quickly disappeared into his apron pocket before he went back to his forge.

A sick feeling settled in Mairead's stomach. Bronagh exchanged glances with her, and even Ciara frowned.

"Bring up the prisoners, one by one," the English captain ordered his men.

Mairead was the first to be grabbed. The soldier dug his gritty fingernails into her arm and pulled her into the shop. A second soldier seized her other arm. Too weak to fight them both, she offered no resistance and allowed them to drag her inside.

"What are you doing?" she whispered, but they didn't give any indication that they heard.

The blacksmith was bent over his forge, heating a long metal rod with a flat end. When he turned around, he held up a glowing red brand. His face glowed inhumanly.

Mairead gasped. "No!" Suddenly, hands were all over her, pulling back her left arm and ripping the sleeve of her dress. She twisted to pull away, but the soldiers had her in a firm hold. They hauled her to the blacksmith's bench.

"Please, no," she whimpered to the blacksmith. "Please—*no!*" She strained against them, but they had her in a tight vise.

The blacksmith paused a fraction of a moment. Mairead's lips moved soundlessly. *Please. You're Irish.* He shuttered his expression and pressed his mouth in a resolute line.

When the hot brand touched Mairead's arm, she screamed. She bucked to get free, but they held her in a tight grip. Excruciating pain burrowed deep into her muscle, and the fire radiated through her skin. The smell of her own burnt flesh turned her stomach, and she gagged on her vomit.

Someone threw water on her shoulder, but it wasn't enough to put out the fire from inside. They shoved her in a corner padded with straw as, one by one, each prisoner was so marked. She watched, unable to turn away, and bore witness to their sobbing and panic. The worst was when they brought Ciara forward. Her cousin's cries sliced through Mairead.

Mairead watched as the last of the prisoners were branded. A hot rage rippled through her. Never would she forget this. *Never.* She dug her fingers into the dirt, curling them into fists. She palmed a smooth grey stone and pressed it into her hand. She was still clutching that stone when the English herded them to a waiting ship.

The ship's movement stilled. Iain pried his eyes open. Above, he could hear the pounding of footsteps and the men shouting orders. It appeared to him that they had arrived somewhere—Barbados, so soon? Dread gripped him in his belly, and yet a small ounce of relief crept in since they'd soon be out of this reeking hold.

The hatch opened, and one of the sailors shimmied down the ladder.

"Are we here?" Glencross called out weakly. "Are we in Barbados already?"

The sailor's brows shot up. "Not bleedin' close. Cork, this be."

Groans rippled through the hold.

Could this get any worse? "You're taking a tour of the British isles, are you?" Iain said. "Be a good lad and swing the ship north to Scotland. There's a bonny set of islands, right." That generated a few mocking laughs in response.

"Aren't you a cracker?" the seaman said with a scowl.

Iain covered his face with the crook of his arm. "'Tis no laughing matter."

"We've found you company," the seaman said. "You can thank us later." He gave a sharp whistle and looked up to the top of the ladder. "Hurry up and get down here, you filthy papist bogtrotter, or I'll yank you down quick as that."

Iain sat up when he heard the rattle of chains and the steady shuffling of many feet.

One by one, a chain of Irish prisoners climbed down the wooden ladder, their shackles hampering their movement. The irons gave them very little leeway, and one man slipped and skidded down the ladder, bringing down another three to crash at the base.

The seaman kicked the first Irishman in the ribs. "Look lively, bogtrotter." He hauled the man to his feet and pushed him towards an empty bunk.

Another dozen prisoners followed in his wake. They were a filthy lot, their lips cut and faces swollen. When the last man climbed down, Iain was about to turn away until he caught a glimpse of a brown skirt, a grey one, and the hem of another brown. Ten women descended into the hold.

Everyone went silent. Iain rubbed his eyes and blinked. Had he gone completely mad, or was this a vomit-induced delirium? Even Glencross's mouth hung open like a fish.

The women were a bedraggled lot and cringed when the seaman hustled them farther into the hold. Their skirts were torn and blackened by filth, and their hair was matted in tangles. They were unshackled, but rope burns ringed their necks, proof that they had at one time been tied up.

The seaman scratched his head and glanced back at the women. Frowning, he marched to the end of the hold and seemed bemused at the planked wall. "Should be another compartment." After a moment, he appeared to come to a decision and made for the wooden ladder. "I want no trouble from any of you," he told the men in the hold before scrambling up the ladder. The hatch slammed behind him.

The women pressed closer together, forming themselves into a frightened knot. Most had the look of country workers, but a few wore clothing that suggested they were a station above—a bit of lace around their bodice, the skirts showing evidence of fine wool instead of homespun.

Low murmuring rippled through the hold. Whores and harlots, a few muttered, with a hint of eager anticipation.

One in particular drew open leers and hungry eyes. A bonny lass, her eyes wide and blue as a summer's day, with hair like ripened barley. Even in her filthy state, her skin looked as silky as new cream. The whistles and calls unnerved her, and her bosom quivered like a snared hare. These men hadn't seen anything like her in too long to remember.

Iain's gaze flitted past her and rested on another—a young wisp of a thing with the biggest eyes he had ever seen. Frizzy brown hair framed a smudged oval face that ended with a little pointed chin. While the other women cowered, this one met the men's stares with open defiance. *A proper sprite, this one.*

"And who said the English were heartless bastards," Dunsmore said with a throaty laugh. His words released the dam of ribald laughter in the hold. "Months without a woman—several more weeks before we dock." Another pleased chuckle. Ignoring the other women, Dunsmore headed straight for the bonny lass, no doubt intending to claim her first.

But the wee sprite stepped between them and nudged the other woman behind her. "Leave her be," she said to Dunsmore. Her English betrayed a distinctive Irish lilt.

Dunsmore looked astonished at the interference. "Look at this, lads. This doxy is a feisty one," he said, recovering. "She'll get your blood up, to be sure. Killean Ross—you'll have to fight Angus Rae for a turn with her first." Some of the lads started clamouring, and the women contracted into a tighter knot, but not the sprite. She still remained between the bonny lass and the bastard.

"You should all be ashamed." That slip of a woman raked everyone with her accusing gaze. "You're no better off than any of us, but you are acting like depraved beasts."

Dunsmore laughter deepened and the others joined in. "Aye, now this one's lecturing me. Move over, lass, I'm after the juicy tidbit. I'll get to you later. Promise."

Iain had heard enough. Dunsmore was a right arse and needed his chain yanked before he stoked these men to carnal violence. Iain wasn't going to sit around and let that happen. As he pushed himself off his bunk, Glencross pulled a Lazarus and found his feet. His brother-in-law swayed slightly before managing to steady himself. With each step, he seemed to gather his strength.

Ignoring Dunsmore, Glencross approached the women. "Come, we'll squeeze in a spot for you," he told them, indicating the available space beside his bunk. The women exchanged wary looks, though none moved. "You'll not be harmed, upon my word," he added pointedly.

Dunsmore shoved Glencross against the shoulder. "What's this? Cutting in, are you? You can barely hold your water down, youngling—not much use to these lasses, are you?"

"Leave them be." Glencross drew the last dregs of his strength and held his ground.

"Hey," Iain called out as he approached the two men. "Don't be a misery, Dunsmore. Sit down, right, and quit your drooling. You've never seen a woman before?"

"You claiming these women as kin, Locharbaidh? These are all Johnstones, then?" He clenched his hand with the broken finger without once flinching and held Iain's stare.

"I told you what would happen if you crossed me again," Iain said in a low tone. Then, raising his voice so that it carried through the hold, he added, "Aye, these women are under my protection."

Instead of slinking to his bunk, Dunsmore faced Iain's moss-troopers and shrugged with a pained smile. "I told you, lads. This is how it is." His tone pierced like vinegar on an open wound.

"Aye, how about *you* tell me how it is?" Iain's eyes narrowed.

"Think yourself the laird, Locharbaidh?" Dunsmore said with a mocking laugh.

"You're the only one who thinks that horseshit." He glanced over at his men, expecting them to be nodding and shouting down this bystart, but, to his growing unease, they remained silent.

Dunsmore turned to Iain's men. "He's dragged you into this mess and spoils what little sport we find. He cares more for these Irish trollops than for your comfort. If he was *my* lord, he'd not have thought so low of his men."

Iain caught the disgruntled mutterings, including from some of his own men. Every man's attention centred on them. Even if he wanted to back down, and by God's death he didn't, he couldn't without losing face. He'd have to grind the snake into the ground before the venom spread.

"Enough foreplay." Iain slammed his fist into Dunsmore's jaw. The man's head snapped back, and he scrambled to keep his balance. Shackles snared his feet, and he fell backwards, knocking a piss bucket into the straw.

Iain stood over the man and slowly dusted his hands. "That's enough of you." He shook his head and began to turn back to

Glencross. The scuffling of the straw alerted him. As Iain whipped around, Dunsmore's fist plowed him in the stomach. The breath was knocked out of him, and pain rushed in to fill the sudden void. Dunsmore snarled and swung again. Iain shook his head and dodged the blow, then elbowed him in the throat. The man coughed and sputtered, dropping to his knees.

Iain should have walked away and let the man salvage his pride, but his blood still raged. He pushed him down and pressed his boot against his throat. "The next time you come at me, you'd better have more than that, for I'll not stay my hand again." Iain stepped away, this time not trusting his back to the man. "Get your arse back to your bench. Aye, I've had enough of you."

Dunsmore staggered to his feet, rubbing his bruised gullet. His flinty gaze locked on Iain. "This ain't done," he said in a low voice and spat on the ground between them. He chewed out an unintelligible word before slinking back to his own bunk.

Iain looked around. A hundred men in the hold, their hard stares riddling his hide. He stood between available women and desperate men. Though he'd dispatched Dunsmore easily enough, how long could he defend these women once everyone's blood heated up? The mood had already soured against him.

Iain squared his shoulders and held their hostile stares. A few had the sense to look away, but some of the bolder ones did not. His gaze darted to his moss-troopers. He could always count on their support, but there were only a few of them against many.

When Iain turned back to the women, the muscles between his shoulder blades twitched. He found Glencross speaking in soothing tones to the women. His brother-in-law offered half his own bunk space for their comfort. A kindhearted gesture, the least that a decent man should do, but something snapped in Iain. With Dunsmore out for blood and turning the others against him, these damned Irishwomen would be the death of him and Glencross. The men would pick them apart like wolves scenting weakness. He had an overwhelming desire to roar his frustration.

At that moment, the sprite placed herself in his path. Undaunted, she looked him in the eye and simply said, "Thank you."

Had Iain been even remotely sane, he would have given her a civil response, but all he could do was scowl. A growl rumbled at the back of his throat. Crazed man that he was, he barked, "Get back with the others and don't venture a toe out on the floor. You're all more trouble than you're worth."

She blinked, and her impossibly large eyes widened. Without taking her attention off him, she backed up and settled beside the blond, regarding him as she would a rabid beast.

Aye, now he felt like a complete arse. *Well done, Locharbaidh.*

The hatch rattled and opened. The seaman who had just left them practically fell down the ladder. The quartermaster followed, his shouts bouncing off the hold walls.

"Damn your blood—putting these women down here." He grabbed the man by the shirt and shook him like a rag doll. "Forward hold, I said, damn you. *Forward.* Now!" He released him and shoved him away. The seaman scrambled to round the women up and hurried them up the ladder like a small dog yapping at their ankles. The hatch slammed shut behind them.

Iain released his breath slowly. It was a long time before the men's sullen glances turned away from him and back to their own misery. Everyone except Dunsmore, who nursed his wounds with a baleful glare.

Chapter 4

————◆————

Mairead prayed for death. There was nothing more in her stomach to throw up. She drew herself into a tight ball, stomach churning with every rise and dip of the ship against the waves. The only solid thing in her world was Ciara's reassuring hand against her brow.

A rat drew closer to Mairead's face, drawn by the smell of vomit. She groaned and forced herself to sit up. Her head swam, and she gritted her teeth against the nausea. She pressed her knees to her chest and wrapped her arms tight around her legs. The brand on her shoulder itched furiously.

"Feeling better, dearest?" Ciara asked her.

Mairead nodded, but that was a lie. From the moment they set sail, Mairead had endured intense seasickness, and it was Ciara who nursed her through the ordeal, murmuring soft words of encouragement. Guilt gnawed at Mairead. She had cursed Ciara, and yet her cousin spent her energy caring for her. Mairead was deeply ashamed at the madness that had momentarily driven her from her cousin, all for a fickle man.

The section of the hold they had been thrown in was narrow and dim—a smaller, secondary compartment with crates piled in the far corner.

A tattered piece of sail formed a curtain, converting a corner of the hold into an alcove where a few of the bolder sailors could slake their needs with the women. Behind the screen, the steady light of a lantern cast grotesque shadows. Mairead pressed her hands against her ears to the sound of rutting and muffled sobbing, but she couldn't entirely block it out.

At different times of day and night, a sailor would appear in the hold and take one of the women behind the screen. Small mercy that, so far, she, Ciara and Bronagh had been spared. The captain wanted them untouched. They had been sold to him as virgins, and he had paid handsomely for their maidenhead. Worry riddled through Mairead—what would happen when she was eventually found out? She usually managed to push the fear away—if she didn't survive the trip, it wouldn't matter. For now, she was spared the ordeal, but it still wasn't easy to meet the eyes of the other women when the seamen finished with them.

All except the former washer-girl, Roisin, who accepted this reality with the pragmatism of a hardened soul. She didn't bother to hide from the others the extra chunk of bread she received or the cup of grog to wash it down. She met the other women's stares with an open challenge. Call me out if you dare, she seemed to be saying. But the other night things had gotten a bit rough behind the screen for her, and when it was over, Roisin had returned with a little less of her usual unshakeable self-confidence. Mairead had watched as she smoothed her skirts down over her dirty legs with a slight tremor of her hand.

Roisin had caught Mairead staring at her. "Don't pity me, girl. Look to yourself. They're saving you and the other manor misses for the brothels." She motioned to Ciara and Bronagh with a toss of her head. "Men will pay for a first night and pay well."

Mairead couldn't stop thinking about this. Bronagh kept muttering that they wouldn't dare, but that sounded rather hollow to Mairead.

Suddenly, the shadows ceased grappling on the screen and the sounds stopped. After a brief shuffling, the screen was pushed aside and the seaman appeared, hitching his breeches. He didn't bother looking at the women as he left the hold. The hatch closed, leaving them once again in near darkness.

"We'll survive this, dearest, never fear," Ciara said to Mairead as she gathered her in her arms.

Mairead closed her eyes and allowed herself to relax in Ciara's promises of salvation. Her mouth was parched, and she had no strength to speak.

"Your da must have the news by now," Ciara continued softly. "Liam O' Coneill will send a captain to come fetch us, of course he will."

If only Galway wasn't being threatened by the English. Ciara had forgotten this detail, but it congealed as a lump in Mairead's throat.

"Can you not see it now?" Ciara's laugh sounded choked. "Your da marching into the local with your brothers. He'll climb atop one of the benches, no matter how the landlord fumes over muddy boots."

Mairead wanted to lose herself in the fantasy and clung to Ciara's words, picturing her father in the Thorned Staff.

"But no one can say that Liam O' Coneill doesn't have a gilded tongue," Ciara said. "Blessed by the fae, no doubt. 'Half my fortune,' he'll shout to the rafters. 'Half my fortune to the man who fetches me darling girl back.'"

"And her kin," Mairead added with a whisper.

"Oh, for sweet Christ's sake," Bronagh said. "Listen to the both you. No one is coming for us. We're lost . . . lost."

Mairead's hope drained. Bronagh was right. Was there any chance for escape?

"Hold your tongue, Bronagh Mulriane," Ciara said. "There is always hope. The plantation owners in Barbados are Christian— surely they will be charitable."

51

First they had to survive the voyage.

Mairead had heard some of the sailors' talk about Barbados. The settlers had been loyal to the King and only recently had been forced to capitulate to the English Commonwealth. Could they beg their help?

"Your sister speaks the truth," Roisin said to Ciara. "Hide your ears and turn your eyes away, won't you? Tell that one," she said, nodding to Mairead, "a fairy tale to keep her spirits high. Won't change anything. How will you explain it to her when she's sold off to a brothel?"

Mairead's stomach heaved, and she turned her head. The threat of a brothel loomed over all their heads. But Ciara was undeterred. "You've a vile, cruel tongue, Roisin Flynn, and I'll not stand for it."

"You won't, you say? Look at you, with your airs. You're no longer my mistress."

Mairead licked her parched lips and said wearily, "Ciara and Bronagh are the daughters of your lord and deserve your respect. They've lost everything—"

Roisin tipped her head back and cut her off with a laugh of derision. "Like the world that was taken from *us*? Where are the Mulrianes who had pledged to keep us safe? We pledged our faith to a long line of Mulrianes, and the only thing they had to do was offer their protection. When did they fight our fights? Feed our babies? We toiled for them for years, gave them our tithes, all for the fantasy of protection. We were better off minding our own affairs."

"How can you blame my uncle for this?" Mairead said, shrugging to sit up. Anger for the smug woman cut through her weakness and nausea. "The weak will look for ways to blame someone for their ills. So easy to blame the man who tried to defend his home over the invaders who stole it from him. You've become soft on these sailors, have you not, Roisin Flynn?"

Roisin scrambled to her feet and looked down upon Mairead. "How dare you!"

"Leave her be, Roisin," Ciara said. "We should all stand together and remember who our enemy is."

The hatch creaked open, and a sailor scrambled down the ladder with their meal. When he reached the base, he stopped to size up Roisin and Mairead. "Having words, are we? Chew on this instead," he said and handed both of a heel of hard bread. Mairead noticed he slipped Roisin the biggest piece. "Be good doxies, and maybe the captain will let you come up above for a turn on the deck."

When he left, Roisin eyed Mairead with a hardened stare before tearing off a chunk of bread with her teeth. She turned her back and reclaimed her corner in the hold.

Mairead's meagre strength failed, and she curled up beside Ciara. She didn't want to think of what would happen to them when they landed in Barbados.

The darkness smothered Mairead like an unwanted embrace. The sour stench of urine, vomit and tar filled her nostrils. The worst of her seasickness had finally passed, leaving only despair. She clutched at the smooth rock she had picked up at Cork, her last connection to Ireland, but it provided little comfort.

The others had fallen asleep to the sound of creaking and straining timbers, but not Mairead. The ship dipped and swayed but could not lull her back to sleep. One of the women moaned, and her cries intensified until it was obvious that she was gripped in her own nightmare.

Mairead had given up trying to keep track of the days. She had managed to keep a week, then two straight, but after that time blurred. The Mulriane kitchen maid had died a few days ago. The ship's tars had rolled up the poor lass in a canvas sack and hauled her away to be dropped over the side into the cold water below.

Far from home. They would all die far from home. Mairead no longer wanted to live and would have welcomed death. She thought of the kitchen maid and envied her release. The lass was now in a far better place.

She leaned against the wall, feeling the rolling of the ship. A sound broke through her dark thoughts. Someone was singing in a deep baritone voice. The melody sounded familiar, and Mairead strained to place it. Then she recalled it was a Scottish ballad. The Scottish minstrel back in Galway had often played it in the garret room above her father's shop. The song brought to Mairead a rush of poignant memories—stacked crates, oak barrels and a familiar scent of cherry and wood from her father's tobacco pipe.

Where did the singing come from? Mairead followed the song to the end of the hold, where it grew louder. She ran her hand along the dark wall until her fingers caught against the metallic lip of a narrow grate.

An inrush of rancid air wafted up, and she clamped her hand over her nose to stop her stomach from emptying. Here the song sounded more distinct, and Mairead pressed her ears against the grate.

O could ye speak, my bonny spier-hawk,
As ye hae wings to flee,
Then ye wad carry a love-letter
Atween my love an' me.
But how can I your true-love ken?
Or how can I her know?
Or how can I your true-love ken,
The face I never saw?
Ye may easily my love ken
Among them ye never saw
The red that's on o' my love's cheek
Is like blood draped on the snow.

The voice had an earthy quality that curled around her senses. The deep baritone wrapped around her like an embrace. Mairead closed her eyes and allowed herself to be carried away by the melody, taking comfort in the strains that washed over her. It reached deep into her core until she hung on every syllable and every beat.

When the ballad finally trailed to an end, Mairead lowered her head and mouthed a silent thanks to the unknown singer. For while the song continued, she forgot about the stinking hold and the ship that carried her towards slavery.

Mairead startled awake. Someone gripped her shoulder. She jerked back, balling her fists as a barrier in front of her. One of the seamen stood above her. A lantern elongated his features so that he resembled a fierce hunting bird.

"Leave me be," Mairead screamed and scrambled backwards. Pressing her back against the wall, she thrust out her hand to ward him off. Her head was foggy, and she couldn't quite make out his words at first. He had to repeat himself a few times.

"Get up on deck," he yelled slowly, enunciating each word as one would to a deaf mute. He pointed to the open hatch. "Time for some fresh air, you stupid chit."

Ciara, Bronagh and half of the others were already climbing the ladder. *Fresh air?* Mairead rose unsteadily to her feet and shied past the sailor. When she reached the ladder, a salty breeze rushed down to her. It cleared her head and washed away the putrid stench that filled her nose. Gingerly, she grasped the side of the ladder and clambered up to the deck. Though the sky was cloudy and grey, Mairead blinked against the unaccustomed light. She stood there, momentarily disoriented and shielding her eyes.

"This way," one of the crewmen said, jabbing Mairead's back and herding her and the other women to the aft deck. A dozen male prisoners had also gathered there.

The wind was chill and laden with salt spray. It stung Mairead's cracked lips. She swayed and felt the deck beneath her pitch and roll. Her stomach lurched. Retching, she clamped a hand over her mouth and dashed for the taffrail, pushing past everyone in her way. She barely made it before emptying the meagre contents of her stomach over the side. Her stomach cramped while she heaved and gagged until there was no more to throw up. Mairead's limbs began to shake, and she sagged against the rail for support. But her legs were too weak to hold her upright, and she sank to the deck.

Breathe in . . . breathe out. Mairead's eyes remained fastened shut as she willed her stomach to settle. Teardrops clung to her eyelashes. When her eyes fluttered open, her stomach dropped like a rock, this time not from seasickness.

He was there. The Scottish ogre. Right beside her at the taffrail. Heat flooded Mairead's cheeks, and she smothered a groan. She hadn't recovered from the embarrassment of his tongue-lashing—in front of everyone, like a crazed man. All she had done was thank him for his intervention, but like a feral beast he had turned on her in a horrible, horrifying manner. Now he stood there, an immediate witness to her mortification. Was she too late to toss herself overboard?

The man stared at her with a mixture of pity and intense fascination. "Are you done?" His Scottish burr carried a rough texture.

Mairead winced. "For now," she answered in a small voice. She attempted to rise, but her stomach churned queasily. Not wanting to give a repeat performance, she had no choice but to remain where she was.

"You're green."

"As good a colour as any," she answered through clenched teeth.

The ogre sniffed. He rested his forearms on the rail and leaned forward. "I had hoped for a bit of fresh air. I get enough of *that* below."

56

Fresh air. The crisp wind started to calm her stomach—as long as she didn't look at the roiling waves. But her irritation with the man was not so easily smoothed over. "Shame that I've spoiled it for you. Best sharpen your knives and prepare to gut me, I suppose."

His mouth twitched—from amusement or irritation? He didn't answer, only remained fixated by the sea. After several moments, he asked, "Will you not rise, Sprite? Take sanctuary with the other women?" His meaning was unmistakable—leave, go anywhere but remain here. That would suit her well were it not for her nausea.

"Waiting for my constitution to settle," she replied stiffly. "Do you wish for me to befoul your boots?" She cast an eye to them. They had definitely seen better days.

"Stay where you are," he grumbled.

Mairead hugged her knees to her chest. The Scotsman didn't betray any interest in conversing, so she took this opportunity to study the brute. He, like the others, resembled more animal than man, though in his case he had the air of a fearsome beast, albeit a chained one, for the irons were still locked to his ankles. Dirt and grease matted his shoulder-length blond hair, and his beard was a tangled mess—the man needed a shearing very badly. His blue eyes flicked sideways before resuming their unwavering stare towards the dark water.

What was he thinking about, brooding so intensely at the parting sea and ignoring her so thoroughly? Mairead began to notice the tenseness around his eyes and mouth—he looked tired and worn. And wounded. She suspected that the force still keeping him on his feet was the solid rail and a stubborn will.

"What are you doing, woman?"

The suddenness of his deep voice startled Mairead. Mortified that she had been caught staring, heat flooded her cheeks. Shakily, she rose to her feet and paused a moment to steady her reeling head. Her stomach flipped, and all thoughts of a dignified retreat were forced to be delayed. She bent over the rail, trying not to think about the churning waves below. At least she was on her feet.

"Cease badgering me," she said, "or I might aim for your boots after all."

At this moment, the red-haired Scotsman who had offered his bunk joined them at the rail. Mairead had not forgotten his kindness, and she was grateful for his intervention. Dark blue smudges darkened his eyes, and his cheeks had been hollowed out, but he still managed a wan smile. "Is he troubling you, lass? You should know Iain Johnstone eats babies for breakfast."

Mairead expected a retort from the ogre—Johnstone, now that she had his name—and in fact he looked as though he was chewing his words before getting ready to spit them out. "I believe it," she replied. "Uses their bones to pick his teeth, I suppose."

"Aye, you ken the nature of the man," he replied. "I'm David Glencross, his keeper."

Johnstone snorted before turning back to the sea. But there was something in his manner, an alertness that suggested to Mairead that his attention wasn't entirely consumed by the whitecaps.

"I'm Mairead O'Coneill." She hesitated a moment before adding, "Thank you for your kindness earlier."

Glencross shrugged and ducked his head. When he glanced up, he frowned. His gaze flitted to the women gathered at the other end of the deck before he turned once again to Mairead. "How did you end up here, lass?"

A simple question, but one that delivered a sudden stab of pain. Unprepared, Mairead shut her eyes against the memory of her family—and Ronan. His handsome face had started to fade, as had the feeling of her hurt and betrayal, only to be replaced by the horror of his death. A hard lump settled in her throat, and her eyes pricked with tears. "English soldiers," she said after taking a deep breath. "They killed my uncle, his wife and son, then seized his land." She noticed that Johnstone's attention was entirely fixed on her, and the intensity of his gaze was a physical thing. "They thought to earn extra coin by selling us to this slaver." Without conscious thought, her hand touched the still-raw brand on her shoulder, hidden under her sleeve.

Glencross's gaze hardened. "We all fought at Worcester under the King. It didn't end well." He glanced at Johnstone, who hadn't said a word. "They saw the same opportunity to earn a coin with us."

Mairead's widened. "You fought against the Antichrist Cromwell?" They shared something in common as she thought about the Tóraidhe and every man who resisted the invading English.

"Is that what you call him in Ireland?"

"We call him worse," she replied. She felt the force of a stare burning her cheek and turned to find Johnstone's gaze fixed on her. This startled her, at first for being so unexpected and for its intensity.

"The war is over," Johnstone cut in roughly. "Best to mind the present, right."

"The past is all I have." Mairead hated the present and feared the future.

"There's all manner of grief down that road," Johnstone said.

"Hypocrite," Glencross replied. A silent communication seemed to pass between the two men, and Johnstone was the first to turn away.

"She best be prepared," Johnstone said sullenly. "Things will get worse than naught."

"I've seen the worst. There isn't anything more." Mairead lowered her head, blinking away the tears. She bit her lip, using one pain to distract her from another.

"Don't be naive," Johnstone said curtly.

Mairead lifted her chin and forced herself to meet his direct gaze. "I'm not."

Johnstone studied her through narrowed eyes. "You have some strength in you. I hope for your sake 'tis enough." His gaze settled on

Ciara, who stood a little apart from the other women. "But your kinswoman," he nodded towards Ciara, "that one won't last long."

A flare of anger ignited Mairead. "How *dare* you?" To speak such vile thoughts and risk cursing her! She had an overwhelming urge to push him over the side. "You are an impossible man," she hissed.

"I'm speaking the truth—get used to it," Johnstone said.

"Never mind him," Glencross said. "He doesn't mean poorly. I find myself always making excuses for Himself."

"No you don't," Johnstone snapped.

"Aye, I do," Glencross said with a wry grimace.

"You should save yourself the bother," Mairead said. "He isn't worth the trouble."

A bell rang, and one of the sailors called out, "Time's up. Form a line. Look smart."

The crewmen started herding them below. Mairead found herself being driven back to where the other women were collected, and it just occurred to her that the worst of her seasickness had passed without her realising it. Anger and irritation were excellent balms after all. In this, she should thank the ogre.

As she crossed the deck to reach the stairs leading to the decks below, Mairead felt a prickling in her skin. When she glanced over her shoulder, she found Johnstone staring at her.

Chapter 5

———◆———

Iain sensed a change. He pried his eyes open and stared at the steady light filtering through the overhead grate. *Still alive. Barely.*

The last few weeks had nearly done them all in. Squalls and storms had made the hold a living hell. Over a third of the prisoners had perished, their bodies dropped in the cold depths of the *Jane Marie's* wake. Iain had lost five of his own men, and those who remained were barely hanging on. Glencross couldn't lift his head without shaking like a newborn lamb; Killean Ross had lost a few stone in weight and could barely keep anything down. Though short, Masterton the Younger had always displayed raw strength from his corded arms to his bushy moustache. Now his arms looked flabby and deflated. Beside him, Angus Rae curled on his side, gangly legs drawn to his belly. Even Dunsmore looked like the fight had been kicked out of him.

Iain had endured marginally better. The last round of seasickness brought on by the rough waters had finally eased a couple of days ago, but the vapours congesting the hold grew increasingly toxic, making it hard for him to draw breath without gagging. He doubted he'd make it through another squall.

Weakly, he sang a song under his breath. It was an old ballad that had stayed with him for years, an overly sentimental piece about love and returning home. Being so far away from Scotland, he could think of no other verse to distract him from his misery.

He strained to listen to the sounds above deck. Something *was* different. Where he expected to hear the creaking and groaning of timbers, an expectant silence filled his ears. Only then did he realise that the motion of the ship had diminished. Instead of bucking and roaring like an untrained foal, the ship rocked gently forward and back. With effort, he propped himself up on his elbows and looked around. "Do you feel that, lads?" It came out as little more than a raspy croak.

"I feel naught," Masterton groaned weakly.

"Aye, that's what I mean."

The hatch opened, pouring in a flood of light. A couple of sailors scampered down into the hold.

"Gar, this is foul," the first man muttered before he started counting heads.

"Where . . . are . . . we?" Iain asked, forcing himself to call out.

"Shut up—you've messed with my count."

"Eighty-two left," the other sailor called out. He approached one of the prisoners in his bunk and knocked his shoulder. No response. "Eighty-one," he said, clucking his tongue.

"Fewer survivors than the last trip," the first man said with a shrug. "The cap'n won't be best pleased. Grab the ankles quick—we have just enough time to toss this one over before we reach harbour."

Iain's vision darkened with rage. He struggled to a sitting position, but his swimming head levelled him. "We're men . . . not rubbish."

"Eh? What was that?" One of the sailors squinted at Iain as he advanced. Drawing a stave from his belt, he tapped it against his own palm. "What did you say?"

Iain turned his head. He didn't have the strength to answer back, nor did he care if the man bashed him through here and now.

"Well?" the sailor barked.

"He asked where we were," Glencross replied, casting a warning look at Iain.

The soldier snorted. He slipped the stave back in his belt and ran the back of his hand under his nose. "Barbados. Getting ready to sail into Bridge Town." He and his mate exchanged a look before they laughed. "Congratulations, you filthy bogtrotters, you haven't ended up as shark meat. But what happens from here is between you and the devil." And with that, the sailors climbed out of the hold and slammed the hatch shut.

"We made it," Glencross said in a low voice. "We reached Barbados."

"You say that like we've reached the blessed isles," Iain muttered. He licked his parched lips. "You didn't need to defend me."

"Aye?

"More of a mercy if you hadn't."

Glencross leaned in closer. "You'd better not give up now, Locharbaidh, or I'll have words for you. You're a cantankerous bastard, and we're all counting on you to see us through this."

The sounds of frenzied activity above deck penetrated through the depths of the hold. The captain's barked commands mingled with a series of shrill whistles and a clanging bell. From the tilt of his bunk, it seemed to Iain that the ship shifted direction. Against the wall of the hold, he felt a vibration before the ship shuddered to a halt. Eager cheers sounded, cries of gladness not echoed in the hold.

Iain lost track of the hours, and it seemed like years before the hatch was lifted again, but this time instead of the two sailors, the captain and another man climbed down the ladder.

"Mind that middle rung; there's a good man," the captain called up to the stranger. When he reached the bottom of the ladder and stepped away, he looked around the hold. What he saw made him scowl. "Sit up and show respect. The factor's here to take his measure of you."

The factor joined the captain and held a linen kerchief to his nose. Speaking through the cloth, he said, "Is this all?"

"The passage was rough," the captain said, spitting a gob on the mouldy straw. "Winter's never a good time on the seas. This will be my last run before the spring."

"You say you've brought Irish too?" The factor's nose twitched above his handkerchief.

"Aye, a few, including women, but this lot is mostly Scottish," the captain said. "Hence my price. Good workers, I warrant. Bred for the march—the fields should be no trouble for them."

Iain stirred himself at that. He wasn't a bloody dray horse. None of them were.

"They hardly look as though they can lift a bucket." The whine in the man's voice grated on Iain's ears.

"They only need a few days of proper food," the captain said.

The factor sniffed. "I'll take them on at twenty-five percent commission."

"What? You've never charged me more than ten. Your greed has tricked you into thinking I'm a fool."

"The commission reflects the poor shape of this lot, Captain," the factor said. "And the market price has dropped since the war. Every ship that sails into Bridge Town is carrying the same cargo. Christian servants are not as scarce as they were six months ago."

Iain propped himself on his elbow, aghast at what he was hearing. These bastards were bickering over them like old fish wives at market. Glencross caught his eye and shook his head, once again with a silent warning to behave.

The captain adjusted the waistband of his breeches and spat on the straw. "You pay for their food and we have an accord."

The factor's gaze raked across the hold with the detachment of a man assessing the quality of wool. "Half the cost of food and no change in my commission."

A pox on them.

The captain scowled but accepted with a curt nod. "Deal."

"I'll make the necessary arrangements," the factor said, advancing to the ladder. "Now show me those women."

When the hatch slammed behind them, silence settled again in the hold. Not even a ragged cough or a moan. Iain rolled his shoulders until he managed to pull himself into a sitting position. His footing was unsteady, and the shackles rubbed the raw, bleeding skin around his ankles. When he reached one of the slop buckets, he drew it back and hurtled it against the hatch.

"*There's* your twenty-five percent, you bloody arseworms," Iain bellowed to the captain.

"Aye, that will be sure to change their minds, Locharbaidh," Dunsmore said with a derisive laugh.

True to the deal the captain and the factor struck, everyone's diet improved over the next week. The kirk of commerce ruled where Christian charity quailed. Iain smothered his grumblings about being turned into a fatted calf, and for the first time in months he tasted roasted meat. With the first bite, his stomach trembled at the richness of the pork, but he pushed past the discomfort. Many could barely keep the food down, but by the next day fewer were fighting the stomach cramps. By the end of the week, most had the strength to stand on their own.

Just in time for the auction.

The ship's crew had been busy offloading the cargo, and now things were silenced. Iain suspected that it was only a matter of time before they came for them.

Iain wanted to slam his fist through the hold wall whenever he thought of the humiliation awaiting him. Still shackled, he paced a short loop in the hold, shuffling from one end of the bench to the other. He couldn't sit still; his nerves were afire. With every moment that passed, he was one step closer to being forced into bondage. A proud man should never be subjected to this travesty.

Iain looked around the hold. Despite the decent food and clean water, physically none of them could launch an attack against a beetle. And their will to resist? Purged with the hundreds of vomit buckets tossed overboard during the past eight weeks.

When he went to shuffle past Glencross, his brother-in-law blocked his way. "You're a wee bit skittish and undoing everyone with that pacing."

Iain looked up and noticed his men staring at them. Glencross was right—he needed to settle down, if only for his men's sake. Exhaling slowly, he leaned against the edge of the shelf. "I hate this waiting, curse them."

"Aye, I can wait longer," Glencross said in a low tone. "In no hurry for the auction."

Iain grunted. What he wanted was to fight his way out of this, but he knew all was lost. No future. No chance. Seven years of bondage yawned before him—for the remainder of his natural life. The darkness of that thought pressed like a mountain upon his shoulders. He closed his eyes and lowered his head. Why hadn't he died honourably on the field? 'Twas a cruel devil who spared him for this.

Glencross cleared his throat. "I just wanted you to know . . . it was all worth it. I don't regret the road we followed."

Iain clenched his jaw. "Don't talk like that," he said gruffly. Fool Glencross. Didn't he know that he should have been back on his farm, wooing the neighbour's shy daughter and spending his time siring ginger-haired sons? "This isn't the end of the road." He tried to believe that, but he knew it was a mad promise.

Glencross snorted. "It's a bloody fork, Iain, and who knows where we'll end up on the other side."

Iain wished he could reassure him, but there wasn't enough hope to scrape together. He squeezed his eyes shut. It finally sank deep into his gut that he might never see Glencross again. Too much had been ripped out of his life. A wave of sorrow washed over him, and he felt himself sinking. In a low tone, he said, "Talk to me about Innis. Her last words."

It had been years since he had first asked. Then, it had been a shard of glass twisting in his gut. Innis had died during labour delivering their first child. Iain had not been there with her, had instead been on patrol, helping to gather the Johnstones to repel the invading English. He had sent his brother-in-law to check on his wife—he had promised to return home as soon as he could. When Iain finally did, it had not been to the warmth of a wife and newborn, but to the cold ashes of a broken hearth.

It had been Glencross who had held *his* wife's hand while she died and then buried *his* stillborn son. Iain, not Glencross, should have been there.

"Tell me what she said. I want to hear it again," Iain insisted. This might be the last time he was to be reminded of it.

Glencross squinted across the hold before turning his attention to a knot in the boards. He scraped his fingernail into a groove. "Why do you need to think of this now?"

"Was she in pain?"

Crossing his arms over his thin chest, Glencross said, "Nay, no pain." His throat worked. "The lass passed away peacefully."

"Are you sure?" A shadow passed over Iain.

Glencross nodded and turned his face away. "Aye, I already told you."

The silence stretched between them. When Glencross finally spoke, his voice sounded as coarse as sand. "Take care of yourself, Iain."

Iain's gut wrenched and twisted into a knot, so he allowed stubborn grit to override the pain. He seized on the tether. "You think this is the end between us?"

"Might be."

"Think again." Iain rose to his feet and started pacing again, fuelled by anger and frustration. "We're nae being led to our graves here. They brought us here against our wills, but damned if we have to honour that shite." Many of his men turned their attention to him. "No matter where we end up, all of us," Iain said, pointing to his erstwhile officers, "we pledge here and now that we'll find a way to get back home, and nae forget the others."

Masterton nodded with a harrumph, and Killean sat a little straighter.

"Remember," Iain said. "All ready?"

"Always ready," Glencross said.

"Aye, ready," Masterton added.

Dunsmore sat in his corner, sober. "Your house's motto will nae save you. 'Tis neither shield nor sword. The auld ways won't preserve us now."

Iain looked at Dunsmore almost pityingly. Words mattered—they were the hammer and anvil to the steel. He straightened to his full height and said, "The auld ways are all we have. Without tradition, without kin and country, we're naught but beasts. Give up if you will, but I mean to go home."

Iain Locharbaidh Johnstone would not be defeated.

Mairead watched with growing dread as two strange women descended into the hold. They weren't the first visitors who had come to see them since the *Jane Marie* anchored. Not long after the ship entered Bridge Town harbour, the captain had arrived with the factor. The man had given them a cursory inspection before telling the captain that he'd send the midwife, Mother Lucia, to inspect the baggage.

"Better hope that none of them have the pox," the factor had said, "or are breeding. You claim that three or four are still maidens?"

Mairead's breath had hitched in her throat.

"Aye, three. Untouched and clean."

The factor had sniffed. "They'll fetch a high price, but 'tis Mother Lucia's word I'll have on the matter." He was already at the ladder with the captain trailing behind him like a fawning pup.

When they left, Ciara had glanced at Mairead with alarm. Her arm shot out to hold Mairead steady. "Mairead? Sit down. You look as though you'll faint."

Mairead had sunk to the ground, feeling ill indeed.

By that very afternoon, Mother Lucia arrived with an assistant. The midwife filled the hold with a brusque authority while her drab companion followed in her shadow clutching a satchel. Mother Lucia hardly looked motherly, for she was raw-boned and square-shouldered. Were it not for her matronly shape, the creature could have been mistaken for a weather-beaten sailor in petticoats.

"Get up on your feet so's I can get a good look at you," Mother Lucia told the women in a flat tone. When most didn't immediately rise, the woman planted her hands on her padded hips and pinned them with a hard stare. "Or my Martha will drag you by your hair— makes no difference to me."

Mairead's stomach twisted into knots, and her mouth felt as dry as sand. By the look of her, the midwife wasn't a fool. She only hoped the woman had some compassion.

Shakily, Mairead rose to her feet, wobbling and light-headed. Ciara swayed slightly, but she followed as well. Bronagh, however, remained where she was. If anything, she appeared to dig her bottom firmly into the straw, even though she was the only one still down. Mairead recognised the stubborn tilt of Bronagh's chin and for a moment admired her cousin for it.

But Mother Lucia had other opinions. A pointed nod to her assistant caused Bronagh to be seized. The assistant gripped a hunk of hair and hauled her to the midwife. Bronagh's shrieks curdled blood, and tears of pain streamed down her cheeks

Mother Lucia motioned to the alcove hidden behind a screen. "Take her in the back, Martha. Might as well start with this one." Bronagh disappeared into the alcove.

The lantern cast a writhing tangle of shadows against the screen that resembled grappling gargoyles. Mairead stared at the patched canvas, and an icy chill spread through her. She heard the shuffling in the straw and Bronagh's renewed protests, then her strangled shriek.

Slap.

Mairead started and bumped into Ciara, who had paled. Bronagh's screams became muffled, as though a wad of cloth had been shoved into her mouth.

Several minutes lapsed, and Bronagh's cries faded to a whimper. The midwife finally stepped out from behind the screen, wiping her hand on a rag. A moment later, Bronagh appeared, cheeks streaked with tears and dirt. Part of her skirt was hoisted over her knees before Bronagh yanked it down. With a baleful eye to the midwife and her assistant, she skirted away from them and headed for a solitary corner, her expression a mixture of fear and loathing.

The next woman to be taken behind the screen was Roisin. She marched unassisted with her head held high. The young woman tried to engage the midwife with a casual greeting but couldn't entirely disguise the tremor in her voice. Martha parted the screen and Roisin followed where Bronagh had fought fiercely to avoid entering.

This time there was no shrieking or carrying on. Whatever they were doing to her, Roisin took it in stride, as she did most of the horrible things the sailors did to her behind the same screen. Mairead swallowed hard, and her stomach churned sickly.

Finally, the midwife muttered something, and Roisin's voice rose, strained. "What are you saying?"

The midwife spoke, this time loud enough for Mairead to hear. "You're with child."

"So what if I am?"

"We'll deal with you later."

70

"What do you mean?" Roisin persisted. Mairead could hear the sharp fear in her voice.

The screen fluttered and parted slightly. Roisin was turned facing the alcove while Martha was trying to hurry her along. "Tell me, vile woman."

Mother Lucia appeared at the entrance and faced Roisin with a gathering scowl. "Don't you *vile woman* me. I have worth here, while you're not even fit to be auctioned. None of the planters will support a squalling brat. If you're lucky, you'll end up on your back in a whorehouse—or else you'll be begging twopence at the gutters."

Mairead was stunned, and her mouth parted in surprise. Roisin's condition was the fault of the sailors who had visited her these past several weeks. What the midwife described was no doubt a death sentence.

"Tell them to send me back," Roisin said, trying to grab at the midwife's arm, but the woman shook herself free.

"You're not worth the passage," Mother Lucia replied, shrugging her off.

What was to happen to Roisin? It was hard to imagine how her situation could be any worse than it was now. When Mairead's gaze met Roisin's desperation, she understood. Yes, it could be far, far worse.

Mother Lucia's gaze shot to Mairead. "You next."

Mairead's heart sprang into her throat. She took a step back, but Martha grabbed her by the arm and marched her towards the alcove.

"No, please," Mairead said. Who knew what depravity waited for her behind that screen? She dug her heels into the straw and tried to pull back, but Martha's hold on her did not slacken. With a quick jerk, she yanked Mairead forward and pushed her behind the screen.

Mairead landed in the straw on her knees and immediately twisted around, but not fast enough to outrun Martha or Mother Lucia. Martha pushed Mairead to the ground and pinned her shoulders while Mother Lucia straddled her thrashing legs. The midwife hiked up Mairead's skirts.

"What are you doing?" Mairead gasped, trying to lock her knees. She tried to buck them both off. "What are you doing?"

Mother Lucia ignored her and pried Mairead's legs apart.

"Stop! Leave me!"

"Enough of that." The midwife pinched the inside of Mairead's thigh. It felt as though she had nicked a chunk of her flesh. Searing pain washed over Mairead, and her breath locked in her throat.

That was all the time Mother Lucia needed. Mairead forgot the pain of her thigh the moment the woman inserted her fingers into her seam. She gasped and tightened her muscles.

The woman cast an eye at her and then continued to probe. "Hold still, wench. Hold still."

Mairead bit her lip, and tears streamed down her cheek. She was horrified at this indignity. And the woman's calloused hands hurt. Mairead turned her head into the straw and watched the swaying lantern light. *Please, Blessed Mother. Make them stop. Please.* Back and forth the lantern swung on its iron hook. Dark and light and back again. And still the midwife probed. Salty tears trailed down Mairead's cheeks and pooled in the corner of her mouth.

Just as she thought she couldn't take any more, Mother Lucia rose, and a great weight was lifted from her legs. It took Mairead a few moments to gather herself. She smoothed her skirt down over her dirty thighs and tried to still her shaking hands. With the back of her hand, she swiped away the tears. Mairead had never felt more filthy than she did at that moment. Neither the midwife or her assistant looked at her. They acted as though she were not there. Neither offered an apology for their rough treatment. Mairead didn't exist.

"The chit's lost her maidenhead," Mother Lucia said with a cluck of her tongue. "At least she's not with child." Her eyes flicked over Mairead as she added to her assistant, "Send the next one in."

Mairead returned to her place in the straw and avoided Ciara's worried gaze. Her desire to curl up and cry warred with annoyance with herself. She had to toughen up. She couldn't come undone over a little rough treatment. Mairead had already lost everything—her home, her family, her liberty. Worse things she'd have to face and soon. How could she survive? Would it not be easier just to give up right now and simply pray for death? Without thought, her hand slipped into her pouch and curled around the stone she had found in Cork. Its solidness anchored her; its coolness in her sweaty palm helped her draw an even breath.

Mairead closed her eyes and focused on her bit of Ireland. She'd survive this ordeal. It didn't matter how tumbled and far swept the river of life took her, she'd find a way to survive.

Chapter 6

———◆———

Iain's first glimpse of Barbados left him dazed. He squinted against the stabbing light to focus on the anchored ships bobbing in the harbour and the buildings of Bridge Town hugging the shoreline. The waterfront delivered a hard assault of colour. Sunlight rippled in the lapping blue water and reflected off the red-tiled buildings sprawled along the port. Verdant hills rose from the foot of the town, giving a view of numerous plantations and cultivated fields. A blanket of heat enveloped him with only a light breeze to bring relief. The wind carried the scent of decomposing swamp, fish and burning pitch from shore.

The *Jane Marie* was anchored in the harbour along with five other vessels. A constant flow of traffic ferried goods between the ships and shore, and the entire waterfront teemed with industry. This was the first time that Iain and the others had been allowed on deck since the ship had anchored. They were the last of the ship's cargo to be off-loaded.

"Line up, line up, you Scottish bogtrotters, if you want those shackles struck off," the quartermaster called out, waving an iron hammer. "Don't dawdle like moonstruck wenches, or you'll have to swim to shore with them irons."

After the ship's blacksmith struck off Iain's shackles, he took a step for the first time without the irons and nearly stumbled.

"Step lively," the quartermaster shouted. "Keep the line moving."

The slave factor stood beside the captain. A wide-brimmed straw hat shaded his narrow face as he scratched a mark on a vellum sheet for each prisoner who filed past.

Iain fell in behind Glencross and the line of prisoners that queued up to descend into the ship's pinnace. When Glencross grabbed the top of the ladder to ease himself down, his hands visibly shook.

"All right, lad?" Iain asked.

Glencross nodded. "Aye. If I fall, don't bother fishing me out. Just let me sink."

Iain snorted. "I'll join you, lad."

Glencross gave him a wan smile before the top of his ginger head vanished.

Iain gripped the rail and followed down the ladder. He felt the motion of the boat more keenly, dangling as he was on a length of rope. He had to pause a few times to regain his balance, but he eventually climbed into the bobbing boat. Dunsmore followed close after him, elbowing Iain in the ribs on his way to secure a seat. The bastard needed a swift shove into the harbour.

"All full," one of the sailors called up to the ship. They pushed out and headed for shore. The current was choppy, and the sailors had to put their backs into rowing towards the nearest jetty.

Iain's stomach churned with every rise and fall of the boat. He gripped the gunwale so tightly his knuckles whitened. Tearing his eyes from the surging waves, he fixed his attention to the solid shoreline.

When the boat reached the jetty, the factor's men were waiting for them. Iain climbed out, hitting his shin against the side of the pier. With his first several steps, Iain felt the ground lurch beneath him, and he had to remind himself he was no longer on a rocking boat.

He and Glencross were forced to line up with the others. People had gathered around the shore to gawk—men, women, grubby children and even a few men with skin startlingly black. These must be the African slaves Iain had heard about. He couldn't help but stare at how dark they were, but it was their clothing, or lack of, that shocked him. All of the men were naked except for a swath of linen fashioned into drawers, and their bare feet were grey from the dust of the road.

"Line up, line up," the factor shouted while his men looped a length of rope around each prisoner's neck, tethering them all in a chain. Iain swore as the cord tightened and bit into his skin.

"Not tight enough?" The factor laughed in Iain's face. "Just in case you're thinking of making a run for it. But there's one thing," he said, leaning in closer as though ready to impart a secret. "There's no bloody place *to* run."

"If you're so sure of that, take this rope off then," Iain said.

The man laughed again. "There's always an idiot in every lot who don't know better. I'd soon as not have to run after anyone, especially in this bloody heat. The rope stays till we get you locked up in the merchant's yard." He left to check the others down the line.

The factor led the prisoners down the jetty and into the town. His men were armed with coiled whips, and one or two looked like they itched for an excuse to test it on the prisoners' backs. Iain followed the others along the narrow road. Layers of sunbaked mud and leafy debris clogged the gutters. Flanked on either side of the road, rows of storied buildings leaned against each other, some built from pitted stone, others from bleached timber. Wind-ravaged balconies formed an overhang and provided the only shade along the blazing road, and there women hawkers gathered with crates of crabs.

The factor shouted out to laggards to clear a way for them. Carts and donkeys were urged aside, people parted like water under a determined prow, and as the column of prisoners passed, most paused to stare.

Iain felt the darts of their open curiosity. He tried to clear his mind and focus on placing one foot in front of the other. He locked away the anger and shame into an internal compartment.

Block everything out.

He had been captured before and paraded through hostile streets. This was nothing new, he reminded himself. Twice he had been captured while in England. After Worcester had been the worst. He and the others had been forced to make the long trek to London through towns that regarded them as the devil's agents. He and his countrymen had provided sport for the townspeople. Clods of horse shit, mud and rocks had been hurtled at them. A handful of men hadn't even made it to London and had to be buried along the way.

Iain steeled himself for the taunts and jeers, but nothing came.

People went on their business without paying them any mind. The procession went straight through a crowded market. Stalls piled with produce were spread out with hawkers crying out their wares. The sounds of commerce were deafening.

Here, Iain and the others were as common as sheep.

Through the long journey from England, shackled and chained to a bench, he had considered himself a prisoner—still a man, but a disadvantaged one. These people didn't see him as a man to be pitied or reviled. He was livestock, herded at his master's pleasure.

Iain Locharbaidh Johnstone didn't even warrant a turd missile.

Iain's muscles screamed. Forced to kneel into the hard-packed dirt, his shoulders ached and his thighs burned. The moment when any of them stirred to adjust their position, one of the guards descended upon them like ravenous midges. Dunsmore got the latest cuff to the head, but Iain couldn't even take satisfaction in that.

A sizeable crowd gathered in the merchant's yard for the auction. People continued to pour into the sunbaked square, some riding braying donkeys while others arrived on foot. English men and women in light-coloured clothing exchanged greetings and cast speculative glances at the first ten men on the block. Iain avoided their stares. Contempt was a sour taste in his mouth. He wanted to spit at them, spew them with the fury churning his gut. Instead, he fixed his gaze at the warehouses in the distance.

A bell clanged, dampening the chatter but heightening the anticipation. The auctioneer swaggered across the stage, his rounded belly hanging over his breeches. He lifted a hand to greet the crowd before motioning to one of his assistants. "I'll start with that one," he said, indicating Iain.

"Get up," the factor said, nudging him with his boot.

Iain didn't move. Damned if he was going to make their job easier.

"Look lively." This time the factor gave him a swift kick.

Iain stayed where he was. "Bugger off," he growled.

He heard a movement behind him, but before he could react, the rope that was looped around his neck jerked tight. Iain's hands flew to his neck. The rope pressed against his throat, choking his breath.

"In five minutes, you'll be someone else's problem," the factor hissed in his ear. "But right now you're my concern and damned if I let a stubborn Scotsman bleed my commission." He yanked on the rope, forcing Iain to scramble to his feet. "I'll strangle you first."

"Go ahead." Iain's words came out in a harsh rasp. He didn't much care what happened to him anymore.

The factor smiled grimly, showing a crooked row of teeth. His breath reeked of grog. "Rather die, would you? Play nice or I'll remove you from the block and off-load you privately. I'll sell you to one of the worst devils in the West Indies; then you'll really plead for death." The smile was brittle and hard. "Do we have an accord?"

Iain knew when someone was bluffing, and there wasn't one scrap of a lie showing in the man's rheumy eyes. "Aye."

The factor studied him a moment longer before nodding. He slackened the pressure on the rope. "Wouldn't want to lower your price. The good plantation owners don't like cheek in their servants," he said before shoving Iain towards the auctioneer.

With bitter bile, Iain climbed the block and stood there on display.

The auctioneer stepped forward and whistled to get everyone's attention. "Loosen your purses—this one is a prime fieldworker." The man gripped Iain's jaw and forced him to tilt his head this way and that, showing him off like a prized heifer. "This Scotsman is solidly built with a broad back. He's all sinew and muscle, as you can see. Be assured he'll do more than his share of clearing your fields. Guaranteed to recoup your initial investment tenfold." The auctioneer grabbed Iain's arm and hoisted it in the air. "Look at the muscles on this forearm, gentlemen. He's more than capable of doing the work of two men. The bidding opens at five hundred pounds of sugar."

Iain closed his ears to the offers shouted out for him. His pride ground into the dirt. Was this his value, measured in pounds of sugar? His body might survive the gruelling years to come, but his pride wouldn't survive the next few moments of bartering. Iain Locharbaidh Johnstone reduced to a slave—they might call it servitude, but he didn't see the difference right now. His house had always been proud advisors to the line of Scottish kings. They fought their enemies and never conceded an inch. Iain had once pledged his service to great men—to the laird, his kinsman, to his commanders and then to two kings. And now he was to be sold to a bastard Englishman. The bitterness and gall choked him. These damned Southroners—always causing them grief.

The auction grew more heated as two planters tried to outbid each other.

"Six hundred pounds of sugar," the auctioneer confirmed the latest offer. "Do I hear six hundred fifty?"

"Six hundred fifty," one bidder called out.

"Seven hundred seventy-five," another countered. Several more bids drove the price up to seven hundred twenty pounds of sugar.

A sun-weathered man in a straw hat stood slightly apart from the others. He hadn't cast a bid, but he still followed the auction. While the bidders were warring between themselves, he studied Iain dispassionately. Iain was reminded of the horse fairs back home when he had seen the same appraising look as men considered whether to lay out coin on a horse.

"Eight hundred pounds of sugar," the man in the straw hat called out, his voice in a distinctive Scottish burr.

"Alastair?" the auctioneer said, shielding his eyes. The morning sun slanted in his face. "Did I hear eight hundred?"

"Aye," the man replied shortly. By his speech, he was a Scotsman—from Lanarkshire, no less. "Eight hundred."

The auctioneer touched the brim of his hat and nodded. Grinning, he turned to the other two scowling planters. "Gentlemen? Do I hear a counteroffer?" One man folded his arms sullenly across his chest while the other shook his head. "Eight hundred pounds it is. Sold to Mount Vale." He took a hunk of charcoal and marked *MV* on Iain's forehead before motioning for his men to take him away.

Alastair met them at the platform and handed the factor a slip of paper in exchange for Iain's papers, a rolled-up scrap of parchment. The sum of his worth. Iain turned his head and looked away.

"I didn't agree to that," Iain said stiffly. "You'll not find my signature on that piece of shite."

Alastair's brow lifted, and he shrugged. "I don't care. You belong to Mount Vale now."

Iain studied the man who held the legal title to his person in his hands. He had no more than a score of years over Iain, but his face was heavily lined and darkened by the sun. It was clear to Iain that this man Alastair had been here for years and had likely forgotten their ways. He was no more Scottish than the Welshman who had failed at getting them out of Tothill Fields. Iain's simmering anger roiled to a boil. "How does it feel enslaving your own countrymen?" Iain ground out.

Alastair shrugged. "I don't own you. Mount Vale does."

Something in his tone pricked Iain's ears. "You like whoring yourself to these Southroners?"

Except for the tightening of his jaw, Alastair didn't appear to react. Instead, he took his time to scan the documents. "Iain Locharbaidh Johnstone." He lifted his gaze and narrowed his eyes. "The Johnstones have a long history of reiving and knavery. Spare me your outrage." He grabbed Iain's arm and pulled him roughly through the crowds. "In the future, mind your tongue. Only warning you'll get from me."

He nodded to one of the factor's men. "Take him to the others. I have more to buy for the estate."

Iain was led to a large building, straining against his tether like a dog on a leash. The inside of the building was blessedly cool and divided into a series of pens. One man appeared to be the gatekeeper, checking everyone's passes and turning away those whose only business involved gawking at the sold chattel.

"Mount Vale? We've a spot reserved for them over there."

Alone, Iain made his way to the wall and slumped down with his back against the boards. The last of his energy seeped away from him. It had already been a long day, but he didn't fool himself into thinking that this accounted for his bone-deep weariness. He shut his eyes and tried to conjure the memory of his home with the dry-stacked stone wall that always needed repairing. Only this time the image hovered vague and indistinct.

"Well, Locharbaidh," Masterton's voice made Iain crack open an eye. The grizzled moss-trooper stood over him, grinning widely, with Angus Rae hovering beside him. "You haven't rid yourself of us, have you now?"

Fierce relief swept through Iain, and he gave them both a wry smile. "You always need someone to look after you both, right." He looked around to see who else had been rounded up for Mount Vale. A few of the Highlanders from the hold arrived, but not a sign of the one he wanted to see. "Glencross?"

Angus shook his head and shrugged. "We were split up—he might still be back there."

Over the next hour and a half, more men from the ship came, including, to Iain's chagrin, Dunsmore. With each new addition, Iain lifted his head, hoping to see Glencross. One time he saw a shock of ginger hair and he grinned, about to call out a greeting to his brother-in-law. But he quickly saw his error. Killean Ross.

"The last of the lot, I guess?" Dunsmore muttered to someone.

Glencross would have been sold by now. He closed his eyes and rubbed his knuckles against his chin. Someone knocked him in the shin to move over. Blasted Dunsmore. Iain turned to bite the man's head off but stopped when he saw who it was. "Glencross?"

His brother-in-law stood above him, grinning like a fool. "Thought you got rid of me, didn't you?"

Iain swallowed the sudden lump in his throat. He smothered the stupid, pleased grin that threatened to betray him and instead scooted over to make room for Glencross. "Guess not."

Mairead and the other women were cordoned off inside a grass hut with a guard posted outside. Several people had tried to take a look at the soon-to-be-auctioned women, but the guard turned everyone away.

"Factor's orders," the man claimed to any who tried to get past him. Curiosity was the factor's way of keeping his price high.

Mairead sat on the dirt floor with her knees drawn tightly to her chest, watching the midwife knitting on her stool. The woman had been assigned to mind them until the auction. Her knitting needles flashed and clacked away in a semicircular dance. Mairead watched with sick fascination as the woman's nimble fingers threaded the yarn around the needles, looped and tucked the strands into an intricate pattern.

Outside the door, a commotion broke out, and Mairead leaned forward to hear.

The guard poked his head inside. "Time to show yourselves."

Ciara pressed close to Mairead's side. Mairead wished she could give her a word of hope, but she had none. The terror and uncertainty had burrowed deep in her stomach like a squirming worm.

When Mairead stepped outside, she flinched at the blinding light. Through watering eyes, the throngs of gaping people swam before her. The guards hurried them towards a raised platform situated in the centre of the market. Mairead shut her ears to the lewd calls and climbed the steps after Bronagh and Ciara. Instead of being led to stand at the back of the platform, all the women were first paraded across the front.

A dandy in a cream waist coat made his way to the front. He had the swarthy complexion of a Spaniard and swung an ivory cane with each step. Clearly an affectation since he had no sign of a limp. When he saw the midwife, he raised his hand to the brim of his hat and saluted her.

"Lucia, my love, you're looking fine this day." To Mairead's surprise, his accent was pure-born English.

The old woman pretended to be stern, but Mairead saw her suppressing a smile. "Still outrageous, Julius Burke." If she had lashes, the vile woman would have fluttered them.

"I don't want to disappoint," Burke said, rubbing his cane against his thigh. "What's the catch today? Will I be pleased?"

"Oh, you might at that," the midwife said, coming up between Ciara and Bronagh. She clamped her talons on both their shoulders before shoving them forward.

Burke leaned against the platform, and a slow smile spread across his swarthy face. His attention was fixed on Ciara. "Tasty. Where you from, sweet?"

Ciara winced and turned her head, but Mother Lucia pinched her arm, and Ciara cried out. "Eire—Ireland," she stammered.

He nodded as though he'd guessed it. "I'll not hold it against you, luv. Many of my best customers prefer the Irish girls." He looked to the midwife. "Are they clean?"

"As the first snow." She grinned.

His smile widened into a leer. "Excellent." His appraising gaze touched Mairead. "And that one?"

The midwife's smile stiffened. "She's broken in, but barely. You can't do wrong with that one too." Mairead felt Ciara's and Bronagh's eyes swing to her; she kept her gaze averted.

Burke's smile widened, and he winked at her. Mairead turned her head. Her stomach roiled from disgust.

The auctioneer climbed the platform and took centre stage. "And to start today's business," he called out, "we'll be starting with the women: seven Irish women who arrived on the *Jane Marie* a sennight ago. The first two are maids—that Mother Lucia will vouch for." He motioned to the midwife, who grabbed Bronagh and pulled her forward.

Bronagh tried to squirm out of the woman's grasp, but the midwife was a canny one. With a quick motion, she twisted Bronagh's arm behind her back and won a cry of pain out of her.

"She's a feisty one," someone called out from the crowd.

"Come visit the Little Bristol tomorrow night," Burke called out to the man with a laugh. "I'll have a special first night rate for you."

A ripple of laughter accompanied his quip, and without breaking stride, Burke called out, "I'll offer four hundred pounds of sugar. The day promises to be as hot as Satan's tits. To move this along, throw in the other two," he pointed to Ciara and Mairead, "and I'll give you nine hundred for all three."

The auctioneer gave it a moment's thought before he shook his head. "I'm not cutting a deal, Burke. We're doing this one by one."

"Have more imagination than that, my good man," Burke said, eliciting more bawdy laughter from the crowd.

Mairead realised she had been holding her breath, waiting for the auctioneer's verdict. But then the horrible thought hit her that it didn't matter. She'd likely be sold to this whoremonger eventually—whether this instant or an hour later. The despair rose in her gorge to choke her, and she swallowed back tears.

The auctioneer cleared his throat and said, "Burke's offered four hundred pounds of sugar. Do I hear four hundred twenty-five? Four hundred twenty-five for the dark-haired maid."

"Wait!" Bronagh said. "I must speak."

The factor snapped his head up, interrupting his conversation with one of the planters.

Bronagh continued in a rush. "I am a Mulriane, descended from great chieftains of Ireland. I was abducted from my home and brought here against my will. A reward will be posted for my speedy return, far more than any profit from this debauchery."

The factor bounded towards her. Bronagh darted away from him, causing a few chuckles from the crowd. "You will be rewarded—" she managed to cry out before the factor seized her and slapped a hand over her mouth. Bronagh struggled against him and twisted to kick his shin, but the man was wiry and avoided her foot.

"And she's a spritely one," the auctioneer said to the crowd, clutching a fixed smile while his employer struggled to contain the damage. More laughter erupted. "Julius Burke, she will be a hot-blooded addition to your stable. See how she bucks and squirms."

Burke laughed, his white teeth flashing against his tanned skin. "My offer stands at four hundred."

As Bronagh continued to struggle, more offers started firing in, and Burke was forced to keep increasing his bid. When the price reached six hundred fifty pounds, the interest suddenly cooled, and there were no new bids.

"Six hundred fifty, gentlemen," the auctioneer called out. "Do I hear seven hundred?" He scanned the crowd. "Six hundred seventy-five? Nay? Going once," he paused a fraction, "Going twice . . . Final price six hundred fifty pounds!" The auctioneer pointed to the swarthy man. "Julius, she's yours."

The factor released Bronagh, and for a moment she stood there staring at them, stunned. The midwife grabbed her arm and led her away. Only when they reached the steps did she turn around and search for her sister. "Ciara! Help me."

Ciara's lips were bloodless, and she trembled like a leaf. Mairead found it hard to watch when the midwife handed Bronagh over to Burke. His open perusal of his goods made Mairead sick to her stomach. She reached over and squeezed Ciara's hand, as much to give her cousin comfort as she could reassure herself. Mairead feared for Bronagh and was very conscious that she and Ciara could soon be joining her.

Ciara's turn came next. Mairead gripped her cousin's hand, desperate to hold her back. The midwife seized Ciara and pulled her towards the block. Mairead strained to maintain her contact with Ciara, fingers grasping, then slipping apart. Mairead choked back a sob.

The auctioneer gave a wolfish grin as he lifted a lock of Ciara's blond hair to show the crowd. "This one is a charmer, my good men, the sweetest, most docile morsel you'll ever find in Barbados. Bidding starts at five—"

"Five hundred pounds," Burke called out. He pressed closer to the platform, pushing aside two other men.

The bidding became hot very quickly, and the men behaved like a pack of slavering dogs circling a female in heat. Ciara kept her eyes downcast, and she grew whiter with each passing moment. Mairead clasped her own hands tightly and cringed at the ribald comments directed at Ciara. She could do nothing for her cousin—or for herself, for that matter—and the frustration made her want to rage and cry all at the same time.

"We have a new bid of seven hundred twenty-five from Julius Burke," the auctioneer said after several moments of frantic bidding. Burke leaned against his cane, staring down anyone who would raise their voice. "Seven hundred fifty? I have seven hundred twenty-five . . . Once, twice . . . "

"Seven hundred seventy-five," a woman called out.

Burke spun around, and the auctioneer peered over the heads of the men gathered at the front. An older woman approached the platform, a wide-brimmed straw hat perched above a lacy coif. She wore crisp gloves despite the heat. A weathered man in a straw hat walked slightly ahead of her, clearing a path. Though his frame leaned towards the lanky side, a solid strength came through his movements.

"Mistress Wilton," Burke said, no longer smiling. "What does Mount Vale need with a wench like her? Bid on the fieldworkers, but leave the sluts to me."

"I'll not be lectured by a half-breed whoremonger."

Burke flushed and narrowed his eyes. He tapped the end of his cane against the side of his boot. A low buzz spread through the crowd. "My lady, you're not setting up a rival trade. Your son—"

"That is none of your concern," she said, her tone colder than chipped ice. Turning her shoulder to Burke, she addressed the auctioneer, "My offer was seven hundred seventy-five."

Burke's lips were drawn in fury. "Eight hundred, then."

"Eight hundred fifty," the woman said without hesitation. "Money is no concern to me, Burke. I mean to have this one, no matter the cost."

Burke clutched his cane, his knuckles showing white. He looked as though he would snap the cane in two. With a curt shake of his head, he gave up the contest for Ciara.

87

"Eight hundred fifty pounds of sugar. Final bid goes to Mistress Wilton of Mount Vale." The crowd politely clapped.

Before the midwife could lead her away, Ciara broke free from the woman's clutches and flung herself into Mairead's arms.

Mairead held her tight and squeezed her eyes shut. "I'm so sorry, Ciara. It's all my fault. I'm so sorry." She was openly crying now, and her vision was blurred by her tears. In the next instant, the auctioneer and midwife ripped them apart. Ciara was hurried across the platform and to the woman who purchased her, leaving Mairead behind.

"Next one," the auctioneer called out.

The factor grabbed Mairead and forced her to stand facing the crowd. All eyes were fastened on her. Grins and leers covered her like burrs, and she felt unclean and sullied. Though she wanted to curl within herself, she forced her shoulders back and fixed her gaze over the crowd's head.

I will not break down. Mairead's eyes darted to a tearful Ciara, and she swallowed a painful lump. There was every chance that this would be the last time she'd see her cousin. Biting her lip, Mairead tore her gaze away.

I must prevail. Mairead recited the rosary under her breath and prayed for the strength to survive this ordeal. The next few moments would determine her life. No matter who would buy her, Mairead vowed that she would find her cousins, and together they'd return to Ireland. A curse for the English formed on her lips, but she remembered herself in time and bit it back. She didn't need another curse lashing back on her.

"Another lass from the *Jane Marie* and kin to the first two maids," the auctioneer announced.

"A bit of a plain chit compared to the others," someone called out. For once, Mairead blessed her plainness. Maybe it would save her after all.

"How old is she? Such a small thing," another shouted. "She'd be crushed by a wee man."

More laughter erupted.

Mairead tugged at her skirt and scrunched the fabric in her fist. She tried to shut out the jeers. She couldn't lift her eyes from the deck, felt their probing gaze touching every square inch of her.

"Three hundred pounds," Burke offered shortly. He still looked annoyed over losing Ciara. He frowned at Mistress Wilton, who still hadn't left. The woman watched the proceedings with a great deal of interest.

"Three hundred fifty," another man called out. He had spectacles perched atop his nose, and he kept adjusting them. He looked like a clerk or a barrister. Mairead held his gaze, hoping to encourage him. His clothes were wrinkled, and he had a distracted air. He looked kindly—surely he could use a housekeeper.

"Four." Burke waved a dismissive hand to the other bidder. "She's not a book, man. She's completely useless to you."

"Four hundred . . . twenty-five," the clerk stammered.

Burke rolled his eyes. "Four fifty. You'll not outbid me, wretch."

The clerk chewed on his bottom lip and looked conflicted. Mairead stared at him. *Please. Just a little more. Please. I'll cook and clean for you and will never complain. Don't let him buy me.* The clerk shook his head and stepped aside. Mairead's stomach dropped, and she stared with horror at the whoremonger who was about to purchase her.

Burke grinned and started walking up to the platform until Mistress Wilton halted him when she called out, "Five hundred pounds."

Burke growled and spun around. He whipped his hat off and strode angrily to her. "What in *hell* are you doing?" Had the woman's manservant not stepped in front of her, he would have likely shaken her.

"I need a scullery maid," she replied, unfazed.

"And I need her to warm some sheets," he said, brandishing his cane at the woman.

"There are others."

"Not if you keep bidding against me." The man bared his teeth. "Are you going to do this for the remainder of the auction? You're just doing this to sell them back to me for a profit, aren't you? How much do you want to leave me to my business?"

The woman's smile was cold. "I'm above filthy profit, Burke."

Burke's eyes narrowed. "But not above trying to ruin me." His voice dropped, and Mairead had to strain to hear what he said. "I've told you before, old woman, you can't control how your son chooses how to entertain himself, and you'll not hold me hostage for your spite. Shall we air our grievances to these good folk?"

The woman didn't reply, but her mouth tightened into a furious line. Mairead expected her to capitulate, but instead the woman squared her shoulders and stared the whoremonger down. "I mean to have this one. The rest are hardly worth the trouble, but you're welcome to them."

Burke let out an aggravated sigh. He glanced at Mairead and the other women. Mairead held her breath. Her heart pounded in her throat as she waited for his reply.

Burke rapped his cane on the hard ground, then flung his hand up dismissively. "Fine. Enjoy your scullery maid."

Mairead nearly collapsed in relief.

"Last bid—five hundred pounds of sugar to Mistress Wilton," the auctioneer finalised the sale.

In a daze, Mairead followed the midwife and nearly stumbled down the platform. Mistress Wilton waited to receive her. Up close, Mairead could see that she was all blunt angles with an expression as hard as granite. She wanted to thank her for saving her, but the words were cut off by the woman's cold demeanour.

That hardly mattered. She had been saved from the whorehouse, and joy, she remained with Ciara. Her cousin clapped a trembling hand over her mouth and pulled Mairead down into a fierce embrace. "Oh, my dear, oh, my dear," she sobbed. "You haven't been taken away."

"Everything will be fine, my love, as long as we're together."
Mairead smiled in relief. For the first time since they had been
captured, she actually believed it.

Chapter 7

In his life, Iain had been a moss-trooper, an officer in His Majesty's cavalry, a prisoner of war and now he was chattel.

Alastair tethered the new indentures to each other and personally tested the tautness of the rope around Iain's neck. Iain forced himself to not flinch—wouldn't give the man the satisfaction of seeing his discomfort, even though he wanted to snatch at the rope. Stone cold, Alastair betrayed no emotion either as he took his place at the head of the group.

"This way," Alastair called out, then addressed a dark-haired young man at the far end, "Tam, keep them close."

"To be sure," Tam called back, his speech liberally flavoured with a rolling Irish accent. A Monmouth cap covered his head, protection against the sun. He had been standing beside Iain, and he now turned to him and nodded with an impudent grin. "There's nowhere to run, so don't be getting any mad ideas."

Anything that Iain might have said was interrupted when his five-foot tether yanked him forward. Glencross, ahead of him, had started moving.

They left the building and stepped into the merchant's yard under the hard sunlight. Waves of heat rose from the cobbles while the encircling buildings smothered any breeze that might have brought relief.

Alastair's straw hat bobbed at the head of the procession as he led them across the square to a baggage train of donkeys and two monstrous beasts, each nearly double the size of a dray horse. The creatures had long, tapered heads, and instead of a gently sloping back—as any self-respecting horse—theirs were disfigured by a large mounded hump. Thin tails swatted at flies darting around their sand-coloured hides.

"Devil take me," Iain muttered under his breath.

"Never seen a camel?" Tam asked with a laugh. "Useful beasties in these parts. Carry their weight in sugar."

Both camels were laden with goods—bales of cloth, bundles of tools, and one even bore a decorative table that belonged in a fancy parlour. Everything appeared to have been recently offloaded by one of the ships in the harbour. Half a dozen donkeys were similarly outfitted, goods strapped to their packs. Only three donkeys were left unburdened. Iain cast an eye at the arrangement. Between the number of Alastair's men and the new indentured servants—slaves, *call a goose for what it is*—there weren't enough beasts to carry them. They'd be walking, no doubt.

"Hope it's not far," Glencross muttered in a low voice, clearly coming to the same conclusion.

"I'd rather walk," Iain said. Better that than being carried like an invalid on the back of a donkey. Or like a bale of goods. His gut tightened as a mocking voice in his head whispered, *But you are.*

Iain and the others were now tethered to the donkeys, one on either side, and Tam handed the bridle to Iain. "You're in charge of this one."

"One beast of burden over the other," Iain muttered under his breath. No one paid him any mind.

They were all ready to set out, but Alastair still hadn't mounted his horse. After several more moments, he pushed his straw hat back over his forehead and scanned the still-crowded merchant's yard. Iain looked around, wondering what they were waiting for.

Glencross stood on the other side of Iain's donkey, also tethered to the animal. "Must be waiting for more goods." He nodded to the beast between them who hadn't been laden down with any parcels.

"Aye," Iain agreed, shifting from one foot to the other. He looked around at the men absorbed by their own business.

Then an odd apparition cut through the crowd. A mature woman rode a grey dappled horse, and tethered behind her were two familiar figures. The Irish sprite, Mairead, and her blond kinswoman. Both women looked far more frail than Iain remembered them on the ship, especially the sprite.

Iain felt oddly relieved to realise that the sprite hadn't been purchased by a whorehouse. The sentiment surprised him. He hadn't realised he had been worrying about her, or her cousin, until this moment. Then annoyance set in. He had enough to worry about, and these two women weren't his responsibility. He may have announced they were under his protection in the hold, but that was as far as it went. No one had appointed him laird of all the indentured servants on the island.

"Look sharp, men," Alastair said, directing his words to the new slaves. "Your new mistress has come."

The mistress of Mount Vale drew up to Alastair and reined in her horse. "A few more things for the estate," she told him. Whether she was gesturing to the Irish women or the bundles they carried, Iain couldn't tell. Probably both, he thought darkly.

The additional goods were strapped to the other packs while Tam dealt with the Irish women. He bent slightly forward and spoke to them the way a horse handler would treat a skittish foal. He drew them towards the baggage train, and Iain realised that Tam was leading them to his donkey.

"Up you both go," Tam said as he first helped Mairead and then her cousin onto the back of the donkey. The creature didn't even flick an ear, but Iain felt idiotic standing there holding the bridle like a groom. Mairead's gaze turned to him, and she stared at him with round eyes, unmindful of her ratty skirts twisting around her dirty legs.

Iain gave her a curt nod, not trusting himself to say anything, for in his present mood he'd snarl at the blue sky. She already thought him an ogre.

Alastair released a sharp whistle, and the caravan set out. The road out of Bridge Town meandered around bogs and swampy ground, and their pace was necessarily slow due to the congestion of other baggage trains making their way along the same route. Eventually, they left the foul town behind them.

Iain had been walking nearly two hours and felt every footstep he made. The road was broken by half-rotted tree stumps and flanked on either side by thick stands of trees, some he recognised, most he did not. Stretches of cultivated fields were broken by thick stands of arching trees, their glossy leaves ruffling in the breeze.

Occasionally, the woods thinned and yielded to fields of billowing grasses, as tall as a man, before being swallowed up again by more woods. They had not paused once during this time. Mistress Wilton was in a hurry to return to the plantation with her new supplies. New mistress, he thought in distaste. His mouth curled as though he had just bitten something sour.

He maintained a firm grip on the donkey's bridle, and his right shoulder ached with the effort. It was a cantankerous beast that would have liked nothing better than to have thrown the two women. Mairead rode in front of her fair cousin. It was a good thing they were riding—the caravan would never have gotten as far as they had if the two women were on their feet. As it was, Mairead's shoulders were slumped forward while her cousin rested her cheek against Mairead's back.

Weariness set into Iain's bones. He gripped the bridle to turn his mind to the coarse leather strap digging into his palm rather than the burn in his thighs. He stumbled on a thrust-up root. His boots were worn, and there was a coin-sized hole in the sole of each boot. Pebbles collected into the boots, digging into his sore feet.

This weariness angered him—his weakness was a failing, but he couldn't make his muscles work in the way they always had. He had been on more gruelling marches, but the ship had taken its toll on him, and all he could do was put one foot in front of the other. With each step, more of his energy evaporated in the heat.

"Are you well?"

The lilt of Mairead's voice startled Iain. She hadn't said a word to him since leaving Bridge Town. *Am I well?* Here was a wisp of a woman pitying him for his weakness. *Christ's death*, her words were vinegar to an open wound.

"Save your concern," he said a little more gruffly than he intended.

She didn't immediately answer. He guessed she was debating whether to keep to herself. "You're limping."

"The road is uneven." Iain made an effort to walk more normally, but it required gritting his teeth in a grimace.

"I could walk in your stead," she offered.

Iain squared his shoulders. "Are you mad, woman? I am nae getting on top of that beast—even if they cut me down at the knees."

She visibly stiffened, but she held her tongue.

From behind, Iain heard Dunsmore's snort. "That I'd pay good coin to see. Iain Locharbaidh Johnstone being led on a donkey by an Irish slip of a girl."

Iain steamed but kept his mouth clamped shut. He refused to be baited by the cur. Instead, he fixed his eyes on the road ahead and tried to block out the mocking voice that repeated over and over again in his brain, *Iain is weak. Iain is pitiful. Iain is a slave.*

"I'm sorry," she said in a low voice, glancing back towards Dunsmore.

"Do me no more favours," he said. "I can't afford the cost."

Tam pushed forward with his donkey from his place in the rear to ride alongside them. "What's this about?"

No one replied. "That's better." He dropped his tone and added, "The mistress has keen ears—mind that well."

The baggage train plodded along for another couple of hours, breaking only briefly to water the donkeys in muddy streams. Of her new *servants*, the mistress gave the least thought. Iain's feet throbbed, and it took all his compromised strength to rise when Alastair whistled to set them on their way again. They had long since lost the tethers—small mercy, that.

The afternoon was ageing when they reached a stone marker at the top of a rutted lane. The mistress turned off the main road and headed down the tree-lined avenue. Soon the dirt path fanned out past fields of various crops, some tall and grassy, others short and scrubby. The fields were peppered with men and women tending the crops, many of the women with swaddled infants strapped to their backs. Except for the length of cloth used to secure their children, the women were bare breasted. Most of the fieldworkers were African, their black skin contrasting against the pale green of the crops, though Iain caught a glimpse of a few more field hands who were the same sun-burnt colour as Tam.

The road climbed a little, and Iain saw the gabled roof of a manor house in the distance. The building appeared to be of white stone and gleamed in the golden afternoon light. It was surrounded by a dry-stacked stone wall with a wrought-iron arch leading up the main forecourt. Flaunted wealth—that was what that was.

"That be the big house," Tam said, riding alongside Iain. "The servant compounds are by the fields," he continued. "Only those with business will be allowed to go near the big house—all others will get a flogging. You've been warned, you have."

They left the manor behind and followed the meandering road that ran downhill towards a timbered barn. Young African lads rushed out to help with the animals and offload the cargo. The mistress remained on her horse, but Alastair and Tam dismounted from their beasties.

Iain watched Mairead struggle to get down from the donkey. It wasn't a tall animal, but she was a wee thing. She managed to swing her leg over one side, but her skirt twisted, and to Iain's eyes, any moment she would fall flat on her face.

Iain offered his hand to help her down. She hesitated in surprise and looked at it as though he were presenting a snake. "Come on, lass," he urged her with his usual gruffness. "We're no longer in the civilised world. Take the hand. I'll not bite."

Mairead accepted his assistance, slipping her hand in his, like the tentative touch of a wee bird. When she landed, she wobbled a little. She dropped his hand and edged away.

"Thank . . . you," she stammered.

Iain's brow lifted in surprise. Instead of replying, he cleared his throat and stepped away.

"Right, then," Tam called out to everyone. "This way."

They were herded down towards a clearing, following in the mistress's wake as she rode on her horse. Iain took in the rows of outbuildings that ringed the perimeter. Small shacks built of sticks, mud and grass. Barely enough shelter to keep them dry from the rain. Several naked black children gathered to gawk at the new recruits. A few of the bolder ones crept closer.

The mistress dismounted, handing her reins to one of the lads, and fell into step beside Alastair. His gaze swept the group, and Iain got the impression that very little escaped his attention.

"Where's Potts?" Alastair asked Tam. "He should be waiting for us."

"Fetch him, Alastair," the mistress said crisply. "Before I lose my patience. The day is overly hot."

Alastair motioned to one of the black children. "Find Mister Potts." But instead of the lad running off, he grinned and pointed to one of the huts. Iain did not miss Alastair's annoyed expression.

"Potts, you there, man? Enough of that now. We got another shipment of hands needs sorting."

A brawny, rugged man emerged from the hut, tying the laces of his breeches. Iain caught a glimpse of an African woman in the room behind him. When Potts spied the mistress, his expression changed from exasperation to contrition as quickly as a shutter dropping. He slammed the door behind him and greeted the mistress with a fawning smile. "My lady. I didn't realise you were seeing to this . . . business yourself."

"This is my late husband's enterprise, and now my dear son's. If I don't look after Mount Vale, who will?" Her tone brooked no disagreement.

"Aye, my lady." Potts turned to the row of prisoners and folded his arms across his broad chest. "Line them up, Tam. Let's see what we have to work with."

Potts continued down the row alone, inspecting each man, bursting with impatience. "Ragged lot," he muttered, casting an eye to the direction of Alastair and the mistress. "I give them a month."

When he reached Iain, he stopped before him. The others had looked down or away from Potts's challenging glare, but Iain refused to give him that. Instead, he held the man's squinting glare and dug in where he stood.

The overseer appeared at first surprised, then his small eyes narrowed to slits. "What's this? Full of your own piss, aren't you?" Potts had the look of a tavern brawler, with a crooked nose that no doubt had been broken several times. A jagged, whitish scar ran down the centre of his chin, to his thick, bullish neck. Though a nose shorter than Iain, his rugged build spoke to brute strength. He moved closer, crowding Iain, who held his ground. After having endured eight weeks on board ship, another week locked in a hold, and a four-hour walk to get to this godforsaken place, Iain barely had enough strength to keep himself upright. Sheer grit kept him on his feet, and contrary stubbornness kept him from backing down now.

99

"Master Potts, we're waiting," the mistress said, cutting through the tension. "Is there a problem?"

Potts's lips parted in a sneer, and though he answered the mistress, there was no mistaking that his words were directed to Iain. "There won't be, my lady. And if there is, I knows best how to deal with it." With a parting glare, he continued along the line.

When Potts finished his inspection, he nodded to the mistress and returned to stand beside Alastair.

After a moment, the mistress stepped forward to address the company. She didn't have to raise her voice; her words carried down to the far end. "This is Mount Vale," she said. "You will be tied to this land, blood and bone, growing and harvesting cane, indigo and other cash crops. My family's well-being depends on your work in the fields. Sluggards will not be tolerated, and my representative, Simon Potts, is here to make sure Mount Vale is well served." She nodded to the overseer. "You will be provided basic sustenance and two sets of clothes. It falls to you to keep them tidy and mended. We observe the Lord's Day here, and everyone will have the opportunity to attend service." She paused a moment. "Anglican, naturally. I don't countenance that independent Presbyterian nonsense, nor, God forbid, papistry."

Around him, Iain heard the grumbling but wondered why any of them should care. Did any of it change their status? They'd already passed into hell. The Kirk wasn't about to save them now.

Potts quieted everyone down by smacking a stick against a tree stump. "Damn your insolence." A grin split across his face. "The Lord might keep you on Sundays, but the rest of the week, you're mine."

Mairead was unsure what was expected of her and Ciara. The overseer, Potts, led the men away from the compound, and she didn't know if she was expected to follow them or not. The mistress had drawn aside to converse with Alastair. At regular intervals, he nodded respectfully, though his gaze wandered occasionally towards Mairead and Ciara.

Finally, Tam appeared at Mairead's side. "Mistress expects you at the big house." His Irish lilt was a welcome balm to Mairead's ears. Nut-brown hair fell across a tanned brow, and his shoulders were slightly stooped, as though he had known the meaning of strenuous labour. He had introduced himself at Bridge Town as Tam O'Grady, and Mairead assumed he held a position of authority at the plantation. Her curiosity stirred to find out how he came to be here and where in Ireland he had come from, but that would have to wait for another day. All she could muster was a grateful bob of her head, though Ciara looked far more lost. "I'll see you both later," he said and gave them a friendly wink before jogging after Potts.

Alastair helped the mistress mount her dappled grey. Crisply, she motioned for Mairead and Ciara to follow. "Step lightly and mind the horse dung."

Mairead and Ciara trudged after their new mistress. The way back to the manor was all uphill. Halfway there, Mairead's legs started to weaken, and a sharp stitch worried her side. Nearly two months aboard the ship had stolen her vigour. Worse, the blazing sun pounded down on Mairead, making her lightheaded. Ciara struggled too. Her cheeks were flushed, and a thin sheen of perspiration coated her brow. With every step she took, she visibly wilted.

Along the road, they passed a team of oxen pulling a wagon piled high with freshly cut stalks. The African driver urged his team to the side of the road, giving the mistress ample breadth to pass him. She held her chin high, without even one sideways glance of acknowledgment.

As they neared the manor, they encountered an exotic apparition heading in the opposite direction. A woman led a grey donkey hitched to a rickety cart. Her copper skin shone under the hard sunlight, and her long black hair fell loosely down her back. Except for a swath of fabric decorated with blue beads and draped across her slim hips, she was entirely naked, but she walked as though she wore the finest silks.

Mairead couldn't help but gape. The woman returned her regard openly and gave Mairead a crisp nod in passing.

"A strange woman," Ciara said. She looked around. "Everything is strange—the vegetation, even the beasts of burden."

"To be sure," Mairead replied. A large bird flew past with plumage a riot of orange, red and blue. *Blessed Mother,* even the fowls were strange and colourful.

The mistress drew into the stable block and handed her mount to one of the grooms.

"Don't dawdle," she called to Mairead and Ciara over her shoulder and headed to the manor.

The mistress entered a sunbaked courtyard from a gate situated at the rear of the manor. Herbs and flowering plants were neatly arranged in low-walled beds joined by wide, flat pavers. The cloying scent of peppermint stirred when the mistress's skirt brushed one of the beds. A walkway made of crushed stone linked the courtyard with the manor.

A young blond woman swept the pavers. She paused in her work to cast curious sidelong glances at both Mairead and Ciara. The woman might have been pretty were it not for her snub nose and saucy mouth. When the mistress glanced in her direction, the blond snapped her attention back to her broom and swept harder.

"Lucy," the mistress called out to the maid, "run and tell Providence Moss that I've returned. I have found her two new charges."

"Right away, my lady." The maid's speech carried a strong London flavour. With a last curious look at the newcomers, Lucy darted past them and towards the house.

When Mairead's attention returned to the mistress, she found the woman in front of Ciara, lifting her chin, turning it this way and that—examining her as one would assess a foal in a horse market.

Ciara's face burned bright, and with her eyes downcast, her lashes cast lacy shadows over her cheeks. The mistress took her time considering Ciara until finally she said, "You'll do."

Mairead braced herself to undergo the same inspection, but the woman barely looked at her. Even as far as they were from Ireland, Ciara drew the eye like bees to honey. Mairead winced at her own shrewish thoughts. Jealousy for her cousin had brought her to these straits, while Mairead's wayward tongue had cursed them both well and good. Had she not learned anything yet?

"I want to make this abundantly clear," the mistress said to them, pinning Mairead and Ciara with a hard stare. "Poor conduct from one will reflect poorly on the other. I expect you both to be on your best behaviour—obedient, respectful and eager to please. If either of you disappoints," she fastened her stare on Ciara, "both will suffer repercussions."

Mairead frowned. The woman acted as though she expected the worse from Ciara.

"Understood?" Nothing soft about her flinty tone. Both Mairead and Ciara nodded.

The crunch of footsteps over gravel drew Mairead's attention. She looked over her shoulder to find the tallest woman that she had ever seen, reed-thin, with pale, hollow cheeks, approaching. It was as though someone had taken a perfectly normal-shaped woman and stretched her out a few more feet. The result was a stork. The snub-nosed maid slunk within earshot.

"You've kept me waiting, Providence Moss," the mistress said. "It's been a long day, and I'm out of humour."

The housekeeper dipped her head. "My apologies, my lady. I was setting the table for your supper."

The mistress sniffed. "I've purchased new indentures. Irish wenches. This one," she nodded to Mairead, "can be used in the scullery and the washhouse. You were complaining that you needed more help. This should sort that out."

"And the other, my lady?"

The mistress smoothed her gloves over her hands and shrugged. "Give her duties in the manor. I need a seamstress."

She might as well have told the housekeeper that Ciara was there to coddle pixies, for the woman couldn't have looked more surprised. "Sewing?"

"And embroidery. As soon as she's cleaned, send the chit up to my sitting room."

Providence Moss did not hesitate. "Very well, my lady."

Without a backwards glance, the mistress strode towards the manor. She reached the first herbal bed and paused. "Have you seen my son, Providence?"

"My lord has not yet returned."

The mistress didn't reply and continued inside the house.

Providence Moss sighed and shook her head. "Lucy, get this one scrubbed," she said with a nod to Ciara. "You'll need to change the water several times to get all the bilgewater out of her pores."

Before Lucy led Ciara away, her cousin reached out and squeezed Mairead's hand. *"Misneach,"* she whispered. *Courage.*

Mairead blinked back tears. *"Misneach."* They could both use it.

Providence Moss started a rapid tapping of her boot while Lucy pulled Ciara towards the manor. The housekeeper's mood remained sour as she pinned Mairead with her dark eyes. "Do you speak a civilised tongue? I certainly hope you do. What do they call you?"

Mairead bit back what she wanted to say, that she did speak a civilised tongue—Irish. Instead, she replied in English, "My name is Mairead O'Coneill."

The woman's mouth disappeared in a tight line, and she gave her a withering look. "I do not hold with papist names," she said in a harsh tone. "Margaret will do for you, even though it is too good for a common bogtrotter."

Mairead flushed in embarrassment and anger, not just for the slur, but for the fact that Providence Moss dared to change her

104

Christian name. The name her mother had given her just before she had died of childbed fever.

"Was there something you wanted to say, Margaret?" Providence Moss pressed, her black eyes narrowed into slits.

Lucy returned carrying a pair of empty buckets. Savouring the tension, the maid taunted her, "Come along, *Margaret*. You can draw your own water."

"My name is *Mairead*. Mairead O'Coneill."

Mairead saw the housekeeper's hand fly a heartbeat before it connected with her face. *Slap.* A million tiny needles tingled from cheek to jaw. She recoiled and lifted her arm to protect herself from another attack, but Providence Moss was quicker. Another slap fell. Mairead's ears started ringing, and she staggered backwards.

Providence Moss grabbed Mairead's arm and yanked her close. Leaning over her, she hissed, "You had best forget your impudent Irish ways, or I shall whip them out of you. *Margaret* is your name as I have spoken it, and *Margaret* it will be."

Potts herded the men away from the compound. "Gan alang, lads," he called out, his accent thick as paste. A Newcastle man. *Damned stubborn buggers.* "Off to the pond. Everyone one o' you needs a good sousing." When they reached the pond, they were ordered to strip off their filthy clothes.

Potts surveyed the men filing past, meaty fists on his hips. He hitched his breeches and squared his shoulders. "Toss all them all in a pile here, I says. Go on. Don't bother laying them out like prissy maids, they'll all be feeding a campfire afore long. Mistress don't hold with lice-infested vermin."

Tam handed out a strip of rough cloth and a sliver of lye soap to each man. "Scrub well, lads. Scrub like your life depends on it."

Most balked at having to wade into the pond, while a few thrashed around in panic when they were prodded into the water by the end of a stick. Glencross waded into the muddy water as far as his knees and flatly refused to go any deeper. He had never been comfortable in water, never having learned to swim.

Iain braced himself for the cold water, but the tepid temperature lapping against his bare thighs surprised him. His toes curled in the fine silt as he waded deeper, waist high.

For once, Iain was in agreement with these Southroners. He heartily scrubbed away the layers of bilge that he had accumulated in the hold and earlier in Tothill Fields. The lye soap rooted out festering cuts and cracked skin. Instead of shying away from the pain, Iain gritted his teeth and continued on, revelling in the sensation of being alive. The fading afternoon sun poured over his bare shoulders, smoothing out every bruise of his strained back.

After he had rubbed himself raw, Iain sank deeper into the water until it lapped under his chin. He closed his eyes and tipped his face to the sun and allowed himself to float on the water. For a moment, he felt at peace, and he allowed his mind to wander.

Midsummer's Day. The first year he and Innis were married. The weeks had been unusually warm, and Iain had dragged her down to the river. He'd shed his clothes on the riverbank, and before she could stop him, he cleaved into the water. When he'd come back up to the surface, Innis was practically in tears from her alarm.

"Join me, lass," he'd called out, trying to spray her with a stream of water.

"You're mad, Iain Johnstone," she'd replied, shaking her head furiously. "You'll catch your death of a cold and drown."

Iain had tossed his head back and guffawed. "Which is it, then? If I drown, I can't very well catch a cold." He'd swum closer to shore and waved her in. "Trust me, lass, I'll not let you sink."

But she wouldn't be told. Instead, she'd found an overturned log, sat down and contented herself with watching him from the shore.

Odd how that still bothered him, Iain thought as he floated on the water. Innis had never let herself take a risk. He had admired her gentleness when they were courting; when they married, Iain had hoped that he could coax out her bolder nature. Iain pushed the thought away, instead trying to reconstruct Innis's face in his mind. The image faded, indistinct and vague.

The sun began to work deep into his muscles, unknotting them with its warmth. For this moment, he was content, and everything else fell away.

"You—hey, you!" A voice finally penetrated Iain's tired brain. "Hey, fish man!"

Iain opened his eyes to find Potts hopping from one foot to another, looking for the world like a stork anxious for his meal. Iain grinned and sank farther into the water. Let the sodden bastard come and get him. The water felt cool against his heated head. He picked up indistinct shouts and came up for air.

Potts waded into the pond, slicing through like the prow of a ship.

Iain pushed his feet against the murky pond bed and stood up. "Aye, I'm coming. Don't get your breeks in a twist." He sighed and reluctantly started back. He shook his head and sent a shower of water scattering from his hair.

But Potts had already reached him, and instead of hurrying him back to shore, he grabbed Iain by the scruff of the neck and drove his head into the water.

Iain pushed hard against the mucky bottom and thrashed, trying to break free of his hold. Potts's grip held him like an iron band, and it didn't matter what Iain did, he couldn't break free. His lungs burned.

Potts finally pulled Iain's head out of the water, but his fingers dug into the back of his neck. "I told you to come out," he shouted before pushing Iain's head back into the water. Iain continued to flail, twisting and elbowing the man, but Potts remained firm. Didn't even lose his footing. Once more, Iain broke the surface and gasped for breath. "When we tell you something—" Down again, before Iain had time to suck in a lungful of air. Again, he pulled him out. "When we give you an order, you will obey."

Potts pushed hard and held Iain under the water. Iain stopped struggling, hoping that the man would accept this as submission, but Potts held him firm. Iain's lungs were ready to explode. The bugger was going to drown him. Now Iain started fighting for his life, thrashing and trying to knock the man off his balance, but he couldn't get any purchase. Just as spots started flashing before his eyes, Potts finally released him.

Iain broke the surface and sucked in a great gulp of air. He bent over, coughing up pond water.

Potts stood with his hands on his hips. The veins were throbbing on the side of his neck. "Defy me again, Scotsman, and you won't live out the moment," the man snarled. "Now get with the others." Not waiting for a reply, he pushed Iain towards shore.

Iain struggled to keep his balance, made more difficult with Potts snapping at his heels. When he reached shore, Tam grabbed his arm, but before he could pull away, Potts came up and seized his other arm. Together, they hauled Iain past the others and marched him to higher ground. They forced him down on a large log, and while Tam held him down, Potts whipped out a blade and held the edge against Iain's throat.

Iain froze.

"Don't think I won't do it, Scotsman," Potts said, applying a little pressure until Iain could feel a slight nick.

Iain held his breath. He felt the sweat beading on his forehead; his eyes darted between Potts and Tam. "Which one of you will be carrying news to the mistress that she's lost her good coin?" Iain said.

To his surprise, Potts laughed. "Your cost in sugar is less than what you'll cut by noon, gaumless wretch." He seized Iain by the hair and pulled his head back, hissing in his ear, "A bad seed will cost us more. She'd rather I crush you now and set an example than allow you to poison the barrel." He moved the blade so it touched his windpipe. "Do you ken, Scotsman?"

Iain wanted to tell Potts to go yank himself, that he'd rather have his throat slit than endure one more moment as an Englishman's slave. But he hadn't survived a battle, the prisoner camps and a gruelling ship voyage only to end it here, thousands of miles away from home. He gave a slight nod, capitulating . . . for now. Iain Locharbaidh Johnstone knew how to bide his time, even if it killed him.

"Good decision," Potts said smugly. "Hold him fast, Tam. This one gets the first shearing."

They forced Iain's head back. He felt the edge of the blade press against his throat. The bugger was going to kill him anyway—forced him to degrade himself for naught. Iain braced himself, but instead of feeling the slice of the blade and the hot seeping of his own blood, Potts ran the knife against Iain's beard and started shaving it off.

Iain tried to break free from Tam's hold, but the Irishman tightened his grip. Potts began to laugh. Iain gritted his teeth, mortified. He hadn't been beardless since his stones had dropped. Then, as a final insult, when Tam finished, Potts grabbed a fistful of Iain's hair and sheared it to the ears.

They might as well have castrated him.

Chapter 8

————◆————

Iain's first day in the fields, the heat slammed him like a sledgehammer. Sweat stung his eyes, and the acres of sugarcane blurred under the shimmering midmorning sun. He had thought he understood the meaning of gruelling labour, but cutting cane had smashed that apart. Already his muscles from lower back to shoulder blades were twisted in knots, and he had sweated more than he had ever in his entire life. Working a few feet away from him, Glencross resembled a burnt gingerroot.

Iain swiped at the sweat dripping from his brow and paused to stare at the fields—endless rows of sugarcane as far as the eye could see. He had only cut a twig's worth out of an entire forest.

Kill me now.

Spaced a few feet apart, the cane stalks were as tall as a man with their grassy tops. The fronds were a light green, but the main stalks were a jewelled red and green, thick as two fingers. Each man was given a billhook to cut through the bottom of the woody stem. Iain's was as dull as water from the repeated hacking, and he had to stop to sharpen the curved blade using the whetstone.

Glencross worked across the row from Iain. While they made their way cutting, three African women gathered the stalks and carried them to the far end of the row to a wagon.

Iain spied Potts on an old piebald garron, working his way towards them. As the man drew closer, his shouts carried across to where Iain and Glencross worked. "Faster, you laggards—keep cutting! If this field ain't cut by the end of the week, the yields will be piss."

The wagoners weren't spared the abuse either. If they didn't hurry the oxen along to the crushing mill to Potts's liking, he rained threats on them too. No mistake, their lives amounted to less than the damned sugar.

Iain had known men like Potts—thugs who caused others to cut a wide swath around them and took perverse pleasure in it. Men who feasted on any sign of weakness. Dunsmore had sprung from the same patch. Iain understood how to handle these upstarts—speaking with the fist was the only language they understood. But he didn't have that luxury, not in these reduced circumstances. Every moment in the fields doing this shite's bidding reminded Iain of how far he had fallen. Indentured bondsman. Chattel. *Less than a man.*

Glencross knocked Iain's arm to get his attention. "Best get back to it. Don't let Potts catch you idle."

The urge to grind his billhook into the ground, consequences be damned, taunted Iain, but he forced it down. Instead, he turned his frustration on the sugarcane with a fresh vengeance, hacking at the thick cane as though every stroke would sever his own bonds.

An hour later, with the sweat stinging his eyes and his head swimming, Iain paused to regain his breath. His back and shoulders ached, and his hands were beginning to cramp. The cane fought back, covering him with deep scratches that attracted the mosquitos. Though he had spent years on a battlefield wielding sword and lance, this pain was different. He was discovering muscles he had never used before.

He squinted at the sky. Not a blasted cloud in sight. Nearby, a pair of African men toiled with practiced economy. Their movements were fluid, and they didn't seem to be bothered by the heat. Their black skin shone with a thin sheen of sweat, unfettered with proper clothes. As usual, they only wore short drawers to cover their privates.

At first, Iain had thought them indecent for being stripped down, but under the oppressive heat, his coarse linen shirt cloyed like the thickest wool. Madness seized him, and Iain peeled off the sweat-sodden cloth. When the breeze touched his overheated skin, he sighed at the sudden coolness. He tied the shirt around his waist, feeling immediately relieved.

"A heathen, you are," Glencross said, but he was already mirroring Iain.

A couple of hours later, he had reached halfway down his row. Panting, Iain bent over his legs and waited for his head to stop swimming. A queasiness twisted his stomach, and he felt like he was going to throw up. He couldn't continue. Only one day and already he doubted that he could survive this.

Glencross returned from the wagon, his movements sluggish, and he seemed to trip over his feet as he walked. Without saying a word, he sank to the ground, finding a patch of shade in the cane.

Iain wanted to join him, but one of them had to mind where Potts was. "I'll keep a watch for that maniac."

"I can't take much more of this," Glencross gasped.

Somehow seeing Glencross's strength spent and his lips cracked and bleeding brought clarity to Iain. They would die here. Impossible that anyone could survive this. Across the fields, for every four African slaves, there was only one indentured servant. Tam, the sub-overseer, had mentioned that Iain and the others were the third shipment of servants from England in eighteen months. The implication was obvious.

In the distance, Iain heard Alastair call out and Potts answer him, all meek and mild. Next to the mistress, the only person for whom Potts fawned like a dog was Alastair.

"What's his story—Alastair, that is?" Iain asked Glencross.

"He indentured himself ten years ago for a bit of land."

"Sold himself out," Iain sniffed and swiped his nose with the back of his hand. *Ten years?* "Where's his parcel, then? Why's he still here?"

Glencross shrugged. "No land—they gave him the living of a master brewer. Not many who know more about working the cane juice than Alastair."

"More fool to put his faith in these Southroners." *Forewarned was forearmed.* "A canting auld wife, you are, Glencross. Where'd you hear that?"

"Tam. You'd hear more too if you didn't scowl your way through the compound." Potts's voice rose over the cane, this time closer, and Glencross rose to his feet. "Our cue."

The sun blazed directly overhead by the time they finished a second row. All shade had disappeared, leaving the air shimmering waves of heat. Iain's skin stretched taut across his shoulders, and he could barely move. Even the Africans down the line had stopped their cutting. He reached for the waterskin and held it over his mouth, trying to shake the last drop of water onto his parched tongue.

Glencross dropped to his knees, shoulders hunched over. His cheeks blazed red.

Through the willowy fronds of cane, Iain caught a glimpse of Potts. "You'd better get up, lad."

"One moment," Glencross wheezed.

"You don't have one," Iain hissed. He grabbed his brother-in-law from under the armpits to haul him up.

Glencross lurched unsteadily to his feet before his strength failed him. He sank back to the ground, panting.

Potts was nearly upon them. Iain swore. He tried to hoist Glencross up again, but his brother-in-law wouldn't move.

Too late.

Potts cleared the last stand of cane and came into view.

Iain stepped in front of Glencross as a human shield. Intending to draw Potts's attention away from Glencross, Iain headed off the overseer, brandishing his empty water bottle.

"You there! We need water!" Iain spat. "You want us to work in these stinking fields and get this cane cut before it rots—then give us more water, dammit."

Potts stopped midstride and faced Iain, first with surprise, then with thundering anger. "No slave talks to me that way." His knuckles whitened as he clutched his tamarind cane.

"Iain," Glencross said in a low tone as he struggled to his feet. By now, others had gathered to watch.

"We're bondsmen, nae slaves," Iain ground out, ignoring Glencross's warning. "You need to remember that."

Potts bared his teeth. "I take no lesson from a stinking turd." Before Iain could dart out of the way, Potts swung his cane and smashed it against his head.

Pain exploded, blinding him with its intensity. Iain stumbled backwards, reeling. Hot blood spurted from his crown.

Potts swung again, but this time Iain managed to catch the staff in his fist. He struggled to yank it out of the overseer's grasp, but Potts hadn't spent his strength cutting sugarcane. He twisted it free, veins throbbing angrily on the side of his neck. "Teach me a lesson, will you? One plus   one . . . " Another two strikes, this time across the temple. "Two, or was that three?"

Iain was now on the ground, shoulders hunched over with his arm lifted as protection. Potts raised his club again, but Glencross placed himself between them.

"Nay. No more. We'll get back to work," Glencross called out, holding his hands up.

Iain shook his head and swiped away the blood dripping into his eyes. He struggled to his feet, though every movement caused fresh agony. He'd stand like a man even if it drove Potts to murder. Glencross continued to placate the overseer. Iain's ears were ringing, and he couldn't settle on what Glencross exactly said, but whatever it was got through to Potts. The overseer's rage eased slightly.

"See that you do, or we'll go over new figures." He pointed the end of his cane first to Iain, then Glencross. "I call it digging two graves in one day." Sniffing, he hitched his breeches. Glaring at the crowd that had gathered to watch, he barked, "Gan back to work, the lot of you. NOW!" The others scattered and returned to what they were doing.

"Thanks," Iain said to Glencross, wiping the blood with his shirt.

Glencross bent over his knees, breathing deeply. "Thanks? You took that for me, and I owe you. But don't push this with Potts."

Iain frowned, looking into the direction that the overseer had gone. "He's a filthy bystart, but worse, a mad one." The man had just demonstrated that he didn't give a fig for their lives. They were as disposable as the bloodied shirts they wore.

The six o'clock bell clanged, calling a halt to work in fields. Two African lads were taking their turn pulling the bell-rope—fighting for their turn, more like. Exhausted, Iain and Glencross joined the others to head back to the compound for their dinner. Masterton's cheeks blazed red, and sweat plastered his thinning hair against his head. Neither Killean nor Angus said a word beyond a grunt and a nod of acknowledgment.

"You think they'll give us meat tonight?" Dunsmore asked to no one in particular when the roofs of the huts were visible. The scent of something wafted in the smoke of the cook fires.

"Only if a dumb beast dies—we might get some of that," Glencross said. "That's what I heard."

Iain snorted. "Aye, is that so? Give me a blade, and I'll have our dinner sorted."

"Gan alang," Potts called out as he passed them on his garron. "Gan alang, or your porridge will be scarfed down and there won't be nowt left."

115

A large cooking fire occupied the centre of the compound with a cast-iron kettle suspended over a tripod. The scent curling up in the steam confirmed what they would get—more gruel, an unpalatable, gelatinous slop unfit for swine. Loblolly, as Tam had called the stuff on their first night here, wouldn't even sustain a dog. Nary an oat or kernel of barley in the pot. Not even a proper hunk of bread or ale to be found. Iain had quickly realised what they referred to as bread was some odd ground-up vegetable, and this drink they called mobbie turned out to be a vile amber brew made from another vegetable. It left a bland, cloying aftertaste on his tongue, but there was naught else to quench his thirst. What he would do for a cup of ale and a hunk of meat.

He rubbed his raw cheek and considered the options. A moss-trooper took what he needed—a chicken, a goat. All fair game.

Iain queued up to receive his bowl of gruel with Glencross a step behind him. A pair of wenches worked the line, and to his surprise, one was Mairead.

He watched as she stirred the contents of the pot over the fire, frowning. The lass was unsteady on her feet—a thin breeze could knock her down. Her cheeks were flushed from the heat of the cook fire, and her oversized shift clung to her back from perspiration. Wisps of light brown hair escaped from a thick braid, hanging limply around her face. When she pushed the strands away, her hand shook slightly. This woman before him at the stew pot had become a shadow of herself, and this disturbed him. Iain hated seeing any woman crushed.

Killean was ahead of them and raised his bowl for his ration. Mairead reached across to give Killean a scoop of the loblolly and missed his bowl. The glob fell into the fire. The gruel hissed over the burning wood, a moderate sound compared to the angry hiss of the other maid, a blond snub-nosed wench. The blond whirled around and yanked the ladle from Mairead's hand before smacking her with it. Instead of turning on her tormentor, the Irish lass flinched and bit her lip.

What had happened to the woman who had the stones to defend her kinswoman against Dunsmore in the hold of a ship?

"Learn her right, Lucy—there's a good lass," Potts called out, cupping his jewels with both hands and making a rude gesture. With one throaty laugh, he continued to his own hut.

Iain shook his head. *Ill-hadden Pig.*

Not surprising, Dunsmore joined in. "You can use that one on me, love, I won't mind. You might even enjoy it."

Lucy arched her back slightly and appraised the oaf from beneath coy lashes.

Angus and one of Tam's Irish lads both chuckled until Angus met Iain's glower. Smothering his amusement, Angus looked elsewhere. He'd have a word with *him* later. At the moment, it fell on him to yank Dunsmore's chain. "Be a man, nae a beast," he called to him over his shoulder.

"Don't be a prude, Johnstone. A man has to have a bit o' fun now and then." He jostled Glencross, who was immediately ahead of him. "Hurry up—I've a hole in my belly."

Iain reached the front of the queue. His gaze shifted to her cheek, and this was when he realised that it wasn't red from only the fire. He could tell that she had been slapped and hard. His anger stirred.

Mairead looked up. Green eyes flecked with brown glanced over his bare jaw before lighting on his shorn hair. Frowning, her brows knitted together as though she were trying to place him. How different did he look?

Iain's irritation stirred, but he still managed a pleasant tone. "The gruel can barely be stomached when warm. I'll have my share before it's stone cold."

Mairead's eyes widened, and she almost dropped her ladle. "Iain Johnstone?" She leaned closer and scrutinised him as she would an ugly bug.

"Gruel," he repeated, tilting the bowl closer to her.

Finally, the lass regained her senses, and yet, as she ladled his portion, she cast furtive glances at him. A corner of her mouth lifted in amusement. Damn the wench, had she never seen a shaven man before?

The loblolly landed with a thud into his bowl. Iain stared at it. The glob turned his stomach.

"What's wrong?" Mairead asked. Her brow lifted slightly. "I cooked it myself."

"'Tis slop," he grumbled. "I'm a man, nae a pig."

Mairead's eyebrow lifted, and the corner of her mouth quirked slightly. Instead of replying, she waved him away. "Next."

Glencross held out his bowl to Mairead. "You well, lass?"

Mairead's eyes darted to Lucy before she nodded. "Well enough. My thanks for asking."

"That . . . smells fine," Glencross said.

"Fair words are always welcome." She cast Iain a pointed look.

"Margaret, keep the line moving," Lucy called out.

Glencross looked around. "Who's Margaret?" Iain wondered the same thing.

Mairead's expression became flat. The life that had lit her eyes faded, and her shoulders had tensed to her ears. "You'd best move on."

"Margaret," Lucy called out again. "Daft chit!"

Then Iain understood. They had taken the lass's name from her. They wouldn't have dared take his from *him*. But then the thought bored into him—they had taken everything else, and he hadn't been able to stop them.

Glencross reached across to win her attention. "There's nothing to that Southron wench. My wager is on Ireland," he said, giving her a friendly wink.

A shy smile flitted at the corner of her mouth. Then, instead of giving Glencross just one shallow scoop, she gave him a heaping serving.

Lucy was now flirting with another lad and missed it, but Dunsmore hadn't. When it was his turn to get his gruel, he planted himself squarely when Mairead only gave him a regular scoop.

"Where's *my* due?" Dunsmore grumbled. "I want what he got." He gave a sharp nod in Glencross's direction.

Mairead paled, no doubt realising her predicament. Appease Dunsmore but cause a revolt in the line when the others didn't get the same. The wench Lucy would no doubt seize on any excuse to cause a row.

Iain stepped between Dunsmore and Mairead and tried to move him along. The fool was going to get the lass in trouble. He gripped the man by the back of the neck and forced him to turn. "This unpalatable crap is not worth the fuss. That's enough."

Dunsmore shook him off and stepped back. "You don't tell me naught, Johnstone. You aren't the laird."

Again with that.

"You want a serious disagreement, Dunsmore?" Iain said, digging in his heels. "First you tell these lads why you're standing between them and the pot." Before Dunsmore opened his mouth to retort, he added, "You act like there's meat on offer instead of this shitten gruel." He snorted. "You want more gruel, Dunsmore? Here, have mine." And he shoved his bowl in the man's hand.

By now, the men had started loudly grumbling, making impatient noises in the queue behind them. The angry murmur made Dunsmore back down. "Keep your bowl." He jostled past him and, in one final peevish action, knocked the bowl out of Iain's hand and to the ground. Facedown.

Bastard.

Glencross grabbed Iain's arm and kept him from going after the man. "Let it go."

Iain drew a deep breath through clenched teeth. Not for the first time did he wonder why fate had taken McCaul and spared a louse like Dunsmore.

When he tore his eyes away, he realised that Mairead was staring at him. Her eyes were impossibly large and entirely fathomless. Taking a ragged breath, he turned and strode away.

Chapter 9

———◆———

Mairead was cruelly awoken when she was pulled from her hammock. She hit the dirt floor and cried out. Providence Moss stood over her in a fury. Her tallow candle cast grotesque shadows across her face, causing her already pinched features to resemble a scowling gargoyle.

"Get up, lazy wench," she said. "I've been trying to wake you— serves you right."

Mairead rubbed her aching side and looked around the hut that she shared with Lucy and the other kitchen maids. No one was there. Outside, the sky was black as soot. Mairead blinked at the housekeeper. "But it's still dark."

She gasped when Providence Moss yanked her to her feet. The woman's fingers curled like talons and bit into the tender flesh of her arm. "I don't hold with lazy wenches."

"It's not yet dawn," Mairead said as she tried to pry herself from the housekeeper's grasp.

"If it were, you'd have slept in," the housekeeper hissed and finally released her. "There's porridge to cook, fires to stoke, night buckets to collect. You'll be in the washhouse today. Get a move on, Margaret. Start gathering the firewood." She pushed Mairead to the door.

Mairead floundered, thoroughly disorientated. "You don't want me in the scullery today?" Since her arrival, she had been dealing with chores pertaining to all manner of pots—scrubbing, emptying and polishing. Her hands were cracked and burned from the harsh lye.

"Don't you dare question me, Margaret."

Mairead had barely enough time to grab her apron before flying after Providence Moss across the courtyard and into the kitchen house where the wood basket was kept. The other women were already working at the trestle tables.

Aline, one of the kitchen maids, gave Mairead a sympathetic smile, which proved to be a balm against Lucy's smirk.

Lucy waited until Providence Moss left the kitchen before saying, "There she is, the sleeping wonder. We had to fetch our own wood—you've put us behind. I've never seen Providence Moss so livid. The Duchess is expecting guests later today." This was what the kitchen maids called the mistress behind her back and far from Providence Moss's hearing.

"I didn't know," Mairead said. "Why didn't you wake me?"

Aline leaned closer and said in a low voice, "Lucy wouldn't let me. She threatened to throw me in the swine trough."

Providence Moss poked her head in the kitchen. "Margaret—the wood!"

Mairead dashed outside and hurried across the courtyard. Dawn finally broke, and a rooster crowed, followed by another. She hurried towards the woodpile behind the barn. The hens scratched in the dirt while a pair of cocks strutted around the yard, no longer concerned with being a herald. One fixed his beady eyes on Mairead and flew right at her, talons extended. She shrieked and jabbed a log at it.

Mairead heard a sound behind her, and she whirled around to find the copper-skinned woman she had seen her first day. This time the woman wasn't leading a grey donkey; instead, she held a medium-sized clay jug. Mairead had since learned that she was one of the Arawaks, a local tribe. Mairead hadn't been entirely sure of their status when Aline had spoken of them to her. The girl hadn't referred to them as slaves. They came and went, she had said, like no other servant, paid or indentured. Lucy spoke of them as though they were mostly wild and unpredictably dangerous, to be avoided at all costs.

Mairead didn't know what to make of the woman. She remained stern and somewhat fierce, and yet Mairead sensed that the woman was equally curious about her.

The Arawak gave Mairead a crisp nod before heading for the well. Mairead watched her go with an inexplicable fascination. Ciara had thought the woman was immoral for not covering herself up, but Mairead wondered at the woman's boldness.

From the direction of the kitchen, Providence Moss's scolding voice jarred Mairead out of her reverie. She hurried to fill her wood basket.

Mairead spent most of the morning feeding the fires in the washhouse and boiling the sheets. The washerwoman was named Hengist, a pear-shaped Dutch woman. She reminded Mairead of a gnome, complete with leathery skin and ruddy cheeks.

As Mairead hung the wash along a line, a lump rose in her throat. Hot tears sprang to her eyes. The sheets reminded her of old comforts—her home, her father and brothers. She had taken everything and everyone for granted. How she had hated to share quarters with Ciara and Bronagh, but she hadn't considered the inconvenience to them of welcoming a homeless relation. How stupid that she had once thought of that arrangement as a hardship.

Home. Just the thought of it cut her at the knees and pulled her down into hopeless despair. She swiped away her tears. *Selfish, pampered twit.* Here she stood bemoaning her fate, but hard work wouldn't kill her. Bronagh was in far more desperate straits. *Poor Bronagh.* Mairead's stomach twisted when she considered what evils her cousin had to face.

Mairead glanced at the direction of the manor. She hadn't seen Ciara since they had arrived, but Mairead couldn't help but worry about her. Surely, the Duchess wouldn't be entirely unkind to her cousin. Ciara had a pretty hand for fine needlework, and she would have no cause to give the woman dissatisfaction.

And still, something about Ciara's arrangement with the Duchess caused Mairead's spine to tingle with suspicion. She had always had a knack for uncovering things that people didn't want her to know—at least most of the time, she thought ruefully, remembering Ronan. Her brother Niall had claimed she had an uncanny intuition, to be sure, and often grew frustrated by her constant, probing questions that uncovered his half-truths and dissembling redirections. When caught, he'd whip off his hat and slam it on the ground. "Dammit, Mairead—why don't you just leave well enough alone? Your nose twitches, don't it?"

The breezes fluttered the clean sheets that were drying on the line. Mairead returned to the washhouse to collect the next set of washed linens when she saw a dishevelled young man bent over a bucket of water and splashing his face.

That wouldn't have bothered Mairead, but to her horror she saw that he had pushed aside the sheets she had left on the bench and trampled them underfoot. Her clean linens now ground into the dirt!

Mairead gave a strangled shriek and flew to the trampled sheets. She picked them up to find them fully soiled. Hours of work destroyed. Mairead whirled around to confront the vagabond. "Do you know what you've done?" She held up the sheet and practically shoved it in his face. "Ruined!"

"This is the washhouse, and that is laundry," the man drawled. His stained shirttails hung over wrinkled grey breeches, and the laces of his shirt were half-undone. "I fail to see the problem, wench."

Mairead wanted to gnash her teeth in frustration. Any moment, Hengist would return and would blame her for this disaster. She'd be sure to turn Mairead over to Providence Moss. She cringed to think of it. "I should get you to wash them. Then you tell me what the problem is."

"'Tis too early in the day to engage with a waspish female," the man muttered to himself. A tangle of curly brown hair hung to his shoulders, and a shadowed hint of a beard outlined a weak jaw. He had a lazy droop to his bloodshot eyes. Even a few feet away, Mairead could smell strong spirits and tobacco on him. "Wherever did they find a scrawny chit like you?"

The drunkard had unerringly touched on a sore spot. Mairead burned with shame. She would not be baited. "Providence Moss will not be pleased that you are filthy and drunk," Mairead said, allowing her tongue to run away from her good sense. Besides, she didn't want the woman to blame her for encouraging this vagabond. "You had best get on your way."

The man ignored her and instead settled himself on the bench, holding his head. He had taken one of the Duchess's fine linens from the line and pressed the damp cloth to his head.

Oh no, that would not do. "Did you not hear me, sirrah? Away with you!"

"Fair warning, wench, you're annoying me to no end. Shut your mouth and fetch me a cup of ale from the buttery."

Mairead crossed her arms. "You go on a bender and expect me to draw you a cup of ale so you can get even more drunk? Hie yourself down to the docks where they are used to serving lowlife scum."

"Scum?" The man bounded to his feet and threw the cloth to the muddy ground. His anger built to palpable heights. "You *dare* call *me* scum?"

Just then Providence Moss returned with Hengist. The woman froze when she saw the young wastrel. Instead of chasing the drunkard away, a fawning smile transformed her dour features. A cold chill scraped down Mairead's nape.

"Master Wilton. You've returned home," Providence Moss said with a respectful nod.

Mairead's stomach dropped. He couldn't be—not the Duchess's son? *Blessed Mother Mary.* What had she done?

"Obviously, as I am here." The corner of his left eye twitched, and his glare pinned Mairead. "I have been slandered in my own estate by this Irish wench. Is this the quality of maids you keep Providence Moss?"

Providence Moss's lips became a tight, quivering line. Sharp eyes swung to Mairead, who quailed. "My apologies, my lord. I will take matters in hand. This will not happen at Mount Vale again."

Wilton drew himself up to his full height. "It had better not," he said, "or we'll need to find a new housekeeper."

"Indeed, my lord."

"After you discipline the wench, send a jug of ale to my quarters. I don't wish to be disturbed for the remainder of the day. Can you manage that?"

"Aye, my lord."

The moment he left, Providence whirled to face Mairead, snarling, "What did you do, idiot girl?"

Mairead swallowed and shook her head. "I didn't know. He didn't say who he was . . . I thought he was one of the field men—"

Providence Moss raised her hand, and Mairead braced herself for a slap, but instead the woman grabbed her wrist and dragged her across the courtyard to the kitchen. "I've had enough of your impudence, Irish witch," she spat through white lips. "Time you were taught a proper lesson." The housekeeper didn't slacken her pace, and Mairead thought she'd yank her arm from its socket.

"Lucy!" Providence called when she pulled Mairead into the kitchen. "Lucy, fetch my switch."

"No!" Mairead panicked and tried pulling back, but the housekeeper had her in a vise grip. "I'm sorry—I didn't know."

"*Lucy!*"

The moment the housekeeper's hold relaxed, Mairead tried to snatch herself away, but she was slammed back down against a trestle table. The breath emptied from her lungs.

"I will teach you to embarrass me," Providence Moss hissed.

"I'm sorry," Mairead pleaded. "I didn't mean—I didn't know—" Her skirts were hiked up, exposing her buttocks. Lucy held her down with an iron grip. "Please, no—" Mairead cried out and tried to squirm away, then *whack*! She jerked away and smothered a shriek. A line of fire spread from her leg up along her hip, and she tasted blood where she bit down on her lip.

Whack! The switch landed straight across her bum. A scream wrenched from her throat, and tears of pain coursed down her cheeks.

"Margaret will learn to never." *Whack.* "Insult." *Whack.* "Her." *Whack.* "Betters." *Whack.* "Margaret is a lazy Irish whore." *Whack.*

Mairead bit her lip to keep from crying out. Her backside was afire, and she felt the hot trickle of blood trailing down her legs. Unbearable pain. Mairead's fingernails dug into the surface of the table. Her mind blocked the bite of the switch and instead focused on the housekeeper's furious words.

Margaret, Margaret, Margaret.

With every crack of the switch, Mairead repeated under her breath, over and over again: *My name is Mairead. My name is Mairead. MY NAME IS MAIREAD.*

Mairead's backside burned. She must have fainted in the end, for she woke to find herself lying on the hard dirt ground. Whoever had dragged her back to her hut hadn't even bothered to set her into her hammock.

She stirred to rise, but knife shards of pain caused her to suck in her breath and brought salty tears to her eyes. She couldn't do it. Not yet. Instead, she remained where she was, cheek pressed against the hard-packed earth.

Why was she here? What had she done to deserve this? The answer, of course, was bitter bile. Mairead had prayed for forgiveness over the fury and the jealousy that had made her spew the words she could not take back. During the long march to Cork, crammed in the foul hold and most especially those nights when she didn't know if she would awaken the next morn, she had prayed for a lifting of the curse. Clearly, no one listened. It was up to her to change things, if she could, or die trying.

Mairead pushed herself up to her knees, gritting her teeth against the pain that flooded her with every slightest movement. Her arms shook, and she nearly gave up and collapsed again, but she blew out a slow breath and straightened, rising to her feet. Heat pulsed across her backside, and she could feel where Providence Moss's whip lingered the longest. Her petticoats were still bunched up against her thighs, the rough cloth glued in places by dried blood.

Slowly, Mairead made her way to the hammock. Just the sight of the rope mesh made her stomach turn when she contemplated how easily it would bite into her raw skin. She gripped the hammock and managed to flop into it in such a way that she lay forward. That was all she could manage for now. She hung there limply with the rope mesh crisscrossing her cheek, watching the sunlight creep across the floor.

And then Ciara appeared at the door carrying a jar and a small wooden bucket. She rushed to Mairead and pressed her cool fingers to Mairead's wet cheeks. Mairead couldn't help crying, seeing Ciara there.

"There now, my love," her soft voice was a sweet balm. "Don't distress yourself. I'm here."

"You shouldn't be here, Ciara. What if they find you?"

"Don't fear for me, dearest. The mistress lies abed with a headache. She often does poorly in this heat, so she won't be looking for me now." Ciara stroked Mairead's hair and Mairead squeezed her eyes shut at the gentle touch. "You'll be right as rain soon enough. I'll see to that."

Ciara tugged at Mairead's petticoats, causing fresh pain. "One moment," Mairead said and lifted her hips. A slight breeze brushed across her bare skin. Ciara stopped talking, and it seemed to Mairead as though she held her breath.

"I'm glad I thought to bring a cloth." Her breath was oddly hitched.

Ciara bent over and dipped a cloth into the water in the bucket, wringing it out with clever, supple fingers. The first contact of damp cloth against inflamed skin made Mairead suck in her breath. But Ciara's touch was light, and soon Mairead was getting used to the relief the cool water brought her. Patiently, Ciara cleaned up the dried blood. When she finished, she dropped the cloth, now stained pink, into the water. Mairead stared at is as it fanned out before it sank to the bottom.

"One of the kitchen maids—Aline, I believe her name is—gave me this salve from the mistress's own cupboards," Ciara said. "It smells horrible, to be sure, dearest, but let's not put us off it." She wafted the salve under Mairead's nose. Mairead shuddered at the foul stench. "Aline, swears it will help," Ciara continued, "and I have no cause to doubt her." Sweet, trusting Ciara. Fortunately, Aline had stepped forward first and not Lucy. It wouldn't be above that witch to have given Ciara lard mixed with piss and sworn beautifully of its sovereign properties.

With cool, circling fingers, Ciara worked in the salve, massaging the paste into Mairead's outraged skin. She took care to apply liberal amounts to the most inflamed stripes. Mairead expected the salve to sting, but instead the softness of the lotion brought relief. She allowed herself to relax under Ciara's touch.

"I heard what happened with the young master," Ciara said as she worked on Mairead's back. "You need to be careful, my dearest. Don't draw their ire, can you promise me this?"

The Duchess's words rose like oil in Mairead's memory. Their poor behaviour would reflect ill on the other. Mairead turned her head, craning to look at Ciara.

"Did they harm you? You weren't punished for my actions? Were you?" Mairead bit her lip, a cold fear clutching at her chest.

Ciara paused a moment, so fleeting a moment that Mairead wondered if she imagined it. She gave Mairead a comforting smile. "Perish the thought. Don't you worry about me, my love. I'm well aware of how Providence Moss torments you, but the creature keeps a civil tongue in her mouth to me and is sweet as butter when the mistress is around. It's you I worry for."

Mairead closed her eyes, relieved to hear that no harm had befallen Ciara. Then her eyes flew open as another worrisome thought darted into her head. "Ciara, be sure to take care around the master, that horrible man. He is a drunkard and a wastrel."

"And a notorious gambler; yes, I've heard."

"Keep a fair distance lest he harass you too." Mairead's fingers wrapped around her cousin's wrist. "Be vigilant."

"Don't worry. I work under the sharp eyes of the man's own mother, a fearsome woman if there ever was one." Ciara shut the tin of salve and gathered her bucket. "I must return. Feeling better?"

Mairead hesitated, her earlier worries about the curse and confessing tying her tongue. Her soul had been flayed worse than her backside and all by her own doing. Should she confess now to Ciara, beg her forgiveness? Allow this to be the salve that would soften her soul?

Looking into Ciara's blue eyes, Mairead realise she couldn't. Ciara was the only link she had to home, and Mairead cared too deeply for her. She couldn't risk Ciara turning away from her in disgust if she found out about the curse—if she found out how hateful Mairead had been to her. It occurred to Mairead that confession only helped relieve the burden of the bearer, never anyone else. Relieving herself would only hurt Ciara. No, she'd not say a word. She'd lock this confession deep inside her chest.

"I am feeling better, thanks to you, dear Ciara." And she'd do her very best so that Ciara wouldn't suffer on her account.

Chapter 10

Mairead passed an agonising night with her shredded backside, even with the application of the salve. In the morning, she dressed slowly, for every movement freshened the pain. As she tightened her petticoat's drawstrings, she gritted her teeth. The rough cloth rubbed like sandpaper against her raw wounds.

"Take your time, Miss Dainty," Lucy said with a smirk. "Providence Moss will be sure to give you matching stripes across your back if you're late." She blocked the doorway and stood with her hands on her hips. "Now that you've received a taste of the switch, I hope you'll be served up more."

"Get out of my way." Mairead pushed past her, but not before Lucy delivered a parting slap on Mairead's bum. Sharp daggers of pain ripped through Mairead, and she nearly fainted. She leaned against the wall of the hut to keep herself from collapsing.

Lucy strolled past her with airy laughter. "Don't be late."

Mairead swallowed the waves of nausea and made her way to the scullery as quickly as she could. With every step, she kept repeating, *They will not break me.* Her resolve faltered when she found Providence Moss waiting for her.

The woman's long nose twitched in aggravation, and her thin mouth had all but disappeared in a white line of irritation. She pinned Mairead with a withering glare. "Where do you think you're going?"

Mairead edged away from the woman, feeling that she trod on marshy ground. Lucy openly gloated, but Aline had the decency to look uncomfortable. "The scullery . . . " Her words trailed uncertainly.

Providence Moss crossed her bony arms across her chest, and a gloating smile played across her slitted mouth. "You've offended the master, stupid chit, and the scullery is too good for you. Time to learn your place. You'll be collecting all the night buckets for the laundry, starting with the slave quarters."

That was how Mairead found herself leading a nut-brown donkey down the centre of the African compound.

A cask had been strapped to the side of the animal where she could collect the contents from the night buckets. As Mairead emptied the buckets into the cask, she held her breath and leaned slightly away. She quickly replaced the lid before moving on to the next hut. No matter how many night buckets she emptied, she couldn't keep herself from gagging. This had to be the worst duty on the entire plantation. A pox on the master.

The African huts were built close together, smaller than the ones used by the Christian servants, even though there were triple the number of African slaves. Since no one cooked for them, every other hut had an iron pot suspended over a tripod. Several fires were already stoked with the noon hour meal burbling away. All the able-bodied slaves, including the older children, were already in the fields, leaving the elderly and infirm behind in the compound, doing chores and minding the very young.

Mairead went through her task, painfully aware of all the eyes that followed her. Providence Moss had likely spent half the night thinking up degrading chores for Mairead. The housekeeper made no effort to hide where she considered Mairead's place on the plantation to be—the lowest of the low.

Mairead hurried through the last of the huts and turned the donkey towards the boiling house. The last place she had to visit was Alastair's cottage, just downhill from the crushing mill and the boiling house, where he ruled. Mairead prodded the donkey to keep moving. Mostly, it complied, but occasionally it insisted on stopping to graze on a patch of turf.

Passing the boiling house, she glanced inside. A dozen African lads were stirring the simmering cane juice. She didn't see Alastair, but normally he paced along each cauldron and checked that the process of cooking the cane sugar didn't fail. She never spoke to him during the course of her duties. Their paths rarely crossed.

Alastair's cottage was the largest on the plantation and could easily have housed a sizeable family, even though the master boiler lived alone. Blue shutters were parted to freshen the inside of the hut, and a cream-coloured goat grazed on the turf beneath a guava tree. A tripod had been rigged up over a campfire with an iron cauldron poised over it. The scent of fish stew wafted from the pot, causing Mairead's stomach to rumble. She hadn't had her meal yet, and she didn't expect anything as appetising as this when next she sat down to eat.

Mairead hurried to finish before Alastair returned. As she headed for the bedroom, her gaze touched on a large work table along a wall, and what she saw made her freeze. Aside from the various bottles and jars that cluttered the work surface, something entirely wonderful rested upon it.

A violin!

Mairead's breath caught in her throat, and she approached it carefully, as though it were a wild, living thing that would startle at any sudden movement. Two strings were missing, and a crack ran along its side, but to Mairead it was utterly divine. She hovered over it, drinking in its rich brown colour and sleek body. The heady combination of resin and wood filled her senses. How did such a civilised wonder find its way to an uncivilised world?

Mairead reached over and dared to pick up the treasure. She cradled it in her hands and tested the sound of the remaining strings. Without thinking, she turned the whorl to tune them until they thrummed just right. The sound resonated deep inside of her.

"Careful, it might bite," a man said.

Mairead whirled around, clutching the violin to her breast. Alastair stood there, his expression revealing nothing except for the slight raising of his bushy white brows. His hair, silver and stone grey mingled with dark, was tied back by a leather cord. If Mairead were to guess, she would have said that his expression looked curious.

"I suppose it would serve me well if it did," she replied, carefully returning the violin to its place. "Forgive my impudence. I shouldn't have touched it." Mairead backed away before heading towards the back room.

"Do you play?"

Mairead halted. *Did she play?* A sad, wistful longing tugged at her heart. He might as well have asked if she breathed or loved. "I do," she answered softly. "I haven't since . . . a long time. I haven't played for a very long age."

Alastair picked up the violin and turned it over in his hands, examining it critically. "I used to play too. It's not often that a proper instrument finds its way here. I'm restoring this one. A little worse for wear, but it's travelled far enough." He looked down his hooked nose at her. "Not unlike some other imports," he said with the first sign of a smile. "What do they call you, lass?"

"Margaret." She resisted the urge to lower her eyes and instead held his steady gaze. "But . . . my name is Mairead."

He nodded gravely. "Aye, you'll hear no Margaret from me."

"Thank you," she said in a low voice. Alastair put the instrument down, and Mairead's eyes were riveted. "Have you a bow for it?"

"Nay, that came splintered in two. I've given it to the carpenter. He tried to repair it, but it can't be fixed. Promised to craft me another."

"But you haven't given him the violin—it still needs to be repaired."

"Nay, lass, that task falls to me. I'll nae give it to another."

Mairead smiled, fully understanding. "I had better go," she said. "Hengist will be wondering where I've run off to." She tore herself from the table and dashed to retrieve the night bucket. When she returned, Alastair was leaving the cottage.

Mairead followed him out to the front yard to find the Arawak woman working at the cook fire. She looked up from her stirring and nodded a greeting. Alastair joined the woman, and to Mairead's astonishment said something in her language. The woman's expression softened, and when she responded, even though Mairead didn't understand a word, it sounded affectionate to Mairead's ears.

"What's her name?" Mairead asked Alastair with a sudden impulse.

The woman answered herself with simple dignity. "Uini."

"Nice to meet you, Uini."

Mairead smiled, then, feeling foolish, quickly skirted to the donkey, where she emptied her last night bucket. As she snapped the top of the cask shut, her gaze lingered upon the violin's direction.

"Just leave the bucket on the stoop, lass," Alastair said. "I'll take it in later. Return on the morrow after the supper hour. I'll need some help with the violin strings, if you've a mind."

Mairead broke into a wide smile that she could not contain. "On the morrow." And with a lighter step than when she'd come, she led the donkey down the road.

She headed down the pathway, humming a tune under her breath. The same tune that she had heard in the ship's hold in what seemed a lifetime ago. Even the donkey seemed content—or just anticipated a watering and decent rations at the end of this trip.

135

It was the fault of her good spirits that she didn't hear the rider approach from the road behind her until the horse nickered.

Mairead glanced over her shoulder, and a cold chill snaked through her body. Master Wilton approached her, riding a fine dappled grey. He sat at ease in the saddle, his wide-brimmed hat tilted at an arrogant angle. His hair hung in lustrous waves to his shoulders over a frothy white cambric shirt. His doublet was made of the finest brocade, and his boots were now polished to a lustrous shine. He held the reins in his gloved hand with a carelessness that spoke of his horsemanship. Mairead hoped he choked from the heat.

Tugging at her donkey's bridle, Mairead urged her beast aside to let the wretch pass, but instead of sweeping past, he halted alongside her.

"In charge of asses and night buckets, I see," he said. "A fitting employment for your tart tongue, wench."

Mairead didn't answer. She clutched the bridle until the leather straps bit into her palms.

"What, no response?" he asked. "Strange, you had more than enough to say the other day."

Mairead held her tongue, remembering her vow to do nothing to cause harm to Ciara. She hoped the louse would eventually tire of baiting her and continue on his way. Unfortunately, he appeared entirely at his leisure.

"I heard they whipped you," he drawled. "I took Providence Moss to task over that. She should have waited until I had my bath. I should have liked to see you squirm."

Mairead's mouth went dry. The man was worse sober than he was drunk. "I had better get back to my work, my lord, before Providence Moss returns."

"Aye, we wouldn't want her switch to taste your backside again," he said, adjusting his seat. "That would be a shame, even if you are a slight thing. Very different than your kinswoman. Ciara, they call her? A pretty one."

"She's a good lass," Mairead blurted out, realising too late that she shouldn't have spoken.

The master's smile widened. "I'll take your recommendation under advisement."

Fear washed over Mairead at the double edge of his words. Leave her alone, she screamed in her head. Instead, she forced herself to remain still and unaffected, even though she wanted to retch.

"Well, Margaret, you better get back to your night buckets. I expect my drawers to be extra clean on the morrow." He clicked his tongue and urged his horse past.

Mairead watched him disappear down the road, feeling sick and dirty, far dirtier than the contents of the buckets.

Wilton's veiled threats alarmed Mairead. No matter that she tried to convince herself that he only stirred an empty pot, she grew increasingly desperate to warn Ciara.

But how to do it? Mairead solicited Aline's help.

"Your cousin has a room in the garret," the girl told her when they were cooking their dinner of plantains and sweet potatoes that evening.

"How could I slip upstairs unnoticed, do you suppose?"

Aline gave her an anxious look but still answered, "Wait until after the eleventh hour, and use the back staircase. When you reach the third floor, turn left. Your cousin's room is at the far end of the corridor. Best you mind Providence Moss though. You'll have to pass by her door to reach your cousin, and she has the hearing of a bat."

Mairead waited until the suggested time, when the kitchen fires were banked, the maids let off their leads and Providence Moss drifted off to sleep to dream of fresh ways to torment her charges.

Night transformed the compound into another world, with the campfires doused and the huts shuttered and dark. Overhead, the midnight sky blazed with the fury of a million stars. Mairead followed the winding pathway to the manor until she reached the courtyard.

The sweet, cloying scent of exotic blooms perfumed the night air. She took care to flit between the shadows, far from the open windows of the manor. A light still shone in Master Wilton's study.

Mairead found the back door that led to the vestibule. She opened the portal slowly, grateful that the wretched thing didn't squeak. Equally carefully, she eased it shut behind her. Her heart pounded in her throat while she dreaded to hear the sharp clacking of Providence Moss's boots doing her final rounds. Yet all was silent.

A narrow staircase ran up to the servants' quarters, and Mairead climbed slowly, cringing when one of the risers creaked, an earth-shattering sound in an otherwise still house.

She reached the top floor and followed Aline's instructions. Mairead crept down the corridor, keeping a wary eye on the shut doors, fearful that at any time one might swing open.

Mairead reached the last door and halted outside. She leaned into the wooden portal and heard someone moving around in the room. Then she heard it. The lazy laughter of a man. Mairead's breath hitched in her throat. A few more muffled words, and Mairead was certain of Ciara's midnight caller—Wilton. *Oh, Ciara!* There could be no innocent reason for Wilton to be in her cousin's room.

Wilton's voice grew louder, and Mairead realised that he headed for the door. She backed away and looked around wildly, searching the austere corridor for a likely hiding place. One of the other rooms? Which one was Providence Moss's quarters? Oh, why hadn't she thought to ask Aline?

The door handle rattled, then stilled. No time to flee down the stairs—she'd not reach them in time. Just as the door started to open, Mairead darted into the closest room, praying she hadn't jumped from fry pan to fire. Weak moonlight showed that the room was empty, and Mairead sagged in relief against the closed portal. In the corridor, Wilton's footfalls passed by the room and continued down the hall towards the stairs. Then silence.

Mairead counted to ten before leaving the room. Shocked, she stood in the dark corridor and stared at Ciara's closed door. Debating whether to leave and bury her knowledge under a moth-eaten carpet, or go to her cousin . . . And then what? Had Ciara been swept away by the charms of a reprobate, or had he given her no choice?

Blessed Mother.

Mairead couldn't, wouldn't turn her back on her cousin, not when she most needed her. She hurried back to Ciara's room and, as loudly as she dared, knocked. The door opened by a timid Ciara, a weary, wary Ciara. Her hair was not bound in her usual braid and instead tumbled dishevelled around her shoulders. When she saw Mairead, she shrank back. Red-rimmed eyes widened. "Mairead? What are you doing here? You shouldn't have come." Ciara looked over Mairead's shoulder, her fear unmistakable. *Oh, Ciara.*

"Will you let me in, my love? I'll be discovered otherwise."

Ciara gave a reluctant nod and stepped aside to let her in.

Mairead looked around the room, grazing over the simple clothes press and washstand. Her gaze settled on the bed with the rumpled sheets. A cloying scent lingered in the room. Ciara crossed the room, and instead of sitting at the edge of the bed, she chose a chair near the washstand. As she tugged at her chemise, her hands shook.

"I saw him," Mairead said. She couldn't bear to defile her tongue on his name.

For a moment, it looked as though Ciara would pretend pretty confusion, but she merely nodded. "Did he see you?"

"I hid before he could." Mairead approached her cousin, and her heart turned when she noticed how Ciara's shoulders tensed. She took one step at a time, approaching her cousin as one would a wounded creature. Slowly, she lowered herself to kneel at Ciara's feet. Mairead didn't know how to manoeuvre these waters, nor did she have the benefit of a mother's advice to rely on. Aunt Fianna might have known how to comfort her daughter, but Mairead was glad that the woman had not lived long enough to see where they were. "Are you . . . are you well?" Mairead cringed at her poor choice of words. Of course her cousin *wasn't* well. "Are you hurt?" What could she say? Remembering the shame she felt when Ronan threw her over guided her now. This must be a little of how Ciara felt. "This is not your fault, my love."

Ciara wouldn't meet her gaze. Instead, she focused her attention on her clasped hands resting on her lap. "You're wrong. It is my fault. He has no control where I'm concerned."

A surge of anger shot through Mairead, but she curbed it. "Is that what he told you?" Mairead covered Ciara's hand with her own. Her cousin flinched but didn't try to pull away. "Dearest, you are the loveliest lass and a jewel of Ireland. The only thing that outshines that beauty is your kindness." Then her voice hardened. "Only a hateful wretch would turn your gifts into an excuse for his own failings. A man has better control over his passions."

Ciara sniffed and swiped away a stray tear. "Don't worry about me. I am not poorly off." She glanced around the room. "I have some comforts, while you," she turned Mairead's calloused hands over in her own, brushing over her cuts and abrasions, "you are forced to labour in the fields." Her gaze sharpened. "You are well, Mairead? No one has forced you—"

Mairead shook her head. "They pay me the least attention." She knew how fortunate she was. Potts might occasionally leer, but he didn't push his limits. But who could draw limits around Ciara? "What of the Duchess? If she knew, would she—"

Ciara's expression stiffened. "She knows." Her round lips curled down bitterly.

Mairead opened her mouth in surprise. The ground could have shifted under her, and she wouldn't have been as taken aback. "This does not concern her?"

"Why do you suppose she purchased me?" Ciara twisted her chemise and picked at the threads. "She despaired of the time her son spent in the whorehouses and gambling dens. She thought to tie him here—with me."

Mairead felt dawning horror and revulsion. *Unnatural, vile woman.* Now the woman's manner made more sense. The interest she extended to Ciara from the moment her cousin stepped up on the block. No small wonder the Duchess expressed so much satisfaction in defeating the whoremonger, Burke. She wasn't saving Ciara from Burke, that woman was in competition with him.

"It's getting late," Ciara said. "You should leave."

"Do you want me to stay with you? I will if you like."

"Best not, my love." She gave Mairead a tremulous smile, the first one with any hint of herself.

Mairead squeezed Ciara's hands between her own and gathered Ciara in her arms. This time, Ciara didn't try to pull away and buried her face in Mairead's shoulder. As she held her, Mairead said, her voice thick, "We will return to Ireland, dearest. Survive. We must both survive. One day, we *will* return home."

Ciara looked away and wouldn't meet Mairead's gaze. "Impossible. There's no going home, not ever."

"Keep your faith, my love," Mairead said. It was important to her that Ciara not give up. She didn't think she could handle her cousin's despair and still struggle against her own. "This is not forever," she said with sudden determination. "They cannot keep us. Eventually, we will be allowed to return home—all of us, including Bronagh, even if we have to fetch her ourselves."

"Bronagh won't return—not now." Ciara fastened her attention on the window and the night beyond. "You've tarried long enough, Mairead." She pressed a tremulous kiss on Mairead's cheek, then held her at arm's length. "Please. I couldn't bear it if someone found you."

Mairead gripped both of Ciara's hands in her own. A desperate grip. "I will always be here for you," she told her fiercely. "Do not forget that. Look for me at the dovecote. I'll be there every evening, an hour after sunset. Look for me there if you need me. Come anyway."

When Mairead slipped out of Ciara's room, her feet dragged, her leaden heart weighing her down. She didn't take especial care to mask her movements, but no one caught her treading down the stairs or even stopped her at the vestibule.

Only when she reached the courtyard did she allow the tears to flow. She had to find a way to get her and Ciara away from here.

Iain lay awake, staring at the beam above his hammock. Sunburn layered over sunburn, making lying in this sausage casing a teeth-clenching misery. This he could suffer, but having to swallow his pride whenever Potts appeared was nearly beyond Iain's capability.

Whenever the overseer came to inspect their progress, he'd loom over them atop his garron, tapping the side of his dusty boot with a tamarind cane. Glencross drilled pointed stares at Iain, silently urging him to hold his tongue. Iain's forced submission chipped away at his self-respect, and Dunsmore's relentless digs further salted the wound.

Iain repeated his personal mantra: *Bide your time. Lull them into complacency. Get off this fockin' island.*

A chorus of snoring in the hut further chased away sleep. Iain's thoughts drifted back to Tothill Fields and the Welsh barrister, Nathaniel Lewis, who had tried to recruit him for the Highlands. During the darkest hour of the night, Iain often wished he could have been an unprincipled bastard who didn't give a farthing for anyone other than himself. Then he'd have taken that pass and been in Scotland by now.

The thought of home haunted him. Every day it worsened, but it also drove him to keep going. By sheer, stubborn will, he'd see that they'd all get out of this hellhole—each one of his men. He didn't have to be an unprincipled bastard after all.

Better do it than wish it done.

Iain rolled out of his sausage casing and shook Glencross's shoulder. "Wake up, lad."

Glencross startled. "What?"

"Council time."

"Now?" Glencross rubbed his eyes and looked around. "Christ's teeth—it's late."

"Masterton, Killean. Get you all up." Iain went around waking the others too. He hesitated before approaching Dunsmore's hammock. The man wasn't one of them, and he detested the lout, but they were now stuck with him. "Dunsmore, you too."

While his men grumbled and yawned, Iain stepped outside to relieve himself. A full moon sailed over the night sky, bathing the compound in soft blue light. On his way back to the hut, he thought he saw a slight shadow flit past. He halted and peered closely, but he saw nothing more.

When he returned inside, he found Dunsmore occupying the centre of the floor as proud as bull-beef, as though he had been the one to call the council.

Iain settled himself a distance directly across from the bugger. He hid his irritation, not wanting to hand Dunsmore even a small victory. Damned if a Johnstone would concede a farthing to a Maxwell, never mind one of their by-blows.

"What's this about?" Dunsmore asked. "We were all sleeping."

"You'll see."

The others finally gathered around Iain. Seeing that he was now on the periphery, Dunsmore had no choice than to scoot closer.

The chirping of the whistling tree frogs filled the night air. The sound had driven Iain mad from the first night, but he considered it an asset tonight. The grating sound would effectively cover their talk. But they still needed to post a lookout for Potts. The Southroner frequently roamed at night.

"Dunsmore, keep watch for us," Iain said.

"You keep watch," Dunsmore said, folding his arms across his chest. "I didn't wake up to be sentinel."

Iain's eyes narrowed, drilling him with a glare that usually forced a weaker man to squirm in his seat. Curse him, the bastard didn't flinch. "My word is the one we go with," Iain finally said through gritted teeth. "You don't like it, there's two other huts. No one's begging to keep you here."

"Why don't one of the younger lads keep watch?" Dunsmore said with a grating whine in his tone. He was a cur with a bone. "I cut more cane than any of you today. Admit it, you have it in for me."

Iain held Dunsmore's gaze. "You're a bloody-mouthed rogue, and that's the truth." Throwing him out would give him more satisfaction than he'd had in months. Let him swim back to Scotland.

Killean exhaled a long, frustrated sigh, then rose to his feet. "I'll take the watch, Locharbaidh. There's a rank stench in here. But next time is on Dunsmore."

It had been on Iain's tongue to tell Killean to sit where he was and not give Dunsmore the victory, but he grudgingly conceded that the morning bell would ring before the whoreson would give in. He didn't want to be arguing about this all night.

Iain gave a curt nod. "Aye, so it will be. Of that, you can be sure." He waited long enough for Killean to get into position before he turned to his men—and Dunsmore, the hanger-on. Iain had prepared a speech in his head, a call to action to motivate his men, but Dunsmore had put him off his game, and his impatience rode him hard. "We need to get off this shitten island."

"Hallelujah," Glencross said with a grin.

"What of the indentures?" Angus Rae asked, looking around nervously. "We'd be outlaws to a man."

"Wouldn't be the first time we had a price on our heads, lad," Masterton the Younger said with a wolfish grin. "And we've been pardoned on more occasions than I can count."

Iain gave Masterton a knowing nod. Moss-troopers, mercenaries and outlaws. All had their turns at being useful to a king. Iain turned to Angus, but his words were meant for all his men. "Damn those papers. Damn the ink and the wax that sealed that worthless scrap of paper. The indenture isn't fit to wipe my arse. That faithless baggage Cromwell sold us into slavery, plain and simple, instead of treating us with honour as prisoners of war. May he rot in hell." He leaned over and spat on the floor. Several others answered the same. Iain's blood rushed through his veins. "We never signed their indenture, and we're nae bound by it. We're moss-troopers, not slaves, and I mean to get out of here." He paused to let his words roost. "If caught, they'll string us up. I'll not force anyone to follow me. Every man has the right to decide what his life is worth."

"A Masterton has never been a slave. They'll nae keep me here," said Masterton, setting his grizzled jaw to a stubborn angle. "I'm in, even if I have to swim the way back."

"Aye, I'm in," Glencross said. "I'll speak for Killean Ross too."

Dunsmore still hadn't replied. He chewed on his lower lip and took in the flow of conversation. Iain wondered why the unnatural reticence. Discretion was not one of Dunsmore's virtues. Finally, the man nodded. "Aye, I'm in, but I'm not following any of you caw-handed louts blindly, not afore hearing the plan."

For the first time in ages, Iain felt a measure of control returning to him. Here was something that he could do—plan and strategise to get them out of here, to get them home where they were masters of their own fate and not beasts of burden purchased on the block. "Same as planning a raid," he said. "Scope out the terrain, then gather resources any way we can. What do we know about the estate?"

"Except for Potts and a few o' Tam's lads doing a turn or two, there aren't any guards protecting the perimeter. I haven't seen any," Glencross said. "It would be naught to slip away."

"And yet there's a hundred slaves still here," Angus Rae said. "Everyone acts as though they're chained to the place."

"It's a damned island. The planters know we can't hide indefinitely, cocky bystarts," Iain said. "Hypocrites too. The majority of these arseworms favoured the King against Parliament until Cromwell's navy blasted them into submission. Had they any principles, which they don't, they'd nae be indenturing prisoners from the King's own army."

"Greed before loyalty," Glencross said bitterly.

"You expect more from Southroners?" Iain snorted.

"If these fields were yours, you might think twice—unless you were a thrice fool," Dunsmore cut in. Seeing Iain's glare, he shrugged. "Every acre is worth a fortune. Have you any idea how much they're making on the sugar? They're growing pure gold."

"They were making a greater fortune before," Glencross said reluctantly, as though he hated to agree with Dunsmore.

"Where'd you hear that?" Iain asked sharply.

"Heard Tam and Alastair talking," he replied. Then with a lopsided grin he added, "While you and Dunsmore are trying to throttle each other, I listen and pay attention."

"Hallelujah," Masterton said under his breath. When Iain glanced at him sharply, he turned back to Glencross with an innocent expression. "What changed for the planters? The war?"

"Parliament wanted to prove their stones. They passed an act, forcing the planters to sell only to English merchants. Lowered their price since the English aren't willing to pay as much as they were when they had the Dutch to compete with."

Masterton snorted. "I'm nae feeling too poorly for these whoresons."

Iain rubbed the heel of his palm against his forehead, feeling the irritation pounding in his head. He didn't care about the politics of the planters, only that they held his bond. "I've had enough of this damned sugar, no matter its worth. You can have it."

Dunsmore whistled, staring up at the rough thatched roof. "Johnstone speaks, and Fate, that faithless bitch, listens. If it were only that easy. What I wouldn't do to get a share of that myself."

"We're talking about escaping, not running a plantation," Iain snapped.

Dunsmore's nostrils flared, and his mouth compressed in an ugly scowl. "I know what the goal is, *Johnstone*."

"I had my doubts." Iain sniffed in dismissal before focusing on his men. "Escaping from the plantation is the least of our worries. We'll need to find passage on a ship heading home." *Home.* There was that word again, that kindled a fire deep in his gut. Focus on that. Work for *that.*

No one spoke at first, then Glencross broke the silence. "The closest port town is Speight's Town. Tam picks a few of the bondsmen to run up there with a shipment of ginger or indigo now and then."

"Speight's Town? I thought the shipments went to Bridge Town," Iain said.

Glencross shook his head. "Only the sugar, and Tam has a dedicated crew for that. Can't pry those lads apart. But Speight's Town serves our purpose better. It's about a couple of hours away— closer than Bridge Town, at any rate. We could stowaway on a ship— not all will be well-guarded."

"Aye, but there's five of us, lad," said Masterton. His eyes flicked to Dunsmore, and he corrected himself. "Six. No matter. We can't all hide between bales of indigo. They'll find us before we leave the harbour and toss us overboard."

"We can bribe our way aboard," Angus said.

"What prevents an oily Southron captain from selling us at the next slaving island? We'd be no better off than now." Masterton spit on the ground. He chewed his bottom lip, and his moustache twitched.

Iain turned the idea over in his head. Masterton was right, as usual. An honest captain would hardly agree to the arrangement, which left them with having to place their trust in the hands of an unprincipled rogue. Iain didn't like those prospects, not without leverage. "What other choice do we have? It's a risk, but—"

"We steal a ship, then," Dunsmore spoke up.

Everyone stared at him, astonished, until finally Iain said, "Aye, and first we sprout feathers."

"I'm serious."

"You're off your head." Iain's ire flared. "Do us a favour, on your way out, send in Killean. The lad won't be yanking our chain by spouting doughy plans."

"You lack imagination, Johnstone," Dunsmore said. "We commandeer a ship and throw those buggers overboard—or keep a few and press them into helping us get back to Scotland."

"Six men can't commandeer a ship, you geit," Iain said.

"If you were Maxwells, half would do."

Masterton growled a warning to Dunsmore, but Iain didn't move. He wasn't about to be goaded into making a rash decision by a manipulative bastard. "Your plan will fail."

"Says you."

"Dunsmore, don't be an arse," Glencross said. "We won't get a rowboat out of the harbour. None of us know one end of a ship from the other."

"I do," Dunsmore said smugly. "I ken the running of a ship."

"Oh aye?" Iain couldn't entirely hide his scepticism.

"I spent a couple of seasons sailing Solway Firth."

"Those waters are different," Iain said.

"As I said, we don't throw all the crew overboard," Dunsmore replied with a shrug. "It can still work."

Normally, such a bold plan would have appealed to Iain. The Southroners would never expect such a turn. If Masterton or Glencross had suggested it, he might have considered it, even decided to risk it, for it *would* be a staggering risk. But this was Dunsmore, a braggart full of his own piss. He'd have to be desperate—and simple—to place his faith on the man. "I'm not about to risk my men on a foolhardy venture. My answer is no."

"Do you have a better idea?"

"Not yet," Iain said flatly, hating to admit that. "But you don't just swim up to a ship and steal it. It's not apt to respond to a handful of oats and a honeyed voice. There will be guards posted on board and on shore. Moreover, if Speight's Town is remotely like Bridge Town, there will be a gun battery, maybe two, protecting the harbour. One shot from a sixteen-pounder and we'll all be at the bottom of the bay. Do you want me to continue or do you ken that we stand a better chance in convincing the Wiltons to book passage for us on a barque and send us on our merry fockin' way?"

"So we just sit here and cut cane?" Dunsmore muttered sullenly. "Is that what Himself will have us do?"

"For now."

Dunsmore scowled. "That has the sound of building roots. I'll nae be an old, bent man by the time you decide the time is nigh. You claim to be moss-troopers, but I'm looking at a bunch of fishwives."

"You go too far," Iain ground out.

"Every man has a voice—that's what you said." Dunsmore turned to the others. "You going to follow him blindly?" No one answered. "By the time he gauges the time right, half of us will be in our graves, ken?"

"I have never led my men into a skirmish without charging alongside them, and I've never led my men recklessly," Iain said. "We get only one chance—just one—and I mean for it to count."

"Aye, quite right," Masterton the Younger said.

"I'm with Locharbaidh," Glencross said.

Angus Rae bobbed his head. "Aye."

"Are you with us or no?" Iain asked, his voice hard and flat. "Choose, Dunsmore."

Dunsmore looked around sullenly at the others, avoiding Iain's glare. He found no supporters, not even Angus Rae. Finally, Dunsmore muttered, "I told you I was in."

Iain nodded. He'd have to be satisfied with that. "Until another opportunity rises, we prepare ourselves. We'll need weapons. Billhooks are fine for cutting cane but useless against a pistol or swords."

"There must be weapons on the estate," Glencross said. "With over a hundred slaves, they must worry about an uprising. I'll see what I can find."

"Right. We'll need more info on this Speight's Town—defences, the ships that ply these waters and how to get into the town without being spied," Iain said. "Glencross, Masterton, find out what you can from the Irishmen. Don't give away your interest. I'll see what I can learn from Tam."

"Aye, that will get us far," Dunsmore snorted. "Relying on the Irish now, are we?"

Iain tried to pretend the man away and turned to Angus. "We'll need extra food. These poor rations won't sustain us. We'll whittle down to naught and won't be able to fight off a midge. When we leave, it'll be at a run and not a crawl."

"Won't be hard, being that we're on a farm," Angus said. "I'll see that we get a proper meal."

"Be smart about it though," Iain said. "They watch the stores like hawks. Potts probably counts every bowl of gruel."

"Too bad we're afraid of Potts," Dunsmore said, staring pointedly at Iain. "I wager that caning you got was nae pleasant."

Iain's knuckles shone white. He clenched his jaw and counted to three. "We're finished here. Someone fetch Killean and fill him in with what he missed." Iain rose and went to get back to his hammock when Masterton halted him. The grizzled moss-trooper had stopped Dunsmore from walking away too.

"Put your differences aside, lads."

Dunsmore took a long moment before answering, "Anything to get out of here."

"Shake on it like men." Masterton nodded to Iain, his bushy brows drawing together.

Iain knew Masterton was right. He still didn't like the turd, and he never would, but to get back home, he'd suffer the man. Anything to get home. "Truce." He held out his hand.

"Aye." Dunsmore accepted, but instead of a quick shake, he gripped Iain's hand with a bone-crushing hold.

Iain didn't flinch, nor was he entirely surprised by it. Instead, he locked his wrist and squeezed hard until Dunsmore winced and finally relented.

Chapter 11

Mairead headed back to the compound after waiting a couple of hours by the dovecote for Ciara. Another night, and her cousin had not ventured to meet her. Worry gnawed at Mairead, but there was very little she could do except linger there each night.

With her mind still on her cousin, Mairead didn't see the figure coming towards her until the last moment. She considered darting away until she recognised David Glencross.

He greeted her with a grin. "Aye, did I startle you, lass?" Under his arm, he carried a small wooden cask.

Mairead pressed her hand against her throat. "A little."

"You shouldn't be out here alone, not at this hour," he said. "What are you doing?"

Mairead hesitated, but the man's open gaze reassured her. "I had hoped to see my cousin, thought she might slip away for a visit."

"Oh aye?"

"And yourself?" Mairead pointed to the cask tucked under his arm. "What have you there?"

He glanced down and grinned. "The last of the mobbie. An acquired taste, but better than naught. The lads have already gone through a cask."

"Lads?"

Glencross canted his head and regarded her, as though coming to a decision. Finally, he smiled. "Are you hungry, lass? Have you had enough of the gruel?"

Mairead's hand touched her empty stomach. "What a question."

"Well then, come along with me. I've a wee surprise." Glencross swept past her and continued several more feet until he realised she wasn't following. "I'll not beg you. Come if you will."

Mairead chewed her lip, considering a number of reasons why she should decline and return to her hut. "Where are you going?"

Glencross winked. "You'll see. Are you coming, for if you're not, you never saw me if anyone asks, ken?"

Mairead decided right then that she'd take the chance. Her curiosity demanded appeasement. "Very well," she said, falling into step beside him.

Glencross led her towards the pond, then struck along a well-worn path that followed the banks of the water. Small stones gave way to larger rocks, and with the pond levels low, more of the bank had become exposed. The terrain plunged downwards into a gully, swallowed up by a gnarled stand of trees, and it was at this point that Mairead decided that she should not have come. Where was he taking her? Glencross had always been a pleasant man, but what did she really know of him?

She slowed down, preparing to let him know that she'd changed her mind, when the faint scent of roasting meat tickled her nose. Her mouth began to water, and she inhaled deeply. All her caution dissolved. "Is that—?"

"Aye," Glencross said. "We'd best get down there before the heathens finish it off."

Mairead hurried after him, needing no further prompting. As they went deeper into the gully, the trees thinned out, and through the leaves she saw a glowing light. A campfire with several of the Scotsmen gathered around it, including Iain Johnstone.

Fashioned out of fallen boughs and branches, a crude spit hung over the fire with four roasting fowls speared through the centre of a stick. Dripping juices hissed and sizzled in the flames. Mairead's head swam with the tantalizing aroma.

Johnstone was the first to realise that Glencross had brought a guest. The others were tearing out hunks of the roasted meat and blowing on their fingers, more concerned with the meal they were about to stuff into their mouths. Johnstone sat on a log across the fire, his legs slightly spread apart as his elbows rested on his knees. The light of the campfire played across his features, making his face appear chiselled from stone. "What's this you brought, lad?" he called out to Glencross, though his eyes still rested on Mairead. "A keg of mobbie, we told you, nae a lass."

The others turned their heads, some twisting around to get a look at her, and greeted her with mixtures of surprise and amusement. To her dismay, their company included Dunsmore, the man who often managed to bring trouble down upon her.

"You can hardly blame him, Locharbaidh. A bonny lass like that," said one man, the oldest of the group. His bristly moustache twitched in poorly suppressed laughter, and his short but husky frame reminded Mairead of a gnarly gnome. "Come, girl, sit yourself down. None will harm you here, and there's enough for all."

Mairead hesitated, feeling awkward and uncertain. Johnstone's expression was unfathomable, watching her steadily. Then he shrugged. "Do as you please."

"Don't be so dour. I invited her," Glencross said with a vein of defiance and promptly introduced her to the group, including to the gnome, who was called Masterton the Younger. She stifled a smile at the irony.

Glencross settled down on an empty log, making enough room for Mairead to join him. Johnstone handed him one of the skewers with a cooked fowl. Glencross sliced off some of the meat with his

154

billhook and presented it to Mairead on the flat of the blade. "Go on."

Mairead's first taste of the roasted bird made her sigh with pleasure. Its juices dribbled down her fingers, and her only vexation was that she couldn't lick up the grease. She would have, except that six men were pretending not to stare at her.

"Tastes like chicken," she said between bites. "What manner of fowl is this?"

Johnstone gave her a rare, though wry, smile. "Chicken."

Mairead was halfway through the next bite when she realised the provenance of their dinner. "You raided the hen-house—the Duchess's hens?"

Johnstone scratched his stubbled cheek. "They were ill-mannered creatures. The one you're eating was one of the roosters."

Mairead almost choked—with laughter. She slowed down and chewed thoughtfully. "I wonder that the Duchess has any chickens left if men help themselves as you have."

"Aye, 'tis perplexing, lass," Masterton said. "Fools they be for not taking their due."

"No need to tell anyone," Killean said with a lopsided grin. He was an endearing, fresh-faced man.

"Especially not the Wiltons," Glencross said, offering Mairead another slice of roasted heaven.

As Mairead ate her dinner, she enjoyed the flow of their easy conversation and found herself relaxing. Their good-natured banter teased a smile out of her. Someone handed her a cup of mobbie, and over the rim of the cup she considered Johnstone—Locharbaidh, as the men called him. His byname, they explained when she asked. Though the meat and mobbie appeared to have softened his disposition, he still held himself apart from the others. Not physically, for he sat closer to their circle than even Dunsmore, but Mairead sensed that he wrapped an invisible barrier around himself.

The only time the shield lifted, just a little, was when he addressed Glencross.

Dunsmore chewed on a bone and fixed his attention on Mairead. She ignored him as long as she could until finally he spoke to her directly. "So, lass, do you often wander about at night?"

Though his expression gave nothing away, Mairead detected a faint mocking tone in his voice and something deeper and darker. She didn't know how to answer, not sure if the mobbie had muddled her judgment and the man simply asked an innocent question, or if he was in fact baiting her. None of the others seemed to pay his manner any mind, except for Johnstone, whose attention sharpened. Mairead decided to give Dunsmore the benefit of the doubt and answered, "I hoped to meet with my cousin at the dovecote. She didn't come."

"Shame you haven't seen her," Glencross said.

"I have, last week."

"How did you find her—your cousin?" Johnstone asked.

Mairead paled. *He knows—he knows how Wilton is ill-using Ciara.* She braced herself, expecting him to repeat the harsh predictions he had made about Ciara on the deck of the *Jane Marie*, but he held his tongue.

"Ciara is well," she lied, not bearing to admit otherwise. "She would have liked a bit of roasted flesh, to be sure."

Johnstone and Glencross exchanged a brief glance before Glencross cleared his throat and said, "I'm sure she's getting enough food, lass. They'll see to her needs."

"And if they don't, I'm sure one of us—" Dunsmore began, but Killean knocked him on the arm and nodded in Johnstone's direction. "I see. Himself is not amused," Dunsmore said with a smirk. "Still under your protection, are they?"

"I'm laird of my word," Johnstone replied with a hard edge.

Dunsmore gave him a mocking grin but didn't answer.

"Accept it, Dunsmore. These are our ways," Killean said.

"Scruples for moss-troopers? I doubt that." Dunsmore sniffed and rubbed the back of his hand under his nose.

"Believe it if you will or no, makes no difference," Johnstone said, "but if you share our food, you respect every man—and woman—here."

Dunsmore held Johnstone's gaze for a moment before finally nodding. "Aye." Mairead didn't understand why the sudden change, but the man's bluster evaporated, and she was glad for it. "Lad," he called out to Angus. "Pass me more of that mobbie. My cup is dry."

As the tension eased, Mairead's curiosity still pricked. Turning to Glencross, she asked, "What are moss-troopers?"

The others heard her question and exchanged amused, indulgent glances between themselves. All except Dunsmore.

"Moss-troopers are . . . enterprising lads," Masterton said, tipping his cup to Johnstone.

"Beholden to none," Glencross said, following Masterton's lead.

"Rebels?" Mairead asked.

"Horse thieves," Dunsmore said bluntly. "*Common* brigands."

"Your jealousy is showing, Dunsmore," Masterton said. "To be sure, the only horses we took were English ones. Scottish nags were safe." Guffaws broke out, and even Dunsmore laughed.

"Confusion to our enemies," Angus Rae said, tipping his cup too.

Mairead wasn't their enemy, but her confusion must have reflected in her expression because Glencross said, "Moss-troopers are very like your Irish Tories."

This she understood. "Freedom fighters—patriots."

Dunsmore snorted, but Johnstone finally broke his silence, "Aye, in a fashion. At first we were soldiers—until the army commanders objected to our less-than-godly opinions. Then we were dirt and purged from the ranks. Uninvited to drive the English from our land."

"You weren't allowed to fight for your own country?" Mairead asked.

"Not by their rules," Johnstone said. An angry tic played in his cheek. "A godly nation could only be defended by a godly army, so the Kirk said, and what the Kirk demanded, the army commanders did—like sheep." Bitterness dripped from his tone.

Mairead couldn't imagine the Church throwing away good fighters. "What happened?"

"We took to the auld ways, lass," Masterton said. "Since Central Command didn't want us, we found another manner to harass the enemy."

"Until they begged us to return and fight for them again," Angus said with a smirk.

"They finally accepted that the Kirk was wrong," Johnstone said, though he didn't look triumphant or smug about it. "But they had to lose thousands of good men at Dunbar to learn that lesson."

"But you fought at Worcester?" Mairead asked, remembering what Glencross had told her on the ship.

"Aye, a year later. The King didn't care for a man's religion as long as he was willing to pick up a musket for his sake. And there were still English on our shores," Johnstone said. The firelight illuminated his lines and shadows, accenting the bleakness of his tone.

"And now we find ourselves here," Killean added. "With a stolen chicken dinner."

Masterton snorted. "We should have kept to moss-trooping."

"Count yourself fortunate, old man," Angus said with a lopsided grin. "Now you have an excuse for nae being home." The mood lightened, and scowls turned to chortles.

"Aye, my wife, the auld hen, probably doesn't realise I'm gone yet," Masterton said with a wide grin. "Give that woman another year afore she wonders. When she kens the English have sold me, she'll be put out—"

"That she hadn't thought of it first," Johnstone said. "Aye, she'll have wanted a share of *that* bond."

Chuckles spread around the campfire, and Masterton's grin deepened. "You know my Agnes well."

Laughter spilled over, and Mairead joined in the mirth. When she glanced up, she caught Johnstone laughing openly. She held her breath in astonishment. His whole face lit up, and a small dimple played in the crease of his cheek. As he continued to needle Masterton, he met her amazed gaze and gave her a quick wink. Now *that* stirred butterflies in her stomach. She glanced away, feeling the heat flush through her cheeks.

"My Mary will be beside herself, sweet lass," Killean said, becoming sober. "We had an understanding, but she might well think me dead."

"Same with my own da—he must be wondering," Glencross said with a sigh. He and Johnstone exchanged a look before Johnstone studied his feet.

My da. A tight pain constricted Mairead's chest until she could hardly breathe. Word of Uncle Mulriane's death may have reached her father in Galway, but had he learned what had happened to his only daughter? Did he even know she was alive? A hard, jagged lump settled in her throat.

"We're making the lass uncomfortable," Johnstone said to the group. There was a quality to his tone that unsettled her further— understanding, perhaps? Rising to his feet, he glanced skyward, studying the stars. "Time we leave. The morning bell isn't far off."

"Aye, best we douse that fire first, lads," Masterton said. They smothered the embers with soil and sand but left the fire stones as they were, along with the crude spit. "Maybe next time we'll liberate a wee goat."

Mairead followed them back to the compound, wrapped in her own thoughts. Most of the men walked ahead of her, but both Glencross and Johnstone fell into step beside her. No one spoke, and since the terrain was rocky and sloped upwards, Mairead concentrated on where she was going so as not to embarrass herself

159

by falling flat on her face. By the time they reached the pond, Masterton and the others had already disappeared.

Johnstone turned to Glencross. "See that the lass gets back to her hut and that she doesn't fall in with another party." He glanced at Mairead and nodded his farewell before he headed off.

Mairead watched him go, a solitary shadow in the deepening gloom. He made no effort to catch up to the others; instead, he seemed content to walk on his own terms.

Iain spent the next week keeping up with Potts's manic demands for cutting the back lot of cane. The overseer's voice had grown hoarse from his constant threats to whip anyone within an inch of their lives if they didn't keep up the gruelling pace.

They were behind in their harvesting, and the Duchess was worried. Instead of each cutter having two women to gather the cane in their wake, they had to make do with only one so that the hardiest, and more experienced, wenches could cut their own rows.

Churning grey clouds hovered in the distance far to the north, and the winds were blowing in the wrong direction. A sudden storm would put them off even more.

Though Wilton didn't once appear, the Duchess inspected the fields on her dappled gelding several times a day.

"What have you been doing here, Mister Potts? This cane should have been harvested by now." Mistress Wilton's scorn carried past the overseer to those who stood near him. "Every day those stalks aren't crushed is losing Mount Vale valuable pounds of sugar. Get it done, no matter what it takes."

A few sharp words were enough for Potts to poach workers from every corner of the estate. He pulled most of the hands who had been tending the other crops to help with the sugar; the yams and cassava could wait a week. But when Potts assigned Mairead to him, Iain knew they were truly desperate.

"Oh aye?" Iain lifted a brow at Mairead, then turned back to the overseer. "She'll blow away with the chaff."

"Ain't no other," Potts said from the loftiness of his horse. His palm hovered over the grip of his cane. "Clear your allotment, or I'll flog the *both* of you. I'll take great pleasure in doing it too, Scotsman."

Iain's eyes narrowed as he caught Potts's speculative gaze dart to Mairead. She didn't seem to be aware of the man's lascivious expression. Damn, but Iain didn't want to be responsible for defending her too.

"Why not assign her to Tam?" Iain knew that Tam would do a better job at shielding the lass.

As Potts turned his horse around he said, "'Tis work I need, not fellowship."

Iain smothered a curse. "If you care for the work, give me another. One of them African wenches will do. I'll get twice as much done."

"Twice the yield?" Potts said with a smirk. "Aye, I'll take that."

"I didn't mean that," Iain said quickly. Christ's death, what had he done?

"But I am, and that's what counts, Scotsman."

"You can't really expect me—us," Iain said with growing alarm, "to clear twice as much cane as the others?"

Potts leaned forward in the saddle and tapped his cane against his booted thigh. "Twice as much, and you'll need to get it out of the Irish wench. You'll get no other. And I'll not be sparing either of you the lash if you fail." Potts rode down the rows. "All of you, get working."

Iain's frustration made him want to throttle Potts. He swore and turned around to find Mairead facing him with her enormous eyes. She flushed and averted her gaze. Iain raked his fingers through his hair. *Damn.* He clenched his teeth and counted to ten. This wasn't her fault.

"Come on." He didn't even bother to soften his gruff tone. "We've enough to do." He strode to his section without glancing back. In the distance, he caught Dunsmore's amused smirk. When Iain stopped to yell at the sot, the lass bumped right into him. "What the—" He whirled around to face her. "Do I look like empty air to you? Give me space, woman, instead of tripping me up like a mouse skittering at my heels."

Instead of shrinking, Mairead squared her shoulders and jutted out her pointy little chin. "What has gotten into you, Locharbaidh?" The use of his byname surprised Iain, but she used it as though she had the right to it. "You stop suddenly, then blame me for your injury? Daft man." She rested her hands on her hips in ill-disguised disdain, but a fly buzzing around her freckled nose ruined the effect.

"Listen here, Mouse, we've got enough cane to cut and load on that damned wagon." Iain jabbed his finger in the direction of the oxen dumbly waiting. "Just to be clear, I'm not getting my back flayed on account of you."

"I'll keep up," she said flatly. "I'm not a mouse. Stop calling me that."

Iain snorted. "You'd better keep up—*Mouse*." He rolled his shoulders and stretched his back before bending down to grab the first bunch of cane. His billhook cut through the stalk, leaving a foot from the ground for regrowth.

He had progressed four feet along the row before he glanced back to see how she was doing. Most of the bleeding cane was still lying in a heap on the ground while she was only carrying half of what the others normally picked up.

Iain hung his head and rubbed the bridge of his nose between thumb and forefinger. This was going to kill him. Damn that Potts.

When she returned from the wagon and picked up another small batch, he decided that he'd better step in.

"God's death, woman—can you not pick up more?"

Mairead's expression darkened, and her lips began moving silently as she muttered under her breath. This time she gathered more than she could reasonably manage. Some cane threatened to spill from the stack in her arms, but she shifted her weight and got a better hold of the bundle. She headed to the wagon with a slight sway of her hips, accentuated by the load she carried.

Iain stared, fascinated. To his surprise, he couldn't look away. His loins tightened, reminding him how long he had been without a woman. He continued to watch as she reached the wagon and handed over the bundle to the one of the lads in the back. Her smock stretched, drawing Iain's attention to her trim waist. Though he often growled and glowered at her, her looks were not as plain as he liked to pretend. Just as she was turning around, he mentally shook himself back into action and returned to cutting the cane. For the next while, he hacked at the stalks with an undisguised ferocity.

As the morning progressed, she matched her pace with his. The figure of Potts inspecting the fields made Iain cut faster. He ignored his protesting shoulders and back and pushed on. *Twice the yield.* When was he going to remember to keep his mouth shut?

To her credit, Mairead managed to keep up. Back and forth, from cane to wagon, she trotted. Once she even managed to grab the bundle just as he'd cut it.

"You're lagging, Locharbaidh. Tsk." Her tone was smug and laced with suppressed laughter. "Should we trade places, perhaps?"

"You're testing my patience, Mouse."

Mairead's laughter drifted in her wake as she hurried to the wagon.

When her back was turned, Iain's glower faded, to be replaced with a wry half-smile. He returned to his work before he could betray himself. A perverse desire to make her eat her words possessed him, and he turned his focus on mowing through the cane as quickly as he could.

A little later, a group of African lads came by with clay jugs filled with cool water. Iain tucked away his billhook and dropped to the ground with his precious cup of water. He chose a spot of shade.

After a moment of obvious indecision, she made up her mind and flopped beside him. Her cheeks were flushed, and damp curls lay flat against her forehead. She shut her eyes when she took a draught of water, then sighed. She tilted her head and turned to him.

"How is it you are kin to Glencross?" She scratched the side of her nose.

"Aye, you've noticed we don't look alike."

"That, and he has a sweeter disposition."

Iain quirked a brow and debated whether he should ignore her or not. Finally, he gave in, "Related through marriage."

"Yours or his?"

"Glencross doesn't have a wife, if that's what you're asking." Her questions were beginning to irritate him. "There—I've made your day."

She shrugged. "Neither my concern or no. But I do find it curious."

"Why?"

"You, with the disposition of an ogre, have found yourself a wife, yet a sweet man such as Glencross remains alone. Proof that the world lacks justice."

"Had." The admission was hard, even after all this time.

"Pardon?"

"*Had* a wife. I don't have one now. There—justice restored." He squinted up to the clouds as though he cared one jot about them.

She straightened, and her hazel eyes grew round. "I'm sorry. What happened?"

"None of your business." He immediately regretted his words when her lashes fluttered in hurt confusion. "Time to get back to work." He did try to soften his tone, but it came out as a thick rasp. Giving up, he rose and went back to cutting cane.

For the rest of the morning, they worked in silence. Iain continued his punishing pace, and he looked for a chance to chide her for lagging, but she never gave him the opportunity. She hustled between field and wagon.

The heat was getting to Iain, and he found his strength waning. When he looked back to offer her a truce, he grew alarmed. She had bent down to pick up a fresh bundle, and when she straightened, she began to sway. Her face was alarmingly pale. She dropped the bundle and struck her hands out, as though scrabbling for something solid to hold on to.

Iain caught her before she collapsed. He steadied her and led her to a shrinking patch of shade. "Sit," he commanded and helped her to the ground.

She closed her eyes and tilted her head back. Her mouth was slightly open and she panted in short breaths.

"Here." Iain unstoppered his canteen and pressed it to her mouth. "Drink."

Mairead clutched at the canteen, her fingers curled around his as she drank the water. The contact jolted Iain, and he released the canteen as though it were a hot coal.

He glanced up and noticed that her head was uncovered. Small tight coils of wispy curls had escaped her braid and framed her face in a frizzy halo.

"What happened to your kerchief?" He was sure she had worn something to cover her head.

In response, she held up her hand to show him. Her kerchief was been turned into a bandage. In the curve between index finger and thumb, blood had seeped through the linen.

"You should have said something, damned stubborn wench," he muttered. "Of all the stupid things, working without anything to top your head. No wonder you were ready to collapse." Iain swore again and shrugged off his shirt.

"What are you doing?"

"You'll see." He applied the tip of his knife to the linen and cut through about an inch. He held the hilt of the billhook between his teeth and tore the lower half of his shirt with his hands. He wound the linen around her head until most of her head was covered. Then he tied it at the back in a tight knot.

"Better?"

Mairead nodded. "What of your shirt? It's ruined."

"I'll manage, but if we don't get this cane cut and piled in the cart by the end of the day, both our backs will be ruined." And she would not survive that. He draped what was left of his shirt across his shoulders, giving no mind to his back and stomach being exposed. He held out his calloused hand to her and helped her to her feet. "Let's get back to work."

They barely spoke the rest of the day as they pushed themselves to get the last rows cut. The moment the final bell of the day rang, Potts made straight for them, ignoring two other groups on his way.

"Done," Iain gritted out. He couldn't have said anything more without giving away how winded he was, and he'd not give Potts that satisfaction.

Mairead leaned against the wagon and said nothing. Half her hair had fallen loose down her back, and damp tendrils were plastered against her neck and flushed cheeks. She looked like she had crawled through the hayloft. Though she was slight and looked like she could be carried away by a middling gust of wind, she had managed to keep up with him without a word of complaint. Not many women would have been able to do it. The lass had a backbone of steel, he realised with grudging respect.

As soon as Potts had ridden off to inspect the others' progress, Iain and Mairead headed back to the compound together. Neither spoke. Mairead limped slightly, her slender shoulders drooping. When they reached the first hut, Iain turned to Mairead and said, "Good work, Mouse."

Chapter 12

———◆———

Iain sat on a log and stared at the dying cook fires. Another long day in the fields, and he could barely move now that he had settled here. Every muscle screamed in agony. His shoulder blades felt twisted, and his sunburnt skin stretched taut across his back. Too exhausted to even eat, the bowl of porridge was left to congeal on the ground. A pair of mosquitoes hovered over his forehead, and he kept swatting them away. There were nearly as annoying as Potts raging up and down the rows of cane screaming at them like a madman. A couple of the African slaves had felt his annoyance today. One had been left in the field, his body a bleeding, pulpy mess.

Iain clenched his fist. He had tried to shield Mairead from the sight, but she'd stubbornly refused to turn away. He didn't think it was morbid curiosity on her part. Her little, pointed face had been resolutely set, as though she considered it her duty to *not* turn away. To her credit, she hadn't fainted, but no woman should have been in a position in the first place to decide whether to turn away or no.

Potts deserved to be buried in deepest hell, and Iain wanted nothing better than to deliver the bugger there himself.

Iain hunched forward, considering his fate. He didn't know how long he could suffer this place before losing his fockin' mind. The only thing keeping him sane right now, oddly enough, was working with Mairead—even though it still meant double work for him. The lass seemed to enjoy baiting him with her unquenchable wit almost as much as he enjoyed being baited. She kept him on his toes, and few could manage that.

Whistles and laughter from the Irish hut drew his attention. A bit of wagering centred on a couple of men fist-fighting for a bit of sport. Tam sat on a log with a cup in his hand and called out his wager.

Iain had noticed that when Tam needed goods to be carried to Speight's Town, these lads were usually picked. Just last week this lot of them delivered a shipment of ginger. Shame he couldn't have hidden in a sack of ginger. The only thing getting off this godforsaken island was produce.

The fistfight grew more raucous. An elbow to the nose, a mouthful of blood spurting, and things got dirty. They continued to beat the pulp out of each other. At this rate, neither man would be fit to transport a thing.

Iain scratched his growing beard. An idea took hold. There would be more shipments on the morrow. A trip to Speight's Town would be invaluable. He could survey the harbour, how many ships were anchored, and what the defences were.

Time to get his head out of his arse and get something done.

Iain hadn't gotten very far with Tam. He tried several times to develop a friendship with the man, but a tight group of Irishmen normally surrounded the sub-overseer. But now Tam sat alone while his bulwark of Dubliners were all turned to the fight. Time to make a friend. Betting on the common hatred of the English to grease his way, Iain crossed to the other camp and headed straight for Tam.

"What are you drinking?" Iain asked. He had long stopped hoping that they had ale—what he'd do for just a cup of a proper drink.

Tam shifted over, giving him leave to join him on the log. He handed him a spare cup and poured a healthy draught from a clay jug. "Kill-devil. *Sláinte.*"

Iain sniffed the brew. His nose twitched at the rich and spicy aroma. He took a generous draught, and the liquor burned all the way down his throat. He coughed and cleared his throat. Not unpleasant—strong enough to make him forget for a while, which was probably its virtue. He tossed the rest down.

"What is this?"

"Rum—fermented from the cane. You'll get used to it," Tam said. He chewed on a slim piece of wood.

"Alastair?"

Tam nodded. "I do a few small jobs for him, and he keeps a few jugs aside for me and the lads."

Iain took another swig. Warmth spread through his stomach. "You've been here for some time?"

"Six years five months."

Iain scowled. "A lifetime." He poured himself another draught and welcomed the burn down this throat.

"A man can get used to anything," Tam said with a wry smile. "Seven more months and my indenture is done. I might stay on here. The Duchess will pay me, same as she does Potts. Well, almost the same. That living and my sugar portion will set me up nicely."

That was what Iain feared. That he'd get used to all of this. That home would be a distant memory. This place would either kill him or kill his drive to return home, and that would be the same as being laid in the grave. An image formed in his mind, years from now sitting on the same log, sharing a drink of rum with a new servant and giving him every damned excuse for why he didn't return to Scotland. The thought soured his gut.

Iain swirled the liquor around his cup, considering how to approach his subject of getting on Tam's crew. He pointed to the fighters. By now, they were taking sluggish swings at one another. "Your lads won't be much use tomorrow."

"They needed to vent." Tam shrugged. "No use to me, they are, bursting at the seams."

"Aye, fair," Iain said.

Iain accepted a refill and braced himself for another taste. This time it went down a little smoother. "What's the wager?"

"A week's ration of sweet potatoes."

Iain could see the currency in that. Those strange vegetables broke the monotony of the loblolly.

One of the boxers had a burst of energy and drove his fists into his opponent's nose, jaw then stomach. Iain noticed how Tam sat up straighter, his attention entirely transfixed. The man crumpled to the ground. A few of the men were screaming at him to rise. He managed to prop himself up on an elbow before crumbling into oblivion.

Tam chuckled and lifted his cup to the winner. "Two sweet potatoes you owe me," he called out to one of the lads.

The man answered back in Irish before giving the loser a swift kick in the arse.

After a few moments, Iain said, "I heard you're carrying goods to Speight's Town in the morning. You'll need men."

"Got the men I need."

"Him?" Iain snorted. "His eyes will be swollen shut in the morning."

Tam shrugged his shoulders and didn't reply.

He wasn't getting anywhere with subtlety. Time for a more direct approach. "I need to be doing something more than fieldwork. A little variety now and then. How do I volunteer for that duty?"

"You don't. I only pick those I can trust. Right now I barely trust you with cutting the cane."

"But I'm not the one bleeding in the dirt."

"Fair," Tam said.

Iain opened his mouth to further his case when Tam added, "Alastair has to approve, and he don't care for you. Thinks you're too full of yourself."

Iain grimaced. "Aye, I had just been sold and said a few words. Not my finest day, right."

"Friendly advice—to survive here, you need to be in Alastair's good graces. Nothing happens here without his permission. Not even Potts would dare cross him." Tam tapped his cup against Iain's. *"Sláinte."*

Iain pondered this as he stared at the dirt at his feet. Could he lower himself further to flatter Alastair? It didn't look like he'd have a choice, but the prospect nearly defeated him.

The sound of whistling tree frogs mellowed as the dawn approached. Mairead stared up at the beams that formed the underbelly of the hut's roof. Gaps between the slats and thatch revealed the growing light. She picked out the central melody in the tree frogs' song and tried to match her voice to it just under her breath. *I'm mad, truly.*

How she longed for Alastair's violin, ever since first seeing the battered instrument in the cottage. Mairead had accepted Alastair's offer and ran over there as often as she could. The repairs were nearly complete. The yearning to play it bore itself deep into her heart. She flexed her fingers, moving them in the pattern of a favourite tune, imagining the strings pressed beneath her fingertips.

Her hammock swayed back and forth, and from a forgotten corner in her mind the song that she had heard on the ship ran through her head—she remembered the singer's earthy tones and the memory enveloped her like a cherished blanket. The lyrics floated in her mind.

An' what will be the love-tokens
That ye will send wi' me?
Ye may tell my love I'll send her a kiss,

A kiss, will I twae;
An' ever she come to fair Scotland,
I the red gold she sall gae.

She closed her eyes, and her fingers moved along the phantom fingerboard to pluck out the notes of the melody.

Suddenly, Mairead had an urge to break free, taste the dawn and breathe in the early morning air, the way she did in Ireland. No one would come looking for her—this being Sunday morning—nor was she expected to attend the Duchess's church sermon, being fully Irish and mostly heathen in the woman's eyes.

Mairead snuck outside the hut and carefully shut the crooked door behind her. The morning was fresh, the sun not yet a scorching ball. She crossed the compound and found Uini outside her hut grinding dried cassava root in a wide mortar. The woman gave a slight nod and bent her dark head to continue what she was doing.

Without a clear destination in mind, Mairead's feet found the well-worn path to the pond, and when she realised where she had been thoughtlessly heading, she hurried with more purpose. She imagined the cool water lapping against her legs. Mairead relished the idea of a quick swim before everyone stirred.

So thoroughly did she imagine the guilty pleasure that awaited her that when she heard a splash ahead, she felt keen disappointment. Had someone already beaten her to it? Mairead crept forward, careful to not make a sound. She reached the edge of the brush and carefully parted the leaves, hoping to see waterfowl.

Sunlight sparkled on the water. A slight breeze rippled the otherwise still water. Another splash. At first, she didn't see anything, then someone surfaced. A man, skimming across the pond, arms and legs slicing through the water. Even before he turned, she knew who it was. *Johnstone.*

Mairead knew she should back away and leave before he caught her watching—he'd be insufferable otherwise. That, or bark her head off as any self-respecting ogre. And yet something pinned her to the spot.

He dove into the water, his body curving with a flash of his naked buttocks.

Mairead's eyes widened, and she edged closer. When he split the surface of the lake, he caused a spray of water drops to splatter. He stood facing her direction, eyes closed. Raising his hands to his head, he slicked back his dark blond hair.

Mairead didn't dare move. She watched how the muscles in his arms flexed. Her eyes travelled across his broad chest with its light mat of hair. A trail of darkish hair ran down from chest to stomach until it disappeared below the pond's surface. Mairead craned her head to peer into the pond, but the water was murky and brownish-green.

Johnstone dove under again. Mairead sat back on her heels and nibbled her fingertip, considering her options. She really *should* leave. A smile played at the corner of her mouth as she made herself more comfortable.

Johnstone surfaced and began to paddle lazily in the water. His head was tipped backwards, his face presented to the sun. His skin had become tanned and gleamed against the lapping water.

Mairead watched, captivated. He seemed at one with the water. She didn't know too many who could swim, and none so well. Her own brothers had enjoyed a quick barrelling leap into the river back home, splashing like mad puppies and thrashing in the water. They had taught her to float, but swimming across the water as this Scotsman was now doing, with strong, purposeful strokes, was an art, and one she admired greatly. So she told herself.

After a few moments, prudence whispered that she had stayed long enough. Mairead rose from her crouch, careful not to rustle a leaf, but just as she moved Johnstone finished his swim and headed back to the bank. Mairead dropped to the ground again so he wouldn't notice her.

Johnstone slowly waded out of the water, all glorious and dripping. Mairead's breath locked in her throat. She took in that expanse of chest, the tapered waist then . . . *Blessed Mother of Jesus.*

She made a slight choking sound, and Johnstone stopped to look around.

"Who's there?" he called out in her direction.

Mairead's face flooded. He would *never* let her live this down. She had to get away from here without him seeing her.

No time for discretion.

Mairead darted for the trail. She risked a glance over her shoulder to catch a glimpse of Johnstone yanking on his breeches. And that was her downfall. Literally. A root hooked her foot, and she crashed to the ground with a cry. Then she heard him thrashing through the brush behind her. Mairead scrambled to her feet and managed to take a few more strides before he caught up with her, grabbing a fistful of her petticoat in his hand.

Mairead twisted around and found herself face-to-face with Iain Locharbaidh Johnstone. It was one thing to gawk at the man from a distance but to be this close to his still-wet chest squeezed the breath from her lungs. She averted her eyes, not sure where she could safely look, and her gaze landed on his unlaced breeches. More wet skin. Heat flooded her cheeks.

"Oh!"

Johnstone released her and swore under his breath while he laced up his breeches. "What were you doing, woman?"

"Nothing! I . . . I came down for a wash."

"Do you always hide in the shrubs when taking a wash?" His eyes narrowed, causing her to squirm. "Here's a tip, lass, the water works far better. Not sure what they do in Ireland, but that's how it's done in Scotland."

"I was *not* hiding in the shrubs." Mairead hid her crossed fingers in the folds of her petticoat and searched lamely for an adequate rebuttal. "I had only *reached* the shrubs when you starting crashing around like a mad man. And don't you dare disparage *my* homeland with your poor attempt of humour."

"How long were you watching me?"

Mairead felt her face blaze. "I was not watching you, to be sure. Have you not heard a thing I've said?"

He folded his arms across his chest and quirked his brow. "Building a nest in the shrubs, then, like a wee mouse?"

"Stop calling me a mouse," Mairead said, now with true outrage. Small and insignificant—was she always to be thought this way? No one ever compared Ciara to a mouse. Not even Bronagh—a shrew, perhaps, but never a mouse.

The corners of his mouth lifted slightly. "Aye, you were watching."

She knew it—she *knew* he'd be insufferable! "I didn't know who was in the pond and the moment . . . *the moment* I discovered who it was . . . For certain, it could have been anyone . . . even . . . even Masterton the Younger."

Johnstone quirked a brow, amusement playing across his features. Mairead's gaze latched on to his deepening smile, and she only now noticed the firmness of his jaw and how the droplets of water clung to his blond whiskers.

Mairead tore her eyes away and forced herself to meet his eyes. "What? What do you find so amusing?"

"Not sure where to start." Was that laughter in his voice?

Mairead's inner voice sat her down and delivered a stern lecture. *Concede the field, Mairead. Retreat now. No shame in admitting defeat.* And yet she dashed the voice of reason and found herself saying, "Make an effort. Explain it to me."

"You thought you were ogling *Masterton*?"

Mairead's jaw dropped. "I never said—"

Johnstone's teeth flashed in a smile. "He'll be flattered, lass, but I'd steer clear of his wife, were I you. She'll not think twice to chase you off the croft with a broom."

"I never said I was ogling him!"

"Oh aye? But you *were* ogling someone?"

Mairead sucked in her breath. "You. Are. An. Impossible. Man!" She finally did what her good sense had urged her to do earlier. She whirled around and fled the field.

Chapter 13

To Mairead's immense relief, Johnstone didn't tease her about the pond incident. True, a few times he regarded her quizzically, and she braced herself for a provoking comment, but it never came. She did, however, sneak glances at him, remembering all too clearly how he looked wading out of the water. When had she become a shameless hussy?

Fortunately, or unfortunately, she didn't have time to dwell on the matter. Sugarcane needed to be harvested. After a long, gruelling week in the fields, Mairead had earned an aching back and a crisscross of scratches and welts over her arms. She lost track of how many wagonloads of cane Johnstone had cut and she had gathered.

One more hour until the last bell tolled, the final one before the Sunday rest. She had survived another week. As soon as the clanging started, everyone would scramble to gather tools and return to the compound. Back at the boiling house, the slaves would be extinguishing the furnace fires, and for one day there would be no sugar work—cutting, crushing or boiling. Tomorrow, Mairead could stay in her hammock all day if she pleased and slave for no one.

"What's the matter with you, woman?" Johnstone said gruffly. "I've been talking to the wind. What are you about?"

"Nothing," she said, making a face at him. "I'm wondering where Glencross is." She hadn't even remotely, but telling him so proved to be a curious and convenient manner to set him back on his heels.

"Time enough for mooning later," he grumbled.

"Mooning is it now? Wherever did you get *that* idea, Locharbaidh? Even if true, it's none of your concern." This wasn't the first time he had accused her of sweet-hearting with Glencross, which puzzled her greatly because she spent more time with him than his brother-in-law. The only difference was Glencross never failed to be amiable. Mairead found the younger man pleasant and engaging, a bit more of a flirt than comfort allowed. She had been stung by that nonsense once before, and although she wouldn't insult Glencross by comparing him to Ronan, Mairead refused to be a twice-over fool. But she wasn't above teasing Johnstone. Someone needed to pull his tail now and then.

"Never mind," he said brusquely. "Get the last stalks loaded in the wagon."

Potts drew closer on his horse, and Mairead saw the wisdom of doing as Johnstone bid. The overseer made her skin crawl. Always hovering close, looking for an opportunity to beat them, only in her case Mairead suspected he'd particularly relish exposing her backside. Suppressing a shiver, she hurried to finish her work. He had made no attempt to hide his dalliance with a few of the female slaves, and lately the beast had been hovering too close for comfort.

The blessed bell finally clanged, and Mairead heaved a sigh of relief. "Can I hitch a ride?" she asked Tam, who drove the oxen and wagon back to the barn.

"Hop on, lass."

Mairead hoisted herself up to the back of the wagon and settled down, her legs dangling as the oxen plodded along. They hadn't gotten far when Johnstone caught up to them and hopped up beside her.

"My feet hurt," he said by way of an explanation. "Move over, Mouse." His thighs pressed close to hers and radiated heat. Tipping his head back, he shut his eyes.

Mairead watched him curiously, noting the lines etched on his face from fatigue and sun. Streaks of sun-bleached hair mingled with darker blond. His beard had come in, parts of it lightened as well.

"What are you staring at?" Johnstone opened one eye and then the other.

"Nothing." She abruptly turned away and forced herself to focus on the dust churning in their wake.

"Hey, lass," Tam called over his shoulder. "Come by the crushing mill on the morrow. It's been a long week, and we could all use a bit o' frivolity. Alastair has something special planned. The lads have built a few instruments, and they're ready to try them out."

"Instruments?" Mairead's eyes widened, and she perked up. "What sort of instruments?"

"Nothing too grand," Tam replied. "They've stretched some hides to fashion a drum. We've whittled a few homemade pipes too."

Mairead scooted into a half-turn. "Will Alastair be bringing out his violin?" She hadn't managed to visit the cottage all week, and she wondered if he had finally finished the repairs. She caught Johnstone looking at her curiously. "What?"

He gave her an odd smile and shook his head. A single dimple played at the crease of his cheek.

Tam led the oxen into the stable, and Johnstone was the first to hop off the wagon. He held out his hand to help Mairead down, but the uncharacteristic offer flustered her. Distracted and in a hurry to jump down without his assistance, she caught her toe in the half-torn hem of her petticoat and pitched forward. Right into his arms. He caught her effortlessly, strong arms encircling her waist. The heat of his body seeped through the rough linen of her smock.

"Ease up, lass." He seemed equally surprised to be holding her, but instead of releasing her, he cradled her a little longer than necessary. "A bit eager to be off, aren't you?"

Mortified, she put up her hands like a shield. "I'm fine, Locharbaidh. Fine." Her voice sounded a little shrill even to her ears.

"Right, then. Next time I'll let you fall on your arse." Shaking his head, he walked away, heading in the direction of the compound.

Mairead watched him leave, torn about letting him go or running after him. He had only been trying to help her. No doubt that had been the source of her confusion. "Locharbaidh!" She hurried after him. "Wait!"

He didn't slacken his pace.

Mairead tried to match his very long stride with several of her shorter ones. The path dipped sharply downwards, and she nearly tripped but managed to settle her balance in time. "About that, I'm sorry."

"But?" Johnstone eased his pace.

"But what?"

"I'm hearing a *but*."

Mairead stifled a smile. "Well . . . now you know how it feels for someone to turn into an ogre on you."

"Oh aye?"

"Not very pleasant, is it?"

Johnstone sniffed but didn't reply. Still, Mairead sensed a slight crinkling at the edges of his eyes. Stopping, he turned to her. "Is that what you call it?"

Mairead frowned, wondering what he meant.

"Never mind, lass," he said with a shake of his head and continued towards the compound. "Coming?"

Mairead fell into step beside him, and this time he slowed down to an easier pace.

"What was that about a fiddle?" he asked.

"Oh!" Excitement bubbled inside her, and for a moment she was about to blurt out everything about Alastair's violin, but then she stopped herself. This meant something to her. She couldn't bear it if he scoffed at it or made fun of her over it. Even her own had never understood her passion for the instrument. "Something he's fixing."

They reached the fork, one path heading to the compound, the other to the crushing mill. Mairead didn't care about loblolly and stewed fish bones. Instead, she had a driving urge to see the progress Alastair had made on the instrument. She hung back, then turned down the other path. "I have to go," she told him.

"What are you on about now, flighty woman?"

Mairead waved at him, not giving him a chance to question her further, before she dashed down the hill towards Alastair's cottage.

She found Uini working over hot stones at the cook fire, baking thin rounds of cassava bread. The woman looked up, and before Mairead could ask her about Alastair, she motioned to the cottage. "Inside," Uini said in a low, throaty voice.

Mairead gave an impatient knock before stepping inside. Alastair sat on a stool by his workbench applying rosin to the new bow strings.

"There she is," Alastair said with a pleased grin. "Wondered when you were going to show up."

"The bow is ready," she said, admiring the solid lines. "The carpenter has done fine work."

"Aye, but not nearly as fine as this." Alastair bent down, opened a wooden chest and from it drew the violin. Whole, repaired and gleaming. He held it up for her. "I gave it a final polish last night."

Mairead pressed a hand to her chest, suddenly getting misty. "Could I try it?"

"How cruel would it be if I said no?"

"Very." Mairead reached over and took the violin in her hands. She ran a finger down its body, touching the wood that had been repaired. Alastair had done a masterful job of it. Though a scar remained, he had filled in the split seam well.

"You'll need this," he said, handing her the bow. "It'll need a bit of breaking in."

Mairead positioned the violin so it rested above her collarbone and aligned her fingers over the D string. But when she held up the bow, ready to play, she hesitated.

Nerves fluttered in her heart, and blood pounded in her ears. The last time she had taken up a violin, the very last time she had played, her entire world had changed. She had discovered Ronan for a fickle man, playing one cousin over the other. And then the English had arrived. Her last song had been soured by so much tragedy.

"Is there a problem, Mairead?" Alastair asked.

She shook her head, willing her racing heart to calm. "You've done a fine job with it. It's been a long time since I last played."

"Worried that you've forgotten the knack of it."

"That must be it."

Mairead moistened her dry lips and turned her thoughts from the past. She was here now with a new instrument, fully determined to enjoy it.

She lifted her bow and ran it across the strings experimentally, as an overture of engagement. This violin had a different sound than her lost cherished beauty, but not unwholesomely so. A slightly lower timbre gave it a more mature tone. Poor instrument, she thought, it had gone through a great deal of trouble to find its way here, not unlike herself.

While Mairead ran through scales, the instrument warmed to her touch. She found her fingers stiff and out of practice, but to her joy, she didn't need to think about the notes before she played them. As she ran through a few more flights, she found her finger pads to be a little sensitive, an oddity considering how work-toughened the rest of her body had become.

Uini had drifted in and sat cross-legged on the ground. "Good sound," she said when Mairead lowered the bow.

"Aye, the lass plays well," Alastair said in a low, distracted tone with a wistful expression.

"Alastair?"

His expression cleared, and he glanced at Uini. "I am suspecting that dinner may be ready. Will you join us for a bowl?"

"Thank you, I will," she replied. Too many nights she'd had to suffer Lucy's shrewish digs, which soured the poor food that Mairead could barely stomach. For once, it would be a nice thing to share a meal, no matter how sparse, with people not looking to lay fault.

"Tuck the fiddle away in that chest; there's a good lass. The humidity won't get to it in there," he said before he walked outside with Uini.

Mairead knelt on the ground and opened the chest. Inside, she found carefully folded linens, including the finest Holland cloth she had ever seen, so fine that it hitched against her roughened skin. She didn't stop to consider the value of the fabric other than it would make a soft bed for the fiddle. She closed the chest and hurried out of the cottage to join Alastair and Uini for the evening meal.

The energy changed in the compound late Sunday afternoon. Iain sensed this shift long before Tam appeared carrying a stick, rapping against logs to get everyone's attention as he strode along the row of huts.

"Hie yourself up to the crushing mill," Tam called out as he passed. "Where the finest music in the West Indies will be played."

"Come on," Glencross said, kicking Iain in the foot. "The *cèilidh* will do you good."

"Go on without me," he muttered. "I'm tired." No more than usual, but he had been edgy all day.

"You brood too much."

"My back hurts, and you want me to do a jig? Are you daft, man?"

Glencross ignored his protests and nudged him out of the hut. "Out with you."

Iain didn't resist, but all along the uphill march to the crushing mill, he was plotting when he could slip away and return to the comfort of his sausage casing.

All the indentured servants and African slaves had gathered at the crushing mill. Tam and his lads had pooled their freshly distilled mobbie and were filling cups as they were passed around. Alastair stood at the head of the crushing mill, helping some of the others set up their hide-stretched drums. One of the men gave a tentative rap, and the sound bounded off the conical stone walls and back into the crowd.

Iain went straight for the keg of mobbie.

"You've developed a taste for it, have you?" Tam laughed and filled a cup for him.

"I'll take what I can get." Iain took a sip and grimaced. He quaffed his drink as he scanned the crowd. He wasn't aware that he was looking for someone until his eyes settled on Mairead. She stepped into the clearing with her cousin, Ciara, beside her. Mairead's brown hair had been gathered in a loose braid that hung down her back. Wispy tendrils curled around her face.

While a number of heads followed Ciara as she passed, Iain couldn't turn away from Mairead. Her step was light and her movements fluid. She headed straight for the musicians setting up their instruments. Iain had not seen her this animated; she was a veritable arrow set to fly.

Glencross called out to her. He reminded Iain of a puppy taken off his leash. Mairead and Ciara looked up together. Mairead hung back, her gaze lingering on the musicians, but after her cousin said a few words, the pair headed over.

Iain wondered if his brother-in-law wasn't a little besotted by Mairead. Iain took a long draught of mobbie and mulled on it. So what if he was? She was a bright lass with more than her share of spirit, and the lad deserved some happiness, wherever he could find it. Iain took a longer draught of mobbie, only this time the drink had a bitter edge to it. He tipped his cup and watched as the mobbie dribbled to the parched ground.

If he were honest with himself, a touch of envy soured his gut. *Too long without a woman. Nothing more.* And yet he had an uncomfortable suspicion that had he caught Glencross tupping the chit Lucy behind the shrubbery, he'd not spare a thought.

Iain forced his attention elsewhere and settled on Ciara. There was a quality in her that reminded him of Innis. He searched his mind for what it was. Physically, the two women bore little similarity to one another, and in all ways not at all to Mairead. Then it occurred to him—fragility. That was what it was. As though he were looking through a piece of thin glass.

As Iain continued to muse about Ciara, Mairead turned to ask her cousin a question, and she responded with an answering smile. Iain could understand how men could be half-smitten with Ciara because there was sweetness in her glance. She even laughed briefly at a story Mairead recounted with lively animation, but the moment Mairead turned back to Glencross, Ciara's face fell. It was like watching a shutter being latched.

The first pounding of the drums cut into his thoughts.

On the platform, a few men had gathered, including some of the African lads. One sat behind a homemade drum and nestled it between his thighs. He started to experiment with the sound, tapping on the skin with the flat of his palm and with his fingers. Soon he had settled into a rhythm that made a few women move in time. A second man took out a crudely carved pipe and tested the sound, closing his eyes and adjusting his mouth until clear notes filled the air.

The two started to play together, merging the higher wind melody with the baser rumbling of the drum. The sound carried Iain away from this cursed island, back to his laird's home, when travelling musicians would gather what instruments they could find to play for their lord's pleasure.

The pipe hit on a melody that made Mairead's feet move while she clapped in time to the drum. Iain admired the way her skirt swirled around her ankles and felt his interest stirring. He tore his eyes away and put the cup to his mouth, realising too late that it was empty.

Sitting alone on an upturned barrel, Alastair watched the performers, keeping time to the music by tapping on his knee. Iain had rarely spoken with the boiling master since the day of the auction. He couldn't help but associate Alastair with having been sold on the block, even if Alastair didn't own his indenture. This holding a grudge prevented him from getting on the right side of a man who could mean the difference between survival and defeat. Time to act like a man and swallow his pride—again.

Iain refilled his cup and headed over to Alastair. He found an empty spot to stand beside him and greeted him with a nod. "They play well. Have they been at it for long?"

"When they can," Alastair replied.

"Tam mentioned they fashioned those drums with skins." Iain searched for common ground. Dropping Tam's name couldn't hurt.

"You play?"

Iain shook his head. "I've had other concerns in my life."

"Shame," Alastair said with a curl of his lip. "Look around. Music can make life bearable."

Iain didn't answer. Nothing would make this place bearable. The old ballads never failed to trigger memories of childhood and a simpler time, but music was what you did on a winter night during winter quarters. It passed the time; it did not change the world.

186

His attention lit on Dunsmore standing with Masterton and Angus. Dunsmore crowded them both, leaning in close and speaking intently. Angus nodded at times and glanced often over at Masterton for his reaction, but the latter only chewed on his bottom lip. Classic Masterton the Younger crafty expression. Usually reserved for dealing with something thorny and unpalatable. A common enough reaction to Dunsmore, but something about this didn't sit well with Iain.

A new tune started, this time with the pipers leading the chorus. Iain tore his attention away from Masterton and Dunsmore. He'd speak to Masterton later, but in the meantime he needed to win Alastair over.

"Were you a musician before?" Iain asked the boiling master.

"Not hardly," Alastair said. Iain detected a slight bitterness. "I was a chandler in Glasgow."

"How did you end up here?"

"On my own," he said grimly.

Mairead hovered close and drew Iain's attention. She watched the performers as though the rest of the world mattered naught. She kept her hands against her thighs, and Iain couldn't help but notice how her fingers moved in a strange pattern with the music.

"She's a good lass," Alastair said, pulling Iain's thoughts back.

He muttered his agreement and took another sip of mobbie.

"I've heard you look out for her," Alastair said.

Iain hadn't realised that had been obvious. He shrugged. "She doesn't deserve to be here."

"Aye, she doesn't, but she is."

"Nor me or my men. You know this."

Alastair shrugged. "But we're all here now. Fate can be a bitch."

Iain gave a grudging smile and lifted his cup. "Do you not miss Scotland?"

Alastair snorted. "The damp, the cold? My old bones welcome this heat. This place will either destroy you or make you a fortune—

which one depends on the strength of one's mettle. In the end, few return back from whence they came."

Iain tossed back the rest of his mobbie. *Damn that.* Not only would he survive, he'd find his way back to Scotland. If Alastair wanted to feel better about staying in this hellhole, let him square that with his conscience.

"You don't believe me," Alastair said. "Think only a fool would remain, given the chance?" He hopped down from the barrel and gave a nod to Iain. "Right, then. I'm off."

Well done, Locharbaidh.

The song ended, and Iain watched Alastair as he entered the crushing mill. He disappeared for a moment, and when he reappeared, he cradled a violin in the crook of his arm.

Iain couldn't sit there any longer. Passing by the keg, he dropped the cup on top and manoeuvred through the crowd to head back to his hut.

Tam stopped him. "Where are you off to, Scotsman? You're truly sour, man."

"I've had enough." Iain patted the man on the shoulder and attempted to move past him. Before he did, he glanced to the crushing mill in time to see Alastair handing the violin to Mairead. The rapt expression on her face made Iain pause. She handled the instrument reverently, as carefully as a woman cradling her bairn. Iain had never seen her eyes so round, her normally wary expression soft.

Mairead lifted the violin to her collarbone and adjusted her grip. She tried a few tentative plucks and adjusted the tuning until the chord sounded right. She lifted the bow against the strings and started to play.

The sound that came from her violin was low, wistful and with a melody that stirred long-buried hopes. Both light and dark notes rounded each other out as she pushed the tune farther along. A low drumbeat joined in, and she adjusted her rhythm slightly to hit the rising notes with the downbeat.

Then the main melody started.

Iain knew this song. An old Scottish ballad, one of his favourites. It called to mind the longing of home. It had been the song that he had sung to himself during the gruelling journey from England.

How was it that she stood there playing that very song?

The melody had always stirred him, providing comfort during all those times he had been away on campaign, far from home. But Mairead's rendition added layers he had never heard. The mournful tone of the violin spoke of the wind in the firs and smoky twilight clinging to the mountains. A flight of swallows darting in a cold twilight sky and the cry of terns riding a lonely sea breeze. It called to memory swiftly flowing burns bordered with purple heather, and the hope of love reunited.

As she played, the lyrics flowed through his mind: *An' what will be the love-tokens that ye will send wi me . . . A kiss, will I twae an' ever she come to fair Scotland . . . I the red gold she sall gae . . .*

Iain felt it deep in his bones. Each note ripped through his defences, stone and mortar. Everything melted away. He forgot the crowd, forgot his situation and the harshness of the sugarcane fields. Only Mairead and her song remained.

He moved closer to the platform. Mairead stood several feet away, her eyes closed and head tilted sideways. Her lashes fanned her flushed cheeks, and her mouth was slightly parted. At times, a smile flitted across her lips, while at others her brow puckered into a frown, but always her expression remained enraptured. He watched, fascinated, as the bow danced over the strings, directed by nimble fingers.

Iain hung on every note as though it were the last. Good, sweet Lord, he didn't want it to end.

The song finally ended, and Mairead drew her last pass with the bow. Her hand stilled, and her shoulders went limp. A single tear traced down her cheek. When she opened her eyes, her unfocused gaze found his, and the look shot right through him.

189

Around Iain, men whistled and clapped, not realising that the earth had just shifted.

Chapter 14

———◆———

Iain sat on the bank of the pond, the sounds of the *cèilidh* in the distance. A light breeze ruffled the surface, and pair of green-and-brown ducks paddled lazily through the muddy shallows. The setting sun caught the water and caused it to sparkle like diamonds. The lapping water should have soothed him, eased the pain deep in his chest. Mairead's blazing, earnest face seared in his brain. The look she'd shot him when she played her final note had destroyed him.

He had fled right after she finished playing, needing time to sort out his churning thoughts. His emotions were too raw. Dazed and not a little shocked, he faced what was finally as plain as porridge. He had feelings for Mairead. When—*how* had that happened?

Iain exhaled slowly. A part of him couldn't accept it. The music had bewitched him into forgetting that they were thousands of miles away from home, indentured and bound. He faulted the *cèilidh* for bringing the illusion of normalcy to a lonely, bleak existence.

And is that so bad, Locharbaidh?

For a wild moment, he thought to hell with it. Live in the moment. No one expected him to be celibate. After all, he was a man, not a gelding. Lately, he had sensed Mairead softening towards him. Competition had transformed into friendship—when, he couldn't be sure—but there had been several unguarded moments when she looked at him with warm affection. Her gaze had found his when she finished playing, flushed with the triumph of her accomplishment—not Glencross nor Tam.

You are a mad, stupid fool.

He should be more focused on escaping this cursed island than mooning over an Irish wench like an untried lad. His men counted on him to stay true to the course, relied on him to keep a clear head and not make a misstep that could get them all killed—trusted *him* to lead them home to Scotland. At best, any dalliance could be a fleeting thing, and Mairead deserved better. Innis had deserved better too.

Iain sensed rather than heard someone approaching. He turned his head to find Mairead picking her way towards him as one would approach a bear in a cave. He couldn't decide whether to warn her off or accept her company.

She stopped several feet away from him, still holding the violin and bow. The sunlight caught the frizzy curls that framed her face and highlighted ruddy tones. The sun had darkened her skin, and a new crop of freckles sprinkled across the bridge of her nose. She had never looked more striking to him than she did now. Damned endearing imperfections.

"What are you doing here?" It came out harsher than he intended. Clearing his throat, he added more kindly, "You should be back at the crushing mill playing another set."

"There were others who wanted a turn." Mairead's toes curled in the loamy soil, fine, freckled toes.

"Rout the others." Iain could've listened to her for ages. He wondered at Alastair for not keeping her there to play out the night.

Mairead lifted a hand to shield her eyes from the last rays of sunlight that slanted across the water. "Why didn't you stay? You departed so abruptly."

"I'm not one for crowds."

"It's a cheerful gathering, and your friends are missing you. They've already broached a few kegs of mobbie." She sat down beside him.

"They're welcome to that rot." Iain raked his fingers through his hair. He didn't need spirits in order to be knocked on his arse. A slip of an Irish woman was potent enough to do that alone.

Mairead lowered her head and traced an idle finger along the body of her violin. Iain watched in fascination as her fingers caressed the wood. He couldn't wrench his eyes away. A thought flared in his mind—how would those fingers feel against his own skin? His groin tightened in answer. Iain exhaled slowly. What was wrong with him? He was a seasoned man, for God's sake.

The silence stretched between them until she finally broke it with a tentative question, "Did . . . did you enjoy the music?" She tilted her head, and Iain sensed a vulnerability in her glance that tugged his heart.

Did he enjoy it? When had music gone through him like this—when had it the power to remind him of all that he had lost? Iain shifted so he faced her properly. "You play very well, Mairead," he said softly. "It reminded me of happier times."

Mairead gave him incandescent smile that snatched his breath away. "Music makes everything bearable."

Iain lost the ability to turn away. Her hazel eyes were the very shade of leaf-green. "Where did you learn 'The Gay Goshawk'?"

"Is that its name? The song has been in my head for some time."

"Oh aye? 'Tis an old ballad. One of the few where no one is slaughtered for infidelity and whole bloodlines aren't destroyed."

"Is that how the other ballads go?"

"Aye, usually." He couldn't help but smile.

"Why am I not surprised?" There was a suspicion of laughter in her voice. It occurred to him that he had never really heard her laugh, and he really wanted to. Her smiles were rare and usually reserved for Tam or Glencross.

Iain's gaze settled on her lips. Her mouth fascinated him. Her upper lip had a delicate bow shape, while the lower lip, fuller and pillow soft—that, he could almost taste. He wondered how her mouth would feel parted against his own.

They both stared at each other. He shifted, leaning in a fraction closer. The fresh earthy scent of her filled his senses, and her warmth, radiating like heat from sunbaked stones. Her face tilted up, and her lips parted slightly. Eyelashes dipped downward.

Raucous laughter and off-key singing shattered the silence. Iain jerked back in time to see Glencross and Killean bursting through the trees. In that moment, he wanted to throttle the pair of them.

When they spotted Iain and Mairead, they released a whoop and loped over.

"There she is," Glencross called out. A high colour flushed his cheeks. "Hiding her, are you, Locharbaidh? Greedy bastard."

"Come, lass, we're here to spirit you away," Killean said. "The lads are threatening to demolish the crushing mill if you don't turn up soon. Alastair has offered a reward for the first man to fetch you."

A rosy red flushed across Mairead's face. She turned to Iain. "My audience awaits. Will you come?" Her eyes were wide and searching.

"Best if I don't." Best if she did leave. Iain drew a deep breath, trying to clear his mind. "The ducks, you ken." He nodded to the pair foraging in the shallows. "I'm the laird of them, you see."

"Very well, Locharbaidh." Before she passed him, she touched her palm to his shoulder.

Iain watched her leave, his eyes following the swaying of her slim hips until she disappeared through the trees with Glencross and Killean. He exhaled slowly. Better this way, he thought. No ties. No complications.

And yet her handprint still burned on his shoulder.

After the second bell of the day, Mairead chose a roundabout route to the compound by way of the kennels. It was an excuse not to walk with Iain and subject herself to more of his painful, brooding silences. He had been unusually taciturn all morning, and normally this wouldn't have bothered her. She'd have accepted the challenge to draw him out of his shell and shake him up any way she could. But not this day. The air between them was heavily textured with strain, ever since the *ceilidh*.

She found it quite maddening. For a moment at the pond, she sensed interest from Iain, a fond tenderness even, before he shuttered up again. For a moment, his normally gruff voice had softened. Was it her imagination, or would he have kissed her had Glencross and Killean not barged in at that moment? Mairead's pounding heart suspected so.

When she reached the kennels, Mairead ran into the kitchen girl, Aline, hauling a kettle full of scraps for the hounds. The moment Aline saw Mairead, she sagged in relief. "Oh, Margaret, you've come to save me."

"How so?" Mairead asked, trying to shrug off her annoyance with Aline for calling her Margaret. English Margaret. Obedient Margaret. Beaten Margaret. But she knew that Aline didn't use this name out of spite.

"Lucy foisted the hounds on me, and I still have to feed the chickens and the swine, or Providence Moss will beat me. Could you be a dear and give the hounds their bone meat for me? I'd be ever so grateful!"

"No trouble at all," Mairead said. "Leave it with me."

Aline thanked her profusely and dashed down the lane towards the henhouse.

Mairead hoisted the kettle and rested it on her hip as she unlatched the gate to step inside the kennel. The rusted hinge winced and alerted the hounds.

A pack of brown-and-copper Liam hounds bounded up to her, prancing for their dinner. They were a friendly lot, and even though the hounds were large enough to reach her waist, they amused rather than startled her. One of the Liam hounds, an older dog with a touch of silver in his chocolate-brown muzzle, bumped her arm with his wet snout to encourage a scratch behind his floppy ears. In a thrice, she had strewn the scraps on the ground and stepped quickly aside so as not to get trampled.

"What are *you* doing here, Margaret?" Lucy appeared on the other side of the gate with a basket dangling from the crook of her arm. "Where's Aline?"

"Doing her own work," she replied, noting Lucy's crisp white apron. Mairead paid the English maid little mind as she tried to juggle, kettle, latch and gate while keeping all the hounds inside the kennel. One of the pups launched himself against the gate, rattling the boards. Mairead didn't fail to notice how Lucy jumped back and maintained a wary distance from the hounds.

"What are you grinning at?" Lucy asked, but Mairead ignored her. "Nothing to say, papist swine?" Lucy continued. "Do you not understand good, proper English? I *am* talking to you!" Lucy grabbed Mairead's arm and dug her nails into her skin.

"Don't touch me." Mairead pried herself from Lucy's grip and shoved the girl away.

"Or what? You'll tell Providence Moss? She'll have you emptying night buckets again."

From the kennel behind them, the old hound began to growl deep in his throat and advanced towards the gate, baring his teeth.

Lucy reacted instinctively. A strangled shriek escaped her, and she nearly tripped over her heels. When she realised that the gate was still latched, she flushed an angry red and skewered Mairead with narrowed eyes. "You are little better than those hounds. I wonder that Providence Moss hasn't insisted you make your bed in the kennel. No wonder you Irish end up as fieldworkers and whores."

Mairead stiffened. "How is a scullery maid any better than a fieldworker? And you have no right to call me a whore!"

Lucy's smirk dripped with cream. "I didn't call *you* a whore. Your cousin, on the other hand, is a filthy trollop, spreading herself for my lord Wilton."

Mairead stared at her with revulsion. The blood pounded in her temples. "Shut your mouth."

"The entire plantation already knows your cousin is a whore. Potts can't wait until Wilton tires of her so he can get his latest cast-off. Did you know that I can hear her coy whimpers each night, pleading?"

Mairead advanced on Lucy, her fists balled. "Say that again, you wretch, and I'll rip your tongue from your mouth."

Lucy's eyes widened, and she backed away. "Touch me and I'll tell Providence Moss. She'll beat you within an inch of your life."

For once, the threat of the housekeeper didn't deter Mairead. "You are a vile witch of a woman."

Lucy scrambled back a few steps, kicking up a small cloud of dirt. "Providence Moss will beat you, then strip you in the compound and flay you with a cat-o'-nines. And just because she can, she'll hand you over to Potts to do what he will to you. And I will be laughing the whole time."

Mairead trembled with rage. Instead of rushing at Lucy, she whirled around and strode back to the kennel.

"That's right, hide with the hounds," Lucy crowed. "Providence will find you and haul you up to the whipping post."

Mairead turned to face Lucy, her hand poised on the latch. In that moment, Lucy's face blanched. Mairead flipped the latch, and the gate sailed open. With a baying yelp, the old hound bounded straight for Lucy, followed closely by the rest of the pack. A chorus of energetic barking and howling erupted amidst the surging mass of eager dogs. Lucy screamed and dropped her basket. She stumbled back several feet, flapping her arms to keep her balance and ward off the dogs. Still shrieking, she tore down the lane with the hounds giving chase.

Normally, Mairead would have laughed, glad to have given the English girl her comeuppance, but Lucy's poison tainted her satisfaction.

A whistle split the air, followed by a shout. Tam and his lads hurried to the kennels, holding a few of the dominant hounds by the collar.

"Who the devil released them?" Tam yelled before his gaze landing on Mairead, who still stood by the open gate. Tam shook his head, pained. "You?"

Mairead winced, knowing she wouldn't be able to deny her guilt. She lifted her chin and said, "Lucy deserved it."

"I believe that, I can. But of all the times to teach the English lass a lesson. Potts will be here any moment, and it won't be Lucy's backside he flays if he finds out." Turning to his men, he said, "Round them up right away, for Sweet Mary's sake. We need to get them on leash before the man arrives."

"What's happened?" Mairead asked, grabbing the old hound's collar.

"Escaped slave," Tam said. He hooked the long leash in place. "One of the Africans." He worked at untangling the leads from the eager dogs. "That one's tried it twice before. He won't go far—the hounds will find him—but it's a bother I can do without, being a damned hot day."

Before Mairead could ask any more questions, Potts rode down the laneway with three other horses on a lead, barrel chest puffed out and shoulders thrust back. Instead of being furious over an escaped slave, the hunt clearly excited him. His horse sensed his mood and pulled at the bit, eager to run.

"Gear up, lads." Potts tossed the reins of the other horses to the men. "Wilton has offered a reward for bringing in the runner—dead or alive. He doesn't care which." He swept a glance at Mairead and leered. "Nothing better to get the blood up than a hearty chase—

almost nothing." The hounds were yelping and straining at their leads. "The hunt is on," Potts called out.

Men and hounds raced down the lane, kicking up dust in their wake.

Mairead couldn't hide her shudder of revulsion as they disappeared down the lane. She prayed that the African would not be caught. *Godspeed to him.*

The final bell of the day rang, and Iain headed back to the compound with the others. The day had been hotter than hell, with nary a breeze or a cloud to bring reprieve. To his right, Mairead appeared mostly wilted. Iain wished he could have spared her the long walk back, but Tam and his wagon were nowhere to be found. Glencross shuffled to his left, exhaustion written in the forward slope of his shoulders. Masterton, Killean and the others lagged far behind.

When they reached the first row of huts, a great commotion broke out. The baying of hounds combined with the shrieks of hysterical women. A throng of bondsmen and slaves crowded in the compound, making it difficult for Iain to see what was happening.

He pressed through the crowd and reached the front in time to see Potts leading a gruesome procession from astride his garron. In one fist, he clutched a rope with the other end tethered around the neck of an African slave. Tam and his lads followed, and the Liam hounds ran loose, their blood running hot. The slave stumbled past Iain, bleeding from the head and arms, the rope pulled taut around his neck. A couple of women walked alongside the captured slave, calling out to him in their language. The man didn't respond; instead, his head jerked this way and that as he looked for a way to break free. The panic shone in the whites of his eyes.

Iain remembered well the bite of the rope around his neck, knew the shame of walking through horse dung—how hard it was to shut out the taunts and jeers of a crowd.

Mairead brushed against Iain's shoulder, and she leaned in to see past him. He didn't know exactly what Potts planned for this escaped slave, but mercy wouldn't be an option.

Iain pulled her back, determined to shelter her from this. "You don't want to see this."

She slipped away from him. "Likely not, but I should," she replied grimly before stepping around him to follow the procession.

Infernal woman, Iain swore under his breath and followed after her.

Potts halted in the clearing outside the boiling house where a whipping post stood. Alastair appeared at the doorway with his assistants crowding around him. Potts dismounted and reeled in the slave, hauling him over to the whipping post. Once within arm's reach, the overseer slammed the African against the wood beam.

"This man," Potts bellowed to the gathered crowd as he restrained him against the post, "this man dared to run from this plantation—no better than a criminal and a common thief, to withhold from my lord Wilton the use of his rightful property. Fifty lashes as punishment." A wolfish grin split across his face.

Iain clenched his jaw against the kindling rage. It soured his gut to call a man thief for trying to reclaim his freedom.

Another pair of horses approached, and the gathered crowd parted. Wilton and his mother rode into the clearing. One of the Irish lads rushed up to take the reins and hold the master's bridle while Wilton dismounted. The Duchess waved away assistance, choosing to remain on her horse.

"Doesn't want to soil her fancy boots," Mairead said under her breath, only loud enough for Iain's ears.

"Well done, Potts. You and your men will receive a little extra at the end of the month," Wilton said as he smoothed his waistcoat.

Potts glowered. He chewed his lower lip before saying, "My lord, you promised us a reward for our troubles. Now, not later."

"We shall speak of this at another time."

"My lord—"

While Potts's attention focused on haggling with Wilton, the slave seized his opportunity. He elbowed Potts in the side and yanked his tether from his grasp. Before Potts could seize him, the man bolted past him and Wilton.

"There he goes again," Potts said, but he didn't go after the slave. Instead, he turned to Wilton with an ill-disguised sneer. "My lord, shall we give chase now or wait till the end of the month?"

Wilton scowled. "Get him, beggar."

"He'll no' go far, my lord Wilton," Potts replied with a laugh and waved Tam's men to close in.

Too many had gathered together in a circle, hampering the slave's progress. The desperate man darted around the tightening space, dodging everyone who lunged to grasp him.

Potts's men finally penned him in. The slave backed up against his own people, his eyes wide and darting. The African feinted to the left, and when Potts lunged to seize him, the slave darted the other way. Finding a break, the man shot through and dashed for the boiling house, past an astonished Alastair.

Potts laughed. "The bugger is giving us a merry chase—"

Laughter turned to shouts of alarm. Frantic yelling erupted inside the building, followed by a bloodcurdling scream.

Iain had a clear view of the horror. Rather than allowing himself to be caught, the cornered slave had leapt straight into the first boiling vat of sugarcane juice. His agonising howls curdled even Iain's blood.

"Pull him out—get him out," Alastair barked.

"Oh my God," Mairead gasped.

Iain drew her into his arms, turning his body so as to shield her from the sight. "Nay, you'd better not." She pressed her small face in his chest and covered her ears from the horrible screams.

Iain forced himself to watch. The slave collapsed on the floor, contorted and steaming. He writhed in excruciating pain, and eventually his cries faded to a gurgling whimper. His muscles continued to spasm until he lay completely still.

"Dead," Alastair said in disgust. His voice cut through the shocked silence.

"Dead or alive, my lord," Potts called out to Wilton. "Just what you promised."

Glencross appeared at Iain's side. Iain considered handing Mairead over to him while he helped with the body, but Mairead clutched at him as though she had grown talons.

"They were only going to whip him," Glencross said in a low, questioning tone. But Iain understood the African's despair. It was never about the whipping. It was the chains the man couldn't endure. His own situation choked him every moment of every day.

Wilton strode up to the body and gave it a casual nudge with the tip of his polished boot. The Duchess finally deigned to dismount from her horse and marched up to Alastair.

"He had better not have ruined my sugar," she said in a tight voice. "Alastair, tell me the sugar isn't ruined."

"This batch is ruined."

Wilton released a strangled curse and kicked the dead slave with more force. He smashed his cane against the dead slave's skull, splattering blood and bone. With one last kick, he turned to Potts. "You know what to do with him."

The overseer snapped his fingers, and Tam and a helper came forward to drag the dead slave into the clearing. Instead of following them, Potts turned aside and disappeared into the crowd.

When the men dumped the slave in the clearing, an African matron fell to the ground beside the body, rocking and wailing. Another woman joined her, wrapping broad arms around the matron's shoulders. Someone started singing a dirge, and others joined in.

"What are they saying?" Mairead asked Iain. Only now did she realise she was still in his arms. She disentangled herself and stepped away.

An elderly African woman leaned in and said, "Welcome him home. He goes home. Tears over." A grim smile spread across her broad face. "When man dies, man reborn in the land of our fathers. Goes home."

Home. Call him mad, but Iain thought there had to be a better way to manage that than to die. Maybe not.

Iain caught a movement at the edge of the circle. Potts had returned with an axe. The overseer hefted it in his hand and strode to the body. "Back off," he said to the women, who needed no further warning. He lifted the axe and pointed to the crowd. "No one touch this body."

"What is he doing?" Mairead asked.

Potts raised the axe over his head then swung the blade to connect with the dead man's throat. *Crunch.* Blade connected with bone. Three more swings and he severed the head.

Mairead gagged and clamped her hand over her mouth. Too late. Vomit spewed between her fingers. She turned away and retched until she had nothing left in her stomach.

Iain tried to remain stoic, but when Potts gave the head one last kick, Iain's stomach turned. If he didn't step in now, he'd be less than a man. Pushing his way to the centre, he called out to Potts, "That's enough."

The overseer turned around, astonished. "You challenging me, Scotsman? Gan back to your place." His Geordie accent was thick from excitement.

"No man deserves to be defiled in death," Iain replied.

Potts lifted the bloody axe and pointed it to Iain. "This ain't none of your business unless you want to see the wrong end of my axe." He bent down to seize the severed head. Lifting it, he turned around so everyone could see the dripping mess. "A warning to you. If anyone takes their life and thinks they'll escape to the otherworld, they won't be going with their head. Just try finding your next life. Your body will wander the darkness for all eternity. Remember that."

There was fresh wailing from the two women. The elder one flung herself at Potts's feet and begged for mercy. He pushed her away, and defeated, she crumpled into the dirt.

"Fetch me a spike—you lad, go!" Potts thundered. "His heid will be a warning to all."

Iain stopped the boy and faced the overseer. "He'll fetch us a shovel to bury the man as he deserves. He's nae a dog. You've made your point."

Potts looked incredulous. "You're right. Didn't know what I was thinkin'." He turned slightly, and then without warning, his fist shot out and caught Iain under the chin. Iain flew backwards and landed on the ground. Before he could regain his wits, Potts pinned him with his boot, grinding his entire weight upon Iain's chest. "I don't need no gaumless Scotsman telling us our business." He then spat in his face before snarling at the others, "Hoist him to the whipping post!"

Chapter 15

———— ◆ ————

Crack.

Iain jerked against the whip; fire ripped down his back. He pulled against the ropes and bit down a cry of pain.

Potts stood at the edge of his vision, shaking out the whip for another pass. Iain braced himself for another lash.

"You've been a troublesome bastard since you came here," Potts said, his voice loud enough to please even the Wiltons. "Just because you're a Christian servant doesn't give you the leave to show disrespect to your betters."

Iain opened his mouth to tell the man to find his betters in hell when the second lash ripped across his back. He strained against the post, hands fisted. He forced down the cry that threatened to wrench from him.

"How many lashes shall we give him, my lord Wilton? One for every man who has witnessed his insolence?"

Crack. Another kiss of the whip. Iain bit down, tasted blood. He would not cry out. He would *not* give Potts the satisfaction of breaking him.

"Or until he begs for mercy?" Potts asked, moving so that he was square in Iain's vision. The overseer's feet were braced apart, and he held up the whip lined with blood and bits of skin. "What will it be, my lord?"

"A dozen, overseer," Wilton said in a lazy voice. "We need him for the fields in the morning."

Iain caught the sneer on Potts's face a moment before he felt the lash. He jerked away, and this time a small groan escaped him. His back was on fire, tendrils of pain leaching across his flesh like a disease. He panted through clenched teeth, smothering the scream that built at the back of his throat.

Having not been given free rein, Potts made up for it by putting muscle into every lash. No mercy. With every single pass, the strokes landed more fiercely than the last. The rope bit into Iain's wrists as he writhed and jerked away from the cat-o'-nines. Iain's entire focus centred on not crying out—not giving Potts any victory from this. He had never been whipped before—only beasts and slaves were whipped, and Potts was drilling this into Iain's flesh more deeply than any word written on an indenture.

By the tenth lash, Iain's strength began to fail him. He hung limply against the post, head lolling on his shoulders. His muscles quivered. Through the blur of pain and sweat, he saw a figure hover in the crowd behind Potts. Dirty petticoats and freckled toes. His eyes lifted. Mairead. He moaned under his breath and turned away. His lips started moving. *Get her away from here.* He couldn't bear for her to see his shame—worse than the lash.

"What's this?" Potts yanked Iain's hair and forced his head back. "Are you pleading for mercy, Scotsman?"

Iain struggled to speak. He spat out the blood in his mouth. It dribbled down his chin.

"I didn't hear you. Speak so everyone can hear."

Iain formed the words that he should have said long ago. "Go to fockin' hell."

Potts roared and slammed Iain against the whipping post. Another lash fell and then another. A scream finally burst from Iain's lips.

His head swam, and he felt consciousness slipping from him. Through the haze, he dimly heard Wilton say, "Enough, overseer." The strokes finally stopped. "Someone cut him down."

Iain felt the press of a blade against his arm. He jerked away, and he heard Tam's voice, "Easy, Scotsman. Give me a moment." The blade sliced through his bonds, cutting him down from the post. With nothing holding him up, Iain's legs gave out from under him, and he crumbled to the dirt.

Iain panted through the excruciating pain. Someone touched him on the shoulder, and he drew back in a snarl, hands raised.

"It's me, Locharbaidh," Glencross's voice cut through Iain's rage. A hand floated above his face—the hand of his brother-in-law. "Take it." Iain hesitated a moment before grabbing Glencross's hand. He struggled to his feet. Every movement brought fresh pain. Glencross ducked under his arm and helped him back to the direction of the hut.

Iain passed the group of people who remained. His own men were there, all of them watching with shocked expressions. Iain forced his legs to keep moving.

Glencross got him back to his hut, and when he peeled the blood-soaked shirt from Iain's back, sharp shards of pain flooded his brain. Darkness overwhelmed him.

When Iain finally regained consciousness, he found himself lying facedown in his hammock. The meshing bit into his face and chest, but his back throbbed with fire.

He couldn't lift his head, but he heard voices talking near him. Unconsciousness drew him in again. When he awoke again, everything was silent. He struggled to pry open his gummed-over eyelids. At the edge of his vision, he saw the hem of a dirty petticoat and bare feet peeking out from under the skirts. Delicate, freckled feet. Cool fingers rubbed something on his back in a slow circular motion, light as a butterfly's wing.

A tin was placed on a wooden stool, and the soft patter of footsteps retreated. When he lifted his head, he found himself alone.

The moment the final bell sounded, Mairead hurried away from Iain and his tight-lipped seething. A couple of days had passed since Iain's punishment at the whipping post, and except for those first hours when he had been insensible, he sullenly rejected all her help.

When back in the field, he grimly applied himself to cutting cane with nary a word to her or any other. Mairead could see the white tenseness of his jaw and knew that every movement caused him fresh pain. Except for being slower than usual, nothing else betrayed him at first—until the blood seeped through his coarse shirt and spread in a slash of crisscrossed veins. She suspected that only jagged rage kept him on his feet. He wanted no pity, least of all from her.

She was surprised by how much that stung.

As she made her way down the hill, she saw Ciara in the distance drawing water at the well. Every night Mairead slipped into the dovecote and waited for her cousin, hoping that she'd finally come to see her, but she rarely did. Instead, Mairead had to rely on bits of gossip, which tended to be breathtakingly vicious. Lucy made sure everyone on the plantation knew about Ciara. Finally, here was her opportunity to gauge for herself how her cousin fared. At the very least, Ciara would know that she was not alone.

Mairead hurried to the well. When she approached, Ciara turned her head, and for a brief moment froze like a cornered hare. Her cousin's gaze darted, as though looking for an easy route to flee.

Mairead pretended not to notice, though it tore right through her heart. When she reached the well, she forced herself to adopt an overly bright greeting. "Ciara, my love. Here, let me help you," she said, reaching across to help her cousin hoist the full bucket from the well and place it on the ground.

"I can manage," Ciara said. She must have regretted the sharpness of her tone because she attempted a smile, though it came out strangely. She reached out and plucked a stalk from Mairead's frizzy hair. "You've been crawling through the fields, I see."

"It's hard work, to be sure," Mairead said. "I've been haunting the dovecote. You've not come by as I thought you might."

"I cannot," Ciara said. Her arms were wrapped around her waist as one might hold up a shield.

An awkward silence enveloped between, broken only by the blackbirds twittering from the tall trees. Mairead didn't know what to say next.

When Ciara bent down to pick up the bucket, her neckline slipped slightly, drawing Mairead's eyes to a purplish bruise on her shoulder. Mairead's forced good humour dissolved instantly. She could just make out the shadowed imprint of a man's hand. The brute must have dug his fingers deeply into her skin. "He did that to you?"

Ciara glanced over to her shoulder. Quickly, she adjusted her shift to cover up the bruising. "It's nothing, dearest," she said with a fixed smile. "I bumped into the doorway." She continued prattling but refused to meet Mairead's eye. "I had an armful of linens and didn't mind where I walked. I'll be more careful next time."

"A doorway with five fingers? Oh, Ciara."

"It's nothing, I tell you," Ciara said sharply. Then she softened. "It's nothing. He's usually not . . . like that." She seemed to shrink within herself. "'Tis only that he lost a great deal of money gambling in Speight's Town."

It wasn't his fault? Same as it wasn't Ronan's fault that his eyes wandered, nor the English soldier's fault for running a blade into Uncle Mulriane's belly. She looked around this place with its exotic plants and the lizards that darted across the cobbles. A paradise on the surface, but rotten to the core. A fiefdom built on acres and acres of sugarcane fields, fertilised by human misery. She thought of the stripes on a proud man's back, there because he dared to condemn the inhuman treatment of another.

Mairead felt sickened by it all. A painful war waged inside her. She wanted to tell Ciara to fight back, only she knew the harsh reality of their situation. No one would stop this monster from preying on Ciara, or anyone he chose to for that matter.

If they couldn't fight, and they shouldn't capitulate, where would they find salvation? Perseverance. Courage. Hope, if there was such a thing left in this strange world.

Mairead would not turn away, no matter how often Ciara closed herself off. If Ciara couldn't find a piece inside her that would allow her to resist, to fight against her essence being ground into the dirt, if she was too weary to do it, Mairead would have to be her shield.

She took Ciara's hands in her own. "Hold on to this, never stop believing in *this*. We will return home. Trust in that. They can't keep us here forever. We're indentured, not slaves. And at that time when we sail from these shores, we can put this aside in the box where all nightmares are locked, and we will face a new day together. The Tóraidhe are fighting to purge Ireland of the English disease, and they will succeed. They must. When we finally return home, you will reclaim your family's lands, and I will return to Galway, where my brothers will continue to plague my life." Mairead won a fleeting smile from Ciara, though it lacked her usual lustre. A victory nonetheless. She squeezed her cousin's hands. "And until that day, we have each other."

Tears shone on Ciara's lashes. She nodded and wiped away a stray tear. When Mairead moved to hug her cousin, Ciara hurriedly turned aside to gather her bucket. "I'd best be returning," she said, toying with the handle.

Mairead fell in beside her cousin, misery dogging every step, not knowing what more she could say. She tried to shine a light, but the mine shaft was too deep. When they reached the courtyard gate,

Mairead stopped Ciara. "If you ever need me, my love, I am here for you. I will always be here for you. Do not forget."

Ciara gave her another glancing smile. "I won't." But like a cloud passing under the sun, her face soon darkened. She squared her shoulders, and her expression hardened. "I had better return. They'll be looking for me." With one last parting glance, she left Mairead and made her way across the courtyard, careful not to spill the water she had fetched.

Mairead stood at the gate watching her cousin slip into the rear entrance, entirely sick at heart.

Chapter 16

———◆———

Iain lay on his stomach in the hammock. His lashed back had started to heal, but the skin was still too raw to allow the hammock's rope meshing to rub against it. Though his skin knitted, his pride remained macerated. He could barely meet Mairead's questioning glances for fear of seeing disgust or worse, pity, reflected in her expressive hazel eyes. His only salvation—that he hadn't pressed his suit after the *cèilidh*. He couldn't bear to go from lover to a waste of a man in her mind.

A hot breeze wafted through the open windows—no comfort from the unnatural heat. Iain longed for the cool glens of home and swore to himself that if he ever got back, he'd never complain about sleet, ice or snow again. He'd welcome it all, just to breathe in the blooming heather.

His men drifted into the hut, laughing with one another as though they were set up in clover. Even usually dour Masterton chuckled over the tail end of a story spun by Dunsmore. Iain's mood darkened. *They* must have had a trifling day, he thought sourly. Only Glencross remained sober. Without even a grunt of greeting, his brother-in-law crawled into his own hammock, face flushed red.

Then Iain picked up a smell—a heavenly scent that made his nose twitch. Roasted meat. He struggled upright, wincing at the movement, and met Masterton's amused grin. The man showed him a bowl with still-steaming meat coated with running juices.

"Where did you get *that*?" Iain said. For the moment, his ills forgotten, he stared at the roast, salivating. This was more than the scraps of bone meat they were tossed as a Sunday treat.

"I told you lads he'd rouse when he smelled this," Masterton said.

"If he can stomach it," Dunsmore said. "He might only be able to handle gruel. Best to save the meat for those not crippled with pain." His spearing glance told Iain that his words were carefully chosen. Since Iain's shaming at the whipping post, Dunsmore had become emboldened.

"Nothing like solid meat for putting more hair on your chest," Masterton said with a good-natured laugh.

When Masterton offered him the bowl, Iain hesitated. He wished for the willpower to send them both packing. Their words, intentional in the case of Dunsmore and less so from Masterton, spoiled the prospect of a decent meal. But his stomach balked at sacrificing proper sustenance on the altar of ravaged pride. He took the bowl from Masterton with a sullen nod. "Where'd this come from?"

"One of the goats died, and they carved it up for everyone," Killean piped in. He had remained quiet through the exchange. A thoughtful frown creased his brow. "The Africans only got the entrails, poor bastards."

Iain tore off a large bite and closed his eyes against the exquisite juices that filled his mouth. Slightly gamey, but it didn't matter. If only they had ale. "Found dead? You think it was diseased?" Not that he really cared. At least he'd die with a full stomach.

"I'm willing to risk it," Killean said, echoing his thoughts. "Didn't sit well with Glencross over there. He tossed up his first bite."

Iain forced himself to slow down, to savour each mouthful. "All right, lad?" Glencross murmured something. "Too rich after that loblolly crap, likely." That gruel they fed them was enough to leach the staunchest man of his vigour. They daren't steal any more chickens—the housekeeper locked the coop up herself at night, and no one volunteered to cosy up to *her*—and it was impossible to roast a pig or a goat without anyone catching wind of the venture.

They needed to get out of here before they were reduced to begging for scraps of meat. That would be the final ignominy. Bowl in hand, Iain wandered over to the door and cast a glance outside. Everyone was huddled by their respective campfires, attending to their share of the roasted goat.

Iain turned to Dunsmore and asked, "Found out where Wilton stores his weapons?"

"Nay." Dunsmore's eyes narrowed while he chewed his meat. A dribble of hot grease trailed down his chin. "Before you huff and glower, I can't just go to the Southron bastard and ask to see his sabres."

"Don't get your breeks in a twist," Iain said. "I only asked."

"What of you?" Dunsmore said. "Did you manage to wheedle information about the port of Speight's Town?"

Iain glowered and didn't respond.

"Just asking," Dunsmore said with a mocking sniff. "You gonna eat that?" He pointed to Iain's bowl and added, "Or you gonna woo it?"

"Back off. This isn't for you." Iain looked down at the last hunk of meat in his bowl and over at Glencross, who hadn't moved from his hammock. The cane fields must have knocked the wind out of the lad. When Glencross finally roused himself, he'd be put out if no one saved him a bite. And yet if the lad slept through the night, it would go to waste. Iain walked over to Glencross. "You want me to keep you a bowl, lad?"

Glencross didn't stir. His cheeks were ruby red, an unnatural colour. Iain tried to shake him awake, and it was then that he realised his brother-in-law burned with fever.

Iain dropped the bowl, and it clattered to the ground. "Wake up." Glencross didn't stir. Iain shook him again more forcefully. Alarm seized him by the throat. Glencross groaned but wouldn't open his eyes. *"Wake up!"* Nothing except a weak moan. Iain yelled over his shoulder, "Someone fetch a healer." No one moved. They all stared blankly. *"Now!"*

Glencross tossed in his hammock, burning with fever, while Iain watched completely powerless to help. Had his brother-in-law been shot or stabbed, he'd know what to do—staunch the flow, try to make him more comfortable. But how to win a war that raged from the inside?

Killean returned with the Arawak woman, Uini. When she passed the threshold, Iain realised a throng had gathered outside. This agitated rather than reassured him.

"Curious buggers—get thee gone!" he bellowed.

At that moment, Mairead stepped into the hut. His outburst startled her, but she stood her ground. "You won't chase me out so easily, Locharbaidh. I've come for Glencross, and I'll only leave when *he* tells me to go."

Iain couldn't trust himself to speak. She had often called him an ogre, for good reason, and he had no desire to be called a madman too. Her presence unsettled him, an unwanted reminder that she had seen him brought low. "As you will." He stepped aside, allowing her access. His gaze followed her progress across the hut to where Uini stood at Glencross's hammock.

The lad pried open his eyes and blinked at everyone around him. He seemed to be particularly startled to see Uini bending over him. "Leave me be." He licked his dry lips. "I need rest—hurt all over." He burrowed deeper into his hammock and drifted in and out of a fitful sleep.

"He's been in the fields all day," Iain said, more to convince himself. But that didn't account for the fever. He had been hale and canty earlier in the day.

Uini made a slight clucking sound with her tongue as she shook her head.

"Don't do that, woman," Iain snapped. "Why are you doing that?" If she couldn't help, why the hell was she in his hut?

Uini turned to him and said, "Yellow fever."

"I don't care what it's called—help him."

"I heard the bellows of an enraged bear, and it led me here. Imagine my surprise," Alastair said, entering the hut.

"The crowd outside did nothing to alert you?" Iain said, not bothering to hide his irritation. "Imagine my surprise."

"You won't help him that way." Alastair crossed the hut to reach Uini. "What do we have here?" The two conversed in her language, haltingly on Alastair's part. He questioned her a little more before he said to Iain, "Aye, 'tis the fever. We had an outbreak last year—a particularly virulent one. A few years ago it killed most of Uini's family."

"Don't talk like that," Iain said. "There must be something she can do—must know of a cure, like the juice of some miserable berry."

"If only it were that easy."

Uini said a few more words to Alastair before she left the hut. "She says she'll fetch one of the African wenches to make a strengthening draught," Alastair said. "'Tis the best we can do."

"Aye, good. That will cure him?"

"Depends on the lad's inner strength. Some survive. Pray that he's one of the fortunate."

Iain rubbed his beard, clamping down on his alarm. Glencross was strong—he had survived the bloody carnage of Worcester, the pestilence of Tothill Fields and the depraved conditions of the slaver, even when nearly half of them had died. But all that had already

216

taken a toll on Glencross. Did he have any strength remaining? "You had better pull through, lad, or I'll have words for you, ken? Selfish bastard, leaving me in this mess." Glencross didn't open his eyes. Iain wanted to shake him until he did.

"Don't worry—he's a feerdy one. He stands a chance," Alastair said. He looked around the hut, noting the men gathered inside. "Pack up your hammocks and hie yourselves over to Tam's. Tell him I sent you. This lad could use a bit o' space right now, and you don't want to catch what he got. Out you go."

"He's just dodging a bit o' work, right, lad? Aye, he'll be fine." Masterton laid a hand on Iain's shoulder. "Come on laggards, time to invade Ireland." He cleared everyone from the hut. All except Mairead.

"You heard Alastair," Iain told her. "The fever is virulent. You need to leave. "

Mairead considered that a moment. "I'll fetch cool water for compresses. We'll need to bring the fever down, strengthening draught or no." Without giving him an opportunity to argue the matter, she left the hut.

Now alone, Iain pulled up a stool and brought it beside his brother-in-law's hammock. Glencross's cheeks blazed alarmingly red, and his skin felt parchment dry. He twitched in his sleep while his breathing sounded short and ragged.

Get better, damn you.

Iain propped his elbows on his thighs and hung his head, staring at the hard-packed ground. As he sat with Glencross, thoughts of Innis haunted him. In the end, a raging fever had claimed his wife too. Complication following childbirth.

But Iain hadn't been there.

It had been Glencross who had sat with Innis, holding her hand and bathing her forehead through the hours of her delirium. He had kept from her the knowledge that the bairn had been stillborn. This, Glencross admitted, had been the hardest thing he'd ever had to do.

In her fevered state, Innis had peppered her brother with questions about the bairn. *"Does he look like Iain?"* The very spit, Glencross had assured her. And as she travelled deeper into the valley of death, her voice cracked, *"David, I can hear him crying. Bring him to me."*

It had taken every grain of Iain's strength to not break down when he heard this. The memory stabbed fresh, and he buried his face in his hands.

Glencross moaned, and Iain lifted his head. Pain rippled across the lad's blazing face.

"Don't flee me now," Iain whispered to his brother-in-law. He'd lost enough already. No more.

Mairead returned with a basin of sloshing water. "The water is rather tepid, but cool enough to bring relief."

Iain rose to his feet and turned away from her, needing a moment to compose himself. He headed for the grass-shuttered window. Meanwhile, she settled herself on the ground and dipped a clean scrap of linen into the water.

"Are you all right?" she asked, glancing at him over her shoulder. A frown puckered her brow.

"Aye." His throat felt raspy.

Mairead wrung out the cloth. He watched as, with the lightest touch, she dabbed at Glencross's flushed forehead, cheeks and neck. He flinched and shuddered. His body began to shake as though she bathed him in ice water.

Glencross started to cough, a gurgling, wheezing gasp. Before Mairead could fetch the night bucket, he vomited on the dirt floor. A few minutes later, he threw up again before going limp. His breathing was ragged and his face a blotchy red and white. He muttered something indistinct before settling into an uneasy sleep.

"Are you going to say it?" Iain said.

"What?"

"The world lacks justice—to inflict a fever on Glencross while sparing me."

After a long moment, she said, "I don't think you've been spared. You have a different illness eating at you from the inside."

Iain looked at her, startled by her words. He opened his mouth to refute them but held his tongue as they burrowed deeper inside. She turned her attention back to Glencross as she sponged his forehead.

Uini finally returned with one of the African wenches and a bowl of steaming broth. Iain found himself shunted aside while they tended Glencross. The three women blurred together for a moment: Mairead, sunburnt but still fair; Uini, gleaming copper and beaded; and the African woman, ebony dark.

Completely oblivious, Glencross's teeth chattered from the cold, and his entire body shook, but the African woman managed to trickle some of the brew between his cracked lips.

"Give man more soon," the African woman said to Mairead, handing her the wooden bowl. "Little every time. Ajla brew more. Return when sun rises."

Before she left, Uini tucked a wooden carving the size of a child's palm beside Glencross. A heathenish relic, but Iain didn't care. Whether magic or a favour of the devil, if it helped his brother-in-law, he'd welcome it. As if reading his mind, Uini gave him an approving glance.

Iain expected Mairead to leave with the women, but as before, she made no move to follow. "You don't need to stay." He managed this time to sound neither gruff nor enraged.

"Nonsense. You'll need help this night," she said, tilting her head up at him. "It's been a long day, and I suspect 'twill be a longer night. Get some rest. I'll take the first shift."

"I'm not taking my ease while he's like that," Iain replied, then less harshly, "I owe it to him to stay here."

Mairead looked as though she wanted to argue her point further, but instead she nodded. He followed every motion of her hands as she freshened the compress, swirling the cloth in the water, squeezing out the excess. He was soothed by the flow of her hands, the way she spread the cloth over Glencross's forehead.

Sometime during the night, delirium set in. Glencross began to thrash around in his hammock, flinging his arms violently. While Iain pinned him down, Mairead hummed a tune to soothe him. While the worst of his agitation eventually subsided, Glencross continued to mutter under his breath as the fever raged. The same name over and over. *Innis.*

Iain paled and loosened his hold on him.

"Who's Innis?" Mairead asked.

A sudden lump formed in his throat, and he took a few moments before replying. "My late wife."

Mairead gave an audible sigh. "Ah."

Glencross started mumbling louder. "Innis . . . Innis, lass . . . " His voice trailed off, leaving Iain straining to hear. Then Glencross popped his eyes open and stared at an empty corner. "I'll be back a moment . . . no need to be scared . . . Water . . . must get water for you."

Iain didn't want to hear this, but he was imprisoned by the delirium of an ill man.

Glencross's agitation intensified. "The pain will end soon, Innis...promise...so much blood. Dear God . . . Midwife! She's lost too much blood . . . her strength is spent . . . hold fast, lass." His voice trembled

Iain's insides twisted, and he forced himself not to turn away. Memories flooded back of his return. Seeing his empty bedroom, with the pallet stripped from its frame and the fire in the grate that did not warm. He remembered the faint tang of blood in the air. He could see it all now, how it must have been with Innis —ill, scared . . . in pain . . . and Glencross the only one to comfort her. Iain had always sensed that Glencross hadn't told him everything, had glossed over details for his sake. Iain hadn't pressed the issue, instead clinging to the sterile, soothing account that Glencross had given him.

Mairead bent over Glencross, smoothing his wet hair from his forehead. "Shush, David. Everything is well. No need to worry. It's all over now."

"Innis? Is that you, lass?" Unfocused eyes searched Mairead's face. "Prayers have been answered . . . Iain's come home." Another shard sliced through Iain.

"He's right here, David," Mairead said.

"Just like I promised," he said in the tone one reserved for soothing children. "He's come home to you . . . aye, I swear to you . . . while you were sleeping . . . sat with you . . . held your hand . . . hush, Innis, don't cry."

Though Glencross spoke in a whisper, his words slammed into Iain. His throat constricted, and his eyes burned. This wasn't what Glencross had told him. Iain had been assured that Innis had been at peace when death claimed her, that she understood why he wasn't back in time for the birthing—though she hadn't known the real reason for his delay. He had been told that she had whispered words of love for him before her life slipped away.

Instead, Glencross had been forced to give his beloved, dying sister a lie, telling her what she needed to hear—so she wouldn't know that Iain had abandoned her.

"He's with the bairn now . . . a proud father . . . he'll be back in a moment," Glencross continued his ramblings, each word lashing Iain bone-deep. Then he stiffened and tried to launch himself out of the hammock. Iain grabbed his shoulder to hold him fast while Glencross fought against him with a final burst of strength.

"The midwife," Glencross yelled hoarsely. Iain struggled to keep him still, struggling to subdue a violent thrashing of arms and legs. "The goddamned midwife . . . wrapped up the wee dead thing in a blanket . . . " Sobs cut through his whimpers, and he finally stopped fighting back. "Laid it in Innis's arms . . . " His eyes were wide and glassy, staring unseeing, past Iain who bent over him. "She didn't know . . . didnae realise the wee little man couldn't move."

Stop. Someone make this stop. Iain couldn't take this anymore. He released Glencross and backed away. It had been *his* duty to protect his wife, his family, his home, but he failed. What kind of man did that make him?

"Sister . . . wake up . . . wake up . . . "

"Drink some more of this, David." Mairead gave him a sip of the broth to ease the last of his agitation. He moaned and shifted, crying out in pain, but eventually his mutterings faded into sleep.

"Leave," Iain said to her hoarsely, not wanting her to hear any more. "Please leave." He needed space to lick his wounds.

Mairead seemed to consider it, but then she shook her head. "I can't."

"I'm telling you to go." Was it her intention to see him unmanned?

Mairead didn't reply. She turned her back to him and took her time applying a fresh compress on Glencross's forehead.

"Goddamn it, woman, did you nae hear?"

She sat back on her heels and folded her hands in her lap. Her hazel eyes were full of expression. "I'm so very sorry, Iain. It's not your fault. Many women die of childbirth—"

"You don't understand—how could you?" Iain paced the length of hard-packed floor, trying hard not to ram his fist into one of the beams. "You heard that bit about me being there, holding my dead son? Didn't happen. I wasn't there." He stopped his pacing and stopped a few feet away from her. "Glencross gave a lie to his sister, *my wife*, because I wasn't there in her hour of need. He lied to give her a peaceful death *because I wasn't there.*"

"It was a kindness, to be sure."

"He shouldn't have had to do that." How it must have gnawed at Glencross, this knowledge. He should have spit in Iain's eye, but instead he'd followed him blindly into war and now into hell.

"A small lie gave her peace—"

"I *abandoned* her, goddamn it."

That shocked her into silence, and he could see her expression flit between confusion and disappointment. It was time she knew him for the bastard he was.

"Were you not fighting against the English?" she asked.

Iain sank down on the stool and stared at the remaining water in the basin. Candlelight reflected in its surface. Easier to look there instead of her questioning eyes. He rubbed his palm against the flat of his forehead. Weary and past caring, he told her, "The English invaded when Innis was in her sixth month. She had been fretful for days before I left, having strange dreams. Ill-omens, she called them. Every week she had the village scrivener write a letter for me, at first imploring me to return, even for a short leave, and then the letters grew more desperate." How he hated that someone else had been a witness to his wife's petitions—to her fears. How he resented her for not being stronger—made it look as though he couldn't take care of his own family.

He groaned and tried to push the thought away. "I sent Glencross to look in on her, even though he was spoiling to fight the English. He was only to look in on her and hurry back. Instead, she was brought to bed early. Glencross arrived in time. I did not."

"You didn't abandon her, Iain—you had just cause."

"No just cause." Stupid cause. Goddamned prideful cause. He dug his fingers through his hair. "At a place called Dunbar, my men and I were purged from the army—told to pack up our gear and leave camp before the battle. We weren't godly enough—not pious enough for their liking. There were others too. Many others. Those stupid, misguided grandees were so confident that God would march with them in glory to defeat the English, only if they swept away the rubbish."

Iain clenched one hand into a fist and ground it into the palm of the other. "I wasn't going to wait to see how it turned out." He glanced at the rafters and released a bitter, furious laugh. "Turned into a goddamned slaughter—but we didn't know that at the time. I gathered my men and convinced them to strike out like moss-troopers and harass the enemy on our terms. Like the auld ways." Iain had wanted to raze the ground. He remembered his men gathered around a campfire, plotting how they could shove it up both grandee and English arses. "We raged over a month of defiance before I thought to go home."

He met Mairead's gaze defiantly, and his voice dropped to an angry hiss. "We had a choice, we could have gone home, but our pride—*my* fockin' pride—wanted to prove something to those Kirk whores. This was why I didn't make it home in time. This was why my wife had to die thinking she held our newborn son in her arms while her husband sat in the outer room."

She didn't speak at first, then she touched his knee. "Let it go, Iain. You can't keep fighting against yourself."

"You don't know me well enough if you think that."

"You'll never win that argument, to be sure."

He didn't answer. Was she right? Had he fought a battle he couldn't win, the skirmish of gnawing guilt?

Mairead rose slightly and leaned in, pressing a tender kiss against his lips, soft as silk. Her mouth parted slightly under his, and her breath tasted of dates and honey. Then she eased back and tilted her head, hazel eyes searching. Her fingers brushed his cheek, and she looked as though she wanted to say something. Instead, she lowered her lashes and frowned. "I should fetch us fresh water." She rose to her feet and, after a final parting glance, slipped out of the hut.

It had been a fleeting brush of a kiss, but Iain still felt where her mouth had pressed against his. He stared through the door where she had departed and wondered if he hadn't taken a little fever too.

Chapter 17

———◆———

Iain found it difficult to stay focused for the next few days with Glencross feverish in his hammock. Alastair had reassigned Mairead to cook for the fieldworkers, which kept her in the compound. While Iain found that he missed her company and their spirited competition, her new duties allowed her to check in on Glencross throughout the day. For this, he owed Alastair.

Eventually, Glencross's condition improved, and his delirium passed. His diet switched from broth to thin gruel. There were many times that Iain considered confronting his brother-in-law about his ravings, but he figured it would be best to leave matters alone for now. When the lad was back on his feet, he'd have it out with him then. At that time, he could finally lay things to rest.

Meanwhile, Iain's thoughts centred more and more on Mairead. He found himself constantly searching for her, as daft as a green lad. He enjoyed stirring her—to laugher or exasperation, it hardly mattered. He simply enjoyed seeing her cheeks flush and how her large hazel eyes appeared greener.

A new energy possessed him, a "throw it in your face, I'll do as I wish" kind of defiance. Why shouldn't he court her? Some of the African lads had two or three women. He'd be satisfied with one wee sprite. His inner voice reminded him—no ties, no complications, but this he steadily choked into submission.

And then on the fifth day, after the onset of Glencross's illness, Iain found his brother-in-law shaking in his hammock and curled up as weak as a kitten. The fever had returned, though fortunately not with its former strength.

The morning bell rang, announcing the start of another miserable day. "I have to go, lad," Iain said. "Mairead will be in shortly to check on you."

"I'll be fine," Glencross murmured and turned over on his side.

Iain gave Glencross's shoulder a reassuring squeeze before he joined the others gathering in the compound.

Alastair stood in the centre with Tam and Potts standing on either side of him. "There's a shipment of ginger that needs transport to Speight's Town today," he said. "Tam, gather your crew."

Iain tried to catch Tam's eye, but the Irishman avoided him. He pointed to a number of his regular mates, picking one man after another until a final position remained. One of the regular lads whose name hadn't been called started walking towards the crew. He had been fist-fighting last night and wore the badge of his loss around his eye.

"Not you," Tam said.

"What do you mean?"

"You cost me four sweet potatoes last night." A look passed between Tam and Alastair before Tam gave Iain the nod. "You're in, Scotsman."

Now Iain had a clear path—get to Speight's Town, survey the port. Get off this pox-ridden island.

Iain smiled to himself, then caught Potts's glower. The overseer made no attempt to hide his annoyance with this morning's lottery. Iain kept his expression neutral, taking every ounce of self-restraint not to gloat or sneer. Potts sniffed, hitched his breeches and ambled off to where his garron was hitched. Good riddance to poor trash.

Before Iain followed the others to the barn, he ducked into Mairead's hut and caught her as she prepared for her day. "Have a look in on Glencross today, lass. I'm off to Speight's Town with Tam and Alastair. We won't be back until late."

"However did you manage that?"

"It's an art. I'll not miss the cutting."

"So you think. You'll have twice as much cane when you return."

Iain snorted but allowed himself a brief smile. "I wouldn't put it past the irritating sot." Tam called out to him to hurry him up. "Right, I'm off."

"Godspeed," she said.

Iain stared at the fullness of her bottom lip, slightly parted and moist. The urge to pull her into his arms and kiss her thoroughly, until she flushed as the dawn, shot through him. But another shout from Tam put paid to that fancy.

"I'll see you later."

Iain spent the early part of the morning loading burlap bags filled with gingerroot onto several donkeys. As he carried the last bag, slung over his shoulder, he glanced up at the manor house, which was separated from the barn by an expansive courtyard. A movement at one of the gabled windows caught his attention.

Ciara stood alone by the window. Her blond head rested against the windowpane, and even from this distance Iain detected her forlorn expression. *A bird in a cage.* The thought bothered him until he recalled Mairead, with her face burnt, hands blistered and fingernails torn. No, Ciara was indeed worse off. Better a wild sparrow than a pet bird.

Tam's shrill whistle reminded Iain to get a move on. He readjusted his burden and hurried to secure the last sack atop the donkey's pack saddle.

The morning was already getting hot when their caravan started down the tree-lined lane. Iain gripped the donkey's bridle and followed alongside Tam. Alastair maintained the rear, no doubt keeping a sharp eye on both servants and goods.

The hills were broken with gullies and rocky slopes. The road to Speight's Town took them past acres of green sugarcane ruffling in the wind. Few trees provided shelter from the blazing sun. Their path followed a meandering creek that ran downhill northwest. The waterway expanded and flowed more strongly.

At every step of the way, Iain paid attention to the landmarks. Fields of sugarcane stretching along the road for a half-hour walk. To his left, a tumble of rocks marked a fork of the road. *Don't take that— leads to Bridge Town.* He closed his eyes and thought of the slope of the land and considered the direction of the wind that blew straight in his face. The breeze carried a slight taste of salt. There were few places to hide, only gullies not even deep enough to provide shelter. If they ever made it this far, they'd have to do so in the night with perhaps little moonlight to find their way.

When they reached a stone cairn of tumbled rocks, they left the stream and turned due west. They soon struck along a gravelled trail that widened, and then they met with another caravan, from a different estate, heading towards the busy port town.

By the time the sun soared directly overhead, they reached Speight's Town. The main road ran along the shoreline, the water dark blue and then lighter green near the shoals. A small fort guarded the southern end of the town. Iain counted three sixteen-pounders, with four, no—five men manning the fort.

Alastair took over as head of the procession when they entered the town proper, and the streets sharply narrowed. The reek of gutted fish mixed with the salty tang of the water. Wooden buildings leaned one against the other with second floors jutting slightly over the gutters. A number of buildings showed signs of recent damage— exposed charred beams, walls crumbled and pockmarked by musket fire.

228

Iain turned to Tam, who walked alongside him. "What happened here?"

Tam pushed his Monmouth cap back and scratched his forehead. "Last autumn. Parliament sent a fleet down to seize the island. Their first attempt didn't go down well. The garrison drove them back, wouldn't even allow a single boat to land. Fighting was fierce, as you can see. Didn't matter in the end; eventually, they came back with more ships. Everyone knew we couldn't hold out for long, but it don't do to have a man think you're soft."

The Speight's Town harbour had formidable defences after all. He tucked that piece of information away in his belt.

Ahead, one building stood out, a brazen green against its drab neighbours. Hung over the main door, a crude sign marked the Little Bristol. From somewhere inside, ribald laughter mingled with an off-key pipe playing.

Burke, the proprietor and whoremonger, stepped outside and paused to lean against the doorjamb. He puffed on a pipe, lazily blowing tobacco smoke into the air. A froth of lace over a rich brocade vest showed off his swarthy skin.

"Worthy Alastair," Burke called out. "You be sure to give your master my warmest regards. I have a card room, and other diversions, waiting for him; tell him that."

As a reply, Alastair touched his hat's brim, and Burke's raucous laughter followed after them.

They finally reached the warehouse district in the centre of town, strategically positioned between two batteries of cannon. A steady procession of wagons and donkeys made their way, laden with goods. Two dozen hogsheads and miles of stacked crates lined one length of a courtyard.

Iain's attention lingered on the schooners anchored in the dark blue bay. Their tenders ferried goods back and forth from ship to shore. All flew English flags—all except one ship anchored farthest out in the harbour, which flew the Dutch Republic flag.

One ship. That's all he needed—any ship. He didn't care if the vessel was headed to the Azores or to France. As long as it was away from here.

Alastair led them to the warehouse yard, where they were forced to wait for the warehouse master to finish with another shipment. When it was Alastair's turn, the master tallied the shipment, confirmed the price and then directed them where to unload their ginger.

They had only just started when a boat rowing to the nearest jetty caught Iain's interest. The boat docked, but instead of crates and bales, it carried half a dozen sailors and one barrel-chested man who stood out from the others. A wide-brimmed hat had been set at a jaunty angle on straw-coloured hair, and his sapphire coat contrasted with the sailors' rough gear. This man had the look of being the captain.

After exchanging a few terse words with the men, the newcomer headed towards the warehouse, strolling as though he owned the town. A number of the dock workers behaved as though he were a leper. Rather than taking offence, the man nodded to them amiably and continued on his way. Iain found himself admiring the man's swagger.

Tam came out of the warehouses and stopped in midstride. As the man strode past him, Tam tugged on his cap and greeted him, "Morning to you, Captain Hogendorp."

Hogendorp. A Dutchman. Iain looked across the harbour and realised that the foreign ship must be his.

The warehouse master proved to be less than admiring. The little man rushed to intercept the captain, and Iain pretended to busy himself close by. Something about this little drama nipped his curiosity.

"Captain Hogendorp, what are you doing here?" the warehouse master said.

"Naturally, I am enjoying a fine day." The man spoke English generously flavoured with Dutch.

"There are no goods for you here. We cannot trade with Dutch vessels," the warehouse master blurted, then reddened. To Iain, he looked damned uncomfortable. "There are rules we are obliged to follow." The man sputtered and squirmed, even though Hogendorp's expression didn't change. "It's not personal. No trading unless you fly English colours, that's the law——"

"As you say, it is not personal, only restrictive to my countrymen. Shame that an English Parliament, thousands of miles away, can dictate the nature of honest trade to an enterprising colony. Such nonsense." The captain placed a large hand on the man's thin shoulder and continued as though tutoring a pupil. "Such restrictive trade is not healthy, my friend. The price of sugar has doubled on the market but is halved for the plantation owners. Tell me, do you think that is fair?"

"I can't speak about that," the warehouse master said.

"You should, friend. An opinion separates man from beast." The captain smiled. "But if you cannot speak in a professional capacity— of course you cannot, that is clear. I will ease your mind, however. The *Zeelandia* will be anchored only long enough for us to purchase fresh supplies."

"Purchase?"

"Correct. What I need for my voyage. Water. Hemp. Rope and a few other necessities. I'm willing to pay in coin. Surely, this is not objectionable?"

Tam knocked Iain's shoulder and gave him a sharp look. "There's more that needs offloading."

For the next hour, Iain lugged crates of ginger with the others, stacking them precisely where the fussy warehouse assistant demanded they go. When they finished with that, they turned to loading up the donkeys for the return journey home with household supplies—bolts of coarse linen, tools and crates of Spanish wine.

"Don't forget candle wax," Tam told Iain. "Three boxes."

Iain returned into the warehouse to find the wax. When they first arrived on the island, it had struck him as odd that they were given wax candles to burn, even in the African huts. Since the planters couldn't keep cows or sheep to make tallow, they made their candles from good, imported wax. A strange luxury.

The particular warehouse assistant couldn't be found, and Iain searched up and down the rows for the blasted wax. Not that he minded. Stretching his legs felt good, at any rate. He turned down a narrow passage carved out between kegs of ale and stacks of more ginger when he heard the Dutch captain speaking on the other side of the kegs.

"The rumours persist, my friend. War is imminent. The English have become bolder in their posturing. My country will not allow their aggression to go unchallenged."

"What then?" To Iain's surprise, he recognised Alastair's voice. Where he might have continued on in search of the wax, now he decided to stay quiet. And listen.

"My trips will, naturally, discontinue. I shall not risk my ship on any venture," the captain said.

Iain's ears pricked. Though the two men spoke of matters that could be shared over a tankard of ale along with the price of mutton, Iain latched on to one word: venture.

"How soon do you think?"

The captain didn't reply immediately. Iain pictured him rocking on his heels as he contemplated an answer. "A few months."

"Three quarter moons then."

"A guess, my friend. For all we know, the first shots may have already been fired. And if so, news of war will take a couple of months to reach us."

"Two quarter moons then. A third, possibly."

"Reasonable."

The two men walked away, leaving Iain to mull on what he'd overheard. He hadn't spent years moss-trooping and border raiding without developing a nose for subterfuge. He had spent enough time in disreputable taverns where all manner of illicit trade had been arranged. This conversation could have come from any one of those holes.

A short time later, Iain re-emerged with the wax, and he did his best not to attract Alastair's notice. He checked the donkey packs, tightening the straps while he observed Alastair from the corner of his eye. The Dutch captain was nowhere to be seen and his boat no longer at the jetty.

All the way back to Mount Vale, Iain pondered the possibilities. There was one truth when it came to governments, no matter their ideologies. When they tried to monopolise trade to line their pockets, equally enterprising men usually found a way around it to line their own. He thought of the little luxuries that had found their way to Alastair's cottage, like the violin. They had to have come from somewhere.

Alastair the freebooter. Iain would wager anything on it. The only question that remained—how could he use this for his own gain?

The sun had just set when they arrived at Mount Vale. Iain was still deep in thought with plans and possibilities when he returned to his hut.

Mairead startled him when she appeared in the doorway. He smiled and lifted his hand to greet her when her expression halted him. Her eyes were impossibly large. Even from his distance, he could see that they were red-rimmed.

Iain braced himself, but it still hit him like a sharp drive to the gut.

"I'm sorry, Iain," she said. "David has died."

In the Mount Vale graveyard, none of the graves were marked, leaving Mairead to wonder how many servants and slaves had been buried here over the years. The site had been selected for its broken, rocky terrain. Ill-suited for any crops, the goats pastured there, roaming across multiple hilly mounds, though they gave the recently dug grave a respectful berth.

David Glencross had been laid atop a wooden plank and carried to the hill by Killean Ross holding one end and Angus Rae holding the other. Masterton the Younger rang a bell with every several steps as he led the procession to the gravesite. The Wiltons hadn't spared a blanket to enshroud the body. David's hammock would be needed for the next servant. This appalled Mairead, but Uini had offered her own solution. The Arawak women had woven a crude covering made with plantain sheaves. At least David would not be unduly exposed.

Iain stood apart from the others at the grave, grim and stoic, his face cut in all hard angles, as though hewn from granite. He didn't once look at Mairead, hadn't said much of anything since she told him that David had passed away. She didn't dare approach him, sensing that this was the only way he could survive his grief.

That moment when she had given him the news remained branded in her mind. He'd looked as though she had stabbed him in the gut. Mairead knew what he must be thinking. Iain hadn't been there for David on his deathbed, as he hadn't been there for his wife. And he had just started to come to terms with that.

Mairead had urged David to hang on. *Iain will be here shortly*, she kept promising the dying man. But the fever had locked him away in a world where words were meaningless. He was already far away long before his body surrendered.

Mairead blinked back tears as they lowered David's body into the hole. Iain stared ahead, stony and unmoved. Mairead ached for him. David had been released from this hellish life, but what comfort eased those left behind?

Masterton, being the eldest amongst them, stepped forward and fulfilled the role of *seanchaidh*. Killean leaned in and explained it to her in a low whisper. "We honour the dead in this way." Masterton recited Glencross's genealogy as far back as several generations. When they reached his immediate kin, Iain's composure slipped a fraction. Everyone's attention had been turned to the grave, except for Mairead. For a heartbeat, she witnessed the brief shudder of pain mirrored in Iain's blue eyes before he squared his shoulders and stared ahead.

Iain stepped up to the grave and dropped to his knees to scoop up a handful of dirt. Standing over the grave, he clenched the soil in his fist, then slowly released it in a steady and deliberate stream.

While the others filled the grave, he stood apart, unmoving.

The grave was covered with a cairn of stones. Mairead did her part to lay a few to top it off. This would be David Glencross's memorial, at least until the worst of the storms swept through and disturbed the cairn.

Mairead sensed someone staring, a feeling as persistent as the brush of fingers on skin. She looked up and found Iain's gaze resting on her. Her breath caught in her throat. He didn't turn away when their eyes met. His expression remained unfathomable. Then after a moment, he gave her a brief nod and headed back to the compound.

Mairead wasn't in a hurry to leave. She tried to come to terms with how quickly David had passed away. The returning fever had spiked midmorning, and by early afternoon jaundice had set in, and he started to vomit everything he had consumed. Blood and bile turned his vomit a shocking black.

Iain had counted on her to keep an eye on David, and she couldn't help but feel that she had failed him.

It's not your fault.

Mairead sighed. She canted her head and listed to the rustling of the leaves in the wind. There had been no pipes or songs to hasten David's soul. *That shouldn't be.*

An idea came to her. Hurrying down the slope, she headed for Alastair's cottage, hoping he wouldn't be back yet. The men had plans to share a cup of mobbie in David's honour in the compound.

Mairead considered finding Alastair to ask his permission to take the violin, but she didn't want this to be a public display. Everyone would insist on listening, and this was for David alone.

Mairead reached the cottage and darted inside, now self-conscious. There was still time to run back and obtain Alastair's permission, but a quick glance at the sky quashed that idea. Rain clouds gathered on the horizon. It wouldn't be long before they emptied here.

She retrieved the violin and bow from its protective chest, folding back the soft Holland cloth. Then, tucking the instrument close to her breast, she slipped out to return to the grave on the hill.

The stone cairn showed white against the slate-grey sky. The wind had shifted slightly, carrying a salty taste. Mairead raised the violin and poised the bow over the strings. She closed her eyes and cleared her thoughts. She held an image of David in her mind, his easygoing and friendly manner, and allowed it to guide the melody that shaped in her mind and turned again to the tune that had haunted her from the first time she'd heard it in the ship's hold, "The Gay Goshawk."

Mairead lifted her bow and began to play.

She followed the main melody but layered in variations until a new song emerged. The interplay of high and low notes struck a chord deep in her belly, and she followed the threads where they took her. Playing swept Mairead through her grief and expressed what she could not say in words. From her fingers came a charming song for a charming man, with a bittersweet melancholy rounding out the tribute.

When she finished, she opened her eyes and realised she was not alone. Iain stood in the field, twenty feet away from her. Their eyes locked for an unguarded moment. Iain's stoic expression slipped. He lowered himself slowly to the ground, and his shoulders hunched forward. Bowing his head, he buried his face into his shaking hands.

Chapter 18

————◆————

Iain hid within the shadows of a stand of seagrape trees and watched Alastair's cottage. A single light flickered through the window. Wrapped around his shoulders, a donkey blanket hid the pale colour of his clothes. Overhead, a waning quarter moon began to clear the treetops.

Glencross's death had strengthened Iain's desire to get off this infernal island, and deep in his bones, Iain felt that the master brewer held the key to unlocking his fate. He turned over in his mind Alastair's conversation with the Dutch captain, Hogendorp.

Smuggling required goods. Iain considered that if there was anything worth hiding, it wouldn't be found in the boiling house, not with the half-dozen slaves feeding the fires and boiling the cane juice six days a week. He couldn't see how the cottage could hide aught either, but the man spent most of his evenings there. A fortnight and nothing yet to show for it. No matter. He had all the time to piss on.

At least here he wasn't lashing out at his men. In the days following the burial, Iain's temper sparked like a powder keg set under a lit match. It gnawed to bury Glencross in a foreign, hellish land, and he didn't have anything of his brother-in-law to bring back to Scotland. Iain refused to accept that this would be his end too. Masterton and Angus made the mistake of offering their condolences. Iain hadn't raged, but he had frozen them out with a withering glare. He didn't need their sympathy, he needed their resolve. The hut stifled him—everyone stifled him. He couldn't bear to see Glencross's empty hammock, and yet he had shredded Killean when the man suggested taking it down.

Iain almost welcomed this time alone. On most nights, he waited long past the time that Alastair doused his lights. The only highlight of his vigil was the evenings that Mairead paid Alastair a visit.

He had said very little to her since the burial. He couldn't find the words—his grief tied his tongue. The mournful tones of her violin playing a funeral dirge had been his undoing. After the last strains of the instrument had trembled to silence, she had knelt in the dirt beside him and placed her hand upon his arm. He had never shown his weakness before, never allowed another to see his grief, not even when Innis died. His first instinct had been to recoil from Mairead's touch and throw up the barricades—a man should always have better control of himself, no matter the situation. But the warmth of her hand locked him in place. A moment of grief. Could he not allow himself this one small luxury? Then he would gather himself and march onwards as ever he had before.

She hadn't lingered long, a small blessing and yet a hollow one. With a final squeeze of his shoulder, she'd quietly withdrawn before his pride had been completely ravaged.

Iain looked towards the trail that led to the compound and wondered if this would be one of her nights to visit Alastair. He hadn't before realised how much time she spent here. She'd often slip down to the cottage well after night settled in and spend an hour or two playing on the violin. The strains of her melody curled around Iain, and while he couldn't see her playing, he pictured her enraptured expression as when she had performed at the crushing mill. Sitting alone in the dark was a blessing. He didn't have to guard himself or risk anyone, especially Mairead, seeing how moved he was by her. His conflicted feelings hardened—this was the wrong time and the wrong place. If he didn't concentrate on the matter at hand, he'd never find a way to get them off the island—Mairead included.

The only time Iain interrupted his watch was when Mairead headed back to her hut. He followed close behind, quietly so that she wouldn't know, and made sure she reached her shelter unmolested. Iain hadn't missed the attention Potts had been paying Mairead. She hadn't said a word to him about it, but he saw how she shrank whenever the overseer was around.

If Potts touched Mairead, Iain would kill him. They could hang him later.

The light inside the cottage extinguished, and the darkness rushed in to fill the void. Iain glanced up at the sky and considered the passage of stars. The tree frog chorus was particularly loud and hypnotic. Time spun out, and exhaustion caught up with him. It had been a hard end to a long week in the fields. His eyes felt heavy, and he shook his head to clear the fog. A few more moments and he'd end it for the night . . .

Iain startled awake and looked around, wondering how long he had drifted off. He rubbed his eyes and stretched his back. By the height of the moon, he gauged an hour had passed. What had woken him?

His ears pricked by the sound of someone lurking around the cottage. More than one—a few people. Everything was dismally dark, and Iain strained to see who was out there. The door of the cottage opened, followed by a clinking of bottles and a low murmur of voices. Iain picked out Alastair's voice and Tam's, and they hovered outside near the well.

"The lads are coming," Tam asked.

"Why so late? We should have been on the road already," Alastair said.

"Potts."

Alastair's reply was low and indistinct.

Iain heard a group of men approaching along with muffled clopping. A donkey brayed.

"Keep that beast quiet," Tam hissed.

A long train of donkeys materialised from the deeper shadows. Iain counted ten—nearly all the plantation's donkeys. The animals were rigged up to carry goods, but none of them were burdened, except for the bottles that Alastair slipped into one of the packs. The men set off.

Iain waited a few moments before following. His blood pumped, and he was aware of every sound and every movement in the dark. Finally, action.

It wasn't hard to follow the slow, plodding donkey train. Though unlikely that they would see him trailing behind them given the weak moon, Iain took extra care. His moss-trooping instincts took over.

The donkey train headed south towards Bridge Town, through gullies and across fields. In the open meadows, Iain crouched low and tried to keep his head below the tops of the high grasses as he loped along. It didn't matter that his knees protested and his back ached.

One of the donkeys stopped, and Iain sensed that one of the men looked back. Iain flattened himself on the ground and held his breath. Someone called out a brief question, then a response. A few more moments stretched before the train continued. Iain released his breath. When he continued his pursuit, he did so with more caution.

Where were they going?

They were about an hour or more on the road when the donkey train took a narrow footpath and headed towards a ridge of hills that loomed black against the dark sky. The ground grew more broken and rocky. Iain paused to catch his breath. Jagged-edged pebbles collected in his canvas shoes, and his feet throbbed. What he would trade for a proper set of leather boots. And a horse. He'd do anything for a horse. *Keep going, Locharbaidh.*

Thicker brush shielded Iain's view, and the trail wound along and twisted. For several uncomfortable and frustrating moments, he lost sight of them, then to his surprise, they appeared on a lower trail. He quickened his pace.

The donkey train continued for another hundred yards before finally halting.

Iain crouched behind a stunted tree and waited for them to continue, but they didn't. Instead, they disappeared into the hill itself. He smiled to himself with growing certainty. *From Scotland to Barbados, things never changed.* How much contraband had he himself hidden in a convenient hillside?

A half hour later, the donkeys re-emerged in single file, each one laden with several canvas bags. Iain had seen those distinctive sacks in the curing house and knew very well what they contained. *Sugar.* The only currency on the island.

The donkey train continued but this time struck a westerly course. Not Bridge Town, then. Iain kept on their trail despite the bone-grinding weariness that slowed him down. By the progress of the stars, Iain gauged that it had been a couple of hours since they headed west. He lifted his nose and breathed in the distinctive salty tang in the breeze. Not long after, the donkey train turned off the main road and picked up a narrow tract leading towards a cove.

Iain crawled to the top of a rise and carefully lifted his head to see. There in the cove, a ship lay anchored while a boat with half a dozen men rowed to shore. Alastair's donkey train halted on the beach, waiting. A late quarter moon shone high in the sky and made the water sparkle.

Quarter moon. He remembered Alastair's words as though he had just spoken them. Back in Speight's Town, Alastair had specifically mentioned quarter moons. And Iain knew, without any doubt, whose ship was anchored in the cove.

Iain crept down the side of the hill. Keeping his head down, he picked his way to the cove towards an outcrop of rocks. He had to get closer, had to hear what was being said. There'd not be another chance.

A few scrubby bushes provided minimal cover. With the approaching boat drawing close, all heads were drawn to the water, and none minded the road.

As Iain descended the hillside, the soil became looser, and his next step caused a small shower of pebbles to tumble down the hill. The sound of rolling shale echoed loudly in his ears.

Damnation.

Iain dropped to the ground and ducked below the grass fronds. One of Tam's men whipped around and peered up to the darkened hillside in the direction where Iain hid. Slowly, the man advanced towards the hill.

"What's the matter?" Tam's voice rose distinctly from the beach.

"Did you hear something?" The man started walking up the hillside.

A sudden flutter of wings beat through the air, and a bird shot out from the hillside. The man recoiled with a startled cry, followed by Tam's low laughter. "You mean that?"

With a mutter, the other man abandoned the hillside and followed Tam to the beach.

Iain released his breath slowly, his blood pumping through his veins. It was good to feel alive. He waited a few moments before edging closer until he had a clearer view of the beach below.

The boat reached the shore, and men ploughed through the surf to haul the boat on the sand. Iain recognised the burly figure of the Dutch captain leap out of the boat and approach Alastair. The two drew aside before walking over to the donkey train. A purse exchanged hands, the signal for the sugar to be offloaded from donkey to boat.

Iain continued to watch. *Two quarter moons. Possibly three left.* This is what Alastair had said about the threat of a war on the horizon. Good. He still had time.

While the men were unloading the contraband, he retraced his steps and picked up the trail leading away from the cove.

All along his long trek back to the plantation, he determined his next move. The canny option would have been to return to the hut and consider how he could use this information—examine it from all angles and plan twenty steps ahead. But Iain Locharbaidh Johnstone relied on his gut, and he had to admit it mostly served him well.

When Iain returned to the plantation, he headed for Alastair's cottage and let himself in. The darkness began to recede as dawn approached. While he waited, Iain wandered through the cottage, opening drawers. In a cupboard, he found a plate of cold meat, a knife, some cassava bread and a few bottles of rum.

As Iain chewed on the meat, he studied Alastair's quarters. The appointments were better than he had expected: a trestle table with a pair of benches, a large framed bed, two armchairs, roughly made bookcases and a small side table. On the table, a tin of tobacco was left beside a pipe. He opened a chest and found Mairead's violin nestled inside. Iain lifted out the instrument and turned it over in his hands. The smooth wood had been polished and buffed, and as he ran his fingers across the wood he felt an inexplicable connection to her.

Iain poured himself a cup of rum and settled in the chair, still cradling the violin. He had been giving a great deal of thought about how they could have moved so much sugar without Potts or the Wiltons knowing about it. Of that he was sure—Potts didn't know. They couldn't have done it at night. Iain had been watching the cottage, and he hadn't seen anything stir. Besides, with the time they needed to load up the donkeys, there would be too great a chance that Potts would have caught them at it. No, Alastair was too clever for that.

Iain took another sip of rum. The best way to hide something was in plain sight—or under the light of day. Lately, the camels and donkeys hauled the sugar from the plantation to Bridge Town twice a week with Alastair in charge of the shipment, there and back. Iain's eyes narrowed in thought. Alastair was particular about the lads he took with him to Bridge Town. He mostly left the Speight's Town runs to Tam's discretion, but never Bridge Town. And the caves were situated conveniently midway.

Not hard to divert a donkey or two with each run if you were sure of your men. Within the month, an enterprising bastard could have enough to make it worth a Dutch captain's while.

Iain smiled to himself. Leverage.

A quarter of an hour later, footsteps climbed the steps to the cottage. The door opened, and Alastair halted in the threshold. His gaze swept the room before resting on Iain.

"I hope you're comfortable. There's another bottle in the pantry when you finish." His tone betrayed his annoyance.

Iain tipped the cup and smiled grimly. "These are quality spirits. Far better than the shite you give Tam. You don't want to know what I think of the rotgut they let the rest of us have."

Alastair pulled up the other chair. It had been a long night for both of them, but Alastair had a score of years on Iain, and he looked stretched thin. "It's late—or early. What's this about?"

Iain savoured the rum on his tongue before he answered. "I'm curious about Captain Hogendorp." He tipped his glass to examine the liquor. "A handsome ship, the *Zeelandia*—Dutch, isn't she? Shame the captain's not allowed to trade on the island—that *is* illegal, right?" Iain quirked his brow and smiled. Alastair hadn't moved an inch. "That bastard governor, so far up Cromwell's arse," Iain continued, "cutting off good, honest trade. The plantation owners must be fair wrocht over the prices they are forced to accept for trading exclusively to Southron merchants. The Wiltons would be especially ill-pleased to hear that an indentured servant is making more on the same sugar they're forced to sell at half the price."

"*Former* indentured servant," Alastair said.

244

"Not Tam or his lads—at least not yet," Iain said. "How many years would the Duchess add to their terms if she knew?"

"You think she doesn't know?" Alastair arched a brow and smiled.

Iain scratched the side of his nose and considered the man. He had played enough card games to recognise when an opponent clutched at a useless suit. Alastair's smile intended to disarm Iain, to make him think he'd welcome having his bluff called. "Horse shite," he replied. "If that were so, you'd be loading up the sugar straight from the curing house instead of using the caves." Iain leaned in his chair and noted with satisfaction the hardening of Alastair's jaw. "Nay, what you are dealing in are the skimmings. The bit of overflow no one is going to notice."

Alastair folded his arms across his chest and glanced outside the window. The sky was turning a golden blush. "You want a cut? Is this what this is about, Locharbaidh?"

"I want tae get out o' this pisshole."

"In time. Several years, or more in your case, if you keep pushing Potts."

"I don't mean to wait that long," Iain said.

"None of us do, but the years stretch ahead of us anyway."

Iain leaned forward. "And yet you're here—why is that? Once they released you from your bondage, why not reclaim your manhood and shove off?"

Alastair's eyes narrowed, and his nostril's flared. "You're testing me, Locharbaidh."

"My time to test you then," Iain said. "How much influence do you have with Captain Hogendorp?" Alastair's expression hardened, but he didn't reply. Iain smiled and continued, "If you were to ask him, would he find space on his ship for extra passengers bound for Holland, or anywhere he happens to be sailing?"

"He won't, and I'll not ask," Alastair said. "And you won't tell your story."

"Because you won't let me? That's what you're thinking, isn't it?" Iain rubbed his stubbled chin. "Think I was alone last night? Take me for a fool, do you?" Iain moderated his tone so as not give away *his* bluff. He knew he played a dangerous game.

Alastair rose to his feet and fetched a second cup. He poured himself a draught of rum, took a leisurely sip and said, "Hard work will do you good. I'll not help you."

The man was calling his bluff, pretending not to care about his position or any repercussions for siphoning the Wilton's sugar. Iain glanced down at the violin, regrouping his thoughts. He didn't really expect that Alastair would blithely and cheerfully allow the whole lot of them to leave over a threat, but he'd still nurtured a forlorn hope. He wasn't yet ready to accept defeat, so he drew his last card. "If not for me or my men, what about for Mairead?"

That surprised Alastair. "Mairead? What about her?"

"You're fond of her—we can agree on that." He kept his tone neutral. It wouldn't do to show the depths of his feeling for her—he didn't want Alastair to use that against him. "She's a good lass and doesn't belong here. You sold yourself, only the devil knows why, and I for the sake of a king. We're here by our own actions, but she did nothing. Ripped away because some English bugger wanted land. Help me get her away. Use your influence to secure passage on Hogendorp's ship for all of us, and I vow to get her home."

"To what end? The English have taken her home. At least here she's clothed and fed," Alastair said.

Iain's anger stirred. "Oh aye? Slavery is palatable as long as we're all clothed and fed?"

"Don't twist my words. That's not what I meant."

"Explain it to me, then. Clothes, poor rations and Potts slavering over her like a hungry wolf. Have I missed anything?"

"Potts won't step out of line. I have my eye on her."

"Aye, that settles it, then," Iain said testily. It rankled deeply that *he* wasn't the one keeping the overseer in line. Drawing a deep breath, he tried to refocus. "The next quarter moon, when you meet Hogendorp at the cove, bring us with you—my men included. With the profit he's made on your enterprise, he should be amenable to taking on extra passengers. If you truly care for the lass, you'll want to see her home with her kin."

Alastair didn't reply. He poured himself another glass of rum. From somewhere in the distance, a cock crowed, followed by another.

"I'll see."

Iain scowled. The last time someone told him they'd see what they could do, he had been subsequently packed off to a ship. "That's not good enough. I need your word on it."

Alastair slammed his cup down. "You won't get it. I ask this of Hogendorp and he finds another freebooter, one with at least one less demand."

"Arseworm," Iain ground out, rising to his feet. He held up the violin. "What is this, then? You give her cruel hope and a misplaced belief that you're on her side, but the first chance you get tae prove it, you think more of your ill-gotten profits."

"Get out," Alastair said, his mouth in a tight, white line.

"I'm off." Iain kicked over the table, sending the rum bottle crashing to the ground. He paused long enough to leave the violin in the chair. He didn't look back as he strode out of the cottage and across the yard. He didn't stop until he reached the seagrape stand, and only then paused long enough to check that he still had the stolen dagger tucked under his waistband.

Iain returned to the hut and found everyone awake and gathered around Dunsmore. "What's this?" he asked.

"And Himself deigns to return," Dunsmore said with a shallow laugh that ended in a snort.

Iain looked around at the others. Killean avoided his eye, and Angus, normally jovial, sobered when he met Iain's gaze and looked away. Only Masterton dared look him in the eye.

"Are you having a council without me?" Iain demanded.

"Where have ye been?" Dunsmore asked.

"I don't answer to you," Iain said.

"Perhaps cutting deals with Alastair? Don't think we haven't noticed you hanging around there?"

Iain stiffened, his ire rising. "You've the hearing of a stone, Dunsmore. I . . . Do . . . Nae . . . Answer . . . Tae . . . Ye." He turned to the rest of them. "I asked you all a fockin' question. Do any of you bastards have the stones to tell me?"

"We were discussing plans, lad," Masterton blurted with a touch of defiance.

"Without me."

"You haven't been around, Locharbaidh," Masterton muttered.

Iain folded his arms across his chest and glared at Dunsmore. "Convenient for you." Turning to his men, he said, "A man recently loses a kinsman and instead of giving him a reasonable time to deal with it, you blame him and throw it in his face. Glencross is not even cold, and you've made me redundant."

"It's been a month," Masterton said.

That hit Iain in the gut. Of course it had only been a month. But they didn't realise that he didn't just lose a kinsman and a friend—he had lost his last connection to the past. A man didn't just move on from that overnight.

"It's not like that," Killean said, clearing his throat. "We've thought to give you time for a bit of grieving."

"I don't need time to grieve. I need to leave this shitten island."

"Only you?" Dunsmore said, looking around to the others. "What I told you."

Iain's anger coiled. He had been up all night, walked ten miles there and back trying to find any leverage to secure their freedom, and they dared questioned *him*? "What have you been telling them, Dunsmore? Face me like a man instead of like a slinking dog, turning my men against me."

Dunsmore's nostril's flared, but he didn't snap at the bait. Instead, he remained where he was with the others clustered around him. "I had to keep things going while you were moping, Locharbaidh." He glanced around and received a few agreements.

"Is this what he told you?" Iain said. Could they not see this viper for what he was?

"It's nae like that, Locharbaidh. Settle down," Masterton said. "You've been absent since Glencross died. You can huff and rage and go all cross-eyed on us, but it's the truth, plain and simple. Now sit yourself down, and we'll tell you our plans. No one's cut you out, man."

Iain reined himself in. Masterton was right. He had allowed himself to be played by Dunsmore. He was better than that. Iain nodded and joined the others, but he still felt as though there was an invisible dividing line between himself and the others, with Dunsmore being the fulcrum. "Very well. I'm listening."

"Dunsmore managed to get the spare key to the storeroom where Wilton keeps his weapons—muskets, swords and daggers."

The dagger he had taken from Alastair's cottage pressed cold against Iain's skin. Dunsmore smirked, full of his own piss. Iain could hear the man's mockery if he admitted to securing only one weapon. "Who did you have to toss to get that?"

"Lucy is very accommodating."

"I've heard."

"Better a Southron wench with access to Wilton's effects than a scrawny Irish fieldworker," Dunsmore said, shrugging.

Iain's eyes narrowed. "Go there, and I'll rip your tongue out."

"Enough, the both of you," Masterton said. "That wasn't all." He cleared his throat. "We've decided to go with Dunsmore's plan to commandeer a ship."

Iain rubbed his throbbing temple, and the muscles on the back of his neck bunched up. Lack of sleep was starting to affect him. Masterton couldn't have just said that. Dunsmore's stupid, reckless plan? He looked around at the faces of his men, all turned to him, waiting for his reaction. "We've already agreed that this is fool's play. We might as well string ourselves up from a tree and spare the Wiltons the hangman's fee."

"You'll have us wait for Judgment Day to get out of here, Locharbaidh," Dunsmore said with a sneer. "Unless you've made your own plans."

Iain's pride seared his mouth shut. Now was the time to tell them about the caves and Alastair's enterprise, but right now he was too furious with them all, and it rankled that Dunsmore had shifted the stage on him.

"I didn't think so." Dunsmore sniffed and ran the back of his hand under his nose. "It's agreed. We commander a ship ready to sail. Moreover, one with a hold full of goods."

Iain's eyebrows shot up. "What did you say?"

"Why should these Southroners get all the profit? Sugar, ginger, indigo. They're sitting on a bleeding fortune. Imagine how much we'll get for the lot. Forget Scotland. There's a bleeding war going on there. But the Dutch and French will pay dearly for top-quality goods. We'll secure our fortune."

"Aye, you think that will work because a full ship will have no men guarding it. This is a mad jest, right?" Iain turned to Masterton, but the man remained stoic. "You've purchased a steaming pile of shite from this turd."

"Most of them will be whoring on shore until they are ready to sail," Dunsmore said with a laugh.

"You willing to risk our lives on your assumption?" Iain demanded. "And next you'll be telling us that the garrison men will be sending us a proper send-off. This is the harbour that held its own against the might of Cromwell's navy. I've seen the condition of the town."

"There will be a diversion," Dunsmore smirked. When Iain didn't say anything, he continued, "There's fewer of them than us. It would be naught to seize the bugger Wilton, hold the Duchess hostage and take what we're owed. We can fire up the place to give us enough run time."

"How far do you think we'd get?" Iain snarled, losing the last shreds of his patience. "We do away with one of them, and the entire island will hunt us down. And don't think you'll be greeted as the grand liberator by Alastair, Potts and the other servants. Too many have bowed and scraped before these Wiltons for so long that their wings have been clipped, and they wouldn't know what to do with an open cage even if you shook them out. Factor that in and you'll ken that we're up against more than one whoreson planter."

"I don't see a clipped bird," Dunsmore spat. "Only a whipped cur, and Potts holds the leash. You piss your pants whenever he barks out a command."

Both Masterton and Killean placed themselves between Iain and Dunsmore, preventing Iain from launching himself on the bastard.

"I've enough of the both of you," Masterton said. "You're ripping your own throats when the enemy is without."

"And you still believe Dunsmore will see you through? He'll be guaranteeing our own deaths."

"It's better than remaining here as a slave," Killean finally spoke up.

"If we die, we do so as men," Masterton said.

Iain found himself helpless against that argument. He believed the same himself, but *he* meant to get them all home, not twitching on the end of a noose. Shaking himself loose, he said, "You're all fools. Dunsmore is a reckless, self-centred bastard who will sacrifice any of you to save his own hide. Did you nae wonder why none of the Maxwells would have him? Follow him if you must."

"They've already said they would. The question is—are *you* with us or against us?" Dunsmore asked in a mocking tone.

"Of course he's with us," Masterton snapped. "Get some rest, Locharbaidh. 'Tis Sunday, and the bells won't be ringing. We'll talk about it some more in the day. You'll see this is a good plan and our best chance."

Iain left the hut to cool his steam. Had he stayed any longer, his fist would be through either a wall or Dunsmore. It didn't matter which.

"Locharbaidh, hold on, lad," Masterton called out behind him.

"Come to drive the dagger deeper?"

"You deserve a cuff to the head for that," Masterton said. "Acting like an outraged maid, you are."

"I did not expect this defection, not from you," Iain, said clenching and unclenching his fists. "I expected more loyalty."

"And you have it; that hasn't changed."

"You're throwing in your lot with that arse."

"Aye, he's nae my choice for a companion," Masterton admitted, "but his wits are sharp, and no one else has come up with an idea."

"Me, you mean. I've not come up with an idea."

"Aye, put baldly. Nor should we be relying on yourself alone to get us home. No one man can bear such a burden."

Iain looked away. Masterton placed a hand on his shoulder. "Glencross knocked you off course; we ken that. It doesn't matter the means to get home, only that we do."

"The man is reckless."

Masterton gave a snort that ended with a low chuckle. "So were you. Butting heads with our commanders—calling them out for their nonsense. I lost track of how many times they disbanded us. You're not too different from Dunsmore."

That bothered Iain, and he felt his temper rising. "Don't compare me to an ill-begotten Maxwell—not when he's digging on us for not being like them."

252

"He doesn't say much about the Maxwells—only when he wants to yank your chain," Masterton said with a wide yawn. "Sleep on it. You'll know we're right."

Iain watched Masterton return to the hut. The sun's rays crept over the tops of the trees, and the day's heat had already started. He'd do anything to get off this island. But he'd follow his own rules.

Chapter 19

————◆————

Mairead trudged back to the barn, leading a donkey laden by bags of cassava root. With most of the sugarcane harvested, she had been reassigned to helping Uini and her kin in the cassava fields. Though this task proved easier than hauling cane, her spirits scraped the bottom of the pond. The Arawak women mostly left her alone, and at first she thought this contributed to her flat mood. Then the truth finally crept upon her. She missed bantering with Iain and missed him keenly.

He'd kept his distance from everyone since Glencross's death. She tried baiting and prodding him during meal times, anything to bring out his inner ogre. In the past, Iain's anger kept him going, and Mairead tried her best to ignite that banked fire, but without success. Every morning, she watched him head out to the sugarcane fields with his head down, speaking to no one. It unsettled her, made her feel as though the hard-packed ground beneath her feet had turned to silt.

Mairead led the donkey into the barn and settled the creature in a stall with the other beasts. She latched the gate and leaned against the boards. There wasn't a soul around, and she relished the solitude. A window high up in the rafters caught the late afternoon rays, illuminating the dust motes floating in the air. The smell of animals prodded a memory of Uncle Mulriane's barn, and she could almost picture the Mulrianes' dairymaid drifting in, calling each beast by name.

A wave of homesickness swept over Mairead. It hadn't been that long since she had played her violin in her Uncle's barn and waited for Ronan to join her. The thought of Ronan no longer dredged up the old pain. It had been replaced with the pain of loss for her stolen home.

Mairead stepped away from the stall, and a shower of dirt fell on her head from above. She brushed away the grit and peered up to the rafters. A movement caught her eye—a golden head flashed in her vision before pulling back.

"Ciara? Is that you?" Mairead called up. No answer except a slight shuffle of straw. She stared at the rafters and saw the glimpse of a cream-coloured skirt. "Ciara?"

Mairead went to the ladder and started climbing up to the hayloft. When she reached the top, she found Ciara wedged in a corner, her knees drawn tight to her chest and her shoulders hunched forward. Half of her hair had come undone, and tangled golden strands were glued to her cheeks. Tears streaked her face, and her eyes were red-rimmed.

Mairead's heart lurched at the sight of Ciara's distress. She hadn't seen her cousin since the *cèilidh*. Every night she haunted the dovecote, but Ciara never turned up.

Cautiously, Mairead approached her cousin as one would a wounded creature. "Are you all right, Ciara, love?"

She didn't answer, only stared at the straw bedding as she drew herself into an even tighter ball. "Go away."

Mairead grew alarmed. Ciara spoke in a whisper, but there was a chasm of hurt in her tone. "You know I can't do that." She lowered herself to the floor beside her. "Why are you here?" She touched her cousin's arm, and Ciara flinched. Mairead drew back her hand. She had never seen Ciara this way before. When Uncle Mulriane and

Aunt Fianna were killed, Ciara had reacted with horror and shocked grief, but never despair. "Are you hurt?" Mairead turned her attention to Ciara's arms, looking for signs of bruises. There were none.

Ciara turned her face away, still refusing to meet Mairead's gaze. Her voice was weary. "Leave me. I need to be alone—don't look at me," she said, drawing her legs tight against her chest.

Mairead didn't know what to say. She felt the distance expanding between them as Ciara further wrapped her cocoon around herself. She wanted to shake her cousin, snap her out of her despair. *For the love of God, feel better, get better. How can I help you if you won't speak? This is killing me. If you love me, speak to me . . .*

But this wasn't about Mairead, so she gentled her words. "What has he done?" As soon as she asked, Ciara flinched.

Mairead's heart bled for her cousin. Bright beautiful Ciara, whom everyone loved, to be reduced to this despair. She wanted her cousin back, her sunny smiles—the girl who she had always looked up to, the sister she never had. Mairead wished she could lift some of the burden from her.

"I'm cursed," Ciara said dully.

Mairead sucked in her breath. The curse lay heavy on her conscience, but hearing this from her cousin's mouth seared her with guilt. She opened her mouth to reply but couldn't get any words out.

"You don't understand," Ciara continued. A long silence followed, then in a small voice, so low that Mairead had to strain to hear, Ciara said, "I've missed my courses."

Mairead's eyes widened, but she caught herself from betraying her dismay. She felt pitifully ill-equipped to offer solace. What could Mairead tell her—it would be all right? Would it?

Ciara put her hand over her mouth, stifling a sob. Tears flooded her eyes and streamed down her cheeks. Her shoulders shook as she cried, and Mairead edged closer, wrapping her arms around her. Soon Ciara turned into Mairead and allowed her to cradle her and stroke her damp hair.

"That's right, my love. Let it out. Nothing good will come of keeping it in."

"How can I bring a child into . . . this place? To be a slave?"

"The child would not be," Mairead said, though she wasn't entirely sure. The African women kept their children—then she remembered that those children were slaves. "You are indentured," she said more emphatically. "This child can't be a slave."

"It's better if the child were never born."

Mairead grew alarmed. She knew there were special herbs and potions, but she knew that Ciara couldn't live with herself if she caused her pregnancy to end. But what would happen to her when Wilton discovered her condition? Mairead remembered Roisin, from the ship. They had tossed her aside to fend for herself on the streets of Bridge Town. This couldn't be Ciara's fate.

"I'm here, Ciara," Mairead said. "I will always be here for you, my love."

Ciara disentangled herself and drew her knees to her chest. She turned her face away. "What will become of me when I'm big with child and . . . inconvenient? I can't stay here."

"There has to be a way to leave the island," Mairead said, surprising herself. The idea took hold, and the possibility gave her hope. "Listen, my love. If a ship could bring us here, it can take us away. There has to be a way to find passage."

Ciara met Mairead's gaze directly. "We have no money."

Mairead started warming to the idea. "But the Duchess does and—" She was about to say, "and her good for nothing wastrel of a son," but she didn't dare remind Ciara of the leech, not this moment. "And it would serve her right if we took a silver bowl or two. It doesn't have to be much, just enough for us to pay a captain."

Ciara smiled sadly, but it was a smile, and Mairead rejoiced. She'd sail a rowboat to Ireland if needed. Let hope fill their sails. The rest was fate.

"A fair tale, if I've heard one." Ciara sighed and cupped Mairead's face. "I love you, Mairead O'Coneill." She pressed a kiss on her forehead. "Remember that."

Iain kneaded the stitch in his side and gazed across the ripe cane fields. Storm clouds hovered in the distance. *Come this way.* He prayed for a break from the unrelenting heat. After the final bell, he'd head straight to the pond, even though that water was unbearably tepid.

Across the row, Dunsmore worked cutting his allotment of cane, another reason for Iain's testiness. He still hadn't forgiven the man for upending his authority over his men. Worse, all afternoon Dunsmore continued to needle him. "You cut like an auld wife, Locharbaidh."

"Piss off," Iain muttered under his breath. He didn't even have the energy to get into a proper row. The African wench assigned to help him gather the cut cane was efficient and knew her work, but she was not Mairead.

Iain paused to catch his breath, unconcerned that Dunsmore was significantly ahead of him. In the distance, he saw a horseman approaching the manor. Mount Vale received few visitors, that this new arrival piqued Iain's curiosity.

When the rider drew closer, Iain recognised Burke, the whoremonger. Interesting. It was no secret around the plantation that Wilton disappeared on a three-or-more-day bend in Speight's Town now and then, with Burke's establishment more than happy to host him there. What was a whoremonger doing at Mount Vale under the twitchy nose of the Duchess?

When the final bell rang, Iain didn't wait to exchange barbs with Dunsmore. He headed straight for the pond.

Iain sliced into the muddy water, not bothering to shuck his breeks. Ducks squawked and beat their wings to clear his path. When he reached far enough that his feet didn't touch the bottom, he tipped his body back and floated. He stayed like this for only a few moments, but he couldn't clear his mind from his troubles and entrenched discontent.

Nothing seemed to be moving, not this current, not his life, and certainly not their plans to escape this island. It seemed that every path led back to Dunsmore's half-baked plan to snatch a ship and sail blithely back home. Never mind that there were any number of foreign ships between here and Scotland warily circling each other, hot for war. Depending on the ship out in the harbour, they might have any one of those players chasing them as a prize. Iain hated the hand that chance played. There had to be a better way, but to his increasing aggravation, there didn't seem to be one.

It wasn't until darkness had settled in that Iain headed back, not to the compound, but instead to the manor house. He couldn't say why, only that his restlessness drove him there. The night air carried a touch of refreshing coolness, and the tree frogs chirped under a new moon. In the distance behind him, the men were mellowed out on mobbie, having survived another gruelling week.

Iain reached the rear gate of the courtyard. Through the trees, he could see the twinkling candlelight pouring through the windows. All the shutters had been thrown back to welcome the cooler night breezes, and raucous laughter spilled out. Wilton must still be entertaining the whoremaster.

As Iain was about to turn away, his eye caught a slight shadow flitting in the darkness. He paused a moment, eyes straining. Something was there—someone wee. He moved in to get a better look and suddenly knew who it was. Iain had been watching Mairead from the time she had set foot on the ship. What was she doing here?

Now that his eyes caught the form of her, he had no problem disengaging her from the shadows she easily melted into. She made for the side of the manor and stopped. Right under Wilton's study window. As with the rest of the house, the shutters were wide open. Golden candlelight poured out of the room, and indistinct voices drifted down to the courtyard. Iain knew exactly *what* she was doing, but why?

Iain crept along the wall towards her, careful not to make a sound, intent on getting her away from there. As he neared, Wilton's voice sounded close. He and Burke must be sitting by the open window. Iain's interest piqued further, and he was anxious to overhear their conversation.

Mairead's head tilted upwards with her attention firmly fixed on the conversation above. She gave no indication that she was aware of his approach. It suddenly occurred to him that sneaking up on her wasn't his best idea. One false step and he'd startle her into shrieking her head off.

Iain clamped a hand over Mairead's mouth and pulled her against him. She jerked in his grasp and twisted to free herself. Iain felt her scream building in her throat. Bending down, he whispered in her ear. "All right, Mouse?"

Her eyes widened, and she relaxed against him. Iain didn't release her at once. Pressed against his chest, she felt good in his arms. Her scent seemed to fill his head—not a perfumed, flowery scent, but something earthy, more stirring.

Mairead squirmed away, mouthing an unspoken question. Iain pressed a finger against her lips to silence her. It took all his willpower not to trace his thumb along her lower lip.

The sound of tinkling glasses turned their focus back to the window. In his mind, Iain could see the two men lounging in well-stuffed chairs, drinking their Spanish wine and leisurely smoking their pipes. The sweet smell of tobacco wafted out of the room.

Burke's voice sounded clear as day, though with an unpleasant edge. "I don't give a damn what the sugar cycle is, Wilton, and I sure as hell won't be waiting until all your crops come in. You owe me a large sum of money, and I mean to collect."

Iain's brow lifted. Debt to a whoremaster? *Very interesting.*

"Surely, you could give me more consideration?" Wilton's voice sounded annoyed. "The muscovado yields have been low this season, and my profit is down."

Courtesy of Alastair, no doubt. Idiot Southroner.

"That's not possible," Burke said. "I may be a purveyor of flesh, but I'm not completely oblivious to business, mate. The other planters boast that *their* profits are up, like the state of most cocks in the Little Bristol." There was a pause, followed by the scrape of a chair. "I'm not betting on sugar right now. Too many people seek to shave a bit for themselves. There is a war brewing between England and the Dutch Republic over trade—we're closer to it than ever before. If it does break out, shipments will be disrupted, and I'm out my investment."

"Won't happen, and if it does, you're entirely mistaken about the impact," Wilton drawled. A chair creaked against the wooden floor. "If war is declared, sugar prices will go up, not down."

"Ah, but to get your sugar to market, you'll have to slip past the Dutch. And they've been put out over being shut out of this island this past year. And now there is a new wolf hunting the seas—Prince Rupert, the King's bloody cousin."

"He's all bluff," Wilton said with a short laugh.

"And hungry for a prize," Burke said. "Picking off any ship that hasn't declared for Charles Stuart, which is most of them."

"He's in the Virgin Islands and a long way from Barbados. Our ships have nothing to fear from Rupert." Wilton's voice didn't sound convincing, not even to Iain.

"You're a fool to think that, mate," Burke said. "Those islands are straight on the route to Bristol. Hard to restock water and supplies before the long Atlantic crossing when you're skirting around a hostile fleet."

Too bad Rupert couldn't make it farther south and liberate this hellish island, Iain thought. They were on their own.

A moment of silence, then Wilton said wearily, "Very well. Give me a chance to win the sum back."

"Your luck has soured, mate, but you might consider another arrangement."

"And that would be?" Wilton replied.

"My business is growing, and lately the ships aren't bringing in the cargo I need."

"White or dark?" Wilton asked.

"White wenches are more in demand."

"Good, because I'm not giving you any of the African sluts. They're too valuable to me."

"I am particularly interested in your Irish housemaid—the pretty blond. She'd do well in Speight's Town with my customers. Sell her to me and I'll postpone the settlement of your debts until your income is sorted. Consider her interest on a loan."

Mairead stiffened in Iain's arms. He glanced down—her face paled.

"That won't do at all. I'm enjoying her far too much," Wilton's peevish voice carried across. "Perhaps when I tire of her, but not now. You have her sister, be happy with her."

"Had."

"What happened to her?" Wilton sounded mildly curious.

"Dead. A mean cove played her rough. Don't worry, I was well compensated."

Iain felt Mairead shudder. Her breath hitched sharply in her throat, and she now turned ghastly white. To hear of her kinswoman's death, and in this manner . . .

"If you're looking for a replacement, I have another offer," Wilton said. "I've an Irish field servant who was brought in with the same lot. You bid on her at the auction, I've been told."

"The scrawny one?" Burke said.

"You can have her."

Iain lifted his gaze to the window, rage roiling in his gut. *Bastards.* When Mairead winced, he realised he'd been gripping her too tightly.

"She's not worth as much as the blond, and you know it. Not enough to buy my patience, mate."

Iain gritted his teeth. Mairead was very much worth twice than any one of them.

"You're not getting the blond."

A fist slammed on the table, making Mairead jump.

"You owe me a pissing fortune, and we're here debating about sluts?" Burke snarled. A few moments passed, and when he spoke again his tone was clipped and business-like. "You have one month to get this sorted. When I next return, I expect my money, or I start taking my own pound of flesh any way I can. I will make matters unpleasant for you, mate. Your credit will dry up, and with that, this plantation. You'll be begging me to take your fields."

Iain released Mairead and motioned for her to step away from the window. The men continued to argue, but he had heard enough. He led her away from the house and through the gate, not stopping until they were well away from the house.

Mairead was shivering, and her eyes were enormous. Her distress cut right through him. He wanted to smash Burke and Wilton for even suggesting the exchange.

Shitten bastards.

"I'm sorry about your cousin, lass," Iain said.

She nodded and looked away. Her eyes seemed overly bright. "Bronagh and I weren't close . . . But she didn't deserve that." Mairead paused and glanced back at the manor. "And they wanted me to replace her." Shuddering, she hugged herself.

The urge to throttle all of them with his bare hands ripped through Iain. He cursed under his breath. "You'll not be sold to a whorehouse. I'll not allow that."

Mairead faced him, worry, frustration and grief warring across her features. "How have you any say?"

Her words slammed into him. She had touched acid to an open wound. Iain needed no reminders that he was naught but a powerless bondsman. Less than a man. Worse, it had come from *her*. If they were in Scotland, she would never have cause to say that or even doubt him. He scowled and ground out bitterly, "You're right. I don't." He turned and strode away from her.

"Where are you going?"

He didn't answer.

"Iain?" she called out to him in a low tone.

Iain continued to walk away. He had to get away, not just from Mairead. If he didn't get off this island, he'd be less than a man and better off dead. Dunsmore's half-witted plan might be the only chance he had of reclaiming his freedom. He had nothing to lose.

Chapter 20

Heat sapped every ounce of energy from Mairead. Her head spun, and her breath came out in shallow gasps. She couldn't do it anymore. Life was unbearable. The hurt in Iain's eyes haunted her, and she deeply regretted what she had said to him, knowing that she could never unsay it. She had lashed out at him unfairly. Wilton's cavalier bartering for both her and Ciara had unravelled her. *And poor Bronagh.*

Burke's casual words about her cousin's death had unnerved Mairead. No regret, no concern, except that he had been compensated for the loss of one of his women. Her mind shied away from what her cousin must have gone through—what her final moments would have been like. How was she ever going to tell Ciara? She couldn't—not yet. This would break her cousin. It would be a greater kindness for Mairead to bear the weight of this knowledge on her own—for now.

Mairead's gaze swept across the cassava fields. Acres and acres of waist high plants still to be harvested—she'd *never* reach the end. Wearily, she tugged at a root, but it stubbornly clung to the clay soil. She threw her back into it and pulled with all her strength. Losing her balance, she fell to the ground. Giving in to exhaustion, she collapsed.

She lay there, at her lowest and desperately afraid. She had no desire to get up. One more moment, she promised herself. Then she'd force herself to rise and continue. The wind picked up, but if anything, it blew hotter.

In the distance, the Arawak women called out to one another in their language. Uini had taught Mairead a few words, including the one for *overseer*, but at this moment, she couldn't make sense of their exchange. Her eyes felt heavy . . .

Mairead jolted awake. She realised she had dropped off, but for how long? Sitting up, she looked over the plants to search for Potts. To her relief, he wasn't around—nor anyone else.

The temperature had changed. Overhead, dark clouds blotted out the sun. Storm coming. The clouds changed colour, taking on a sick green cast that was terrifying to behold.

From a distance, Uini called for her urgently, "Mari. Mari."

Mairead scrambled to her feet. The Arawak women were far away now, running towards the compound. Uini paused to call for her again.

A bolt of lightning sliced through the charcoal clouds and filled the air with its thunder. Mairead started running for the road. When Uini saw her coming, she abandoned her search and raced for cover after her kin.

Mairead dashed after her. Big splatters of rain were an ominous warning before the heavens opened and great sheets of water gushed down. Mairead ran harder, but she found herself struggling against the storm. The rainwater cut channels into the clay soil, making the ground under her feet slick. The water blinded her, and she could not see more than a few feet ahead.

Crack! A spidery flash of light scored the sky, instantly followed by earsplitting thunder. Mairead shrieked and dropped to the ground. Water rushed over her legs. She struggled to her feet, but the grasping mud sucked her back down.

As the thunder faded, Mairead heard someone shouting for her.

"Mairead!"

"Here!" she shouted over the wind. *"I'm here!"* Mairead had no idea who called her, but she fought her way in the direction of the voice. Through sheets of rain, Iain materialised. Mairead sobbed her relief and scrambled to reach him. Water streamed down his face, plastering his blond hair against his head. He clamped his hand around her arm and pulled her to him.

"This way!" he shouted.

Together they pressed towards the compound. Mairead slipped and fell to her knees, and Iain hauled her up. Slashes of rain angled horizontally as the storm intensified. She tried to take a few more steps. Rushing water sucked at the mud beneath her feet, and her waterlogged skirt wrapped around her ankles. She'd never make it.

"I can't!" Terror cut her at the knees.

Iain scooped her into his arms and ploughed through the teeth of the storm. Mairead clung to him. He nearly lost his footing, and Mairead's breath locked in her chest. The road was now a raging stream that reached as high as his knees.

He continued uphill, and a building loomed up ahead of them— one of the storage sheds. Iain reached the raised hut. He climbed the wooden stairs and pushed his shoulder against the door. Together, they tumbled inside.

Iain released Mairead and threw his weight against the door to close it against the grasping storm. Finally he managed to secure it. The wind shook the hut walls and threatened to lift off the roof, but the structure held. For now.

Sopping wet and shaking, Mairead opened her mouth to thank him, but he didn't give her that opportunity. He rounded on her in a high fury.

"What in sweet hell where you doing out there alone, woman?" Rivulets of water dripping from his whiskers made him look like an enraged beast. "The others had the good sense to take cover, but not you, daft woman." Without waiting for her to break through her stunned silence, he ploughed on in a proper rage. "You could have been swept away, woman. Have you no ken for your safety?"

Iain the Ogre had returned, snarling his rage and ready to rip off her head. His attack was unfair and wholly unwarranted, but Mairead suddenly realised that fear was driving his fury. For her. A sudden giddy warmth swept through her.

"Oh, you impossible man!" Mairead grabbed his shirt and pulled him down for a kiss.

Iain's surprise lasted less than a heartbeat. He drew her tightly against him, and a groan rumbled at the back of his throat. Mouth slanting against hers, he kissed her back with a ferocity that snatched her breath. The taste of his mouth, the musky scent of sweat and wet linen, the hardness of his body pressed against hers drove Mairead wild. She brazenly wanted more, and there was no question that he did too.

He released her lips long enough to devour a path down her neck. Tickling, teasing her skin. Her breath hitched in her throat, and she tipped her head back, offering him every sensitive square inch. He hitched her higher, and she felt the hardness of his manhood even through layers of smock and petticoat. She needed less fabric— no barriers. His mouth paused its sweet torment, and blue eyes met hazel.

"Don't you *dare* stop," Mairead breathed.

"God, I'm past that," he groaned against her mouth. His tongue claimed hers. She arched her hips against him, rubbing against his arousal. *Good Lord,* she wanted him so badly. She always had. From the first moment in the ship's hold, she had been drawn to him like a lodestone.

Iain's hand stroked her breast, caressing her through the wet, clinging fabric. His thumb circled her nipple slowly, driving her mad. Mairead wanted to crawl out of her skin. Hot, wet heat spread between her legs.

Mairead offered herself openly and without hesitation. Ronan had never made her feel this way. She had been hesitant and shy with Ronan, as though one wrong glance would shatter the fairy tale. But not with this man, who was built of flesh, bone and hard sinew.

She was seized with a need to unwrap him, to feel his bare skin against hers. Tugging at his sodden shirt, Mairead wrestled it over his head. When he was free of the damned thing, she ran her fingers across the light furrowing of hair over his broad chest, then followed a path down his taut stomach. He drew in a sharp breath, and she could feel his muscles tensing. That wasn't enough. She needed to reduce him to a mass of quivering nerves, as he had her.

"You'll undo me too soon, lass," Iain said. He sucked and teased her bottom lip before his mouth slanted over hers to claim her in a thoroughly scorching kiss.

Their fingers snatched at each other's clothing, making short work of drawstrings and buttons. Mairead's smock and petticoats were dashed to a heap on the ground beside his shirt, followed by his breeches.

Sweet Blessed Mother.

Iain lowered her to the floor and settled between her thighs. He claimed one nipple in his mouth, rolling it with his tongue before exploring the other. A million shivers coursed through her. Fire and heat.

Her hands explored his body, running her hands over his shoulders, his arms, careful to avoid his healing back, until she found his buttocks.

Iain fingers parted her thighs and stroked her seam, reducing her to jelly. From a million miles away, Mairead heard the wind howling and the pounding rain. She didn't care. She lost all manner of thought, her world confined to every sensation that fired under Iain's touch.

When he entered her, she gasped and tilted her hips, wrapping her legs around him. He filled her completely. Their eyes locked on each other as he moved deep inside her. She welcomed every earthy stroke and didn't hold herself back. His touch drove her wild with need. He was the master musician coaxing exquisite notes from her, body and soul. Sensation built upon sensation. With the final strains, she shattered and cried out against the waves of pleasure coursing through her. At the last moment, he withdrew from her and shuddered his own release in her arms.

Iain held Mairead and listened to the rain drumming on the roof. After an hour, the storm had slackened. Though it still rained, the wind had lost some of its bite.

The top of Mairead's head was tucked under his chin, and her warm cheek lay against his chest. She fit his arms perfectly, like a key in a lock. He could feel the flutter of her heart, and her soft breath tickled his skin. Idly, he played with one damp curl, twisting it between thumb and forefinger. A deep brown, her hair had a living warmth teased out by the harsh sun.

Mairead's passion surprised him, and yet it shouldn't have. He was discovering that there were depths to this woman that few could match.

He brushed a kiss on the top of her head and sighed. They couldn't remain like this, but he wasn't ready to break the moment. Not yet. For the first time in too long, a satisfying peace settled over him. The instant he released her, their situation would intrude.

Mairead stirred in his arms and lifted her head to look up at him. A warm pink coloured her cheeks. "I thought you were sleeping."

As a reply, Iain kissed her deeply, savouring her closeness, knowing it would soon end. His body had other plans, and for a few moments, he warred a pitched battle with his better judgment. Reluctantly, he disengaged and pulled away.

"Come, lass, we'd best leave."

Mairead gave him an uncertain smile and nodded. She eased from his side and stood up. While she donned her smock, she kept her eyes averted. Her fingers fumbled with the laces of her petticoat.

Iain pulled on his breeches and wondered how he was going to say what he needed to say. If they were anywhere but here, he'd be bending a knee, pledging his devotion to her. But they were here. Reality was a mean-spirited witch that he wanted to smother. "This is complicated, all of this," he blurted out, then cringed. Not the best way to have started. He marshalled his thoughts and tried again, "Mairead—"

"I know. 'Twas but a moment of madness." Mairead kept her eyes down as she tried to work out a knot in the drawstring of her petticoat. She added in a low voice, "What you must think of me."

Iain's eyes widened. Did she think so poorly of him? "That hurts, Mairead. What kind of jackass do you take me for?"

She looked up, startled. "Were you not about to beat a hasty retreat?"

"Have you no faith, woman?"

She hugged herself, still looking uncertain. "Once," she said barely above a whisper. "Once I had a great deal."

Iain lifted her chin and forced her to look him square in the eye. "Aye, it was mad and foolish and all manner of complicated. I can offer you nothing, Mairead, neither house nor name," he said grimly. "This is not what I'd want for you. Neither of us have the luxury of seeing the horizon. But no matter the consequences, I regret nothing where you're concerned. I'll not forsake you, believe in that."

Hazel eyes flecked with green searched his face. She must have recognised the depth of his sincerity, for she finally smiled. "One moment at a time, Iain." She touched her fingers to his cheek.

Iain bent down and kissed the tip of her pert nose, then brushed a kiss on her parted lips. He gathered her in his arms and buried his face in her hair. *One moment at a time.* With a sigh, he released her. "I'd better get you back to the compound before they notice us gone, or there will be an uproar."

Just as she was about to step away, Iain remembered a sensation—a memory of touch on her right shoulder. "Wait." His finger hooked at the shoulder of her smock and tugged it down slightly to reveal puckered skin surrounding a crude mark. "What is this?"

Mairead gasped and pulled away, adjusting her smock to hide the mark. "Don't."

"Mairead?"

She didn't answer at first, only tugged at the sleeves of her smock. "Back in Ireland, when they brought us to Cork . . . they branded us. As they do cattle."

Iain bit back a curse. He could imagine her terrified and in pain, imagine the scorching of her delicate skin. How she hadn't crumbled before now, he didn't ken. With a sigh, he drew her close and wrapped his arms around her, cradling her close to his chest. "It seems that we're a matched pair after all."

Mairead and Iain slipped out of the storehouse, and she waited while he refastened the latch. The rain had slackened and steady drizzle replaced the earlier torrent. The air grew heavy with the heat already. She walked beside him, her fingers brushing against his own. They had to be careful, though. Potts would make their lives a misery if he perceived their affection.

The storm had made a mess of the grounds, broken leaves scattered around like flotsam. Dips and slopes in the terrain had become fast-flowing channels and rivers. The main road was entirely washed out, and they were forced to head in the direction of the pond and circle around.

As they reached the trail plunging down to the pond, the ground under Iain loosened. He slid down a crumbling slope and landed knee-deep in water and mud.

Mairead gasped and held out her hand. "Are you hurt?"

"Nay, but stay back. The ground here is unstable." He cursed and swore as he tried to climb out of the pit. Every step he took only mired him further. "*Argh! I hate* this place! Don't you *dare* get any ideas to help me out, right."

Mairead stifled a laugh and shook her head. "I can fetch Dunsmore if you like."

Iain launched into a colourful series of expletives.

"You're too loud," she said, laughing. Looking up, she glanced at the direction of the pond, only now it was more of a raging river. And there, in the distance at its swollen edge, she saw a familiar figure.

"Ciara?" Mairead stepped away from Iain and headed towards the pond. The water surged perilously high, and her cousin was far too close to it. *What is she doing there?*

"Where are you going, woman?" Iain asked. Mairead didn't answer as she headed to the pond. His tone switched from annoyance to sudden concern. "Mairead, wait—" Iain called out after her. "Damn this—wait for me—I'm coming."

Mairead walked faster. Even from this distance, she could tell that something was wrong. Her cousin paced oddly along the banks holding a fist-sized rock in one hand.

"Ciara," Mairead called out, but her voice was drowned out by the roar of the flowing water. *"Ciara?"* This time louder.

Ciara didn't turn her head; instead, she focused entirely on the swollen pond, unmindful of the water rushing up to soak her petticoat. She slipped the rock into her already bulging pocket.

"Ciara!" Mairead called again, panic spreading through her like ice. She picked up her pace. "For pity's sake, Ciara. *Move away from there.*"

Mairead's cries must have reached her, for Ciara finally turned around at the water's edge. Their eyes locked. Ciara's face was stark white, as pale as the foaming water. The wind tore at her golden hair and lashed loose tendrils against her thin cheeks. No emotion, no tears. No welcoming smile.

Then to Mairead's horror, Ciara began to advance into the water. A cold chill snaked down Mairead's spine, and she gasped as realisation struck her. She sprinted towards Ciara, fending off the drooping branches that slapped her face and snatched at her skirt. "Ciara!" Mairead slipped and skidded her way down the muddy slope to reach her. *"Ciara!"*

Ciara took a few more steps before the strong current pulled her in. The water rushed over her head, churning and swirling into an eddy, before she was swept away. Golden tendrils fanned out before they disappeared below the foamy surface.

Mairead screamed. She reached the water and charged inside. "Ciara! *Stop!*" She floundered, splashing and fighting against the current. The water was cold, turbulent and angry. It kept trying to spit her out even as it welcomed her cousin.

Deeper into the pond, the top of Ciara's hair bobbed just under the surface, her body swept downriver by the raging waters. Mairead lost her footing and a rush of water swept over her head. Her shift twisted around her legs and pulled her down. She pushed against the muddy pond floor and thrashed to break the surface. Coughing up murky water, she croaked, *"Ciara!"* Mairead looked around, but the water blinded her. In the distance, she heard Iain calling her name. Another wave washed over her, and the undercurrent dragged her down again.

A strong arm latched on to her, and she cleared the surface. Iain pulled her against him and hauled her out of the water. Mairead thrashed against him and screamed for Ciara, but his hold only tightened.

"It's too late, Mairead," she heard him say as he brought her back to shore.

"It's not! I have to find her!" Tears poured down her face. She searched the water for signs of Ciara and saw nothing except churning, muddy water.

"She's gone, Mairead," Iain said.

Gone.

Mairead screamed her grief. When Iain reached the shore and released her, Mairead crumpled to the ground.

Chapter 21

—◆—

Iain's gut wrenched to see Mairead unravel. After everything she'd endured, he couldn't allow Ciara's suicide to finally break her. He scooped her up in his arms and headed back to the compound. Hysteria had turned to shock—she couldn't stop shaking. Her wet skin felt icy, and he feared that she was close to losing consciousness.

"Mairead, lass—do ye hear me?" He adjusted her in his arms. She barely stirred.

The first person he came across was Uini, at work outside her hut clearing fallen boughs.

"Uini—she needs your help," he called out to her.

"She hurt?"

"Nay, but the lass has suffered a great shock." With a few words, he let her know about Ciara.

Uini had him bring Mairead into her own hut and lay her down on a grass pallet in the corner. The woman drew the shutters, then mixed a white powder with a cup of water. "Drink, then sleep," Uini said with her customary curtness.

Iain watched Mairead with a fist to his heart. Her breathing was shallow, and she occasionally twitched involuntarily as though her body tensed for action.

Uini came up to Iain and stared down at her charge. "She strong."

"Aye." He understood the depth of what Mairead was going through.

"You strong. For her."

Iain looked up in surprise, wondering how obvious his feelings were. Uini's black eyes reflected her wry amusement. Iain had long since stopped questioning the wisdom of old women. They were all the same, seeing past things that most people couldn't.

"I need to leave her here with you," he said. "I've a matter to attend."

Iain left the hut, but instead of returning to his quarters, he headed for the manor. Rage spurred him on. *Goddamn it*, what a senseless death. Seeing Mairead incapacitated with grief made him want to smash something. He didn't need to know why Ciara had taken her life to guess the source of her despair—Wilton. And Iain wanted to be the one to fling it in the worm's face.

He reached the courtyard and pushed through the gate with such force that it slammed against the post and tore off its hinges. Lucy and another housemaid were in the forecourt cleaning up the ravaged herbal beds when Iain strode past them. He charged up to the front door, taking the stone steps two at a time.

"You can't go in there," Lucy shrieked and chased after him. "Providence Moss will have your hide."

"She could try." Iain strode into the hallway, damn his rights. "Master Wilton," he called out. "You'd best get down here."

No sign of Wilton, but Providence Moss came rushing in from the back of the house, sputtering with outrage.

"We do not allow bondsmen in the manor," she hissed. "Your place is in the fields."

"I have news for Himself." Iain stepped around the witch and went to call out again when he saw the Duchess descending the wooden staircase.

"Never mind, Providence, go fetch Potts." The Duchess stopped in front of Iain, her hands folded over her waist. "You are braying for my son?"

Iain coiled his anger. He didn't have much time before Potts arrived. "Your housemaid, Ciara—" he started, but Wilton arrived from his study.

"What of her?" Wilton asked.

Iain faced Wilton—the first time he had been close to the man. He wasn't impressed. He had the useless look of a pampered weasel. The wastrel had a weak chin and very little backbone, from what he could tell. Wilton's eyes kept darting to his dour mother. "The lass took her own life. Drowned in the rising waters."

"Dead?" Wilton blinked. "Her own life, you say?"

"That is quite unfortunate," the Duchess said, no more ruffled than if Iain had told her the time of day. "Now I suppose I'll have to find a replacement for her."

Iain's mouth tightened. The woman had all the warmth of the North Sea, and her callousness left Iain, for once, speechless.

"You may leave, bondsman," the Duchess said. "You've given us the news, and for that we are grateful. It saves us the bother of searching the grounds for her."

"I wouldn't want to inconvenience you." Let his sarcasm wash over them. He took a ragged breath, suddenly weary. "I'll organise the lads to find the body—give her a decent burial."

"Absolutely not," the Duchess said crisply. "We gave her a decent living and adequate quarters. She had no right to take such a foolish action. Let her rot where she washed up, and to the others a warning—there will not be a decent burial if anyone is foolish enough to take their own life. I care not if they're Christian or heathen. I expressly forbid anyone from interfering, and any who do will be swiftly punished."

This was what it came down to. Control. These privileged people demanded full autonomy over the lives of their servants and slaves.

Anyone who took their own life exercised one final, irrevocable act of rebellion, and this they couldn't stomach.

A pox on them.

"Are we clear, bondsman?" the Duchess said sharply.

"Aye," he ground out.

"That is all, then," she said in dismissal.

Iain clenched his fists at his side. "You'll get no argument from me." He turned around and stormed out of the manor. Wilton was useless. They considered them nothing more than livestock. Every slave and indentured servant only had worth if this pair could get hide, bones and a scrap of meat from them.

Rage coursed through him. The Wiltons could rot. But he knew what he had to do.

Iain waited until night settled before heading out on his own with a shovel and an old blanket. He would have liked to take a donkey with him, but he wouldn't have made it out of the barn before being stopped.

Iain took a roundabout way to the pond and followed its course downriver. Normally, the pond fed a modest creek that ended in a gully over a mile farther along, but the rainwater had swollen the creek into a swift-flowing river. Most of the bank had been eaten away from the storm, so he maintained a respectful distance from its edge.

Ciara's body had washed up at the end of the gully. She had been dashed against the rocks and lay there, twisted and white in the pale moonlight. Her skin was bruised purple and slashed from the rocks and gritty mud that had swept her away. Her clothes were torn and caked with mud.

Iain waded into the water to reach her. He placed his hand on Ciara's shoulder. *Poor lass.* He paused a moment, furious at the uselessness of her end. At least Mairead wasn't here to see this. Couldn't Ciara have found another way? The thought bothered

279

him—it had been on his mind all along his trek. Who could say what would push any of them past their breaking point. Even Mairead.

Grimly, he lifted Ciara in his arms and trudged away from the rocks. When he returned to the shore, he laid her in the blanket he had brought and wrapped it around her like a shroud. He picked a spot close to the slope of the gully, as far from the creek as he could get, then started to dig. The soil was rocky at first, then became harder and clay-like.

As he worked, he thought of Innis and their stillborn son. It should have been his hands that prepared their grave. He'd finally accepted there was nothing he could have done to change things, but at least he could do this for Mairead.

Mairead awakened in the night with Uini sleeping beside her. A full moon poured through the windows and filled the hut with a bluish light. For a moment, Mairead felt nothing. She floated in a world of various shades of blue and grey, bloodless and without emotion. Then the grief flooded her. Ciara's forlorn gaze haunted her, burned into Mairead's mind. Across the pond, she had seen her cousin's despair. Had felt it.

Mairead's chest constricted, and a tight band squeezed her until she could barely breathe. She sat upright, sucking in a lungful of air, heart beating in her throat. Ciara would be forever lost to her, lost to everyone. She'd be forced to wander purgatory until the end of time.

She couldn't stay here. She needed to go somewhere. Anywhere.

Careful not to wake Uini, Mairead left the hut.

Beneath the moon, ringed with a double halo and cradled by clouds, she followed the trail to the pond. The only sound was the steady rushing of water and the whistling of the wind. The creek had turned into a river with the runoff water. She was both repelled and drawn to the place. Mairead followed its downhill course, plunging into the gully. Silvery mist rose up from the water in cool vapours.

In the distance, a man worked with a shovel. Even in the dark, Mairead knew every nuance of his form, from the way he moved to the way he planted his feet solidly in the earth. A mound of dirt had been piled up beside him.

When Mairead approached Iain, he stopped and turned around to face her. Though he was in shadow, there was no mistaking the softness of his expression. Her gaze slid to a shrouded body lying a few feet away.

"Thank you." She couldn't bear it if Ciara didn't have a proper resting place.

Iain drove the shovel into the dirt and walked towards her. He cupped her cheek with his work-calloused hand and wiped away a stray tear. Bending down, he kissed her with a tenderness that caused Mairead to further unravel. She choked back a sob and buried her face in his chest. His arms encircled her.

"I have you, my Mairead," he murmured in her ear. "My strength is yours." He brushed a kiss against her hair.

She couldn't stop crying. She held on to him and sobbed until her throat ached. He was her only safety in a storm-tossed harbour. When there were more tears, Iain hummed under his breath and soothed her further still.

"Come, say your farewell," he said. "Dawn will be upon us soon, and we need to be back before anyone stirs."

She nodded and wiped away her tears. Mairead dropped beside Ciara's shrouded body and drew aside the blanket from her face. Her cousin looked so peaceful, so at odds with the passion that had driven her into the raging waters.

"Forgive me," Mairead whispered, pressing a kiss upon Ciara's smooth forehead. There could be no answer. She wished that she had told Ciara this before now.

Mairead covered her cousin's face with the blanket. She hugged herself tightly as Iain lowered Ciara into the grave. When he climbed out, Mairead scooped up a fistful of soil and sprinkled it over Ciara's body. She watched while Iain covered the grave.

Mairead sat down on a log and hugged her knees to her chest. Iain sat beside her in silence. "Ciara was with child," she told him in a dull voice. "Wilton may not have known, but you heard that his concern with her would have lasted only as long as she entertained him."

How deep into despair must Ciara have descended that living no longer meant anything to her—to end not only her own but an innocent life? Ciara would never reach heaven—she'd be doubly damned. "It's my fault." Her curse, uttered in a rash thirst for vengeance, had devoured her cousin—devoured them all. All for the sake of a thoughtless, fickle man.

Iain took her hand and squeezed it tightly. "Nay, lass, it isn't."

The need to confess tore her apart. He'd probably turn from her, but she could no longer live with the crushing guilt. "There was a man, back in Ireland." She kept her eyes on the ground and avoided meeting his gaze. "He said he loved me." She cringed at her foolishness. "I had been taken by his fair face and silvered tongue." Refreshed pain drew her down. Mairead took a deep breath and continued, "Ronan was mine as long as Ciara wasn't his."

Iain didn't say a word, and Mairead drew her legs up to her chest and hugged them tightly.

"I wished for Ciara to understand what it meant to lose everyone she cared about—like I had. My da, my brothers, my home . . . everything." Mairead stared ahead, gaze fixed at the watery sky that lightened with the dawn. "I cursed them," her voice sounded small. "I cursed them, you see." Finally, she turned to Iain to see his reaction. He remained stoic and silent and gave nothing of his thoughts away.

"The soldiers came soon after," her voice cracked. "I didn't mean it. I never meant to hurt anyone." The tears fell on her hands.

Iain touched her arm and brushed away a tear with his finger. "It's not your fault, Mairead," he said and kissed her head. "If I was to be held to account for all the nonsense I spewed in the heat of the moment, lightning would have struck my sorry arse ages ago." His voice hardened. "You have every right to have been hurt over that arseworm. He was a right fool."

She shook her head.

Iain cupped her chin and urged her to meet his eyes. "We both have our demons. Time to put it away, Mairead. No matter what happens, we will grit this out and fight our way through it. There is no giving up, ken? No matter what comes, we face this together."

Mairead met his keen blue eyes and took strength from his steady fire. She nodded. "Together."

Chapter 22

———◆———

Iain watched Dunsmore with distaste. The man returned late in the evening when the men were finishing up their bowl of loblolly around the campfire. He helped himself to the last of the gruel and shovelled it into his mouth like a starving man.

Tam had bypassed Iain for the shipment to Speight's Town and chose Dunsmore instead. Again. Ever since his confrontation with Alastair, Iain had been frozen out. Alastair couldn't have been plainer with his answer to Iain—he'd do nothing to help them off the island.

And yet Iain told no one about Alastair's activities, not even Masterton. Something told him to keep it to himself. Things had shifted in the group, and the bonds between him and the others became more brittle and frayed.

"Tam's a good man," Dunsmore said, wiping his mouth with the back of his hand. "Has a good handle on his lads, unlike others I know." He aimed his smirk at Iain.

Iain refused to be baited by Dunsmore—he'd only be handing him a victory. It gnawed Iain to see how the damned cur eclipsed him with his own men, but he refused to abandon them to the machinations of Dunsmore. And he needed the sod to get him and Mairead off this island.

Most of the others, including Tam's men, had dispersed to their huts. Dunsmore sat down beside Iain, and as though that was the sign, Killean Ross, Angus Rae, and Masterton the Younger gathered close.

"What news from Speight's Town?" Iain asked.

Dunsmore wiped his mouth with the back of his hand before he answered. "The harbour is full of ships being loaded with sugar. They're anxious to get as much of it sent out as they can."

"We should move soon, then," Killean said.

"Aye." Dunsmore cast a glance around before leaning in. "The *Jane Marie* was in port while we were there."

Just the name of the ship that had brought them to this pisshole left a sour taste in Iain's mouth.

"A few of the lads helped them store the barrels in their holds," Dunsmore continued. "Struck up a conversation with the quartermaster. Same bastard as before."

"Did he know you?" Angus Rae said.

Dunsmore shook his head. "We were cattle to him then."

"Why did you have to help with the loading?" Iain asked. It struck him as odd. "We never did that before."

"They were in a piss-hurry," Dunsmore said. "Besides the natural storms, they were hoping to beat the unnatural ones." After a dramatic pause, he said, "Word came in—England has declared war on the Dutch."

Iain swore under his breath. "Bloody Southroners." Those whoresons had a genius for complicating things.

"What does this mean for us?" Killean asked.

"Dogs will be after more scraps," Iain said tersely. "I wouldn't be surprised if they'd send a fleet down here to protect their interests."

"The *Jane Marie* will be sailing for Bristol in three days," Dunsmore said. "She's loading extra victuals in order to make a clean run of it." A hungry leer spread across his ugly face. "Over the next couple of days, her crew will be in harbour, swiving the tarts one last time while they can. We'll nae have another opportunity to make our move."

Iain looked up at the eastern sky. Too early for moonrise, but he considered the phase of the moon. In two days, it would be a late quarter moon, and the timing couldn't be better. Alastair and his men would be away from the plantation, on their way to the caves and the smuggled sugar. His absence would help them escape after all.

"Midnight," Iain said. "We'll act then. Killean, you fill in our lads in the other hut. No loose tongues."

"We'll need a diversion," Dunsmore said.

"Hit them where it counts," Iain said grimly. "We burn the sugar works. It won't take long for the stillroom to ignite. A single open flame in a room full of rum vapour is all that we need. Dunsmore, can you manage that?"

"Himself has spoken," Dunsmore muttered.

"Himself *has* spoken," Iain ground out. "It's my lead we follow, right?"

Dunsmore's reply came as a grunt.

"And there's one more thing," Iain said. "Mairead is coming with us." Silence. Angus glanced at Dunsmore while Masterton chewed on his lower lip. "You don't agree?"

"Absolutely not," Dunsmore spat. "You've gone mad, Locharbaidh. We can't take a wench with us."

"This isn't your decision."

"Aye, it is. I'm risking my life in this venture, and I will have an equal say in this. If she holds us down, if she can't pull her weight—and you know she can't—then we'll be easy to pick off by the Southroners. There's a full garrison in town guarding the harbour."

"She'll be a hindrance," Masterton said. "We need speed and agility to get past the watch."

"Aye, stealth, nae a skirt," Angus said.

Masterton held Iain's gaze. "The lass will be a damaging diversion. You'll be focused on her."

"Is this what you've all decided?" Iain said, for once completely disgusted with his men. They had been through a great deal over the years, kept each others' back. He couldn't believe they were capable of this. "You're all cowards, then, to leave a lass here in her time of need."

One of Tam's men drifted a little closer, likely wondering what they were discussing, which saved Dunsmore from being throttled. The man hovered close, no doubt on Tam's orders.

Masterton, who had a canny ability to see everything, spoke louder for the benefit of the Irishman. "Three—you owe Dunsmore three plantain."

"You're wrong, old man," Killean chimed in, taking Masterton's lead. "Locharbaidh owes him nothing." The Irishman moved along, losing interest.

Dunsmore held Iain's gaze and said, "I say we put a vote to it. Who agrees that Locharbaidh is full of shite and needs tae get his brains out of his cock? Who's with *me*?"

Everyone nodded, even Killean finally. Iain stared at them one by one in impotent fury. Their willingness to side with Dunsmore was a swift kick in his gut. These were *his* men. They had all bled for one another. They were supposed to be loyal to *him*, not to this bootlicking arseworm.

"This is how it is?" Iain said. His gaze raked across the others, but no one moved. Even Killean looked uncomfortable.

"Aye," Dunsmore replied.

"You'd leave behind a woman to save your cowardly hides," Iain ground out through gritted teeth. "I'm ashamed of you all, I am. You're nae but a scabbit lot."

Masterton bristled at that. "Think, man. Alastair is looking out for the lass. If we take her, we'll put everyone at risk. She'll suffer for it too."

"That excuse make you feel better?" Iain said bitterly. Mairead wasn't Alastair's to protect.

"If she means so much to you, then stay here with her. Find your own way out," Dunsmore said.

"This will be on your heads," Iain said, not bothering to disguise his disgust.

"So be it," Dunsmore said. He glanced around to make sure that no one was near. "This Sunday. We break into the manor and seize the weapons while I set fire to the sugar works. Then we're free men. That's all."

Iain didn't get up when the others did. Dunsmore strutted to the hut with the others trailing in his wake. *Shitten bastard.* Iain waited while the burning embers smouldered to ash and the men settled down for the night.

Instead of joining them in the hut, Iain headed for the pond. His feet found the well-worn path, but he did not stop or linger at the water. He continued farther down, towards the cassava fields.

The storage shed rose darkly amongst the trees. Movement drew his attention. A small slip of a shadow approached him.

Iain pulled her into his arms and kissed her fiercely. He felt her initial surprise before she responded with equal passion. He wanted to devour her, drink in every ounce of her essence. A sovereign cure for a debilitating malady.

"You were so late," she said breathlessly. "I thought you wouldn't come—"

"Ah, lass, I can't stay away."

Her lips parted in a smile. He couldn't resist claiming another kiss that left them both breathless. When he finally paused for breath, he said, "Be ready. We're leaving Sunday night."

Mairead's nerves were afire. In two days, they were going to make their escape.

She barely slept the night, plagued by doubt and fear. The chances were against them. By the early hours before dawn, panic set in. What if they were caught—they would *surely* be caught. Iain would see the end of a gibbet, and what would they do to her? She had to convince Iain to abandon this foolhardy plan.

Then sometime before dawn, when sleep crept over her with its drowsy caress, Mairead dreamt of home.

She saw her father standing outside his shop, crates stacked on either side of him, half a man high. He looked older than she had remembered and dark shadows ringed his eyes. The wind tasted of winter and decay. The shops and houses lining the narrow streets were pockmarked and crumbling. Overhead, a flight of swallows darted across a lead sky. Her father called out a plaintive greeting to those who went by—the egg seller, the wainwright and the draper's young lad. *Have you seen my girl? Have you seen my Mairead?*

Mairead awoke to wet cheeks and an ache for home, no matter the consequences. If anyone could manage the impossible, it would be Iain Locharbaidh Johnstone. She'd gladly put her faith in him.

After the first bell, Potts assigned her once again to the sugar fields. Her pleased smile was her undoing. As she headed to Iain, Potts called out, "Not there. You'll be with the other oaf—Dunsmore."

Mairead stared at Potts, at first not comprehending, then her disappointment twisted like a knot.

"Gan alang," Potts said, "before I send you to the pigpens."

Over the course of the morning, the brash, loudmouthed Scotsman made Mairead more keenly miss working with Iain. Dunsmore often dangled poorly veiled lewd comments like choice morsels and smirked as his meaning became clear. His behaviour puzzled her. Dunsmore had barely given her the time of day before, and Mairead couldn't fathom his dogged interest in her now. She decided her best course was to ignore his innuendos. To respond in any way would serve as a bellow to a fire. But as the morning wore on, Dunsmore became more bold and brash in his verbal assault.

"Know how to please a man, wench?" He kept his voice low so it only reached her ears. She tried to ignore him. "Is Locharbaidh easily pleased, or do you have to work hard on your back?" She couldn't stop the mortified flush that crept up her neck, but she remained silent. "What's the matter, Irish? Don't know how to use your mouth?"

"You are vile." Mairead's stomach turned over. Dunsmore left her feeling dirty and battered.

Dunsmore grinned. "Maybe you'd like that, would you, Irish? I can show you a few things tonight—something you won't be forgetting even after—"

"Have you no shame?" Without another word, she walked away.

The eleven o'clock bell rang and everyone around them gathered their tools to break for their meal. Moments later, Iain appeared. Mairead felt herself unravelling and desperately wanted his arms to wrap around her like a shield, but she forced this down. Iain studied her, and a frown gathered on his brow. "All right, Mouse?" he asked, though his attention was focused on Dunsmore, who stood there cleaning his billhook against his breeches with a lazy smirk.

Mairead constructed a pale smile designed to put him at ease. She knew the smallest hint from her of how horribly Dunsmore had behaved would prod Iain to call the man out. To keep the peace, she replied lightly, "Well enough."

Masterton arrived and slipped between Iain and Dunsmore. "Hurry up, lads. I've a hole in my gut that needs filling. Loblolly is unpalatable enough hot, but cold it's absolutely vile. If I have to choke mine down cold because of you two, I'll stuff it down both your gullets." Just before he led them away, he caught her eye and gave her a meaningful nod.

The rest of the day was made more awkward for Mairead. Dunsmore didn't ease up and took every opportunity to goad her into running to Iain. She didn't know why she thought this, but as the afternoon wore on, she had no doubt. Being on wagon duty, Iain made a point of driving past them to the crushing mill and back, and Dunsmore's most shameful comments coincided with Iain's runs.

The man may have been spoiling for a fight, but Mairead wasn't about to give him one. Though her ears burned, she kept her mouth firmly shut.

Mairead's head ached, and her nerves were ready to snap. The moment the final bell rang, she gathered the last of the cane and carefully piled the stalks in the wagon, hoping to avoid Dunsmore on the way back to the compound. He wasn't in a hurry to move along and stood there mopping his forehead with the tail of his shirt—blocking her way.

She was so concerned with trying to work out how to bypass the lout that she didn't realise Potts had arrived. A horse nickered behind her. The overseer stared down at her in an odd, speculative manner.

"The mistress wants you at the manor," he said, the final rays of the lowering sun blazing behind him. "Get going and don't keep her waiting." Without waiting for her agreement, he turned his horse and headed in the opposite direction to the crushing mill.

Dunsmore didn't say a word, not even when she passed him.

Mairead found it disturbing that the woman wanted to see her, and she didn't know how she'd react when having to face her. Mairead's grief over Ciara's death had fermented into a potent brew of anger against the Duchess and her useless son.

Providence Moss stood waiting for her at the courtyard gate. Her thin mouth was pressed into a tight line, as though she had tasted something bitter. "You took your time, Margaret," she hissed as she grabbed Mairead's arm, pinching it most cruelly.

A yelp escaped Mairead, and she found herself dragged through the courtyard, but instead of heading for the manor, Providence Moss marched her to the washhouse. Hengist stood beside a steaming cauldron of water with freshly washed clothes hung along a line. Behind those, a tin washing tub was filled. The washerwoman added another jug of heated water to the tub.

"That's good enough, Hengist," Providence Moss snapped. "Make sure the chit is scrubbed down well. She's filthy, and the mistress will not be best pleased if she reeks of the fields."

"Ja," Hengist answered.

The prospect should have cheered Mairead, but instead it left her more confused and uneasy.

"Get her a change of clothes too," Providence Moss said before she left the washhouse. "I'll be back for her."

"What is happening, Hengist?" Mairead asked.

The woman shrugged her meaty shoulders and laid a set of fresh clothes on a stool. "Scrub. That is what they tell me." Hengist ducked her head under the clothesline and left Mairead alone.

Mairead stripped off her clothes and sank into the tub. If she wasn't on edge, she might have enjoyed a proper bath instead of the hasty splashing she did with the other women by the pond after the men had washed up. But this—this didn't sit well with her.

The clothes laid out for her were a great deal better quality than what the fieldworkers wore. The bodice was made of soft linen, and the skirt was equally soft. It had been a long time since Mairead had worn material that didn't chafe.

By the time Mairead fastened the apron around her waist, Providence Moss returned, her features cast sharply by the lantern she held. She looked only slightly mollified. She walked around Mairead and grabbed her hands, examining her fingernails. She dropped them with a sniff. Mairead half expected the woman to even check the back of her neck and behind her ears, but she didn't.

"This way."

Mairead was forced to walk quickly to keep up with the stork-like housekeeper. When they walked into the kitchen, Lucy and Aline paused what they were doing to stare.

Providence Moss thrust a tray loaded with refreshments into Mairead's arms—a bottle of golden canary wine, a fragrant loaf of white bread and a plate of creamy cheese. Mairead's stomach rumbled at the smell of the food, reminding her that she hadn't eaten for hours.

"You'll be serving the master. He's requested you attend him."

Mairead's eyes widened, and her stomach dropped. "Why?" Her eyes darted to Lucy and Aline.

"I'm not about to question him. Neither should you if you know what's good for you. Now step lively. He has a guest, and you will do nothing to embarrass Mount Vale."

Mairead's heart began to race, and her mouth went dry. She left the kitchen slowly, her feet dragging. The urge to toss the tray into the bushes intensified. Providence Moss followed close on her heels and forced Mairead to plunge through the side entrance, the crystal wine jug wobbling slightly.

She found herself in a small hallway that led past a grand dining room. Through the doorway, Mairead saw a large table, polished like a mirror, that stretched the length of the room. Silver plate winked in a glass cabinet, and a small rug was displayed across a sideboard. Mairead breathed a sigh of relief. Neither Wilton nor the Duchess were in the dining room.

When she went to enter the room, Providence Moss's hand clamped on Mairead's arm and held her back. "Not there."

Mairead nearly dropped the tray. Where did these useless people eat if not the dining room?

"He's in his study down the hall," Providence Moss said. "This way."

Mairead followed her down the hallway to an adjacent parlour. The shutters were still drawn on most of the windows, not only blocking the heat of the sun, but also the cooling breezes.

Providence Moss paused to smooth down her skirts before she raised her hand to rap on the closed study door. "My lord, the wench is here with your meal." She leaned close to the door, nearly resting an ear against the panel.

"Enter."

Providence Moss thrust Mairead into the study and shut the door behind her. Clouds of tobacco smoke hung in the air between Wilton, lounging behind his desk, and the man seated across from him. Mairead held her breath. *Burke.* The whoremaster. Her mouth went dry, and she felt the blood draining from her face.

"All in good time," Wilton said, finishing off what he had been saying before turning to Mairead. His thickly lidded eyes fastened on her, his gaze assessing. He brushed a heavy lock of hair from his forehead and leaned back in his chair. "Here she is."

Mairead felt their gazes lingering on her back as she crossed the room to reach the sideboard. The sensation felt unclean. Her hands shook as she filled the wineglasses. A little spilled on the surface. Biting her lip, she steadied her hand and finished pouring out the wine in the remaining glasses. She took her time wiping away the spill.

"My guest is thirsty, Margaret," Wilton said. "Don't leave us waiting."

Mairead kept her eyes lowered as she served the wine, not out of humility, but she couldn't bear to see Burke's lecherous smirk. When she finished pouring him a draught of wine, Burke grabbed her wrist and held her there a moment, forcing her to look up.

"She's not as homely as I recall, Wilton," the whoremaster said, his voice low and appreciative.

"An eight-week journey will take its toll," Wilton replied, taking a sip from his glass. His eyes were locked on her. "She has her merits."

Mairead tried to extricate herself and pull away, but Burke tightened his hold and drew her to him until she was nearly on his lap.

"How many lovers have you had, darling?" he cooed in her ear.

Mairead felt the heat rising to her cheeks. *Crude, vile man.* "Release me," she said through gritted teeth.

Burke ignored her. Instead he cupped her chin and turned it this way and that. His black eyes pinned her. "Tsk, tsk. Spirit is admirable, but only when you're under a man."

Mairead's gut twisted. "Please let me go."

Burke further shocked her by cupping one of her breasts and kneading it, oh so casually. She shrank away from his touch, causing him to laugh.

"Firm, tender, but on the small side. Not as fine a jewel as the blond, but I'll take her," he said, finally releasing Mairead. "The wench and the sugar fees you collected from Bridge Town last week."

Mairead backed away and edged to the door. Wilton grabbed her by the back of the neck and forced her to halt.

"The wench and half the sugar fee now," Wilton said. "The remainder in a month's time."

Burke stretched out his legs and appeared to be mulling the situation. His eyes flicked to Mairead, and she cringed. "Throw in one of the kitchen maids—the comeliest one you have. The one that opened the door for us this afternoon—Lucy, was it? Do that and we have a deal. I'll fetch them both on the morrow."

Wilton didn't hesitate. "Deal."

Chapter 23

———◆———

Providence Moss hauled Mairead up the stairs.

"He's sold me to the whorehouse," Mairead shrieked, scrabbling to grab on to the spindles, but her fingers barely made purchase.

"Papist heathen. If my lord deems it fit to teach you a lesson in humility, it's not for us to gainsay him."

When they reached the third floor, the housekeeper yanked open the door to Ciara's old room and pushed her inside.

Mairead flew to the floor. She barely made contact before she twisted around and scrambled to her feet. Providence Moss stood poised by the door, gloating.

"You're finally getting your comeuppance, Irish trollop. You're finally going where you belong. You'll pollute this house no longer."

"How can you not care that they'll sell a Christian woman into depravity?" Mairead said, amazed at the woman's vitriol.

"Papists are idolatrous heathens, not true Christians."

"What have I ever done to you?"

To her surprise, Providence Moss advanced on her in a fury, forcing Mairead to scurry back. "Done to me? You filthy Irish killed my brother during the war! A band of papist mercenaries cut him down, strung him up from a tree—he wasn't even Parliamentarian." The housekeeper's voice cracked, but she regained her composure and continued, "I'll be the one holding the gate when Burke comes to cart you away to the brothel, make no mistake." And with that, she left. The sharp click of a key sounded in the lock.

Mairead stood in the middle of the floor, staring at the locked door. Panic nearly choked her. Come the morning, she would be sent to the whorehouse. What had they done to Bronagh? The depravity that awaited her yawned like a pit before her. They would finally break her, and Burke would no doubt take his pleasure by her defilement—all for the sake of settling the gambling debts of a weak man.

And Iain—Iain wouldn't learn what happened to her until she was on her way to Speight's Town. *Blessed Mother—I'll never see him again.*

Mairead rushed to the window and flung open the shutters. Far below lay the courtyard. The window was small, but she might be able to squeeze out. She leaned over and searched for a likely foothold. There was a narrow stone ledge that separated the third from the second story. She might be able to use that.

Then the cold feeling of dread paralyzed her. Three stories high, one misstep would see her hurtling to the ground. When she thought of what awaited her in Speight's Town at the whorehouse, she decided that she'd rather die.

Was this not what Ciara had done? Would St. Peter judge her poorly if she endeavoured one course of action that had every chance of death instead of trusting to her fate to divine guidance?

Sod that, she heard Iain in her brain.

Mairead hiked up her skirts and prepared to swing her legs through the window when, in the dim light, she caught sight of Aline heading for the bakehouse.

"Aline!" she hissed down to the girl. It wasn't loud enough to clear the incessant croaking of the tree frogs, for Aline continued along her way. Mairead leaned over and dared calling out a little louder, *"Aline!"*

The young woman looked around. It didn't occur to her to glance upwards, and she continued on her way.

Mairead wanted to cry. "Up here!"

Aline finally looked up. "Margaret?"

"Hush!" Mairead waved her over. Aline drew close to the building. "For the love of God, help me. They've sold me to Burke."

"I'm so sorry, Margaret."

"I need help, not sorrow," Mairead hissed.

"I don't know what—"

"Keys—can you unlock the door for me?" Everyone knew where Providence Moss kept the spare set of keys. She knew Aline would know where to find them. All she needed was the girl's agreement. Slowly, measured in heartbeats, Aline nodded. Before the girl darted away, Mairead called out to her, "Tell Lucy they'll be coming for her too." Aline held up her hand and dashed off.

Mairead paced the floor, her mind working furiously. Iain would know where to hide her.

A half hour stretched to an hour, and still no Aline. Then she heard the squeak of footsteps on the stairway leading up to the landing. *Aline!* Mairead clasped her hands and watched the door handle jiggle. The lock clicked and the door opened, but instead of Aline, Wilton stepped inside.

Mairead froze, her heart pounding. Wilton shut the door behind him. His linen shirt was hanging open, and the sweet, cloying scent of tobacco clung to him.

"I've always liked this room. Offers a bit of privacy," he said nonchalantly as he took his time crossing the floor. Lazily, he reached up to trace a finger along the low beams that ran along the sloped roof and studied her, predator to prey. "Your cousin was quartered here, did you know? Shame—I hadn't yet tired of her. She made the most charming noises while I rode her."

Mairead turned her head away, sickened by the lecherous smirk he flashed her. "Ciara did not deserve to be so used," she finally said.

"She came from an honourable house and should have been mistress of a grand manor, not its slave."

"And yet she was *my* mistress." Wilton advanced on Mairead, forcing her to edge away until she backed up against the cold stone hearth. Leaning in, he braced his arm on the wall beside her. Gripping Mairead's chin, he forced her to look up. His watery eyes were bloodshot. "Somehow, I don't think you'll be nearly as docile. I should hope not. In fact, I'm counting on it."

Mairead's heart beat frantically in her throat. "Leave me alone." In a rising panic, she tried to push past him, but he caught her and slammed her back against the fireplace. Shards of pain rippled through her spine. Mairead sucked in her breath, and her legs wobbled.

"That would hardly be amusing, my dear," he said with a slow smile. He undid the laces of her smock.

Mairead gasped and shrank back, trying to block him with her arm. "Please don't—"

Wilton pressed against her as he cupped her buttocks. "I'll do as I please, wench," he hissed in her ear. "Until Burke returns with his payment, I will do as much I please. You see, I hate to pay for something that can easily be taken. Right now you're fresh, but by the end of the week, you'll be just another pox-riddled whore."

Tears sprang to her eyes. It was on Mairead's lips to beg him not to sell her.

Wilton pressed a finger to her lips, and she quaked under that vile touch. "We'll have all night to get to know each other." He yanked her by the hair and forced her against him. "Oh, what I'm going to do to you."

"Let me go," she gasped from the pain. "Your mother—"

"What of her? Oh, you think she'll save you? Chide me for abusing the servants, will she?" As he laughed, his hold slackened. "You're worth less to her than the African wenches. She purchased you for leverage—to ensure your cousin's compliance."

Mairead's eyes widened. No, that couldn't be true. An icy-cold snake of doubt slithered into her mind.

"I should thank you," he said as he hiked up her skirts. "Your cousin was most accommodating."

Something exploded in Mairead. Outrage and anger ripped through her. Iain was right. This was *not* her fault. So much guilt had kept her compliant, had imprisoned her more than any indenture. Damned if she was going to accept the blame any longer.

Mairead drove her knee into his groin, and he doubled over, gasping in pain. She leapt towards the door, but Wilton's foot hooked hers. Mairead slammed against the floor. He grabbed her leg, and she whimpered as she tried to scramble back crab-style. He threw her on her back and pinned her with his weight.

She clawed at his face and thrashed against him, but he seized her wrists.

Mairead spat at him. The spittle ran down his nose and dripped to his chin. He exploded with rage and gave her a backhanded fist. Stars exploded in her head. Mairead tried to buck him off, but his strength was quickly overpowering her. Rage melted into fear, and Mairead whimpered. The fear paralyzed her, and all she could do was pray that it would be over soon.

Wilton thrust his tongue into her mouth, and Mairead bit down and tasted a spurt of hot blood.

"Argh!" He shrieked. "Witch!" But it came out garbled because he was clutching his mouth.

That was all Mairead needed. She renewed her thrashing and struck her clenched fist square in his windpipe. He wheezed, turning red as he gasped for breath. Mairead heaved against him and caught him off balance. Instead of making a dash for the door, blinding madness seized her.

Mairead launched herself on him, rage lending her strength. He fell hard to the floor, slamming his head against the edge of the stone hearth. "It's not my fault!" she screamed in his face.

Over and over again, she pummelled him with every ounce of strength she possessed.

Her vision was clouded in a black haze, and she could no longer see him. She didn't have to take this—this wasn't her punishment. She did not deserve this. Violation was not part of absolution.

"Not my fault," she yelled with every blow. Not what had befallen Ciara, not her uncle—not even Ronan. *"IT'S NOT MY FAULT!"*

At the same time that Mairead realised Wilton no longer offered resistance, the door crashed open. Strong arms lifted her up, clearing her from Wilton. Mairead clawed like a hellcat until she heard a familiar voice cut through her fevered brain.

"Dammit, Mairead! Stop!"

Mairead's eyes flew open. *Iain!* She sagged in his arms.

"It's all right, Mairead. It's over. Did the bastard hurt you?"

She shook her head, dazed. Across from them, Killean stood, eyes wide.

Iain slowly released her and allowed her to sink to the floor. Mairead drew her legs up and stared at her hands. They were covered in blood. Her eyes darted over to Wilton, lying still.

"Oh God—I've killed him. Have I killed him?" Mairead's voice rose in hysteria. "Tell me he yet breathes."

A strange look passed between the two men.

"We have to go," Killean said.

"Is he dead? Just tell me that." Mairead started shaking as shock set in.

"Mairead—"

"No! I must know!"

Iain's expression changed. "I'll check." He crouched down to examine the man.

Mairead held her breath, dreading his verdict.

Iain glanced back at Mairead. "The bastard lives."

Mairead exhaled, but in the next instant Iain whipped out his dagger and sliced Wilton's throat ear to ear. She stifled a scream as blood spurted out in a fountain, pooling on the floorboards.

"*Now* he's dead." Iain wiped his blade on his sleeve. "Come—we have to leave."

Iain had never killed a dead man before. God's death, he wanted Wilton alive—so he could kill the whoreson himself.

Mairead looked panic-stricken over the thought of having done in that piece of shite, and he couldn't let her live with that on her conscience. She suffered from enough guilt issues, and this one would have haunted her for the rest of her life. Better she think him a murderous, unprincipled bastard capable of slicing a man while he was down rather than letting her take this one on her own. Only, when he held out his hand to help her up from the floor, she cringed. Iain grimaced.

His immediate concern, however, centred on navigating the cesspool they now found themselves in. When Aline had come running to him in panic, babbling about not finding keys and the master's plan for Mairead, Iain had bolted for the manor, strategy be damned. Now that Wilton lay dead, he had no choice than to push forward their escape.

Iain exchanged a tense look with Killean. "We have to escape now. Our only chance is to get out of here before he's found."

He and Killean hurried Mairead out of the room and down the empty corridor. The poor lass moved as though dazed.

The landing stood clear, and they made their way down the stairs, careful not to make a noise. If they could slip out of the manor undetected, they stood a good chance that Wilton would remain undisturbed until morning. Who, after all, would be brazen enough to interrupt the master while he was occupied? Rage coursed through Iain's veins at the thought of what the bastard had nearly done to his woman.

Focus.

As they reached the second-floor landing, Iain motioned them to pause. He heard light footsteps and the creaking of floorboards. Peering slowly around the corner, he caught the pale swish of a maid's skirt disappearing into one of the bedrooms. The door hadn't been closed behind her—she'd return any moment.

Iain waved Mairead and Killean down the last flight of stairs while he brought up the rear. Finally, they reached the back vestibule and were out the door. No screams or shouts of alarm stopped them. The only sound disturbing the night was the steady tinkling of a harpsichord from the parlour.

Rage seethed through Iain as he strode across the dark courtyard. The powder was ready and set, waiting for only a match to touch it off. He wanted to be the one to set it all ablaze.

He turned to Killean. "Get her out of here—head towards the gully. I'll rouse the others and follow as soon as I can. If I'm delayed, make your way to Speight's Town and the *Jane Marie* as planned."

"You're leaving?" Mairead said, eyes wild. "You can't leave. Where are you going?"

"Don't worry, my lass," he said, rubbing her cold arms. "I'll not be far behind, right. I need to purchase us time."

"Promise?" Her voice wavered.

"Aye, I promise. Now go."

Iain watched Mairead and Killean disappear down the trail and into the night. Time to get to work.

He struck for the compound, and before he reached the first row of huts he forced himself to slow down so as not to draw attention. From between two buildings, he heard the distinctive sound of coupling and spied Dunsmore. The man had one of the African wenches pinned against the wall, and when he turned his head towards Iain, he froze.

After one final grunt, Dunsmore released the wench and pushed her aside. The woman sidled away. Turning slightly, he adjusted his breeches. "She's warm if you want to try her."

"I don't have time for your games. Wilton forced our hand—we move tonight."

"What happened?" Dunsmore's attention darted to the blood on Iain's hands. "What did you do?"

"Never mind that now," Iain said. "Killean Ross and Mairead are already heading for the gully."

"The Irish wench? Goddamn it, Locharbaidh, you just couldn't—"

Iain grabbed Dunsmore by the throat and squeezed slowly. "No more arguments. Get the others. We meet at the gully, ken?"

Dunsmore gave a reluctant nod, and Iain pushed him away. He massaged his throat, expression black as a storm, then spit on the ground. "As Himself commands."

"Himself does."

"What about the still-house? I'm to fire it up, but I can't be in two places at once. Or are you going soft on the Wiltons too and plan on leaving it untouched?"

Iain tightened his jaw. "I'll be doing that myself. I have a desire to see this place burn to a crisp."

Dunsmore gave him a slow smile. "We are in accord, then. I have a desire to see a great deal brought low." With that, he gave Iain one final mocking laugh before heading back to the compound.

Iain retraced his steps, and as he hurried to the still-house, the plan solidified in his head. No half measures. He'd set the fire there and make sure it spilled into both the boiling and curing houses. It would take hours before anyone realised who was missing.

When he reached the boiling house, Iain found the building unlocked and eerily quiet. During the week, the kettles were constantly fired, but being a Saturday night, the furnaces had been doused after the last day's bell, not to restart until Monday morning.

Iain grabbed a tinderbox and rush from the furnace room and headed for the adjacent still-house. A rusted padlock secured the door, but Iain made short work of it, smashing it with the edge of the tinder box.

Inside, a couple of cisterns and a large still for the fermenting rum occupied the room. Heady fumes filled the air. The cardinal rule in this place—no open flames. The vapours were that flammable, and Iain was counting on it.

Iain felt the shifting of air before he heard the movement behind him. He whipped around just in time to dodge the swing of a tamarind cane. He tucked into a roll and landed in a ready crouch.

Potts bounced on the balls of his feet and smacked the cane against the palm of his hand. "What's the punishment for a Scotsman up to no good?" He grinned with brutish glee. "An' here was I this night, in a fine fettle, with nowt to do."

Iain drew the dagger from his waistband and smiled with grim satisfaction. "Aye, this is long overdue."

One minute Potts was grinning like a fool, and the next he snarled like a rabid beast. He rushed at Iain with another crushing swing from his cane.

Iain ducked, the weapon missing the top of his head by a finger. Before Potts could recover his swing, Iain darted in and sliced his dagger across Potts's arm.

The overseer roared in rage. Potts swung the cane in a downwards arc, giving Iain no time to get out of the way. He dropped his knife to grab the cane. Potts threw all his weight into it. Arm straining, back arching, Iain focused all his strength in driving Potts back. Their balance shifted, and Potts stumbled backwards. He lost his hold on the cane, and it clattered to the ground. When he tried to reach it, Iain kicked it away to the direction of the door.

Potts scrambled to his feet, crouched in a fighting posture, fists ready. Iain's eyes darted to his dagger on the ground. Too far out of his reach. *Fists it is, then.*

Iain cracked his knuckles and settled into his own stance. Both men circled the other.

"Give it up, Scotsman. I've beat you before; you'll go down again," Potts said. "This time I'll cut off your balls and feed them to the dogs. And that Irish wench—I'll fuck her in front of you."

Rage exploded in Iain's head. He released a primal growl and smashed his fist into Potts's jaw. The overseer fell back, but managed to right himself. Shaking his head, he gave the bellow of an enraged boar and charged.

They were on each other, punching and gouging, thrashing about in a dirty fight. Potts was a natural brawler, but Iain had ample experience with his fists and more than enough pent-up frustration to fuel his rage. While Potts relied on momentum and sheer power, Iain proved to be quicker on his feet.

Inch by inch, Iain began to wear Potts down. The memory of the lash, every slur and insult, was the hammer to his rage. His knuckles split Potts's lip open, spraying blood.

Potts started swinging wildly. He extended himself a fraction too far, leaving himself exposed. Iain aimed for the man's throat and struck true.

The overseer choked and bent over, gasping for breath. Iain darted behind him and put the man into a headlock. Potts tried to buck him off, but Iain dug in and tightened his hold. With a sharp movement, Iain wrenched Potts's head and snapped his neck.

He released his hold, and Potts's body slumped to the ground. Iain staggered a few feet, bent over his knees and tried to catch his breath.

A floorboard creaked behind him. Iain froze. *How the hell—?*

He whirled around as the tamarind cane connected with his head. Waves of pain ripped through him, and he hit the ground. Iain tried to shake the stars from his head and focus his vision, edging instinctively away.

Standing over him, a blurry figure materialised. A match struck, then the hiss and flare of light. The figure threw his arm back and pitched something into the room. A whoosh of sound flared, followed by a burst of heat.

Fire.

Iain struggled to rise, aware of the danger he was in. A boot slammed him down and pinned him to the ground.

"I can think of no better diversion than to offer you up to them, Locharbaidh," Dunsmore said. "Ye'll nae hold us up, right."

Chapter 24

———◆———

Mairead couldn't focus on the path ahead, numb as she was with shock. The horror of Wilton's death assaulted her mind—the flash of a knife, his life blood soaking into the floorboards, Iain standing over the prone body. And yet Mairead's hands kept remembering the vibrations of Wilton's skull meeting the stone of the hearth. The crunch still resonated in her ears.

"Come on, lass—we can't stop now," Killean said, running ahead of her. The pond lay ahead, a dark chasm in a very black night. This place was where Ciara had ended her life. That thought alone jarred Mairead from the fog smothering her. She had a chance to escape from here, and she owed it to Ciara, if not herself, to try.

She allowed Killean to hurry her along, but a part of her wasn't there.

"Where is Iain?" Mairead stopped and looked back at the direction they had come. *Where is he?*

Killean backtracked to where she stood and urged her forward. "We must keep going, lass. He'll be here, and the others too."

"What if he's not?" A cold dread seeped into her bones. She didn't like this feeling. It niggled that all was not well. "What if they find him? What if—"

"Locharbaidh? He's as canny as a fox. He won't get caught."

308

And yet he had been captured once before by the English.

"Don't worry, lass," Killean said, trying to coax her along again. "He's the best amongst us. He'll take care of himself—that you may tie to."

But the worry burrowed deeper, and Mairead would not turn away. As she stared in the direction of the plantation, she started to notice a faint glow lighting the horizon.

Mairead went cold all over. "Is it dawn already?"

"Nay, we've a few hours yet." Killean frowned as he looked at the horizon. "That can't be the sun rising. What the—" His expression lightened, and he suddenly grinned. "Dunsmore. He must have fired up the still-house as planned. It'll take them half the night to get the fire under control, long enough for us to reach Speight's Town before they realise we're gone." He took Mairead by the elbow. "The lads will be on their way if that building is afire. Iain will be with them. We'll wait at the gully."

Mairead followed Killean without another word. She did, however, continue to check for Iain over her shoulder.

At the gully, a trickle of a creek tumbled over rocks and collected into a dark pool. Mairead's gaze latched on to the small cairn of rocks that marked Ciara's grave. A chill mist settled here, and together with the thin moonlight, Mairead felt her cousin's presence tugging at her. She shivered and hugged herself.

They waited, but no sign of Iain.

Something didn't sit well with Mairead. Each unravelling moment became an agony. The worry she'd felt earlier intensified into palpable dread. Every skittering night sound made her skin prickle.

Then she heard the tumble of loose rocks and shale. Killean pulled her behind him and hefted a rock he had picked up.

Mairead strained to see. Through the mist, a shadow of a man materialised, followed by several more. They drew closer, and she recognised Masterton, Angus and Dunsmore.

Killean relaxed and stepped forward to greet them. "You're all a welcome sight."

Mairead didn't share his relief. She searched the empty road behind Dunsmore, her stomach twisting in knots. "Where's Iain?"

"He's nae here yet?" Masterton asked, looking around. He put his fingers between his lips and whistled like a bird. A moment passed when nothing happened, and he repeated the call. Still nothing. A frown puckered Masterton's brow, and he exchanged a glance with Angus.

"Something is wrong," Mairead said. "Why isn't he with you?"

"We haven't seen him," Angus said. "He spoke with Dunsmore, told him to gather us up and meet at the gully."

Iain, who never trusted the man.

All eyes turned to Dunsmore. "Aye, that's right," he said gruffly. "He had to take care of a wee diversion."

When Dunsmore's eyes darted to the horizon, the blood drained from Mairead's face. She recalled his words—I need to purchase us time. Iain had set that fire himself, and he still hadn't come. There had been more than enough time for him to reach the gully. *Unless something happened to him.*

"We have to go back." She darted towards the road, but Killean grabbed her arm and held her back. "Release me! He might be hurt!"

"There's no waiting," Dunsmore said, heading down the gully. "He'll catch up. He knows to meet us at Speight's Town."

"Lass, those were his instructions—meet at the *Jane Marie*," Killean said.

Mairead snatched her arm free. "I'm not going without Iain."

"As you wish," Dunsmore called out. "Wait here for him, then."

"We're nae leaving the wee lass here, Dunsmore," Killean said.

Dunsmore whirled around and strode back to him. "She wasn't supposed to be here in the first place. I'm nae staying here to be captured and hanged. Any lads wanting to get the hell out of here, follow me now. I'll get you to Speight's Town and off this fockin' island."

Masterton had said nothing, only chewed on his lower lip and stared at the direction of the plantation. Shaking his head, he said, "Come along, lass, if you will. Dunsmore is right. No more arguments. Killean, you too."

But Mairead didn't listen. She turned her back on them and bolted down the trail, back towards the plantation, with Killean's shouts calling after her. Fear nipped at her heels.

She reached the pond and turned onto the stretch that led to the crushing mill. The road climbed upwards to a crest before plunging sharply down. Just as she neared the top, she halted. Two figures crested the hill, one man leaning heavily on the other. Both their faces were cast in shadow, backlit by the fire licking the horizon. Then the light shifted, and their features became visible.

Iain! And Tam?

Mairead's shoulders sagged in relief.

Iain hobbled along with Tam supporting his weight. As they neared, Mairead saw that dried blood matted Iain's hair. She flew to his other side.

"What happened?"

"His head was nearly smashed through," Tam said. "He's lucky he didn't roast alive. Alastair found him by the still-house getting his backside warmed. Told me to get him the hell out of here."

"Who did this to you?" She ducked under his arm to help steady him.

"Dunsmore," he hissed, and it sounded like a curse.

Mairead gasped, surprised, but not shocked. She was well past shocked this night. "Bastard," she spat, resorting to cursing. "He should be roasted."

"Aye, he'll get his," Iain said grimly.

"Hurry—this way," Tam called over his shoulder. Instead of descending the gully, he led them across the fallow southern fields.

"This isn't the way to Speight's Town," Mairead called out.

"We're not going there. Not willing to be betrayed a second time," Iain said through gritted teeth. He clearly was in pain, but he pushed himself to continue.

The sharp crack of a musket fired from the direction of the plantation. Then another.

"Mother Mary," Tam cursed. "They're sounding the alarm for their neighbours. Run."

Tam sprinted through the tall grasses, setting an unrelenting pace. Mairead grabbed Iain's hand, a tether to ensure he didn't fall behind.

They heard another musket shot, this time from a different direction. Another alarm being sounded. How soon before they were hunted down?

Tam led them off the main road and followed a path close to the ditches and the brush, in case they needed to hide.

Mairead's heart pounded in her ears, and a stitch in her side made breathing painful. Iain kept pace with her. Every so often, she paused to look back and check for pursuit.

She finally halted and bent over, clutching her side and panting for breath. "I can't keep this up." They had been stumbling through the gullies, with only a few brief breaks, for over an hour.

Tam halted and looked around. "I haven't heard another shot. You?"

"Nay," Iain said, rubbing his leg. "But we can't risk it. How far?"

"Another half mile," Tam answered.

"Can you make it?" Mairead asked Iain. "You must make it."

He nodded and pressed on.

Mairead was past pain and exhaustion, and she dreaded to think how hard Iain pushed himself to keep up. One foot, then the other. The terrain was rocky and broken. They had been steadily gaining on a ridge of hills. Tam picked out a winding trail where they were forced to travel single file. The trail climbed steadily uphill.

The slope was extreme and at times very narrow. More than once Mairead stumbled and fell to the ground, scraping knees and shins. Iain lagged behind. She slowed down for him to catch up to her, but he waved her away.

"Keep going." His voice sounded raspy.

"It's just ahead," Tam called over his shoulder.

Mairead had no idea where they were going. When the trail ended at a sheer wall of stone covered with a range of vines, her panic bubbled. *Trapped.* Instead of cursing and leading them back, Tam pushed aside the vegetation to reveal the entrance to a cave.

"Wait here," he said before slipping inside. In the darkness, a spark of light flared before Tam returned with a rushlight. "This way."

Mairead followed Tam inside, Iain's hand resting on the small of her back. Cool air brushed her hot cheeks.

The light of the torch bounced off the ceiling and walls, making them glisten. The cave was rough-hewn, as though carved by an unknown hand. In the far corner, a mountain of canvas bags were stacked atop each other. *Sugar.*

"What is this place?" Mairead asked.

"Storage," Tam said. "There are extensive caves in the area."

Iain lowered himself to the ground. His eyes were closed, and he cradled his head.

Tam crouched beside him and handed Iain a dagger. "Take this. I have to get back before anyone notices I'm missing, but I'll return tomorrow night with Alastair. We'll find a way to get you out."

"Why is he helping us now?" Iain asked him.

"Because, Iain Johnstone, you're a right pain in the arse and a damned loose string. No one likes a loose string," Tam said. His gaze lingered on Mairead for a moment. "That, and she's a tender lass. It's best if she's far from here."

Iain grabbed his forearm. "Thank you."

Tam squeezed his arm in return. "Blessed Mary go with both of you."

Tears sprang into Mairead's eyes. "And with you, Tam."

Mairead caught the distant baying of hounds. She lifted her head and froze. Runaway catchers were hunting for them. "Do you hear that?"

The weak daylight filtering through the vines highlighted Iain's bleak expression. "Liam hounds." He rose from her side and strode to the entrance of the cave, canting his head. As he listened, he grew more grim.

Tam had assured them that Alastair would make arrangements for their safety, but if the bloodhounds found them first . . . Then another thought, a cold, chilling one. "If those hounds are from the Wiltons' kennel, they know my scent. I've fed them often enough from my own hand." Her kindness will have led their trackers right to them. Mairead tried to force her panic down, but she was sick with it.

Iain exhaled a slow breath. Distracted, he returned to her side. "These bloodhounds need less than that to track their quarry." Iain's flat tone made her realise how dire their situation truly was. He would normally have deflected her concerns, told her not to worry. Not this time.

"What can we do?"

"I'm going out to scout a bit, see which direction they're heading. There may be other caves to hide in—something wet and foul to confuse the beasties' noses. This one is too dry and shallow." He glanced over at the stack of sugar. "Perfect for that, but not for hiding. We can't be pinned here like doves in a cote."

"No, please, Iain. Don't—"

He stroked her cheek. "Have faith, lass. They'll not see me unless I want them to."

Mairead's breath hitched in her throat. "Tell me you don't want them to."

Iain brushed his lips over hers. "I'll be back soon, my Mairead." And with that, he parted the vines and left the cave.

Mairead hugged herself to stop shaking, but it didn't help. The hounds of hell were coming for them. Retribution for a murder. Sinking to the ground, she looked at her hands. Under the fingernails, in the creases of her palms, they were still stained. Dirt or dried blood? Mairead scrubbed at them, but she couldn't erase the reminder.

Had she, herself, killed Wilton?

Though her eyes had seen Iain's bloody blade, she still remembered the sick crunch of Wilton's head against the hearth moments earlier, had felt his body become limp a heartbeat later. And then she knew the answer. Iain had been trying to protect her.

A half hour passed, and the baying grew louder. Still no Iain. Then she heard a scuffle outside the cave. A shadow fell at the entrance. The vines parted, and Iain appeared at the entrance, sweaty and out of breath.

Mairead flew into his arms. He held her a moment before disengaging himself.

"They're close and heading this way. A party of ten with a dozen hounds between them," he said grimly. "I recognised a few of the handlers from Mount Vale."

"Is there anywhere to go?"

He shook his head. "There are more caves. The hillside is a right warren of them. But if we try to leave this place, they won't miss seeing us."

"This is it, then." Everything ended here.

"I'm a stubborn bastard, as you've told me many times. Not giving up yet." Iain headed to the back of the cavern where the sugar was stacked and started shifting bags.

"What are you doing?"

"Creating a burrow for a mouse," he called over his shoulder. "It's about fockin' time I fixed a dry-stacked wall. Give me a hand."

Together they cleared a neat little alcove nestled into a corner of the sugar stack.

"Crawl in." He helped her inside.

Mairead looked around and realised that it could only fit one. She started to scoot out when he stopped her. "It's not big enough for two."

"I know." Iain started moving the displaced sacks to cover the alcove—to hide her. Only her. "You'll be able to get out from inside when everyone is gone."

"Iain—"

"You'll be safe there, Mairead. I'll divert them away from here. They won't find you."

The baying sounded as though the hounds were scaling the hillside.

"For me," he said, looking at her hesitation. "Whatever happens, I can bear it as long as you're safe." With one last lingering look, he loosely covered the small alcove with the remaining sacks.

Mairead curled up, knees drawn tightly to her chest, while tears streamed down her face. The cloying sweetness of the sugar lodged in her throat. She heard Iain moving away from the stacks, closer to the door, and imagined him, legs braced apart, preparing to attack anyone venturing into the cave.

The Liam hounds were yelping and barking in a frenzy. They sounded close, too close. A whistle pierced the air, followed by a shout. More yelping, but now distinctive whining. Mairead covered her trembling hand with her mouth. Her own heartbeat thundered in her ears.

Another whistle, this time sharper. The whining ceased, and the yelping began to fade, as though the hounds were leaving the area. Were they truly moving away? Mairead strained to hear. No denying it. The baying grew more distant.

Iain's footsteps approached her hiding spot. A bag shifted, then another. A crack of light, then she saw Iain's dear, dear face.

Mairead scrambled out, sobbing in relief. She latched on to him fiercely. Her heart still pounded in her throat.

"They're moving away," he murmured against her hair. "I don't know how or why, but they've left." It was a long time before he released her.

For the rest of day, everything remained quiet. Iain slipped out a few times to scout the area, the last time bringing back ripened fruit. Mairead found herself ravenous with hunger and thirst.

"What if Alastair doesn't come?" she asked as juice dribbled down her chin. "If those were the Mount Vale hounds, he might not be able to slip away—or they might have found out he helped us."

"We'll wait until moonrise. If he doesn't come by then, we'll make our way to Bridge Town. There may be a ship we can stowaway on."

Daylight faded, and evening filled the cave. They risked a small light from a candle, sheltered within a circle of sugar bags. Mairead lay curled against Iain's chest, counting his heartbeats. Waiting. His body heat made her drowsy, and her eyes grew heavy.

It was the sudden tensing of his body that awoke her. The candle had been snuffed out, and their only light was the weak moon filtering between gaps in the vines. Iain eased from her side and crept soundlessly to the cave entrance.

Then she heard a sound, a shower of pebbles and a scrape of a boot. Footsteps stopped right outside the mouth of the cave. The concealing vines shook, then parted. Iain coiled to strike. Mairead pressed herself against the wall.

Alastair ducked his head to clear the vines and stepped inside. Iain checked himself and lowered his blade.

"What took you so long to get here?" Iain asked. "It's already moonrise."

"I know," Alastair said testily. "I got here as quickly as I dared." He looked around the cave. "Are you all right, Mairead?"

"You're a welcome sight," she breathed.

"The hounds nearly found us," Iain said, tucking his dagger back into his waistband.

"Aye, I heard. I sent one of my lads as a handler," Alastair said. "He knows how to distract the hounds when he needs to." He rubbed his greying whiskers. "What a disaster. The entire island is in an uproar over Wilton's murder. Potts's has barely registered—but the sugar works. Aye, that was a problem too. The plantation owners have organised patrols covering the way to Speight's Town and Bridge Town."

"What of the others?" Iain's mouth curled, as though he tasted something unpalatable. "Caught? Escaped?"

"No word. You told Tam about their plan to pirate a ship? Nothing untoward happened in Speight's Town harbour last night. They must still be out there. I don't frankly care. We need to get to the cove. A ship should be waiting there to pick up my last shipment of sugar." His gaze darted to the canvas sacks, and he shook his head. "If we're fortunate, Hogendorp will take you instead. But first we have to reach the coast before he weighs anchor. There's not much time left."

Alastair surprised Iain with the pace he set. Iain had no trouble keeping up, but he kept a close eye on Mairead to make sure she didn't fall behind. The land was broken by hills and thickly wooded stretches. The only light they had to guide them was the rising quarter moon.

When they connected with the main road, Alastair didn't shy from it. Time, that wicked bitch, stood firmly against them. Iain prayed that when they finally reached the cove, Hogendorp's ship would still be there.

The first tang of salt tickled Iain's nose. "How far to the cove?"

"Not far now," Alastair called out over his shoulder.

Beside him, Mairead stumbled and, with a shriek, pitched to the ground. When Iain stopped to help her, he caught sight of lights in the distance—a dozen, jostling up and down. Then the sound of pounding hooves approaching. "Alastair!"

"To the trees!"

And they were off, skidding down a slope and racing for cover. They reached the woods just as the foremost riders came into view. Iain pulled Mairead down, and together they flattened down into the tall grasses that marked the edge of the tree line. Alastair reached them a hair's breadth later.

He lifted his head and watched as the first few riders swept past, torches held high and blazing in the dark night. Ten more followed closely behind. None of the riders broke formation and continued down the road.

When their torches were specks in the distance, Alastair rose. "Damn. That was the shortest way to the cove." He glanced up at the moon grimly. "There's another route, but we'll have to run."

Alastair led them to a winding pig trail that struck southwest, then due west. They splashed through creeks and a marshy stretch. Squelching mud sucked at Iain's shoes, slowing down their progress. Iain's lungs burned, but he pressed on. They had to reach the cove in time. Beside him, Mairead struggled to keep up. Her breath came in short gasps.

Just as he was about to call out to Alastair to find out where they were, they broke through the trees and found themselves on a small ridge with a view to the shore.

In the distance, Iain saw the dark lines of a ship.

"Hurry, Mairead," he called out to her. "The ship is there!"

They reached the shoreline, and Alastair led them through a winding passageway of boulders and ridges until they struck the road leading down to the beach. Sand gave way under their feet, making it harder to run and exhausting them further.

The cove was as Iain remembered it. A shallow bowl carved between jutting cliffs on either side. The sea inhaled and exhaled, smashing itself on the rocks lining the harbour.

Alastair halted and bent over his knees, panting. "One moment."

"How do we signal them?" Iain asked, trying to catch his own breath. The beach was empty.

Alastair straightened and cupped his hands around his mouth. He attempted a call, but it ended as a croak. Clearing his throat, he tried again. This time he managed a call that sounded like a loon. He repeated it several times, each time louder than the first to overcome the steady crashing of waves.

Iain waited for a sign that the ship heard the call. Prayed that they had. Then the slap of rope and the creaking of oars. As he watched, a small craft edged away from the ship and headed for shore.

"Oh, thank you!" Mairead said in a shaky breath.

They'd made it. They were finally getting off this shitten island.

As they waited for the boat to arrive, Alastair went to Mairead. "About Wilton, lass, if I knew what he was planning, I would have warned you."

Iain looked at him sharply. What did he think would eventually happen? Men like Wilton pulled the wings off butterflies and drowned kittens out of sheer boredom. Maybe Alastair preferred to pretend otherwise and square with his conscience later. Like now.

"I believe you," she replied.

Alastair cleared his throat. "You remind me of my daughter—how she used to play the violin. She was as skilled as you."

"You have a daughter?"

"Aye, back in Scotland," he said, then added in a very low tone, "where I can't trouble her." He turned to Iain. "It's always been my choice to remain here. If I did return, I'd end up in debtors' prison. I'd rather spare my lass that shame."

Iain held out his hand to Alastair. "We all have something we're running from."

Alastair smiled and nodded.

When the boat was halfway to shore, Alastair lifted his hand to the sailors. He started to call out to them when they heard the rumble of thunder approaching from the road.

Iain whirled around to see a flare of torchlights and a column of horsemen heading their way.

Damn!

The rowers saw the horsemen, stopped their rowing and manoeuvred the boat to return back to their ship.

No!

"We have to leave," Alastair called out, running for the shelter of the cliffs.

This couldn't be happening. "Not having that!" Iain turned to Mairead. "Can you swim?"

"I can float."

"My lass, hold on to me—don't let go."

They rushed into the churning water. The Dutch sailors saw what was happening and stayed where they were, though they drifted with the current. Iain waded ahead of Mairead. A large wave surged towards her, sweeping right under her feet and knocking her over. She floundered in the salt water, sputtering as she tried to regain her balance. Iain reached her first and grabbed her arm to steady her. He glanced over his shoulder to see that the horsemen had reached the top of the cliff and were making their way down to the beach.

"Hold my shirt and don't let go," Iain called. He kicked out and started swimming towards the rowboat. Though Mairead was a slight woman, she still caused enough of a drag that made him work three times harder. He gritted his teeth and focused on reaching the boat. Mairead clutched his shirt, using it like a tether as she kicked her legs.

Iain fought against the choppy water. The tide was high and the current strong, forcing him to correct his course several times. Barely keeping his head above the waves, he nearly lost sight of the rowboat and had to follow the calls from the Dutch sailors.

Little by little, they drew closer to the boat. The current lessened, and Iain closed the remaining distance. Someone tossed him a rope, and Iain pulled him and Mairead alongside the rowboat. His muscles were afire, and he could barely catch his breath. Not having the strength to haul himself and Mairead into the craft, he held tight as they were towed. The sailors put their backs to rowing, and they headed to the ship.

The riders now swarmed the beach, and Iain hoped Alastair got away. A musket fired, the shot skipping several feet away from them. Too close. Iain cursed and drew Mairead closer, using his body to shield her.

Another crack of a musket. This time, it landed far shy of the mark.

The rowboat finally pulled alongside the ship, and a ladder was tossed down for them.

"You first, lass. Up you go." Iain grabbed the ladder and scooped her up to reach the first rung. He watched as she scrambled up, slowly at first, and then with more assurance. When she neared the top, he followed.

Iain reached the top and pulled himself over the rail. He collapsed on the deck, then felt the tip of a blade pressed against his throat. His eyes flew open to find a stocky seaman glaring at him over a sword. Beside the man, Captain Hogendorp stood with arms crossed over his chest. His men crowded close. "*Godsamme.* Who are *you,* and what are you doing on my ship?"

Iain's eyes darted to Mairead. She sat in a wet pool a few feet away surrounded by curious Dutchmen. He shift moulded to her skin, and she hugged herself, attempting to shield their view. "Put a leash on your lads, and we'll speak like reasonable men. You're making the lass uncomfortable."

The blade still remained against Iain's throat. "Who are you?"

"Iain Johnstone and Mairead O'Coneill." His eyes flicked to Mairead. "Alastair said you'd help us get off the island. Promised it."

The captain sniffed. "Shame he didn't strike a deal with the militia who have fired on my ship. I would have appreciated that."

The men from the rowboat climbed over the rail and stepped onto the deck. One rushed over to the captain and launched into an animated explanation, albeit in Dutch. Iain recognised Alastair's name, but nothing else. He wished he understood what the man was telling his captain, especially since he hadn't called off his attack dog. Hogendorp questioned him further, and after the man bobbed, *"Ja, ja,"* the captain waved away the seaman with the sword. Iain exhaled slowly.

Hogendorp spoke a several sharp words to his men, and they slunk away to their posts. "You were not included in my deal with Alastair," the captain said to Iain. "Not unless you're carrying your weight in sugar." The cables creaked as the anchor lifted from the water.

Iain rose and helped Mairead to her feet. "We left that behind."

More shots fired from the beach. Hogendorp grimaced. "Their range is poor, and for certain they know it. Which suggests that they hope to attract reinforcements." He gave Iain a warning glare. "Stay there, and don't get in my way or in the way of my crew." He whirled around and rushed to the quarterdeck, barking a series of sharp commands that sent his crew flying to their stations.

Iain pulled Mairead aside as men got to work. Scores of men were scattered across the deck, all working in unison to get the ship underway. Iain had fought on battlefields since becoming a man and had taken part in more organised charges than he could remember. Although the deck looked like utter chaos, he appreciated the flow between the men. He came to the conclusion that Dunsmore had been a fool to think that ten men and a hostile crew of captured men could sail a ship to Scotland.

The wind picked up, filling the sails. The *Zeelandia*'s prow bit into the current.

Iain turned to say something to Mairead and found her leaning against the rail, staring at the the waves. Her hair whipped around in her exhilarated face. Fierce, like the sea. He stood beside her as the shoreline rolled away.

Seven months of his life that had marked and changed him. Iain faced the direction of Mount Vale and pictured a cairn of rocks where Glencross lay. He lowered his head. Would he ever be truly free of this place?

The *Zeelandia* continued on her northerly course, passing Speight's Town harbour. They approached a dark outcrop of land, and soon they were clear of it. The wind shifted, and the starlit sky expanded. Barbados fell behind in their wake.

"We did it," Mairead said softly.

"Aye, we did it." Iain smiled and pulled her into his embrace.

Chapter 25

———◆———

Mairead still couldn't believe it. Barbados had slipped away, and with it the constant grinding fear. She closed her eyes and thought of Ciara. Golden, kindly Ciara, who should have been standing with her and Iain on deck, seeing the last of that hateful island.

"Lass, you well?"

Mairead couldn't answer, so she nodded and turned her face away. Misty tears merged with the salt spray bathing her face. She was glad for the shroud of darkness. Suddenly exhausted, she relaxed against Iain, taking comfort in his strength.

After the ship settled into a steady rhythm, Captain Hogendorp returned. "Come. We have matters to discuss." He motioned curtly for Mairead and Iain to follow him.

Hogendorp's cabin surprised Mairead with its comforts. She had never expected a ship to be so appointed, but then her only experience had been in a rat-infested hold. Fine linens were spread across a generous wooden bed. Dark panelling wrapped around the walls, and in the centre of the room a round table had already been set for a meal. A blue-and-white pitcher sat on a tray beside a loaf of brown bread and a round of yellow cheese. Mairead remembered that she was famished.

"So Alastair promised me sugar, and instead he sends me the two of you," Hogendorp said as he poured ale into a pewter cup. He offered it to Mairead. "Had I known, I would have set sail a month ago. The delay places me in a precarious position without any incremental reward." He passed a cup to Iain, then proceeded to carve out healthy portions of the bread and cheese for them. "Sit. We're not heathens here."

Mairead forced herself to remember her manners so as not to stuff all the bread into her mouth at once. Real wheat bread—something she hadn't tasted in months! It didn't matter that it was brown and coarse. Far better than that grainy cassava slab passed off as bread.

Hogendorp settled in a chair and leaned his elbow on the armrest, studying Mairead and Iain. He motioned to their clothes. "You've come from Mount Vale?"

"Aye, is that a problem?" Iain asked, his tone flat, defensive. Mairead looked up from her bread.

Hogendorp shrugged. "Had not the English closed off the ports to honest merchants such as myself, thereby cutting off my livelihood, I might be more particular about not interfering with the planters. Of course, now that our countries are at war, the matter is philosophical. But I never cared for Wilton, that's the truth. He was not one to pay his debts." A cabin boy appeared at Hogendorp's elbow, and the captain murmured a few words before turning his attention back to Iain and Mairead. "His kind rarely do."

Mairead lowered her eyes, her appetite lost. Iain snorted and crossed his arms. "Aye, and he never will. The piece of shite is dead."

Hogendorp's eyebrows shot up. After a thoughtful silence, he said, "Was that the reason the militia were on the beach at midnight wasting musket shot at your expense?"

A short pause before Iain admitted, "Aye."

Hogendorp pinched the bridge of his nose and sighed. "Ah, that Alastair. I owe that man a tongue-lashing."

"We'll cause you nae trouble, you have my word on it," Iain said, leaning forward. "We only desire passage to anywhere as long as it's well away from the West Indies. I'll work for both our fares, but if it's coin you want, I'll make arrangements when we reach Holland."

Mairead held her breath, waiting for the captain's response. This was the moment she dreaded. They were entirely in his control. He could reject their offer and offload them to any island, or worse, decide to turn a profit and sell them to another sugar plantation.

Hogendorp looked at Mairead, and his dour expression softened. "As I told you, we're not heathens here. I'm not without sympathy." He motioned to the tray. "Eat, *mevrouw*. Don't let Wilton put you off your dinner. Only his creditors will mourn him."

Mairead sensed Iain's tension easing. He reached across the table and sliced another wedge of cheese and offered it to her. "We're in your debt. Where are you headed?"

"We're flushed with West Indies treasure—sugar, though not as much as I had hoped, ginger and indigo. Wiser to return to friendlier and more dependable markets. The *Zeelandia* is returning home, to The Hague."

Home. Mairead's excitement bubbled. Surely, from such a busy port such as The Hague, they would be able to find their way home.

"And where is your destination?" Hogendorp asked them.

"Ireland."

"Scotland."

Mairead and Iain both spoke in unison. Mairead should have found it humorous, but instead the reality hit her like a bolt.

"So you are but travelling together for a time?" Hogendorp asked.

Neither Iain nor Mairead replied. The cabin boy returned balancing a platter of cold meats and a second pitcher of ale.

Iain cleared his throat. "The lass and I have been away for too long." He had shifted closer to her, and she could feel his warmth like a reassuring embrace. "Have you any news of how things fare in our homeland?"

Hogendorp shook his head. "I'm afraid I am no use to you. I have been away from home too long, as well. I trade in neither market. The English are at war with everyone except the French and Spanish, but give them time. A man may live in hope."

As the two men continued to discuss war and trade, Mairead's mind drifted to Hogendorp's question. *Where is your destination?*

Up until this moment, she and Iain had been focused on surviving their ordeal. Their hopes had centred only on escape, a desperate half-formed dream. She and Iain had lived heartbeat by heartbeat. But now they were upon the road, and for the first time, she realised, painfully and clearly, that two divergent paths stretched out before them.

They wouldn't always be together.

Mairead had family to return to, and Iain, she suspected, would not be content to remain passive. At the very least, he had his lands to reclaim. For a wild moment, she tried to imagine him returning with her to Ireland, staying with her there and working in her father's store. The image fell apart. Ludicrous. She might as well expect a wolf to be content in a cage.

Their lives had been entangled together for months. Iain had been a prickly nuisance, an exhilarating sparring partner, friend . . . lover. Mairead didn't know what she would ever do without him. Maybe he was only intended to be hers for a fleeting, ephemeral season.

A warm touch on her shoulder made her start. "You look weary, lass," Iain said, stroking her arm lightly. His expression portrayed his concern.

It suddenly became too much for Mairead. Between the stuffiness of the room, an over-full stomach, and her own confused musings, she could barely lift her head. "I am tired."

"Have you a place where the lass can sleep?" Iain asked Hogendorp.

"Naturally. My cabin boy has already made arrangements. He shares a room with my steward, but it won't harm them to relocate with the other men. The boy will show you the way."

Mairead wished the captain good night—or what remained of the night, for it looked to be nearing dawn. Iain's hand rested on the small of her back, warm and grounding, as they followed the cabin boy to her quarters.

Inside a cupboard of a cabin, a narrow bed occupied one corner and a pallet covered half the floor. The cabin boy lit a lantern suspended from a hook on the ceiling, then darted out of the room. Iain closed the door behind him.

Mairead sank down on the bed, her shoulders drooping. "I'm not entirely sure I believed that we would manage to escape. That we're well and truly away from that place."

"You doubted me, then? Aye, don't answer," Iain asked with a smile in his tone. "I would have doubted myself as well."

Mairead lay down and curled on her side. Iain stood beside her. His fingers traced the contour of her cheek, brushing aside her damp hair with infinite care. Mairead's heart overflowed, and she shivered. The lantern cast shadows in the hollows of his square jaw and the broad slope of his shoulders. When he gazed down at her, his eyes were dark and achingly unfathomable.

"Sleep well, Mairead."

He turned to leave, but she reached out to hold him back. Mairead linked her fingers with his and drew him down to her. "Don't leave."

They had been on board the *Zeelandia* for nearly a sennight, and Iain was getting increasingly anxious over their slow progress. Hogendorp plotted a cautious course north along the Leeward Islands, hugging one inlet after the other. Their last stop had been the island of Saint

Lucia, where they replenished their water supplies and tried to gather information about English ship movements. The *Zeelandia* left Saint Lucia with no useful intelligence.

Iain came up on deck for a brief respite from his work below. He had offered to help the gunner and his assistant swab out the ship's guns and complete other minor repairs. He found Mairead sitting cross-legged in a sheltered corner of the deck. She was trying to play a wooden flute that Hogendorp had dug up from his chest. Sea breezes lifted the curling tendrils that escaped her braid. Copper highlights warmed her brown hair, and sun-kissed freckles sprinkled across her golden skin.

Mairead was dressed in an oversized shirt and old breeks borrowed from the cabin boy. Her shapely legs were an immediate distraction that left him imagining how he would peel them off. He considered the possibility of luring her away to her quarters for an hour or two. Would anyone notice? Probably. Definitely.

Had he ever been so besotted? Iain remembered being fascinated with Innis, determined to win her bonny hand and claim her for his own. A prize to be won. She had been the fairest in all of Dumfries, and even his old friend McCaul—poor McCaul—had competed against Iain for her. Ethereal—sparkling sunlight on a loch.

Mairead was entirely different. Earthy, provocative—deep, beguiling waters that teemed with life. She wasn't a prize *to be* won. Mairead O'Coneill was simply a treasure.

She touched an inner core that he had locked away from everyone. Not even Innis had breached that fortress. Innis had been comfortable, never said an unkind or hasty word. Mild as milk— unlike Mairead, who pushed and prodded and never allowed him an ounce of nonsense without challenge.

Iain didn't want to let her go. He didn't know what would happen in the future or what he could expect when he returned to Scotland. He needed to return to his land and take care of long-neglected lands. Could he ask Mairead to come with him—share his life? Would she be satisfied in Scotland?

Hogendorp strode across the deck and joined him at the taffrail, forcing Iain to tear his attention away from the sprite on the deck.

"Weather conditions are perfect, and a fair wind fills our sails. Nothing more satisfying for a sailor." Hogendorp clapped his hand on Iain's shoulder. "Thank you for your help with the guns."

"It's the least I can do." Iain rubbed his jaw and squinted at the sea. "If there's anything I can do to get this ship moving faster, I'll do it. Even climb up that rigging if I must."

Hogendorp grinned. "Are we progressing too slowly for your tastes?"

"Aye. A wee bit more speed would give me hope that we'll see The Hague before Lady Day."

"God willing, we'll be in The Hague before the eve of Sint Nikolaas. Better to be cautious in these waters. If we were in a sizeable convoy, we would make excellent time, and you'd have no complaints. The news of this war has caught me with my breeches down. Had I only been closer to home when the news reached me."

Iain stared across the sea. Whitecaps frothed in the distance as they passed close to another small island. Uprooted mangrove trees and thick logs were scattered on the shore, like a giant's discarded play things. This had been the same thing they had already seen earlier on other islands. Towns half-destroyed, trees felled and harbours washed out. They had learned from a French ship that a hurricane had passed through the Leeward Islands over a month ago.

"I can't believe the storm damage," Iain said to Hogendorp.

"Not any storm, friend. A hurricane is God's own fury," Hogendorp said, staring at the tangled mangroves. "We were fortunate to the south. A strong storm passed over Barbados a month ago—a trace of this perhaps? It must have been gathering steam, and its full force smashed through here."

Iain remembered that storm, and taking shelter with Mairead in the hut. He glanced over at her. Nightfall couldn't come too quickly.

"It's a shame," Hogendorp said.

"About what?"

"Rupert and his lost fleet." The French corsair had also given them the news that Prince Rupert's entire fleet had either been destroyed by the hurricane or flung wide. The prince had been sighted around Montserrat searching for his brother and the others. After a month, everyone expected that Prince Maurice's ship lay at the bottom of the Caribbean, but no one dared to tell that to the prince.

"Poor Rupert," Hogendorp continued. "Never saw two brothers who were closer. My brother I cannot stand, so I am naturally in awe of those who are close."

"How would you know that?"

"I know Rupert," Hogendorp said.

"You know the King's cousins?" Iain asked.

"Sure. Why so amazed? He drinks like any man. We saw the bottom of a very large cask of ale together one night."

Iain raised a brow and crossed his arms. "Oh aye? When was this?"

Hogendorp squinted at the sky and shrugged. "Somewhere in the Azores—No, I'm mistaken . . . the drink was wine, not ale. My pardon." Hogendorp tipped his hat. "If you'll excuse me. I have to return to my charts."

Lies like the devil.

Iain chuckled and returned to his favourite pastime—watching Mairead. By now, a small group of sailors clustered around her. She was no longer sitting cross-legged, but stood in their midst, playing the flute in earnest.

Iain left the taffrail and headed for her, an instinctive reaction to protect and shield her from unwanted attention. But as he drew closer, he realised that she had gathered an appreciative audience. One man clapped a beat, and others soon joined his lead.

Iain stood aside, enjoying how she shone while she played. The song ended, and Mairead burst into delighted laughter. The men clapped enthusiastically, and she bowed to them. Iain hung back until the crew dispersed to their posts.

Mairead looked up and caught him staring. Her smile widened.

"I enjoyed that, Mairead. Is that your new calling, the flute?"

She shook her head, brushing away loose strands of hair. "The violin can never be supplanted in my affections."

"Ah, Mouse, is there nae a wee hope for me?"

A winsome smile played on her lips. "Are you actually flirting, Locharbaidh?"

"Aye. No shame in that."

Her smile deepened. "A sure sign of the Apocalypse, if there ever was one."

The heat was cloying and oppressive. Iain stared at the frothing waves wishing he could jump into the water to cool down. A shout from the crow's nest shattered those musings.

"Een schip, Kapitein!"

Did they say a ship? Iain saw nothing except turquoise sea and aquamarine sky. One of the men dashed past him, followed by another. Iain looked around and found many of the crew gathered on the port side of the ship, their attention fixed on the horizon.

Another cry from the crow's nest—*"Engels."*

Nervous exchanges rippled across the deck, and many repeated the word *Engels* with obvious dismay. Iain didn't need to understand Dutch to know what that meant. *Goddamn English.*

"Not now," he muttered to himself as he hurried to the port rail. "Absolutely not now." In the distance, a vessel skimmed across the sea like a bird of prey, bearing towards them as though to clip them in midflight.

Hogendorp shouted a rapid fire of commands. A mad explosion of activity erupted as men scrambled to their posts. The bell started ringing, bringing with it fresh crew from below deck. Top sails unfurled, a slight shifting of course, and the *Zeelandia* leapt across the waves.

The deck lurched below Iain's feet. As the crew rushed through their work, he could do nothing except grip the rail and curse his fortune. Useless. Completely useless. He knew nothing about the workings of a ship and could offer no help to speed them on their way, if such a thing was possible. Over the last week sailing on the *Zeelandia*, he'd realised the vessel was at the mercy of tides and winds, fickle twins at best.

Iain gripped the rail, watching the chase unfold. The *Zeelandia* was a sturdy craft, but she wasn't running as fast as he would like. Her holds were stuffed with cargo, and she rode low. By God's death, the *Zeelandia* would make for a healthy prize, and these hounds were fresh on her trail. Iain marked the English ship's progress against the horizon, and a horrible fear settled in his stomach. Could the English be gaining on them? After a half hour of obsessive staring, Iain was convinced of it.

Rage swept through him, and he slammed his fist against the rail. They had come this far, managing the impossible—escaping Barbados and finally heading home. Now *this*. The senseless futility was enough for Iain to throw his head back and howl.

Bloody Southroners. Would they ever stop plaguing him? If Iain wasn't so enraged, he'd laugh over the sheer lunacy of this. These damned whoresons were the iron and he the lodestone.

A touch startled him, and Mairead leaned in to stand beside him at the rail.

"Is it true?" Her gaze focused on the ship growing more distinct by the moment.

"Aye," Iain nearly spat. Frustration tasted like bile in his mouth.

"Surely, we can outrun them?" She scanned his face. Though her tone sounded neutral, Iain didn't miss the tautness of her mouth and the strain around her eyes. She searched for reassurance, and by her look, silently pleaded for it. But they had both been through too much together for him not to be honest with her.

"I don't know, lass," Iain admitted and reached out to rub the back of her neck. Around them, the crew scuttled to adjust the sails, wringing out as much scrap of wind as they could possibly manage. But would it be enough?

As Iain watched, frustration choked him. He lowered his head, and his shoulders hunched forward as he leaned against the rail. "I hate this—I'm completely useless." He should be doing *something*.

"What can you possibly do?" Mairead clasped her hands, her eyes enormous. "What could either of us do?"

"Precisely. Nothing." He hated not having power over his life, hated not being able to act to save himself by his own hands and his own will. All he could do was watch helplessly and throw curses to the wind.

Over the next hour, Iain kept his agitated vigil beside Mairead, gripping the port rail as though his life were tethered to it. Each time the *Zeelandia* picked up speed to surge forward, the English ship found fresh courage and narrowed the distance.

Iain prayed for more wind, more speed. Every ounce of sail had been unfurled, but it wasn't enough. Hogendorp prowled and paced the quarterdeck, barking out angry orders.

What would happen to them if the English captured Hogendorp's ship? If the bastards realised he and Mairead had escaped from Barbados, they'd either hang them or ship them back to that hellhole. His gut roiled with fear, but not for himself. If those buggers got ahold of Mairead, Iain knew where she would end up— servicing stinking English turds in a bawdy house. He couldn't allow her to be sent back.

"Return below deck and stay there," he told Mairead. She opened her mouth to argue, but he pressed a finger against her lips. "Please, Mairead. Below. For me." Where it was safer.

"Come with me," she whispered, clutching his arm. "Don't stay here. I have a horrible dread. There's nothing—"

"I know. Nothing I can do." His jaw tightened, and he glanced away.

"Iain, *please.*"

He looked over her shoulder at the English ship giving chase. "Go down below, Mairead. Don't argue with me on this."

She bit back a reply, then finally nodded. With a parting squeeze of his arm, she left.

When he turned his attention back to the English ship, he realised with a twist of his gut that the enemy had narrowed the gap further. The *Zeelandia* needed nightfall or a storm, anything to slow the other ship down. But the sky remained achingly cloudless, and there were hours yet before the sun would set.

Hogendorp fired off more orders, and a commotion broke out on the quarterdeck. From first mate to bosun to midshipman, the captain's orders rippled through the ship, and every free hand dropped what they were doing and dashed for the hold.

"We need help—" The bosun hurried Iain along. "This way."

Then it became clear. Men were hauling cargo out of the hold and dumping it over the side. Anything to lighten the load—bales and barrels, hogsheads of rum and molasses. Into the water. At first, it seemed to have given them the advantage they needed, and Iain began to hope. They might just escape these bastards.

His hope lasted less than an hour.

The English ship, propelled by the devil himself, made up the distance. By the next quarter hour, it had drawn close enough for Iain to see her name—the *Redemption.* Closer still and he stared at the open gunports, aligned like the maw of a sea monster. A flash of light, then a puff of smoke. *Boom!*

Iain instinctively ducked, but the cannon shot landed far short of the mark, sending a plume of water arching fifty yards off the port bow.

A warning shot. The deadly posturing began.

Iain might not know anything about ships, but he did know battlefields. Two armies facing against each other across a muddy field went through the same rituals—lining up cavalry, pikes and muskets. And stoking up the courage of their men. Iain saw none of that on the deck of the Zeelandia. Why weren't the guns being readied or the men arming themselves? On the quarterdeck, Hogendorp was locked in a heated argument with his first mate and the bosun.

Blast them all. They were going to surrender!

Iain charged across the deck and climbed the few steps to reach the quarterdeck. The bosun moved to block his path, but Iain pushed him aside and faced Hogendorp. "Tell me you're not cowering with your tail between your legs. You have to fight!"

Before Hogendorp could reply, the bosun stepped between them. "You cannot speak that way to our *kapitein*. You should not be here."

A second warning shot fired, this time closer than the last. The bosun grabbed Iain's arm to pull him away, but he yanked it free. "Touch me again and you'll eat a mouthful of teeth."

The first mate spoke tersely to Hogendorp in Dutch, stressing the word, *bloedvlag*. Then he added for Iain's benefit, "Blood flag. I agree, we should hoist the blood flag and declare our intent to engage—"

"Ready the guns. Give the damned order," Iain ground out to Hogendorp.

"To what end?" Hogendorp snapped. "We can't outrun them. This is not a fight we can win."

"I'm nae giving in. Nae having my woman taken by those fockin' bastards," Iain said, his voice thick with anger. "They aren't touching a hair on her head, nae while I have a good fight left in me."

337

"Do you not think that if I could do something to keep my ship from being taken as a prize and my men confined to one of their rancid cells that I wouldn't take it? I have a greater care of my men's lives and will not risk their blood."

"They'll do more than lock you up in a cell," Iain nearly shouted. He had to make the man understand. "You're at war with the English, same as we Scots. We came up poorly against them, first at Dunbar, then at Worcester, and what do you think happened to us? They turned us into slaves and shipped us to their plantations! Is that what you want for your men? If given the choice, I would have chosen to die with a blade in my hand instead of slavery."

"If we don't resist, we may be able to negotiate favourable terms," Hogendorp said, the sweat beading on his forehead. "I am a merchant, do not forget. There is always a deal that may be made."

Iain growled in frustration and paced the quarterdeck. *Fight.* He drove his fist into the rail. He should fight like a man, not roll over in the gutter and be dragged to the gibbet. He hated not having any control of his life. He had always been a man who determined his own path. These past several months had reduced him to the whim of others.

Hogendorp turned to his first mate and, with a heavy voice, gave the order, "Reduce sails."

Iain swore. He bounded from the quarterdeck and practically slid down the ladder that led below deck. He'd have to find a way to shield Mairead from the English. At least let him do this.

When Iain rushed into Mairead's makeshift quarters, he found her sitting on the edge of the cot, elbows tucked in, hugging herself tightly.

"Hogendorp is surrendering?" she asked. The tremor in her voice cut right through him.

"Aye. There's little time." He drew the dagger from his waistband and offered it to her, hilt first.

Mairead stared at the blade without taking it. Her eyes widened with alarm. "What do you expect me to do with *that*?"

"We need to disguise you, Mairead. There's no help for it, you'll need to cut off your hair."

Iain expected tears, shock, even a horrified protest, not the resolutely grim expression Mairead assumed.

"Hand it over," she said. Grabbing sections of her thick, curly hair, she sawed through the tresses until all of it lay at her feet. Her shortened locks were uneven and cut no longer than her jawline. When she finally looked up at him, she bit her lip and fingered the ends of her hair. She looked vulnerable, which only freshened Iain's anger. He wanted to pull her into his arms and promise that she'd be safe, but with the English about to board the *Zeelandia*, the only thing he could do was hand her a cap to complete her costume.

"You still look like a lass to me, but you'll likely fool these Southroners," he said thickly, smoothing a lock of hair under her cap. Her eyes shone with unshed tears. He bent down to gather the cut hair. "I'll get rid of this before someone finds it." He swept most of it into the chamber pot, all except one curling lock. This he slipped into his pouch.

Iain heard the thump of grappling hooks, then the winching of cables. Shouts, clearly in English, signalled that the enemy was boarding.

Iain pulled Mairead into his arms and gave her a deep kiss. He cupped her face, committing to memory the feel of her in his arms, the scent of her skin and the taste of her lips. If he failed her . . . if he couldn't protect her . . . His insides clenched. Their lips parted. She looked up at him, fear in her hazel eyes. "Mairead," he whispered under his breath, then pressed a last kiss on her forehead before releasing her. "You're a Dutch cabin boy, remember that. No matter what they do or what you see, do *not* speak a word. Stay close to me."

When they appeared on deck, they found the English with drawn swords and muskets. Their commander strode up to Hogendorp, his gait rolling like a man born to the sea. He was a stocky man with liberal grey threaded through his hair, and he rested a hand on the pommel of his sword.

"I am Captain Morton, and in the name of the Commonwealth of England, I seize this ship as a prize of war. Every man is under our custody and your goods confiscated."

"I am Karel Hogendorp, captain of the *Zeelandia*. State your terms."

"Terms? What terms? You give me your ship, and I allow you to live." Morton signalled to his men. "Round them up and lock them in the hold. Every last one of them."

"Captain, I demand safe passage to a friendly island," Hogendorp said.

But Morton had already turned his back on Hogendorp, and the English sailors were spreading to carry out their captain's orders.

When they advanced on Iain and Mairead, it galled him to put up his hands and allow them to lead him away, but he did. This was the only way he could protect her. He looked over his shoulder to check that she was close behind him, but instead he found one of the English sailors deciding to have a bit of fun at her expense.

"What's this? They breed cabin boys small in the Dutch Republic." The man gave her a shove. Mairead bit her lip against crying out and tried to scuttle away from him. Her eyes met Iain's, and her fear was a knife to his gut.

He had to do something—deflect attention away from her. So he did what any self-respecting Scotsman would do—pick a fight with the English.

"You bloody-mouthed arseworms," he called out to them in a loud voice, immediately drawing everyone's attention to him—and away from Mairead. "Come at me, ye damned curs." Call him a contentious bastard, but Iain revelled in finally being able to tell the lot of them off.

Bellowing his rage, Iain lunged at the foremost man and knocked him down. But before he could continue his attack, he found himself swarmed. There were more of the bastards than he could fight alone. Inch by inch, they drove him to his knees.

Pain exploded in every part of his body—face, arms, stomach as they pounded on him relentlessly. His ribs were afire, and it felt as though shards of glass sliced through him. He was thrown to the deck facedown. A knee dug into his back, and he could barely breathe from the weight on him. A hand clamped around his neck and pressed his cheek against the deck. Iain couldn't lift his head to see Mairead. He strained his ears to hear her cries, but all he heard was the thud of footsteps approaching.

"What's this?" Iain heard Morton say. A set of polished boots stopped inches away from his nose. "A Scotsman on a Dutch ship? This one we have to question."

Chapter 26

———◆———

Iain was hustled into Hogendorp's quarters, now taken over by Captain Morton. His arms were tied behind his back. He attempted to loosen his bindings, but they had lashed his wrists so tight the rope bit into his skin.

Morton's glance flicked to Iain, but otherwise the man gave no acknowledgment of his presence.

Meanwhile, Hogendorp squared off against the enemy commander. His voice trembled with outrage. "And the *Zeelandia*? What are your plans for my ship?"

"The *Zeelandia* is now the property of the Commonwealth of England and will be flying her flag." Morton had claimed Hogendorp's chair, and as he leaned back his fingers steepled over his rounded belly. "My crew will sail her to London where she, and her contents, will be sold as a prize and renamed to commemorate the glory of the Commonwealth. We are well pleased with the quality of your remaining cargo. It should fetch a handsome price in London."

"*Klootzak,*" Hogendorp spat, followed by an angry spate of Dutch.

"Perhaps it's best that I don't understand your heathenish tongue," Morton said with a mocking laugh.

"And what will you do with my men? I insist you tell me where you are taking us."

"We are at war, Captain," Morton said with a touch of smug indifference. "You are not in a position to make demands. You will be taken where I deem fit."

"Spare us the mystery. What will you do with us?"

Captain Morton paused a moment, then shrugged. "I suppose it hardly matters if you know. We're sailing for Antigua, where it will be decided what to do with you and your crew."

Iain lowered his head and exhaled slowly. Antigua. Another damned English colony.

Hogendorp leaned forward to snarl in the man's face. "You had better not be considering selling any of my crew to one of your colonial plantations. I've heard of the depravity of English morals, but I scarcely believed it. Even in war, there are rules."

"Firstly, I don't need your good opinion, Captain Hogendorp. Secondly, you are not in a position to make demands. England and the Dutch Republic are at war—"

"As you take great pains to remind me—"

"And you are now our prisoners and subject to our policies," Morton continued, his voice rising. "If you persist in being an annoyance, I may decide that I have far too many Dutch prisoners and turn my mind to dropping a goodly number of you over the rail. The sharks, at least, will be pleasant about it. Then you might not be so affronted by the alternatives."

Hogendorp turned a strangled shade of purple. He turned to Iain and muttered, "I should have listened."

Now Morton's full attention centred on Iain. He rose from his chair and walked around the table to rest his weight on the edge. "Is this man your advisor?" His tone was mild, almost solicitous, but Iain didn't miss the flinty calculation in the man's eyes.

"He is nothing. A passenger, naught else," Hogendorp said.

"Indeed? I find this to be an intriguing mystery. How does a Scotsman find himself as a passenger on a Dutch ship?"

Iain pulled against his bonds, but he only managed a hair's breadth of slack.

"Why so surprised?" Hogendorp attempted a casual shrug, but the tension crackled between them. "I am a private merchant. I have had Scotsmen and Englishmen sail with me before. That is hardly unusual."

Morton no longer smiled benignly. "What's your name, Scotsman?"

Iain kept his mouth shut, refusing to speak. He stared past the man's shoulder to the grooves in the far wall.

Morton nodded to Iain's guard, and the man yanked a fistful of Iain's hair and pulled his head back. Needles of pain ripped across his skull. "I ask you again, Scotsman. What's your name?"

Iain pressed his lips in a tight line and spat, "Prince Fockin' Rupert."

"Naturally—a Scotsman who thinks he's a jester."

The guard released Iain's head, but before he won a reprieve, a meaty fist slammed into his lower side, above his kidney. A flood of agony weakened his legs, and he fell to his knees on the floor. He found himself once more hauled to his feet. Sucking in air through clenched teeth, Iain met the Morton's hard gaze.

"We've all enjoyed your humour, but now I need answers. Curious how you are so free with the prince's name. Are you, by chance, one of his agents?"

Iain cursed himself for a mindless fool. Why did he have to choose that particular name? It was common knowledge that Prince Rupert terrorised the English ships across the West Indies. Iain could never resist needling the English where they were most vulnerable, but this time his impulsiveness seemed to have landed him in a hot mess. *Good move, Locharbaidh.* "I don't know the prince," he said simply.

"Perhaps you are an agent of the Scottish King—carrying dispatches, very likely?"

Iain shook his head, amazed at the irony of his situation. Fate truly was a hard bitch. If he had agreed to deliver the King's dispatches to Scotland, without conditions for his men, he wouldn't be here now. He kept his expression neutral. "I have no dispatches, not from Rupert or the exiled King."

"Did you search him for contraband?" Morton asked the guard.

"He has nothing."

Morton chewed his lip, then turned to Hogendorp. "This is what has bothered me from the first time I saw your ship. If you're a merchant, why aren't you sailing in the protection of a convoy?"

Hogendorp kept his mouth shut. What could he say? Admit that he did some privateering on the side to supplement his trade? The English had a poor opinion of such freebooting.

"Privateer or spy?" Morton said, as though reading Iain's mind. "I'll have to determine which it is, but either way you are acting against the interests of the Commonwealth. I'll deal with both of you later, when we reach Antigua." He nodded to the guard. "Take them to the hold with the other prisoners."

Iain tumbled down the stairs and hit the straw-covered floor of the hold, his arms still bound behind his back. He bit back a grunt of pain. Hogendorp followed close behind and landed beside him. The English laughed uproariously, their amusement cut off by the slamming of the hatch door.

"Piss and hell." Iain twisted to his side before struggling to his knees. The rope dug into his wrists

"You are an acute inconvenience, Iain Johnstone," Hogendorp muttered as he hauled Iain to his feet. "They now suspect we're spies. If you do not know, the punishment for *that* is far worse than being a prisoner of war."

"Don't fool yourself, Dutchman—" Iain swallowed the rest of his words when Mairead pushed her way past the gathered men to reach him. She threw her arms around his neck, squeezing tight.

Iain closed his eyes against the relief that swept through him. "Thank God you're here."

She pulled back and smacked him on the chest. "You impossible man! What *were* you thinking? Where else would I be? But you, I'm surprised they didn't stretch your neck," she said angrily as she worked at untying his bonds. "Don't give yourself away, he admonishes," she muttered. "You should have been mindful of your own advice, Locharbaidh."

The moment his hands were free, he cupped her face and pressed a kiss on her lips. At first she stiffened, but then she melted against him. Her lips parted, and in her response he recognised a mingling of anger, relief and fear that echoed his own feelings.

Iain rubbed his thumb against her smudged cheek. "I feared for you; truly, I did. Did they harm you, Mairead?"

"I've suffered worse."

He tipped her chin, forcing her to meet his gaze. "*Did* they?"

Mairead shook her head. "They did not. I blended with the others." She looked around shyly at the attention they drew. Even Hogendorp seemed amused.

Iain thought the Southroners blind for not seeing past the knit Monmouth cap to her sensitive mouth and the tangled lashes that framed her enormous eyes. Suddenly, he wanted to shield her from the amused and curious glances of the Hogendorp's men. A worry burrowed inside—what if they betrayed her, told the English who she was in exchange for preferential treatment. He exhaled a ragged breath. Best not to borrow worries when troubles were at hand.

Iain looked around at the crowded hold. A single lantern swayed on a hook, illuminating their prison. They were crammed with the remaining cargo that hadn't been thrown overboard. Crates were stacked one on top of the other, and rows of hogshead barrels lined the other end of the space.

A great weight pressed down upon Iain's head and shoulders. Now that he knew Mairead was safe, energy drained from him, leaving him to feel the affects of his beating. "I need to sit." Was there a dark hole he could crawl into?

"This way." Mairead led him to a space wedged between bales of indigo and tobacco.

Iain sank to the ground, too weary to speak. He didn't miss Mairead's worried expression. He held out his hand and motioned for her to sit. In a moment, she settled beside him, sitting cross-legged, their knees touching.

"What happened with the commander?" she asked in a low voice. "Did he say what was to become of us?"

"We're for Antigua—for now." He closed his eyes against the futility of their situation. He should be devising a plan to get them out of here, to overpower the guards and fight for their freedom, but right now he couldn't get past the fog in his brain. "They don't know what to make of us—of me, mostly." He looked across to Hogendorp who sat with his own men, his shoulders hunched forward. "They will not allow Hogendorp, and his men to return to The Hague—not while there is war."

"They're bound to discover I'm not one of the crew."

She was right, Iain knew this. He hadn't wanted to be the first to give shape to his fears, but now that Mairead said it, he couldn't smother it. The pressure mounted between his eyes and knotted the muscles between his neck and shoulder blades. For her sake, he gave a lie to his assurance. "They needn't know, Mouse." He motioned around the hold to the men gathered there. "A wee sprout is invisible in the thick forest. The captain will be sure to protect your secret." Iain hoped. With the loss of his ship, Hogendorp faced ruin. Deprivation and desperation were unwelcome weights that could tip the scales against them.

She didn't reply at first. Instead she hugged her knees to her chest. "I'm scared, Iain. I can't return to Barbados. I'll throw myself in the harbour before they hand me over to Burke." She looked away, blinking furiously. No doubt she was thinking of Bronagh. The whoremaster's callous words played through Iain's mind. *A mean cove played her rough.*

"That won't happen, do you hear me?" A fierceness swept through Iain, lifting a little of the exhaustion that smothered him. "I won't let that happen. We will find a way from here." Even to his ears, his words sounded as thin as mist.

Failure.

Iain had led them here, had not even saved her.

Powerless.

He had no plan, no idea how to get them away from the English. She had counted on him, and he had failed her. Just like he had Innis.

"I want to return home, Iain," she whispered so softly that for a moment he wondered if she had said it at all. "I want to so badly I can't breathe."

Finally, she lifted her gaze and turned her brilliant eyes to him. "I want to see my da and my brothers . . . if they're still alive." She drew in a breath before continuing. "If they aren't, I need to know that too. I can't stand this uncertainty, Iain. I truly can't."

Another slice of the blade. Not a clean, hot edge, but pitted and rusted and designed to fester. She wanted to go home, and selfishly his heart bled for his loss. He would lose her anyway, that even if they did escape, she wouldn't always be his. They had at best borrowed moments, not forever. Deep in his bones, he loved her. Enough to move heaven and earth to get her home, if that was what she wanted. Even if it killed him.

"You will return home, Mairead. You will see your people again."

Again, Mairead said nothing, and her silence screamed doubt. In him. He had told her this before, many times while they were on the estate. Always, she rewarded him with an indulgent smile, sometimes

348

a trusting one. Whether she truly believed him then, he didn't know, but she had been willing to *hope*. Now she hugged herself tighter and didn't look at him.

The light in the lantern sputtered before dousing out and darkness ushered in a ripple of groans and protests. It crept in every pore, burrowed deep between the joints and froze the heart.

Iain reached out and found her hand. Limp and unresisting, he took it in his own and laced his fingers through hers. "Don't give up, Mairead, my Mairead. Word of a Johnstone, you will go home." His voice thickened in his throat, but he forced himself to continue. "Tell me about your home. Speak to me of Ireland."

"I can't." She shivered and tried to untwine her hand, but he refused to release her. Here in the dark, this was their only connection, and he wouldn't sever it.

"I'll tell you of my home in Scotland. What I remember." Iain was glad the darkness masked his expression. He felt his throat close up. He hadn't allowed himself to think of Scotland for months, but now the memories rushed in, blade sharp. "I have a modest estate, and peat smoke hangs in the air. Rocky land slopes to a ridge where the view is unparalleled." He swallowed a painful lump and cleared his throat. "There's a stone wall that stretches along the base of the property. It's been there long before anyone can say who built it. A cold spring feeds a burn. The trees are purple at dusk. Yellow broom and rolling green fields. A fox prowls in the woods, a glossy red devil with his share of audacity." Iain couldn't continue. He had neglected his land—that's what he thought of when he thought of Scotland. They had been under siege in one form or another for most of his life. "Braes and rocks. That is my beginning and should be my ending. I've spent too many years away."

Iain rubbed his palm against his eyes and gave up trying to work down the burrs stuck in his gullet. Home. A place he'd never see. He knew it. It was farther away from him now than ever before. He tried to restore her courage, but his own faith remained broken like shards on the hold's floor.

Mairead squeezed his hand, her fingers tightening against his own. "You will go home, Iain Locharbaidh Johnstone," she breathed. "We both will."

Chapter 27

———◆———

Iain's first view of the English colony of Antigua called painfully to mind Barbados, though the islands bore little resemblance to each other. He knew this nightmare—different ship, different island, but a prisoner all the same. Iain's gut churned when he thought of another slave auction. Would they all be sold on the block or just handed out as a reward to the loyal planters?

The *Zeelandia* and the *Redemption* laid anchor in a cove their captors called Five Island Harbour. Its shoreline curved like a generous half bowl, with water reflecting blues and greens and the blending of the two. The sunlight slanted in his watering eyes, nearly blinding him with its brilliance. A settlement sprawled along the harbour, much smaller than Bridge Town. A string of warehouses occupied the centre of town, fed by a steady trickle of carts and donkey caravans.

English seamen herded them across the deck, past a line of dragoons who had their muskets trained on them. Iain scanned the ship until he found Mairead, hugging Hogendorp's shadow. Rationing out a brief, reassuring nod to her, he forced his attention elsewhere lest the English bastards notice his interest in Hogendorp's "cabin boy." Before anchorage, he and Hogendorp had agreed that Mairead must stay close to the captain instead of Iain. Hogendorp could better shield her, and as the English commander's suspicions of Iain had not alleviated, anyone in his immediate sphere would be sure to draw heightened scrutiny.

He and Mairead had to get away before the English discovered they were escaped slaves. After a night in the hold, tormented by what might happen to them and his own failings, he reclaimed a weathered determination—if they could manage, against all odds, to escape from Barbados, by Christ's death, they could find a way to leave Antigua behind too. Iain prayed their small scrap of fortune hadn't entirely deserted them yet.

As Iain waited for the men ahead of him to climb down into the boat, he took the opportunity to study the town's defences. Overlooking the harbour, a stone fort stood on a steep hill with four large cannon guarding the harbour entrance. To Iain's trained eye, they were perfectly positioned to blast any ship running in or out of the harbour. In addition, a generous company of horse and foot were gathered near the town's square, parading their might.

Mairead and Hogendorp had fallen behind, and Iain craned his neck to find them. The Dutch captain had halted, staring at the mast with open disgust. His Dutch Republic flag had been cut down and the English ensign flew in its place. Mairead looked nervously at the guards and tugged Hogendorp's sleeve to urge him to continue, but the man was lost in his outrage.

Iain allowed others to pass him in line, but one of the guards caught his ploy and delivered him a sharp jab. "Keep moving, wretch."

He reached the side and climbed down the ladder. Stepping off into the crowded boat, he glanced up to find Mairead clambering down after him. He dared not wait to assist her; besides the pair rowing, four armed dragoons rode in the prow, standing over the prisoners with the vigilance of hawks. Men shifted to make room on the benches, and Iain soon found himself sitting directly across from Mairead and Hogendorp.

One of the sailors cupped his mouth and shouted to his crewmen above, "All in. Heading to shore." The lines were untied, and they launched the craft.

As they rowed across, Iain and Mairead held each other's gaze. Her knit hat was pulled low over her forehead, and she slouched forward. She had done everything to disguise her sex, but she could do nothing to disguise her fear. Iain's frustration mounted, that he couldn't reach across to reassure her.

The boat reached the shore, its keel scraping against the sand bar. The sailors jumped out of the craft and barked instructions for everyone to scramble out. The surf was relentless, and Mairead struggled against the surge and undertow. She lost her balance and fought against the waves. Iain crashed through the surf to help her, but one of the Southroners reached her first. Grabbing her arm, the man hauled her to her feet, and Iain tensed, expecting the seaman to discover her secret and shout the news to the dragoons. Instead, he turned his back on her, distracted by others floundering in the surf.

It took three trips to offload all the prisoners from the *Zeelandia*, and then a company of militiamen rounded everyone up and marched them, ahead of the horsemen, through the sunbaked town. The residents stopped to stare at the ragged procession. Once again Iain felt his life playing in an endless, demoralising loop—the only difference this time was that he burned with a fierce desire to survive this ordeal. For her.

Mairead walked ahead of him. Half-soaked, she kept her head bowed as she trudged along. Word had spread about their capture through the settlement, and agitated crowds fired dung, pebbles and overripe fruit at them. Mairead flinched as a piece of mango landed on her shoulder. With every step, she shrank more and more into herself. Iain loathed the English troops, the mindless crowds and the whole pox-ridden island.

If only he could give her some strength to get through this, some words that she could seize upon to freshen her courage But words would betray her. Hogendorp's cabin boy would only be spoken to in Dutch.

Then an idea flashed in his mind. It didn't matter if he appeared foolish. Let these Southroners think him a mad Scotsman.

Iain began to hum the song in a low baritone, and the melody soon turned into snatches of words meant for Mairead's ears only. Instead of the lyrics from the ballad of "The Gay Goshawk," he substituted reassurances for her.

"My brave, bonny lass . . . walkin' in the garden green . . . crushin' bastard bones to dust . . . afore our very eyes she became a bonny spied hawk . . . flying aboon our heads to freedom . . . "

Mairead stiffened and turned her head slightly, as though trying to catch his song. Then as he continued, he sensed her smile. Straightening her spine, she walked with more determination.

That's my lass.

He cut off his song when one of the officers hurried to catch up to him. "What was that? A minstrel now, is it?" He snorted under his breath, "Mad Tom."

Iain held his tongue. He kept his attention fixed on Mairead's back and didn't break stride.

The procession ended at a large stone building adjacent to the smallest warehouse. Several more dragoons were stationed at the entrance.

"Where'd you pick these up?" an officer asked the sailor.

"Filthy butter-boxes taken with a prize—and one Scotsman," he answered, driving his elbow into Iain's ribs. "There's also a hold half-full of indigo, tobacco and sugar. Too bad none of that will swell our purses."

"What are we to do with them? The cost of their upkeep will ruin us," the officer grumbled.

"I don't know the captain's mind. Likely sell them to the plantations, either that or ransom them for anything the Dutch are willing to pay? Either way, they won't be our trouble for long."

"Lock them up with the others," the officer said with a nod to one of his men.

The heavy pause made even Iain take notice. "The others, you said?" The guard lowered his voice. "Are you sure, sir? With the bloody murderers?"

The officer smirked. "So? Won't trouble me none if those buggers cull a few of the herd. Go on, throw them in."

Inside the building, the air reeked of sweat and piss. The shutters were drawn tight against the sea breezes and the oppressive heat lay thick like a woollen blanket. The prisoners were led down the dim corridor to the rear of the building. Before a narrow door, another dragoon stood guard. He jumped to his feet and hurried to lift the bolt.

"Oy! Not sure if they'll all fit," the guard fretted. He swung the door open and shouted in the room, "Make room, make room."

"Aye," the sailor added. "You'll be sharing your quarters with Dutchmen. Best get cosy now."

Iain found himself jostled and prodded and pushed inside. He whipped around to bite off the man's head, then froze.

It couldn't be.

Dunsmore.

The bastard's mouth dropped when he saw Iain, the bluster knocked out of him. For once, Dunsmore didn't have a word to spare.

Iain's vision expanded, and he spied Killean, Masterton, Angus Rae and the others too. Masterton paled and blinked at Iain as though he were a ghost. So these were the "others" the English had referred to, Iain thought. A wild satisfaction that they too had been captured—damn well deserved it—warred with freshened anger over their betrayal.

Then the precariousness of his and Mairead's situation set in. Likely, their captors had figured out that his former men had escaped from Barbados. He couldn't afford for the English to connect him and Mairead with them. His best chance to extricate Mairead was to keep the English ignorant of who they were.

Killean opened his mouth to speak, but Masterton elbowed him into silence. At his near lapse, Killean flushed red. They had all been through tight situations before, and the accepted rule was to keep your mouth shut when the enemy was near and give no man away. But Dunsmore, that mongrel dog, never adhered to any code.

"Dutchmen? Did you say *Dutchmen?*" Dunsmore said. He lifted his hand and pointed to Iain. "He's no stinking Dutchman. He's an escaped slave from Barbados, same as us." Now he had the full attention of the English. "He had an Irish wench too—where is she?" He looked around at the gathered *Zeelandia* crew before honing in on Mairead.

Fuck.

Iain released a primal roar and charged at Dunsmore. He slammed his fist into the man's jaw, sending him reeling, straight into a group of Dutchmen.

Dunsmore scrambled to regain his balance, shook his head, then snorted like an enraged boar. In one swift motion, he launched himself at Iain, driving a shoulder into his stomach. The wind rushed out of Iain, leaving pain in its place. Before he could lift his arms to defend himself, Dunsmore threw a hard punch, knocking him to the floor. A squirt of hot blood shot through Iain's mouth. He caught a movement at the edge of his vision, and with a curse he jerked aside, narrowly avoiding Dunsmore's boot slamming down into his gut.

Iain rolled to his feet, crouched low, then sprang. Rage unleashed, Iain drove his shoulder into Dunsmore and threw him to the ground. Through a red haze, Iain pinned the cur into the damp straw, raining blow after blow to his face. Dunsmore howled and tried to buck him off, but Iain's outrage had festered, giving him added strength. Dunsmore's nose crunched beneath Iain's knuckles, spurting a fountain of blood. Iain drove another shot straight into his mouth. It was a scrappy, dirty fight that was long overdue.

Shouting and yelling finally penetrated through Iain's bloodlust a moment before someone hauled him off.

Dunsmore lurched to his feet, spitting out blood and teeth. He was about to launch himself into a fresh attack when Masterton and Killean blocked him.

"Enough!" Masterton barked.

One of the English guards hauled Iain several feet back. "Entertaining, to be sure, but enough is right."

The dragoon officer strode between the two heaving men. "Who are you?" he asked Iain, but he said nothing. "Well?" He turned to Dunsmore.

Dunsmore glared at Iain, his face swelling quickly, but he too said nothing.

"Says he's a merchant with the Dutchmen," the sailor offered.

"Doubt that," the dragoon said. "These two know and love each other, don't ya, darlings? This lot were picked up escaping Barbados. Killed one of the planters and an overseer before setting fire to the plantation. If he's a merchant, I'm a mermaid. The dog must have come from Barbados too. The governor will want to know about this."

The man's words coursed over Iain like ice. They knew about Wilton and Potts. He stole a glance at Mairead. She had edged closer to Hogendorp, and her face shone ghastly white.

The guards left and secured the door behind them. A bolt slid across the portal, locking them soundly inside.

Mairead rushed to Iain's side, her warmth a distraction from the throbbing pain. "Are you broke?" Her fingers touched his cheek, and he suppressed a wince. He caught her hand and gave a slight shake of his head.

"I'm well, Mairead," he said, tensing. His attention was now fixed elsewhere. This wasn't done.

Masterton approached, and Iain froze him with a hard glare. "Where have you been, Iain?"

"You dare call me by my first name, as though you have a right of friendship?"

"Aye, I do. I count Iain Locharbaidh Johnstone as a kinsman and friend."

Iain turned away from him, clenching his jaw while counting to ten.

"Where have you been? What happened to you?" Masterton pressed.

Iain's nostrils flared. "You and the others abandoned me, and you wonder where *I've* been? Back at the plantation where you left me. I escaped, but no thanks to any of you."

Masterton whirled around to Dunsmore, who crouched against the far wall, clutching his bleeding nose. "What's this? Why is he saying this?"

"Why are you asking him?" Iain said, his voice rising. "Look at me—face me. Ask *me* those questions."

Masterton faced him squarely. "What happened to you? We got all the way to Speight's Town, and still you hadn't come. We thought you had fallen."

"Fallen," Iain snorted. "Aye, fallen because of that bastard Dunsmore who knocked me out and left me to roast in the stillhouse fire."

"What the hell is this?" Masterton shouted at Dunsmore. "You left Locharbaidh to die back there?"

"If I wanted to kill him, he'd not be here," Dunsmore muttered.

Masterton, despite his age, was on Dunsmore in a flash. With a swift kick to Dunsmore's knees, he had the man lying on the floor. Before Dunsmore could rise, Masterton drove his boot against his windpipe. "Just because he didna die, doesna mean ye didna try. Useless pissen shit." He stepped off him and kicked him in the ribs.

Dunsmore groaned and rolled over. Slowly, he pushed himself from the floor. When he finally faced them, bleeding and swollen, hands pressed against his side, he snapped with rage. "And what do you call *him*, who puts the life of an Irish wench before his kinsmen?" He spat out, blood mixing with spittle. "He's a weak fool, and he's failed you all. Not one of you is blood, but you're all willing to treat each other as kin. Always taking issue with the accident of my birth, even though I left my house to fight in this bleeding war. You wouldn't let the past go, would you? The war broke auld alliances, and yet you stupid arses were holding on to something that would never be regained. I had more to offer than Angus or Killean, but you all treated me like dirt. I thought you all had balls, but clearly you don't." His swollen face was contorted with rage. "Since Tothill Fields, I had to put up with all your superior airs, as though you were something other than broken prisoners like the rest of us. Moss-troopers, nae sheep, so you claimed. But you followed the commanders just like the rest of us. You're all weak fools. You deserve it, being so blinded by this bastard," he spat, pointing to Iain. "All of you were willing to relinquish the keys to your own fate to him. *Locharbaidh* will find the way—*Locharbaidh* will lead us from bondage. The way you all treated him, a body'd think he was fockin' Moses." He gave a short bark of laughter. "I led you off that island. My plan, my balls. If we'd waited for him, we'd still be there breaking our backs for sugar that wasn't ours." Dunsmore wiped his bloody nose and sneered. "It don't matter, does it? None of us are leaving this place. They'll hang us soon as not, and mine will be the last face you see."

Mairead sat on her heels before Iain. She dabbed at his split lip with a scrap of torn shirt to stem the blood that continued to seep. Iain winced and tried to pull away, but Mairead fisted the front of his shirt to hold him in place.

"Sit still," she said in a brook-no-objection tone.

"Leave it, woman." He turned his head and stared at the far wall with a stoic, stubborn set to his jaw. The wall opposite to where his men stood. Killean hovered close, clearly torn between approaching and giving Iain his space. Masterton laid his hand on the young man's shoulder and leaned in to speak a few words to him.

"Should I administer to Dunsmore, then?" she asked with a lift of her brow.

Iain's eyes darted to hers, startled, then narrowing. "My lip can do with more dabbing."

Amused, Mairead pressed the cloth against his mouth, less gently this time. "You should speak to them."

"I said enough."

"You bellowed enough."

Iain pulled her hand away and frowned at her. "You think I'm in the wrong, is that what you're saying? You're agreeing with Dunsmore now?"

Mairead's expression softened. "I do not." She took time to carefully fold the cloth. "Dunsmore lied. He tried to kill you. Save your fury for him, but for the others, ask yourself what you would have done. Had Masterton been missing, would you have risked Killean to retrieve *him*? Possibly lose Killean in the gamble?"

"*You* came back for me," he replied, and she knew he was avoiding her point. Iain shut his eyes and lowered his head. After a few moments, he said, "Aye, we all know the code, but they shouldn't have been taken by the serpent in the first place." His angry expression faded to weariness.

Mairead glanced over Iain's shoulder to Masterton. She gave the older man a discreet nod to approach. Her hand had been resting on Iain's forearm, and she could feel him tense.

Masterton appeared and sank down on his haunches in front of Iain. Iain lifted his head, and although he didn't greet the grizzled man with any warmth, at least he didn't snarl.

"We mourned you for dead, Locharbaidh, you have tae believe that. Dunsmore told us you were polishing Potts off, swore you had the matter in hand." His sturdy arms were braced on his thighs.

"When we saw the fire and you still hadn't come . . . I know now that we should nae have believed the cur."

Iain nodded. "Aye, you shouldn't have." He caught the force of Mairead's pointed stare and added, "It's behind us." He offered his hand, and Masterton took it with a widening smile.

"How are ye with this group of Dutchmen, Locharbaidh? How did you get here?"

As Iain relayed their adventures, Mairead slid close to sit beside him. His hand rested on her trousered thigh. "And you?" Iain asked Masterton when he finished his story.

"Dunsmore's grand plan to commandeer a ship didna work out," Masterton said, wiping his nose with the back of his hand. "The *Jane Marie* was well guarded, so we stowed away on another ship that sailed out in the morning. They found us a few days out and handed us over to the local militia when we docked in Antigua."

"Any idea on what they plan to do with us?" Iain asked.

"Your Dutchmen? Who knows?" Masterton sniffed. "Our lot, that's no secret. At first, these stick-in-the-arse Southroners debated whether to hang us here or send us back to Barbados to hang there. Everyone heard of what happened at Mount Vale . . . and Wilton." His gaze flicked to Mairead for a second before returning to Iain. "They plan to hang us for it. Only waiting for word from the governor."

Cold dread washed over Mairead. She tucked her hands within the folds of the floppy sleeves and sat there, miserably silent.

"You didn't do the deed. Did you not tell them?" Iain said.

Masterton snorted. "Aye, but it only made us sound more guilty. I wouldn't have believed us either."

Killean and Angus Rae made their way over, greeting Iain with guarded relief. When Mairead would have left them alone, Iain took her hand and kept her beside him.

Her eyes drifted around the room. Hogendorp was pacing around like a caged beast, his men giving him as much room to vent as possible. Occasionally, he banged his fists on the door and fired off a string of angry Dutch words with a few garbled English ones. Whatever he said in Dutch made an impression on his men, judging by their shocked, yet pleased, expressions. Unfortunately, his outburst made no impression on the English guard seated on the other side of the door, for it remained firmly shut.

Hogendorp had long since ceased shouting obscenities when Mairead's ears caught the sliding of a bolt. The door opened, and the officer and two of his men were framed in the doorway. He pointed to each of the Scottish moss-troopers before ending with Iain.

"Governor says we can hang you, one by one, until someone confesses and we get the truth about who murdered Robert Wilton of Barbados. If it were up to me, I'd hang you all at once—get our man one way or the other, but our governor prides himself on his morals. Says he wants justice." He looked around and landed on Dunsmore, who sat alone in a corner. "Start with that one."

Two dragoons hauled Dunsmore to his feet and marched him across the cell. He didn't resist. Though dried blood caked his face and his nose had swollen to twice its natural size, he walked with his shoulders back and chin up. As he approached Iain, he looked long and hard at him with a knowing look on his face. Dunsmore owed Iain no loyalty, and he had every reason to seize upon this last opportunity to destroy him with a word. But Dunsmore kept his mouth shut. He lifted his head and allowed himself to be led past.

They were nearly at the door. Mairead couldn't allow this to happen, couldn't live with herself if she did. No matter that Dunsmore was a horrible, selfish man, he was innocent of *this* crime. If she allowed it, nothing would save her soul. And after Dunsmore, they would come for Masterton, then cheerful Killean . . . until only Iain remained.

Mairead knew what she must do.

She felt physically ill, but she stood up. Her legs barely held her up, but she forced herself to keep walking. All eyes were upon her.

She knew the implications. A horrible fear locked her knees. "If it's justice you want, he's not your man. He didn't do it."

Dunsmore's mouth dropped open, and he gave the impression of being slammed by a thick tree. The guards were also shocked, and Mairead could tell they were mentally reordering their thoughts. Up until now, she had managed to avoid their attention, slinking under their noses like a faded ragamuffin—like the mouse that Iain teasingly called her. Here she was speaking English, not Dutch, and revealing the feminine pitch of her voice, clearly not a boy.

Iain pulled her back and placed himself in front of her. "I did it," he told the guards. "I killed the man. Slit his throat and spilled his life blood, right in his own house. There's no need to continue this farce."

Mairead grabbed Iain's arm and forced him to look at her. She shook her head slowly. "I know the truth, Iain. Wilton was dead before you drew your knife. I *know*." She had suspected, even feared this, but when she saw the raw desperation in Iain's blue, blue eyes, any remaining doubt dissolved. She didn't need to ask him why he had lied to her. A wave of love for him washed over her and strengthened her resolve.

"Mairead—"

She slipped away from his grasp.

"You don't need to do this. Not for him."

Mairead ignored him and faced the dragoons. "I smashed his head before Iain came. I killed Robert Wilton." Then she added, "And I feel no guilt for it. He deserved it, Blessed Mother, preserve me."

"Not true," Iain cried out. "I did it. Only me." He looked around until he spied Killean. "This man was there—he saw me slice the man's throat. He can bear witness. Tell him, Killean Ross."

"Iain, cease—please," Mairead said. "I won't be able to live with myself if . . . I can't." Then she choked out a horrible laugh that only sounded gruesome.

"The bastard deserved it—deserved more. He was a whoremongering piece of shite, and he was going to hurt you. If he stood before me now, I'd split him from gut to gullet."

"Well, this has been . . . interesting," the officer said. "Where I had no one confessing, now there's a scramble to own to this. Damn." He pushed the brim of his hat off his forehead and scratched his head, looking decidedly ill-pleased. He grimaced and said, "The governor will need to be told. If it were me, I'd hang every last one of you and let St. Peter sort you out."

Mairead had seen one hanging in her life, when she had persuaded her brother Niall to slip away with her to the gallows on Eyre Square. The criminal had been a rough brigand, a fearsome creature who had killed twenty honest travellers if a dozen. When the cart rumbled up to the gallows and stopped under its grim shadow, the prisoner turned from defiant beast to pleading wretch. The one sharp memory Mairead had of that day was how the man shat himself as he danced at the end of a rope.

This would soon be her fate.

Her terror mounted, and she felt her nerve falter. How long would it take for her to die at the end of a rope? Would it be a swift end or would her slight body take longer to give up her soul than the brigand who had contorted for twenty long minutes? How had he felt with the rope choking the breath from him, as he scrabbled for air?

Mairead tried to wrench her mind from the gruesome thought, but cold panic had already taken root.

Had Ciara been paralysed with fear as the water dragged her down? Was there one heartbeat of a moment that she regretted wading into the water, praying she could turn back? And poor Bronagh. What terror must have gripped her upon the realisation that she'd never again see dawn's light?

Mercy! Mairead could throw herself on the governor's mercy. The dragoons had said he was most concerned with justice. She had been defending herself, surely that would count for something? But when the governor asked her for an accounting and if she felt remorse, how inclined to mercy would he be if he knew the truth? She was not sorry for it. Wilton had been a cruel, unfeeling bastard, and he deserved his end.

Then Mairead thought of Providence Moss with the anti-papist venom that spewed from her mouth. What made her think an English governor would treat her less harshly? She was still Irish and a woman, one who had struck her English master. Property. That was all she was to them. No matter how fair-minded the governor might be, he would never challenge the right of an Englishman to keep his property.

"Mairead?" Iain's low voice cut through her rising panic. His hand rested on her shoulder before edging up to rub the back of her neck. "You shouldn't have spoke out, lass."

"Oh, Iain." A painful knot spread across her chest. His desperate expression startled her, hard and grey. "I couldn't let them come for you. I couldn't let an innocent man die for me."

Iain sniffed. "He's nae innocent."

"Of this crime he is."

Iain exhaled slowly. He drew her to him and held her. Mairead started trembling, and no matter how hard she tried to still her limbs, she couldn't. "I won't let them take you."

She didn't answer. The last time he promised her this, she had thrown it in his face. They were as powerless now as they were then, possibly worse, but she wouldn't hurt him again with her own fears and despair.

"Do you hear me, my Mairead?" He lifted her chin and forced her to look into his eyes. "They will have to kill me first to reach you." He looked fierce and uncompromising, capable of tearing apart the world by the force of his rage. "Do you trust me?"

Mairead nodded slowly. This wasn't a lie, she did.

"I promised you'd return home."

"You're laird of your word." Not entirely hope but a calmness spread through her.

Iain smiled grimly. "Aye, upon my life." He gave her one last reassuring squeeze before releasing her and stepping away. Scanning the room, his gaze settled on one corner. "Stay here, Mouse."

"Where are you going?"

"To see Dunsmore."

Those three bleak words filled Mairead with even more dread. No good would come out of this.

"You were going to let me hang!" Dunsmore bellowed to Iain as they squared off against each other.

"Deserved it, you shitten bastard, for trying to *kill* me," Iain roared back.

Both men circled each other, step but step, both crouched low. The moss-troopers and the *Zeelandia* crew ringed around them, every man shouting loudly at the impending fight. The din was deafening.

Dunsmore threw a sharp jab; Iain ducked aside. Iain fired off one punch, then another, but Dunsmore blocked each strike with his meaty arms.

"You fight like a Southroner, Locharbaidh," Dunsmore taunted.

Iain shifted his stance and nailed him with a kick to the knee. Dunsmore's legs buckled, and he stumbled backwards. Iain was upon him. He fired off another strike to the head, but Dunsmore arched and jumped back, narrowly dodging the shot.

Iain delivered another hit; this time Dunsmore caught his fist in his own hand. Muscles strained, and both men fought to overpower the other. Dunsmore snarled and flushed beet red, while Iain focused every ounce of his strength on pushing the other man back.

366

The shouting around them exploded into a roar. The doors smashed open, and a company of dragoons rushed in to subdue the fracas.

Iain and Dunsmore exchanged a look, disengaged simultaneously, then turned on the English guards along with the others. Too late, the dragoons realised the trap that had sprung on them.

Dunsmore grabbed one of the guards in a head lock and seized the dagger from his belt With one fluid movement, he yanked the man's head back and slit his throat.

Iain fought, unarmed, against the knife point of another guard. As the man slashed, Iain darted aside and delivered strikes to the other's unprotected side. In a rage, the dragoon plunged his knife downwards. Iain grabbed his wrist and wrenched hard. The dragoon cried out and released his hold on the dagger. Iain yanked the weapon from this grasp and drove it into the man's belly with one final twist. A strangled groan ended with a spray of bloody spittle. The dragoon collapsed at Iain's feet.

Iain retrieved the dagger and whirled around to survey the room. A rush of energy pulsed through his veins. The others had overpowered the remaining guards, who littered the room as dead or unconscious. Either way, none would be in a position to raise the alarm. Hogendorp hefted a stave with unmistakable satisfaction as he stood over an unconscious Englishman at his feet. Mairead, to Iain's relief, stood close to Hogendorp, and she was similarly armed—and unhurt.

Iain hurried over to her. "All right, Mouse?"

"Well met, Locharbaidh." Her hair was in wild disarray, and her cheeks were flushed. "What now?"

"We split up into groups and get our arses out of here," he said, giving her a wink. Time to see his plan through.

Hogendorp, Masterton, Killean and Dunsmore regrouped around Iain. This had been his idea, a desperate bid to turn the tables on the English before the hanging started. He damned well wasn't going to allow anyone to put a noose around Mairead's neck. He'd raze the island to the ground before that happened.

"Remember, four groups," Iain told the men. "Hogendorp recaptures the *Zeelandia*, his first mate takes the *Redemption*, I lead a group to disable the guns at the fort, and Dunsmore will hold the beach and protect the boats for our retreat. When we sail from here, we take both ships—leave none behind to give us chase, and I'll make sure all cannon will be spiked." He turned to Dunsmore and couldn't help giving a dig, "*Two* prizes, not one. That's how you improve on a plan."

"Go to hell, Locharbaidh," Dunsmore said with grudging humour. "Yon greedy bastard."

"Gather your men and grab all the weapons. Find some nails we can use to spike the guns," Iain said.

While Dunsmore and Hogendorp rushed off to organise their men, Iain pulled Killean aside and spoke in a low tone, "Dunsmore played his last hand well, but doesn't mean I trust him with my back," Iain told him. "Be vigilant, lad."

"Aye, I will."

"One more thing—if I fail to get back in time, if the ship must sail without me, I'm counting on you to make sure my lass is on board. Can you promise me this?"

Killean's gaze flicked to Mairead. "She didn't listen the last time."

"This is one choice she doesn't get to make, ken?"

"Aye, I'll make sure she's aboard."

Iain squeezed Killean's shoulder. Stepping away, he found Mairead hovering near. Despite the men scrambling around them, he took her in his arms, unmindful of the urgency in the moment. "I need you to go with Killean, Mouse."

"What?" Mairead said, pulling away.

"It's best this way," he said, cupping her face. "Scaling the fort will be treacherous. With Killean, you'll be with the greater force and

368

will get to the ship faster. I won't have a worry if I know you're with him. Do this for me, lass."

Mairead looked like she wanted to argue. Her eyes were bright, but she eventually nodded—reluctantly, but she agreed just the same.

Near the door, Killean called out to the others, "To the ships!"

Iain bent down to give her a last kiss. They were in a rush, and they couldn't stay here any longer, but this might be the last time he saw her. "You better go."

"Stay safe, Iain, and hurry back," she said, searching his face. "We haven't finished arguing."

Iain grinned. "Aye, to be sure."

As Mairead left with Killean, she glanced back one last time. Grimly, Iain watched her go.

Masterton returned with a handful of long nails and a couple of swords, handing a well-balanced short sword to Iain.

"Ready, Locharbaidh?" Angus said with an eager grin.

"Aye, ready," Iain said. He gathered together his small handpicked crew, with Masterton and Angus and the *Zeelandia*'s cannon crew.

The men quit the guardhouse and kept to the darkened laneways, past the brothels and the taverns. They left the town behind and struck for the steep hill leading up to the fort.

Iain scaled the hill with a dozen men fanned out behind him. Loose dirt and rocks rolled beneath his boots, and he picked his way carefully so as not to alert the guards in the fort. As they climbed, the landscape became steep and scrubby. The moonless sky made it more treacherous, but they pressed on, managing to balance speed with stealth.

They wound their way to the eastern slope where the wind rushed at them, threatening to pick them off of the cliff. Iain crouched low, digging his heels into the sloped ground. Close by, Masterton crept up the hill, fighting against the force of the wind. They reached a scrubby mass of cedars and the wind shifted again, this time carrying a noise to their ears, very like a boot scuffing stone. From somewhere ahead, a man coughed and another responded.

Iain touched Masterton's arm; he in turn mirrored his action until all the men halted. How many militiamen were ahead, Iain couldn't guess—two or ten?

"Did you hear something?" one of the guards said.

"Just the wind."

"I think it was something."

Iain leaned in and whispered to Masterton, "Take a few lads to silence those two. We'll meet you at the top."

Masterton pulled a couple of men with him, and they disappeared after the sentries.

Iain and the others continued the climb, skirting where the sentries were, but now they were forced to cover a steeper section of the hill. From below, nearly lost in the howl of the wind, a short cry rose, then immediately fell silent. They were nearly at the top when Masterton and Angus reappeared.

The walls of the fort loomed ahead, dark in the night. The only light came from a couple of rushes fixed to the harbour side of the fort. The flame danced and contorted in the fickle wind. Laughter drifted from the south quarter, and to Iain's ears, it sounded as though there were more than a few men joining in the jest

The men closed to the top and fanned out, taking the last twenty feet carefully, lest anything betray them now.

Then from the harbour below, a lone bell started ringing, followed by an answering bell from the direction of town, this one more frantic.

Chapter 28

———•———

Mairead kept close to Killean and Hogendorp as everyone headed to the harbour. There was a new moon that night, and the only light to guide them came from the taverns a couple of streets over. Iain had timed their escape for when many would be well into their cups. By the sounds of carousing and laughter, he had chosen well.

They approached the warehouses and spotted a pair of militiamen posted in the courtyard near the main building. Dunsmore and a midshipman darted into the shadows, avoiding the reach of the lantern light, and circled around them. After a few moments of painful silence, Mairead heard a grunt and a muffled cry, then the sound of two bodies being dragged away.

At the harbour, the groups splintered off. Four boats were beached on the shore. A score of Hogendorp's men seized one and his first mate's crew another. Across the water, the two ships lay anchored. On the *Zeelandia*, a single light shone in the captain's quarters while a few more scattered lanterns peppered the *Redemption*.

"Wait here and guard the rest of the boats," Hogendorp told Dunsmore. "When we've swept my ship of the rats who have befouled her, we'll send a signal."

Dunsmore looked ill-pleased by the arrangement but gave a reluctant nod.

"Godspeed," Mairead told Hogendorp as he jumped into one of the boats. She watched as both crafts cut through the surf and darted after their quarry—one to the *Redemption* and the other to the *Zeelandia*. The night swallowed them whole, leaving only the creak and splash of oars to mark their passage.

"We should be on one of those boats," Dunsmore said to no one in particular. "Or headed to the forts. Not sitting here on a beach like a piece of driftwood."

Mairead turned to face the direction of the fort, wondering where Iain and his men were. The steep hill stood black as a chasm, but a few scattered lights were visible from where the fort perched.

Both boats finally arrived at their destination. The weak lamplight from the ships illuminated vague shapes. Like shadowy spiders, one by one the men crept up the ladders to reach the deck of each ship.

Mairead held her breath, waiting. She tightened her grip on the stave she carried. The only sound was the steady crash of the surf on the beach and the distant laughter from the town. The warm wind shifted to the east, and clouds parted to reveal a field of stars.

Muted sounds drifted to them across the water. A short cry, suddenly cut off; a gurgled gasp, then a thud. Dark shapes spread across both ships like ants swarming over dead crickets.

The drama unfolding on the water had so riveted Mairead that it took her several moments to realise Dunsmore's attention wasn't directed there. He stared at the town, towards the guardhouse, his palpable unease tracing down Mairead's spine like an icy finger. Soon Dunsmore's mood spread to others, and many glanced nervously back over their shoulders, shifting from one foot to another. It suddenly occurred to Mairead that Iain and his men climbing up the hill, and Hogendorp with his crew stealthily taking back the ships, were not the most vulnerable this night. She, with the remaining moss-troopers and half a dozen *Zeelandia* sailors left on the shore were pinned between the town and the water.

Dunsmore loosened the sword from the scabbard at his waist. Killean checked the priming on the pistols he had lifted from one of the dragoons. The others saw to their weapons as well. Mairead found herself behind a protective wall of ten grim men.

Then from the *Redemption*, a bell started clanging. Alarmed cries sounded from the ship and shredded the unnatural silence. The bell stilled suddenly. A few long, agonising moments passed, and the town remained silent. On shore, all eyes were fastened to the town. Then an answer sounded from the bell tower.

Shots fired from the *Zeelandia,* and a chorus of bloodcurdling cries broke across the water. The dull clang of metal against metal erupted, and the flash of gunpowder lit the deck. Farther down the harbour on the *Redemption,* a skirmish broke out on her decks.

English soldiers poured out of inns, lodgings, anywhere they had been quartered, and rushed to the shore.

Dunsmore swore. "Launch the boats."

"What?" Mairead said. "What about Iain and the others? They'll be stranded."

"Only a dozen went up that hill—they might not come down," Dunsmore said. "Get in the damned boat—*now.*"

Killean pulled her to the first boat while she kept looking over her shoulder towards the hill.

"They're coming." Dunsmore charged after them. "Killean— leave the wench. Help us get these boats in the water."

"Locharbaidh said—"

Before Killean could finish, Dunsmore scooped Mairead over his shoulders and dropped her into the first boat. "That's how it's done."

Mairead scrambled to sit up. The militia had almost reached their position when Dunsmore and Killean pushed the boat into the surf and leapt inside.

"Row," Dunsmore barked across the water to the other boat. "Past those breakers."

A spat of musket fire whizzed over their heads. Mairead dove for cover.

"Row harder!" Dunsmore yelled.

Another report of musket fire, and Dunsmore grunted in pain, clutching his left arm. "Whoresons." Blood flowed between his fingers.

More shots fired, but this time the boats were safely out of range.

Mairead stared at the shore, and her stomach dropped. A company of dragoons were now gathered on the shore, cutting off Iain's only escape from the island.

"No!" she moaned, gripping the gunwale. "We can't leave without Iain," she cried out to Killean.

"We must," he said, his mouth set in a grim line. "His orders."

Hot tears scalded Mairead's eyes. Through blurring vision, she glimpsed movement up at the fort—were they rushing down even now to the beach? They'd find the boats launched and run into the smoking muskets of the dragoons.

Despair flooded her, and she couldn't turn away as the boats slipped farther and farther from shore. *Farther from Iain.*

"Hold here," Dunsmore finally called out to the rowers.

"What are we doing?" Mairead asked. She clutched the gunwale and looked between the shore and the fort. Militia covered the shoreline.

"Holding here for now," Dunsmore said. "I'm not leaving him, but I'm not a fool to get slaughtered on a beach for him either." He turned to study the hot skirmish being waged on the *Zeelandia*. The clash of steel and occasional retort of a musket travelled to them across the water.

Mairead sat in the boat, miserable with fear for Iain. The men in the boats mostly had swords. Only a couple had pistols. They stood no chance against a shoreline of armed dragoons—who were getting closer. "We're drifting," she cried.

374

Dunsmore turned around and too late understood their error. The current had steadily pushed their boat closer to shore. "Row, damn you."

Killean and another man fired their pistols to shore. The smell of acrid gunpowder filled Mairead's nostrils. The men scrambled to reload in the dark.

Crack. A shot fired from shore and zipped over Mairead's head.

"Get down." Dunsmore pushed her down and twisted to shield her with his body. A moment too late.

Crack.

Dunsmore stiffened, then slumped over. Mairead screamed. She tried to get up to help him, but Killean held her down. He rose slightly and fired his pistol against the dragoons.

They rowed farther out, and the gunfire stopped. Mairead popped her head up. Killean laid Dunsmore down on one of the benches. Killean glanced up, and at her silent question he shook his head.

Dunsmore was dead. He'd died saving her. Mairead bowed her head.

Then Killean gasped. "God's sweet death." That sound sent shards of panic through Mairead. She whipped around to see what had shaken the unflappable Killean, and the blood drained from her face.

At the head of the harbour, around an outcrop of rock, the bow of a ship came into view, followed by taut sails. A sleek three-masted ship sailed into the harbour followed closely by a second craft. The foremost ship fired off one cannon shot, then another. *Boom. Boom.* Then its companion spat out another shot. Geysers sliced between the *Zeelandia* and the *Redemption.* Mairead shrieked. Waves surged, and the boat rode up and down over crests and troughs like a drunkard.

Another shot fired, and this time it ripped through the *Redemption*'s main mast. An earsplitting crack, then half the mast crashed down, dragging a tangle of sails along with it. Men screamed, and a few dove into the water. The vessel lurched and shuddered.

Mairead watched, white-lipped and trembling with fear, as the two ships engulfed the harbour. English reinforcements were now sailing in to put down the resistance.

They were caught.

Poised to strike, Iain and his men froze.

Down below in the harbour, the flash of musket fire lit the water, followed by an answering round. Above, the fort exploded into activity. "Ready the cannons!"

The need for stealth was over. If they didn't disable the cannons, no one was getting out of the harbour.

"Now!" Iain shouted.

He and the others topped the summit, screaming at the top of their lungs. They launched themselves upon the foremost guards.

The English were caught by surprise and fell back against the onslaught. Iain jumped over a fallen soldier, followed closely by Masterton and Angus. The cannon embrasure stood fifty feet away. Several muskets discharged in a haphazard spate of fire. A ball whizzed past Iain, grazing his ear, but he kept running forward. No hesitation. Hesitation meant death.

Near him, Angus wasn't so fortunate. A shot struck him square in the forehead. The moss-trooper crumpled to the ground.

Masterton released a blood-curdling cry and led a charge against the dragoons. No time to reload, the soldiers scrambled to draw out their swords.

Iain leapt aside to avoid a sword thrust, then slashed his blade into the man's unprotected arm. Iain followed through with an elbow to the jaw, and the man dropped to the ground like a bag of stones.

Behind him, a shout made Iain whip around just in time to see the butt-end of a musket coming for his forehead. He dropped to the ground and rolled to a crouch. Another soldier swung his sword, but a fraction too slow. Iain darted ahead, driving his blade into his stomach. The man dropped his sword and doubled over. Iain twisted the blade before pushing him away.

Reinforcements swarmed the fort. Iain's men fought to reach the guns, but they were now outnumbered.

One last push. The image of Mairead vulnerable down in the harbour flashed in his mind. He had to get to those guns or her life would be lost. Everything would be lost.

"With me, lads—with me!" Iain roared over the fighting. He grabbed a pair of fallen muskets and used them like staves, knocking heads and barrelling through stomachs. Masterton slashed his way through the soldiers with the fury of a hurricane. Desperation spurred them all on.

Iain pushed through the last ten feet to reach the first cannon. He retrieved one of the iron nails scavenged from the guardhouse and jammed it into the cannon's vent hole. Using the hilt of his sword, he pounded it in. One gun spiked.

He jumped down from the cannon stand to find one of his own fighting off a couple of dragoons at the next cannon. Iain hefted the musket in his hand and charged. He reached the first dragoon and smashed the butt of the musket against the man's head.

"Hold the line!" Iain shouted to Masterton. They needed more time. The grizzled moss-trooper nodded his acknowledgment, but in the next instant, he and the others were forced to lose ground from a fresh assault.

There were too outnumbered! Iain's men were wavering against twice their numbers.

Then from the other side of the hill, more men sprang up—fifty if a dozen. Iain groaned. There were too many aligned against them—too many to defeat.

This then would be where he died. His greatest fear realised. He gritted his teeth against the futile rage and dug his heels into the ground. If this was where he'd die, then he'd take as many down with him as he could.

"Fight to the death!" he bellowed, throwing his defiance at the English pressing them.

He braced himself against the attack of the new force, but instead the unknown men rushed against the militia.

Devil take him. Who were *they*?

A small group hung back and headed for the guns. Before Iain could stop any one of them, they started driving nails into the vent holes.

None of the guns were going to be firing on the ships below.

The English soldiers now found themselves outnumbered. Their resistance crumbled when one of their commanders called retreat. The English scattered and backed out of the fort.

Bleeding and cut and heaving for breath, Iain finally reached one of the newcomers, a man who appeared to be the authority.

"Who are you?" Both men said in unison.

"You're Scottish?" The man's clipped English accent gave him away.

"Aye," and then a thought, "Royalist?"

The man grinned. "Captain Holmes, in the proud service of His Highness Prince Rupert, illustrious cousin to our rightful monarch, Charles Stuart."

Iain laughed in relief and offered his hand. Christ's death, he'd not been this happy to see an Englishman before. "Iain Johnstone, formerly of Montgomery's regiment. Fought for the King at Worcester."

"Rupert will be keen to speak to you, then."

"Where is he?" Iain looked around, expecting the cavalier prince to spring out of the garrison, and wondering where the rest of the forces were.

"Still on the *Swallow*," Holmes pointed in the direction past the harbour. "Our ships are anchored beyond the bar." He turned to one of his men and yelled, "Give the signal." The man grabbed a torch from the embrasure and waved it back and forth in the direction of the harbour.

In the next instant, a boom of a cannon sounded. As Iain watched, two ships sailed into Antigua harbour, one flying a pair of rampant lions against a blue field.

"Our Rupert." Holmes nodded and gave Iain a wide grin. "He prides himself on his timing."

Another cannon shot fired and hit one of the ships. The crack of timber reached them all the way to the fort.

Was that the *Zeelandia* or the *Redemption*?

"Reinforcements footing it up the hill," Masterton called out. More trouble. "A full company."

"We have to get out of here." Iain called out to the rest of his men, "Gird up, lads. Grab whatever weapons they've left. One last push to get to shore. At least we'll be fighting downhill—that's one advantage."

"I have a better way," Holmes said. "Follow me." He grabbed a torch and led them across the fort to a broken section of wall which gave way to a steep hillside. Crashing waves roared a distance below.

The way down was treacherous, and were it not for the torchlight that guided them down, they would easily have pitched forward and broken their necks several times over. Still, there was no tarrying. English soldiers would reach the fort any moment now.

They half stumbled, half slid their way down the hill, following the bobbing torch ahead of them. Shots fired after them from the fort, but the company was already out of range. Iain risked a glance back and saw a few of the soldiers chasing down after them.

"The bastards are coming, lads."

They finally gained the rocky shore where a pinnace floated in the shallows. Iain ran into the waves, then hauled himself over the gunwale. Others piled into the boat while the anchor was being lifted and her sails were unfurled. The last of Holmes's men pushed the craft out farther before climbing aboard. Wind filled the canvas, and within a few moments they were skimming the waves towards the headland.

Iain's first view of the harbour and shoreline made his gut twist. A company of horse swarmed along the beach, blazing torches in hand. He forced his gaze to the ships crowding the harbour. Flanked by both of Rupert's ships, the *Redemption* had a gaping hole in her hull and appeared broken and crippled.

"There!" Iain cried out to Holmes when he saw the Dutch Republic flag flying on the *Zeelandia*. "She's ours. They won her back."

The captain of the pinnace changed course to come alongside the *Zeelandia*. Iain searched the deck for any sign of Mairead.

A rope ladder was tossed over, and Iain was the first to climb up. He ignored the group of *Zeelandia* sailors toasting their fortune with bottles of rum and turned an indifferent eye to the English, tied up hands and feet. His gaze swept the deck and settled on what he needed to see.

Mairead. Her shirt was stained with blood, but she seemed unharmed. With a happy shriek, she flew into his arms, and he held her with a fierce strength. He continued to hold her tight, murmuring against the top of her head. "We're safe now, Mouse."

"I thought—when I saw the ships—I thought . . . " Her face was flushed red, cheeks tearstained.

Killean Ross limped towards him, looking exhausted and grim. "Well met, Locharbaidh," he said, wiping a seeping cut with the back of his arm. "Masterton," he called over Iain's shoulder.

"You well, lad?" Iain asked.

"Aye," Killean said. "We lost a few men . . . "

"Angus isn't coming back," Masterton said grimly.

"Neither is Dunsmore," Killean said. "He died saving your lass."

Had Mairead's eyes not misted over, he might have questioned his hearing. "Dunsmore? He did that?" He struggled with his feelings over the news.

"Aye," Killean said.

"He shielded me from musket fire," Mairead said with a tremor. "They hit him instead."

Iain still couldn't believe it, though he was grateful. "He died well." The man had regained his integrity in the end. "We'll honour his memory in our way."

"The auld way," Masterton said. "And Angus too."

A thought occurred to Iain, and he gripped Mairead by the shoulders. "What were you doing in the middle of musket fire?"

"You would have preferred that I storm the ships with Hogendorp?" she said with an arch of her brow.

He smiled wryly. *That's my sprite.*

Mairead stayed close to Iain and Hogendorp when they boarded Prince Rupert's ship, the *Swallow*, early next morning. The ship's master greeted them warmly and led them to the Prince's private quarters. Curious stares riddled Mairead's back as she crossed the deck. The old Mairead would have shrunk under the scrutiny, glad for the shield of her oversized coat. But this Mairead, the woman who had survived the horrors and misery of the last several months, held her chin high and walked with the others.

They found Prince Rupert bent over a curling parchment that covered the entire length of the table. In one hand, he held a piece of charcoal, and in the other a ruler. A narrow bank of windows backlit his figure, emphasising a mane of fair hair against an azure velvet coat.

Mairead observed the cavalier prince with open curiosity. She had never been in the presence of royalty before, and she was not disappointed. Prince Rupert was far younger than she expected, but given the legend of his exploits, even if twice his age Mairead would have still marvelled.

"Your Highness," Iain said, giving a respectful bow and introducing himself and Mairead. The prince's interest pinned Mairead, studying her boyish garb as though readjusting his assumptions. "We were grateful for your timely arrival," Iain added.

"Timing is important," Rupert agreed. "Though it hardly runs in my favour these days. Welcome, gentlemen—and mistress. Karel Hogendorp, I despaired of finding you in the West Indies. We haven't shared a glass for a long time."

"I am hopeful we shall rectify that shortly, Highness."

Rupert smiled. "Your fortune continues, Hogendorp. I have a few choice bottles undamaged by the storms." He then called for flasks of canary wine.

When the wine had been poured, Rupert leaned back in his chair and said to Hogendorp, "The *Zeelandia* should be my prize."

"Your wine is excellent, Highness, but not enough to befuddle my senses," Hogendorp said. "You may have the *Redemption*. By rights, she should be mine since *my* men captured her, but I am willing to gift her to you for the sake of our friendship and this extraordinary wine."

"A crippled prize? Your generosity does you credit," Rupert said, tapping the side of his glass. "As it happens, I've already claimed her. My men are transferring the salvageable cargo to the *Swallow*. Let us focus instead on the *Zeelandia*, shall we?"

Hogendorp didn't reply.

Rupert smiled urbanely. "My ventures, as you may be aware, enable my cousin, Charles Stuart to live with dignity. As an exiled monarch, he has little other source of income."

"And my ventures, as *you* are aware, add to the coffers of his royal sister the Princess of Orange, mother and regent of our Dutch sovereign prince," Hogendorp countered.

"We are in a quandary, it seems." Rupert took a lazy sip of his wine.

"Sure, this is not simple, trying to please one Stuart over the other," Hogendorp said, mirroring the prince.

Iain's expression darkened, and he shifted impatiently in his chair. Mairead could almost hear his curses. After further inanities, he leaned forward and opened his mouth for what Mairead expected to be a blistering tongue-lashing. Hogendorp stepped on his foot and gave him a warning shake of his head.

"Highness, I propose the following," the captain said. "Petition the Princess of Orange that a share of her profit for this venture be offered for her brother's upkeep. She may be amenable to the notion given how fond she is of him."

"She is, but I hardly expect to be in a position to present that option to her," Rupert said, all amusement fading. He waved away his steward when the man would have refilled his glass. "I have no plans to quit the West Indies at this time, at least not until I've found my brother and the other lost ships of my fleet." His words sounded hopeful, but Mairead sensed the undertow of despair. She understood. What must her own brothers, even the most troublesome ones, be thinking of her disappearance? Where they still searching for her, or had they accepted that she was dead?

"This is a troubling burden," Hogendorp said with unmistakable regret. "Any word of Prince Maurice's fate?"

"Rumours only. There are reports that the *Defiance* and one of the other ships have been sighted in Tortuga. Being a Spanish-controlled territory, this complicates matters; however, I'd prefer his capture to the alternative."

The prince tossed back half his wine in one gulp, and he still looked miserable. Mairead put aside her shyness and said, "I wish you a joyful end to your search, Your Highness."

For an unguarded moment, the prince's face softened. "Thank you, mistress. You're Irish?"

"I am."

"Ah."

Mairead didn't miss the regretful inflection in his tone. Her stomach knotted. "Have you . . . any news of Ireland, Highness?"

After a moment, he said, "I am sorry to bring you an ill-report. As I understand it, most of Ireland is under English control."

Sweet Mother. "And Galway?" Her voice caught in her throat. "My family lives there—they remained during the siege."

The prince shook his head. "The town surrendered months ago. Also under rebel control."

Mairead closed her eyes as grief choked her. In her wishful dreams, Galway remained whole and untouched. She had never wanted to consider what would happen if the city's defenders failed. But now she had to face reality. "What of the townspeople?" Her voice faltered, and she cleared her throat. "Did they suffer? They weren't punished for their resistance?" *Please say no.*

"I haven't heard that they were. They would have had to deal with the usual starvation and plague." He must have noticed the blood draining from Mairead's face, for he hastily added, "The news was thin and incomplete. A great deal may have changed in five months." Though he said this in a tone that expressed his doubt.

"Five months? That long?" All this time, Galway had been under English control. Was her father still alive? What of her brothers? Iain's warm touch startled Mairead. His hand curled over her hers and gently squeezed.

"We'll learn more when we arrive in The Hague," Iain said, then in a lower tone for her ears only he added, "Don't lose hope, Mairead."

She choked back tears and nodded.

Iain gave her hand another squeeze before addressing the prince. "Best give me the bad news too. Before the rebels sold us, the Highlands still held."

The prince reached across the table for the flagon and filled Iain's glass.

"That bad?" Iain said grimly.

The prince's mouth turned down wryly. "Also occupied."

Iain clenched his fist, and a tic played in the muscle of his jaw. "What of the strongholds—surely, Brodick Castle stands for Scotland?"

Prince Rupert shook his head. "Fell half a year ago."

"Dunnottar? Bass Rock?"

Another slight shake. "All were lost to the cause within a few weeks of each other."

Iain sucked in his breath through gritted teeth.

"Perhaps you should rethink your plan to return to Scotland, my friend," Hogendorp said.

"I don't care how many Southroners are fouling the water," Iain replied. "I'll not forsake my homeland in her moment of need."

"If you must rush off to tilt at windmills like a Spaniard, leave the young woman in The Hague, where she will be safe," Hogendorp said.

Iain's gaze lingered on Mairead. His blue eyes darkened, and a furrow worried his brow. "That is her choice," he finally said. "If she still wants to return home, I'll make sure she gets there. I've given my word."

Rupert's eyes widened, and he shook his head, clearly alarmed.

"No, mistress, I would reconsider—strongly recommend you reconsider. Matters are far more alarming in Ireland than Scotland. The rebels still have a measure of respect for the Scots, and their policy is to eventually seek moderate reconciliation." He ignored Iain's snort. "But there's too much ill-will against the Irish. Your safety cannot be assured."

Hogendorp placed his hand on her shoulder. "Stay in The Hague. You can stay with my family, if you do not mind assisting my wife. She would be glad for the companionship. My son, Pieter, is an energetic lad and quite the trial for her. Ah, boys," he said with beaming pride. "The second floor is let. An English family, if you can stomach them. Iain Johnstone, you are welcome too."

The offer caught Mairead by surprise. "I can't . . . "

"Think on it. I won't press you for an answer now."

Rupert leaned back in his chair and studied Iain speculatively. "Warfare requires keen strategy, as you must know, Iain Johnstone, and one must be willing to employ varying tactics depending on the terrain and situation." He paused a moment. "If it's the rebels you wish to fight, you'd do better to join my crew and sail with us on the *Swallow*. We could use more able-bodied men. Fight under my command and you will wreak vengeance on the rebels who reduced you to slavery."

Iain's gaze lingered on Mairead before answering. "I thank you for the offer, Highness, but I'm for Scotland. The thought of home has sustained me these long months. I've been fighting for the Crown long enough, and I'm not willing to pledge my service to any man. Not now. As for the English, I can be a thorn in their side, but on my own terms."

Rupert sighed, clearly pleased. "Very well, it's clear we cannot move you. But I would ask you for a small service."

"If it's within my power," Iain said.

"It is, I assure you. I have dispatches for my cousin, and there is a gentleman in The Hague who keeps him apprised of news abroad. When you arrive in The Hague, ensure Secretary Nicholas receives them. For your troubles, I'll commend him to you and request that he provide you funds to speed you on your way. He will be only too pleased to do this for me. He can help arrange passage for wherever you must go. I'll have a packet ready for you when the *Zeelandia* sails."

"Consider it done."

Satisfied, Rupert turned back to Hogendorp. "So, my friend, we were discussing prizes. I believe you were about to agree on parting with half the cargo?"

Mairead stared down into her lap, lost in her own worries. She quailed at the thought of all the horrible things that might have already befallen her family, and she wouldn't have known. Plague. Starvation. *Sweet Mother, were they even alive?* For all she knew, she might be the last O'Coneill. Mairead thought of the churchyard where her mother lay buried, and she imagined additional gravemarkers under which the rest of her family were buried. Her hands began to shake, and she shoved them under her thighs to keep them still.

She didn't pay attention to the rest of the meeting and hardly remembered taking her leave of the prince. On the boat ride back to the *Zeelandia*, she gleaned that Hogendorp had won his negotiations and they would be setting sail in the morning. Iain said very little.

When they returned to the ship, Iain drew Mairead aside and led her to her quarters.

"Mairead, you heard what they said about Ireland. Don't go, lass. No shame in reconsidering."

"Would you? Reconsider?" she asked, knowing full well the answer. "If I asked you to give up your home, your family and your lands, would you?" Mairead held her breath.

Iain lowered his eyes and shook his hand. "Nay, I could not either."

"Of course not," Mairead said softly. She looked down as she continued. "The promise of returning home preserved me; you better than anyone knows this. Ciara—she would have wanted me to return—this is for her too. I must be with my family, Iain. I can't let them down, especially now, not in this time of need. They're the only anchor I have left."

"Let me be your anchor," he said fiercely, cupping her face. "Come with me to Scotland. Stay with me—be with me always. One day we will return to Ireland together."

Mairead's eyes filled with tears, and her heart ached. "I can't," she choked out. *Blessed Mother*, she couldn't. The pain mirrored in his blue eyes broke her heart. Her tears fell as droplets on her cheeks.

He bent down and kissed away her tears with aching tenderness. "Don't fret, lass. We've come this far. Best to see it to the end." He stroked her cheek with his thumb. "I promised to get you to Ireland, if that is what you want. I'm laird of my word."

Chapter 29

———◆———

Mairead leaned forward on the rail, watching as the port of Delfshaven drew closer. Frosty December air bit into her thin clothes. A grey mist clung to the deck, carrying with it the taste of rotted fish and tar. Disjointed sounds echoed across the harbour as men barked orders over the creaking of pulleys and the banging of crates. On the *Zeelandia,* the crew rushed to make ready for anchorage.

She squinted through the mist, seeing little more than the ghostly shapes of large buildings in the distance. As they entered the harbour, the fog lifted, revealing all manner of anchored ships—merchant ships, frigates and cargo barges. Shanties and sprawling warehouses hugged the waterfront, drawing teeming masses of people.

After several weeks of journeying, Mairead no longer needed to fear another ominous shout from the crow's nest. She should have been jubilant, even kicked up her heels in a celebratory jig, but a bittersweet agony squeezed her tight.

With the *Zeelandia* slipping into the harbour, a weary but triumphant ship, Mairead and Iain were nearing their crossroads. She'd be going home soon, but her time with Iain was running out. He hadn't wavered in his determination to see her safely to Ireland before rejoining Masterton and Killean in Scotland; but before, where she counted their remaining time in months, now they had but a couple of weeks. She'd have to be content with that.

The tread of boots approached—she knew those footfalls like her own shadow. It didn't surprise her, then, when a warm hand pressed upon the small of her back and a familiar voice curled around her heart.

"We made it," Iain said in a low, throaty voice as his arms encircled her waist.

Mairead closed her eyes and leaned back against his chest. She pushed aside her melancholy, refusing to think beyond the luxury of this moment. "I can hardly believe it."

Masterton and Killean drifted up on deck and joined them at the rail. Masterton was unusually quiet since Antigua, and Mairead noticed that his manner around Iain tended to be tentative. She suspected that the elder had not quite forgiven himself for leaving Iain behind, even if it had been instigated by Dunsmore. Killean, on the other hand, did not suffer from shyness. He rested his elbows on the rail and happily pointed out the different crafts to her. "God, I can't wait to get to Scotland," he ended with a sigh that dropped to his boots.

Mairead turned her head, pretending to examine the grains in the salt-seasoned wood. Tears pricked her eyes. Iain didn't answer, but his arms tightened around her.

"It's nae the Firth of Forth, but this will do—for now," Masterton said with a grunt.

"First thing I want to do is find myself a tankard of ale and a chine of beef," Killean said. As he rubbed his stomach, he gave Mairead a merry wink. "What say you, lass?"

"I can think of a few other things I wouldn't mind savouring," Masterton said, then coughed in his sleeve at Mairead's amused glance. The elder turned his attention to the nearing harbour.

"When we finally arrive in The Hague, first business we take care of is delivering Rupert's dispatches," Iain said. "We have a fee to collect and a ship to secure."

On deck, sails were trimmed, and men rushed about to drop anchor. Hogendorp was at the centre of all activity.

It took another couple of hours for Hogendorp to settle the ship's affairs with the harbourmaster before Mairead, Iain, Killean and Masterton could prepare to finally leave the ship and set out for The Hague, several miles to the north by canal. The *Zeelandia*'s pinnace was readied, and Hogendorp took his place at the helm. Mairead climbed nimbly into the boat and settled herself beside Iain. As Hogendorp's crew manoeuvred the labyrinth of canal waterways, she watched as the buildings slipped past. The air nipped at her nose, and she snuggled deeper into her cloak.

As they drew closer to The Hague, the canal narrowed and the buildings clustered tightly together. A rotted, decaying stench hung in the air, and Mairead was relieved when they finally pulled up to a landing and could leave the canal behind.

"My midshipman, Jan, will lead you to the address Rupert gave you," Hogendorp said, clapping a hand on the young man's shoulder. "When you are finished with your business, he'll see you to my home. I'll send word to my wife to expect guests. She will be sure to have a hearty repast ready for us, yes, and I shall meet you there." With that, Hogendorp strode off to speak to his bosun.

"This way," Jan told them, leading them into the city.

The streets were thick with people, and Mairead felt bewildered by the crowds. She had grown up in Galway, which she had always thought to be a worldly town, but against The Hague it was a mere village.

Carts and wagons clogged the narrow streets; hawkers shouted about their wares over the heads of people going about their hurried business. Mairead and Iain passed an open market with brightly coloured awnings. Normally, she would have been drawn to the stalls, but now she pressed closer to Iain. Jan moderated his stride so they wouldn't lose him in the crowd.

Eventually, the streets grew less frantic. Signs hung over doors announcing apothecaries, drapers and glovers. Jan turned down a different avenue where shops gave way to a meaner section of town. The streets narrowed, and the buildings looked tired and worn, like an overtaxed matron who had long ago given up trying.

Jan stopped before the last house in a row of buildings directly across from a small park.

"Is this it?" Iain asked, looking between the red-brick structure and the paper he had been given with the address.

"*Ja*, it is so," Jan said. He gripped the tarnished knocker and rapped smartly.

Mairead happened to be looking at the lace curtains in the window when she saw them slightly part and drop in a flurry.

After a few moments, the door opened, though just a little crack, and a woman peered out at them. Her plump face was unlined and gave nothing away about her age, but her sharp, dark eyes gave Mairead the impression that she had seen enough in her time. "*Wat wil je?*"

Jan spoke to her, no doubt explaining their mission, while the woman punctuated her response with a cluck of her tongue and a stern shake of her head.

"*Mijnheer* Nicholas is not at home," Jan explained to Iain with a shrug. The sound of voices, decidedly English, that came from the upper floor proved the woman a liar, but her expression remained doggedly stubborn.

She tried to shut the door on them, but Iain's boot stopped her. "Tell her that she must be mistaken." Iain held the woman's gaze. While Jan translated, Iain pulled out the nondescript packet of letters and showed them to her. The wax seal gave nothing of their provenance. "We were asked to deliver these to Secretary Nicholas."

When the woman reached out to take the letters, Iain held them back. "*Directly* to Edward Nicholas," he said and Jan translated.

"Who sent you?" the woman asked, now in Dutch-accented English.

"Och, she speaks English," Iain said.

Mairead stepped forward, impatient to end the impasse. Iain gave no indication that he was prepared to follow the prince's instructions by saying the necessary code words, having allowed the woman to goad him into a stubborn position. If the Dutch gatekeeper and the ill-tempered Scottish man were left to their inclinations, Mairead would find herself freezing on the doorstep.

Stepping in front of Iain, Mairead gave the woman her best smile. "My lord recommended us to Secretary Nicholas. He assured us that your master has a rare volume of Markham's *Arte of Fowling*, where the virtues of water dogs are discussed—specifically the hunting *poodle*." Mairead stressed the last word and watched for the other woman's reaction, hoping she hadn't garbled the message. If the woman threw a dusty tome of dog breeds at her, she'd have her answer.

Instead, the housekeeper opened the door fully, allowing them entrance. "Poodles. *Ja*, we are fond of the breed in this household." She still glared at Iain—out of principle, no doubt.

Mairead and the others crowded in a narrow and shadowed hallway. It was a small and modest house with very little furniture to welcome them. Stone floors had been well-scrubbed with lye, and the dark panelling smelled of beeswax, but a definitive chill occupied the air, lending the household a less than homey feel.

"*Een moment,*" the woman told them as she hurried up the stairs.

"That was daft," Iain muttered when she disappeared. "What's wrong with speaking plainly? Everyone knows about Rupert's fondness for his dead dog. The rebels had a superstitious dread over the poor beastie. Don't tell me that one of them couldn't decipher that nonsense about hunting poodles."

Mairead pressed a hand on his chest and caught his eye. She nearly pinched him. "These are difficult times, Locharbaidh. Tuck away the ogre."

The corner of Iain's mouth lifted, and he was going to reply when the creaking of stairs interrupted them.

An older man descended, his silver-white head ducking slightly to clear the overhang. He wore a black coat, the broadcloth once being costly, but upon a closer look it appeared thread-worn.

The gentleman paused at the last step. "I am Edward Nicholas. Marta says you bring news from a respected acquaintance?"

"Aye," Iain said. "We've only now arrived from the West Indies."

Nicholas's brows shot up when Iain began to speak. "Marta spoke rightly—you are Scottish. Curious." His gaze swept over Masterton and Killean but rested a little longer on Mairead. "Very curious." He turned to Marta and said a few words in Dutch, which appeared to involve Jan. The midshipman brightened and allowed himself to be led down the hallway.

"Marta will fetch him a drink from the buttery. We'll call him when we're finished," Nicholas said. "Will you follow me upstairs? It's rather draughty here, and I have an adequate fire in the upstairs stove."

"She better be getting us something from that same buttery," Masterton muttered under his breath.

Nicholas led the way up a steep flight of narrow stairs. "You must forgive Marta. She was more cautious than usual given that I already have guests. As it happens, your timing is excellent." At the top of the landing, he turned left and headed to a room at the end of the corridor.

Mairead stepped into the room immediately behind Secretary Nicholas. Two men stood near the brazier, a lean, raven-haired man in an exquisite brocade coat and another, his opposite, a rugged man in a buff coat, the kind that cavalry officers were wont to wear. Both their glances slid past Mairead and rested on Iain. The reaction from all three men was instantaneous.

Iain released an earsplitting bellow and, in two quick strides, launched himself across the room straight for the cavalry man. Mairead gasped, expecting Iain to attack, but instead both men embraced each other with the heartiness of brothers.

"Devil take you, James Hart, yon bloody Southroner," Iain said.

"What the hell are you doing here, Scotsman?" Hart asked with a disbelieving laugh.

"I should ask you the same," Iain said. "I haven't seen you since Worcester. A pox on that Cromwell."

"I've been here since then," Hart said, the smile fading from his face. "But you—I had heard ill-news that you were Barbadoed?" He glanced over at the other man with a questioning glance.

"Aye, but the arseworms were bane-idle, so we slipped past them. You can never keep a Johnstone down." Then Iain turned to the other man with building anger and pointed his finger at him. "Och aye? The foppish barrister from London—Nathaniel Lewis. Pretty nigh useless. You were supposed to get me and my men out of that bridewell."

"An unpleasant and unfortunate turn of events," Lewis said. "'Tis not often that someone steals a march on me."

"Is that so? Shamed were you?" Iain squared his shoulders, his tone getting harsher by the moment. *"We were the bleeding slaves."*

"I promised nothing, if you recall," Lewis countered. "And I completely disavow any knowledge of their intention to sell you to the Barbados merchants. That was entirely unexpected." His attention shifted to Masterton and Killean before settling on Mairead. "I see that you are still with company, well done."

"Well done? Only two out of ten men remain," Iain ground out.

Lewis's eyes narrowed, and Mairead could see him mentally readjusting his equation. Then a smile spread on his face. "Welcome to The Hague, mistress," he finally said with an eloquent bow. "Not all companions are cut from the same cloth. And here we have boorishly aired our disagreements."

Iain counted to ten. "This is Mairead—"

"Mairead O'Coneill," she said, coming forward, nodding to both men. "Former indentured servant."

Lewis's mouth quirked. "I hope you didn't leave without references."

"Burned in a fire," she said.

"Speaking of papers," Edward Nicholas interrupted. Until now, he had said nothing throughout this strange reunion. "I understand you have something for me?"

"Aye, right. We're here with a purpose." Iain withdrew a sealed letter from his coat and handed it to the gentleman.

"You've gone from bondsman to courier?" Hart asked.

"Dispatches from Prince Rupert," Iain replied. "Our paths crossed briefly in the West Indies."

Nicholas drifted away from the group, engrossed in his letter, leaving Iain to return to Mairead's side. She felt his hand brush hers. The gesture didn't pass the notice of either Hart or Lewis.

"Where's Glencross? I would have thought he'd be with you . . . " Hart asked, his voice trailing.

Iain's mouth pressed in a tight line, and his answer was brusque. "The lad didn't make it. Died of the fever."

"I'm sorry for that," Hart said. "He was a good man."

Iain nodded.

"It seems as though a great many more didn't make it," Nicholas said. "Prince Maurice has been lost at sea. Hurricane. Though His Highness writes of his hope to find his brother, I fear the worst."

Even Lewis seemed shocked by the loss of Prince Maurice.

"Rupert was left with only his flagship," Nicholas continued. "All the prizes and cargo that he had seized—all lost or sunk to the bottom of the sea."

Lewis shook his head. "This *is* a grave setback. The King must be told."

Nicholas nodded. "I will include the news in my report to him. I'll also write to the Queen of Bavaria about her son posthaste. Though this be troubling news, better she learn of Prince Maurice's disappearance from a friendly pen."

A pall settled on the gathering, and Mairead found her strength beginning to ebb. The excitement of the morning combined with the glowing coals in the brazier made her weary. She looked with longing at the vacant chairs.

"We can't stay long," Iain said. "Our captain's man is below, drinking you dry." It sounded to Mairead that Iain was fishing for refreshments, and even Masterton perked up, but a strange expression flitted across Secretary Nicholas's face.

"I shan't keep you. I understand you had a difficult journey," he said. "I thank you for delivering these so promptly."

Iain frowned. "There's one more piece of unfinished business. The prince said you were to give us funds to speed us on our way— you could help us find passage back home. Did he not write that in the letter?"

Nicholas flushed, his discomfort visibly increasing. He unfolded and refolded the paper. Finally, he sighed in the manner of a man forced to admit an unpleasant secret. "If only I could. The King hasn't provided me with business to my care nor any means to enable me to live. I barely have enough for my own household."

"Typical Stuarts." Iain rolled his eyes and muttered under this breath.

But Mairead was shocked. How was this possible that a king didn't provide for his servants, especially when he relied on them for news? Then she remembered Rupert's preoccupation with providing an income for his cousin.

"The unfortunate truth of the matter is that The Hague is filled with impoverished exiles," Hart said, drawing attention away from

Nicholas. "Iain, you needn't worry about not having a place to sleep or wonder where your next meal will come from, not for you or your companions," Hart said. "You are welcome to stay with my family for as long as you are here."

"That's very kind, but our concern was finding passage home, ken. We've already made arrangements to stay with the captain who brought us here. His man is waiting below."

"I'm sure he won't be troubled if you make alternate plans," Hart said. "Send your guide back to his master with the news. Where are these lodgings?"

"Lau Mazirellaan," Iain said.

"That's my street."

"*Sixteen* Lau Mazirellaan?"

"And my building," Hart said. "If your captain is Hogendorp, then he's my landlord—or rather his wife is my landlady. I don't think I've seen Hogendorp more than twice this past year."

"He was in Barbados," Iain said. He rubbed his beard and exchanged a look with Mairead. No funds. No ship. How were they to keep themselves? Living on charity was not an answer. But a small ray of light bloomed deep in her core. At least they would be together for the time being.

"I can offer a solution," Lewis said suddenly. "I can arrange passage for you to Scotland." That ceased the side conversations in the room.

"How?" Iain asked.

The barrister didn't answer at first. He toyed with the onyx ring on his finger, stretching the tension. "Curious how situations repeat. We find ourselves in the same position as when we last met in London."

"Are you only capable of speaking in riddles? Speak plainly, man."

"Passage to Scotland—in exchange for delivering dispatches—for you and all your companions," Lewis said. "Plain enough?"

"Dispatches for Argyll?" Iain's eyes narrowed.

"That ship has sailed," Lewis replied, flicking lint from this sleeve. For one moment, his annoyance betrayed him. "While you were away, the Marquis of Argyll signed Articles of Agreement with the Commonwealth. His capitulation assures his cooperation and the obedience of every man, woman and child allied to his clan. Not inconsiderable, as I understand Scottish politics."

"That worm."

"We are in agreement, for once."

"Who are the dispatches for, then?" Iain's eyes narrowed.

"The King must once again look towards Scotland for aid." Nathaniel smiled, but both Secretary Nicholas and James Hart looked grim. "There's a resistance brewing."

Mairead was watching Iain, and his expression sharpened when he heard *resistance.*

"The King has signed commissions for the leaders to act in his name," Lewis continued. "We need you to deliver these commissions to the Earl of Glencairn in Renfrewshire. I can have a ship ready to sail within a couple of days."

Masterton broke out into an eager grin. "Better than we expected, lads."

"Aye, Renfrewshire is very close to home," Killean said.

Iain's fingers pressed against Mairead's waist. She looked up and met his steady gaze. "I'll consider it only on one condition."

"Locharbaidh—" Masterton grit out. Iain silenced him with a hard look.

"I need to secure passage to Ireland for Mairead," he said, his voice oddly strained. "The lass has family there, and she intends to return."

Lewis's eyes widened. "I wouldn't recommend it. Strongly so."

"Are we back to that again?" Iain asked.

"Do not doubt I can make this happen, but if you have a care for the lady, you'd not ask."

Mairead felt a cold shiver creep down her spine. "Why do you say that?"

Lewis's cool demeanour thawed a little, and he sounded almost kind. "If you return, mistress, your freedom and your safety will be at great risk. Four months ago, the Commonwealth passed the Act of Settlement, which allows for the resettlement of Irish land. They have the authority to evict any Irishman who has ever fought against Parliament and forcibly relocate them anywhere they deem fit. Even if they hadn't fought, it is enough that they're Catholic. There has been talk . . . Local officials have been overreaching their directive—should come as no surprise. There have been rumours they've begun to transport to the colonies. The West Indies, specifically."

Mairead gaped at him, speechless and horrified. "What you describe is how I became indentured in Barbados. This . . . Monstrosity . . . is now the rule of law?"

Lewis nodded gravely and looked past her to Iain. "Do you understand now? She cannot return to Ireland."

Mairead felt her knees weaken, and if Iain wasn't holding on to her, she would have crumbled to the ground.

"I need a moment alone with the lass."

"You can't go," Iain told Mairead. They were in a small chamber adjoining the library. "I'm truly sorry. 'Tis a bitter thing to bury a dream."

When he tried to embrace her, she blocked him with her hands. "I won't accept this," she said, shaking her head. Her hazel eyes were wild. "I won't—I can't accept this." She covered her mouth with her hand and turned away. "This changes nothing. This can't change anything."

"There's no debate, Mairead," he said firmly. "You must stay here."

"The situation in Ireland is no different than when I left," she said bitterly.

"Christ's death, Mairead," Iain said, struggling to master his growing frustration and alarm. "You were taken by marauders who sold you for gold. Had they been caught by their commanders, they would have been shot. And yet there was enough profit for them to have taken that risk. How much worse will it be now that the English have openly blessed this trade? Greedy bastards will be seizing whatever and whoever they can, make no mistake."

"But my da has very little land—he's a shopkeeper."

"You think that matters?" Iain stepped away, raking his fingers through his hair. It took everything he had not to rage against his own fears for her. He turned back to her. "You weren't anywhere near Galway when you were snatched. Even if you travel to the next village, some whoreson might see you as a coin in his coffer." He held her shoulders and tried to soften his tone. "What if you are sent back to Barbados, lass? I won't be there for you. I won't be there to protect you."

Mairead blinked furiously. "What am I to do?"

Stay with me. Marry me. This is what his heart shouted, but he didn't have that luxury. With this resistance brewing back in Scotland, he didn't know where he'd be from one day to the next. He had failed one woman before; he wasn't about to fail this one.

"You must remain here in The Hague. Hogendorp has offered you a place in his household. You will have a bed and a roof over your head. Here, you will be safe."

"Without you?"

He couldn't look at her. "I've no choice. These bastards keep pulling me back in." A poor attempt to lighten the moment. "I can't walk away from this, lass, you know I can't. It's changed everything."

"Will you not take me with you?"

"I can't—Mairead, my lass. I don't know where this fight will take me. I don't know if I can return to my lands or where I'll make my bed. We'll all be living rough like Wallace." He squeezed her arms. "I'm a solider, Mairead. You need to understand this. My wife

401

thought she did, but what she needed was a gentleman farmer whose only concern was the health of his livestock. She deserved that, poor lass. Instead, she received poor trade."

"You are never poor trade, Iain Johnstone, and I'm not Innis."

"Aye, you are not," he said thickly. "Nor would I want you to be anyone except Mairead." He cleared his throat. "It would break me if anything happened to you; that's the truth. Please. Stay here. For me."

Mairead looked lost and small and thoroughly defeated. Her hazel eyes were dull and clouded. This was how she had looked when Ciara died.

A knock sounded on the door. "Time is slipping away, Scotsman," Lewis said. "We must have your answer."

"One moment, man," Iain barked. When he turned back to Mairead, her shoulders had drooped. "Mairead? What's it to be?"

She looked miserable and lost, but she gave an imperceptible nod. "I'll stay."

Iain closed his eyes and sighed. An empty, though necessary, victory.

When they rejoined the others, all eyes were latched upon them. Masterton bristled with suspicion, no doubt fearing the worst. Even Killean looked piqued.

"Aye, I'll do it," Iain told them. "Make the arrangements."

All the way to the Hart residence, Mairead felt like a heavy fog had filled every crevice in her brain. Voices echoed from far away, and she could barely concentrate. When they arrived at the Harts', she had forced herself to greet their hostess with some courtesy. Mairead's grief may have been outwardly contained, but inside it resembled a slavering beast.

Mistress Hart greeted them with a calm, unruffled air, no matter that she was living in exile and had just welcomed four additional guests to her table. A crisp white apron stretched over her blue woollen skirt, and her rounded middle signified she was expecting a child, her second as Mairead soon discovered.

"Iain Johnstone?" she said with a genuine smile. "My husband has spoken of you often. Did you not once try to steal his horses?"

Iain grinned to the point where the corner dimple in his cheeks appeared. "You can't fault me for trying."

When the woman discovered Mairead came from Ireland, she reacted with genuine curiosity instead of revulsion. Several months with Providence Moss had made Mairead forget that there were decent English in the world.

"We're both a long way from home, it seems," Mistress Hart told her. "We'll make the best of it. Do call me Elizabeth."

The Hart household included their year-and-a-half-old son, who had a genius for getting into everything, an elderly maid who lived as a family member and a father-in-law who reminded Mairead of her own father. She choked back the sudden tears that lodged in her throat.

"Are you unwell, my dear?" Elizabeth touched her shoulder with concern. "Do take a seat by the hearth. You look chilled."

Mairead's eyes skimmed across the blue-and-white Delft tiles that decorated the fireplace as Elizabeth ladled a cup of broth for her. The stock was flavourful and perfumed with a faint scent of fennel. "Broth can be restorative," the woman assured her.

Restorative enough to patch together her shredded life? Enough to change how things stood in Ireland and Scotland—to change her and Iain?

When Iain drifted over to join Mairead, Elizabeth melted away. He dropped to his haunches and searched her face. "Mairead, lass . . . "

She tugged at her fingers in her lap and couldn't meet his gaze. Instead, she focused on the hard line of his jaw. "Please don't. I can't talk, not right now." She could fight down the tears and encase herself in a cold shell, but only if Iain didn't touch her and call her

Mouse. Then her grief would overwhelm her and she'd dissolve into a sobbing mess. Mairead had no defences against him.

Iain leaned in to say something, but a mild ruckus erupted down on the lower floor. Hogendorp had returned home, judging by the pounding of footsteps and a woman's hearty shriek and pleased giggle. Mairead exhaled a shaky breath, grateful for the distraction.

The Harts' maid crossed to the hearth to place another log in the fire. Mairead could tell Iain was irritated by the interruption, but he had the good grace to hide it. He rose and leaned against the mantel with his arms folded across his chest, while he waited for the maid to finish stoking the fire.

"*Mevrouw* Hogendorp is normally reticent," the maid said as she finally hung the poker back on its hook. "She must be pleased to see her husband after such a long absence."

Hogendorp trudged up the stairs and burst into the room. On his shoulders, he carried a young lad with hair so blond it looked white. His son, Pieter, had the look of his father. and Hogendorp beamed with pride.

"Stolen my guests, have you?" Hogendorp said in a booming voice. "You English always encroach on borders." He laughed and clapped Hart on the back before plunking down on the table a couple of bottles of spirits. A chorus of cheers rewarded his contribution.

"They will be occupied for some time," Elizabeth said, drawing Mairead away from the hearth and Iain. "I'll find you a change of clothes." She glanced over her shoulder at the maid, who had hooked a kettle over the fire. "Jennet's heating water for your bath."

"I'd be very grateful for that." Mairead needed time alone. She felt close to shattering, and she couldn't fathom staying in the crowded room a moment longer.

Mairead attended her toilette in a daze. When she finished, she peered into a silvered glass set on the wall. A strange apparition reflected back at her, with shorn locks and stricken eyes.

CRYSSA BAZOS

Ireland, home, family . . . love . . . eluded her like a distant shore. She had been so close to realising her hopes that, for a brief moment, she almost heard the voices of home and tasted the peat smoke on her tongue. But a bank of mist swallowed everything up. Home had been her shield against despair, pushing her to keep going. And now it was gone.

The door opened, and Iain entered. Their eyes met in the glass. Mairead watched him advance to her through his reflection in the mirror. When he touched her shoulder, hot tears suddenly flooded her eyes, and no matter how hard she tried, she couldn't will them away.

Iain gathered her in his arms while Mairead sobbed into his chest, clutching a fistful of his shirt. Grief poured out of her, and she didn't have the strength to fight against it anymore.

He bent to scoop her up and carried her to the bed, where he cradled her in his arms. Murmuring words of comfort, he brushed his lips against the top of her head.

"My Mairead, my love." He didn't try to hush her, only stroked her hair and held her tight. Through the haze of her tears, she heard him sing softly. His baritone voice lulled her with comfort.

Mairead didn't know how long she lay curled in his arms, only that her tears had ceased and a deep weariness enveloped her. The last thing she remembered was being tucked into bed and covered by a quilt.

Chapter 30

———◆———

Iain's boots crunched over the crisp snow. The streets had been blanketed overnight, muddy ruts frozen ruts into hard ridges. He headed for Secretary Nicholas's house to pick up the King's commissions and obtain their passes for the ship. They were to set sail on the early morning tide, and he and the lads needed to be on board that night.

Without Mairead. *Christ's death.*

Masterton and Killean remained back at Hogendorps', both groggy after drinking the captain's strong brew. After Mairead had fallen asleep, Iain had joined them deep into the night, but no amount of liquor could blunt his misery.

Hours away from embarking, how could he do it—leave, knowing he'd likely never see her again? It burned on his tongue to promise her that he'd return for her one day, but while he'd never move on without her, he didn't want her to lose her chance for happiness.

She'll be better here, Locharbaidh.

Iain had made arrangements with Hart to allow her to stay with his family instead of Hogendorp's, if she so preferred. He expected Mairead would be more comfortable with Mistress Hart since Hogendorp's wife spoke only halting English. And if things improved in Ireland, Iain could be sure that Hart would know, could gauge the right time to help Mairead return to her homeland. He could trust his friend to do this for him. Mairead deserved to return to her family, as he would have wanted to return to one. Glencross had been a brother to him, so too McCaul who had been buried in a common grave back in England. Knots had been severed and his life unravelled.

It hardly mattered for the future. He had a task to complete, lands to win back and English to defeat. While Killean looked upon this venture with the rosy eyes of an optimist, he and Masterton knew the fight that lay ahead for them. Sacrifices would be required, and the first one was his heart.

Not paying attention to the winding streets, Iain took a wrong turn and found himself in an unfamiliar quarter. He backtracked and passed a series of trade shops, including one with the sign of musical instruments. The sign creaked and swayed, half of its face dusted with blowing snow. Iain stopped beneath it.

Frost traced its spidery patterns across the shop window. Iain wiped the glass with his sleeve, then cupped his hands against the pane and peered inside. A man bent over a work table sanding a lute, his movements precise and deliberate. A few feet away from him, a young boy swept the floor.

Iain entered to the sound of a jingling bell and a gust of snowy wind. The craftsman greeted Iain with a flow of effervescent Dutch. A cheery fire warmed the workshop, and the room smelled of wood shavings and glue. Along one table, several string instruments, in varying stages of completion, lined the length of a display shelf: violas, lutes and even one gleaming fiddle.

"Do you speak English?" Iain asked.

"*Ja.*" The man bobbed his head. "A little. I do my best."

"This," Iain indicated the fiddle. "May I see it?"

"*Ja,* of course." The man nodded and hovered close as Iain turned the fiddle over in his untrained hands.

The wood was supple and as smooth as silk, its lines fluid and unmarred by cracks. The instrument still smelled of fresh stain. Experimentally, Iain plucked one of the strings, and the sound was crisp and pleasing. He tried a few more strings, searching for the right sequence to match the tune that ghosted in his head. Then he hit upon a sound that resonated deep in his memory. Again he played the same sequence.

The sound returned Iain to the crushing mill in a heady-hot afternoon when Mairead stepped onto the platform, nervously clutching a battered violin. He saw her sunburnt face with poignant clarity—she glowed, enraptured and entrancing. That had been the moment he knew that he loved her. This would be the very image of Mairead he'd carry in his heart all the way to Scotland and beyond. And he'd never hear that damned ballad without it lodging in his throat.

Iain ceased plucking at the strings. The urge to bring her here, to this treasure of a shop, seized him. It would bring a smile to her eyes and one more memory he could hoard.

"Use this." The shopkeeper offered him a bow, and Iain suddenly realised how ridiculous he must look.

"Nay, I don't play."

This confused the shopkeeper, and he seemed to be turning Iain's words over in his head. "I give you permission," he said with an encouraging nod.

"I don't know how to play." This confused the shopkeeper even more, but now the man had a worried crease in his brow, no doubt fearing that Iain might be a snatcher of innocent fiddles. Before he alarmed the poor man further, Iain returned the fiddle to him.

"Have you sold this yet?" Iain asked on a whim. "Is it bespoke?"

"*Nee*—no."

"How many *guldens*?" Iain regretted it, not least because of the flare of interest in the craftsman's eyes, even though Iain didn't have the wherewithal to pay even a farthing. Still, he was curious, and he waited for the man's response. When the man named his price, Iain winced. That sum could comfortably pay for another passage to Scotland.

"Thank you," Iain said to the man, now eager to leave the shop. Secretary Nicholas waited, as did another bend in a rutted road.

This time the gate warden, Marta, welcomed him civilly. Not friendly, but at least the woman didn't barricade the house against him.

Iain found Lewis waiting upon Nicholas. The barrister stood before the brazier, warming his hands against the glowing coals while Nicholas wrote at his desk, his nib scratching the parchment.

"Captain Johnstone, welcome," Nicholas said, looking up briefly. "I'll be but a moment."

He joined the barrister at the brazier, glad for its warmth. "Do you have the passes ready?"

"Naturally. The secretary is finishing them."

"Am I to know where I'm going, or are you including a treasure map for me to decipher?"

Lewis gave a wry smile. "You are not impatient, not at all. It would serve you right if I gave your instructions in invisible ink." For a moment, he looked as though he were considering that. *The bugger.* "Very well, then, since we *are* waiting. The ship will leave you in Fife, where you will make your way to the Highlands to deliver these letters to the MacDonnell of Glengarry, the lairds of Maclain and MacLeod and the chief of Clan Ranald. From there, you will proceed to Glencairn in Renfrewshire to the south."

"After Glencairn?"

"I don't know what you'll find in your home in Dumfries," Lewis replied, getting to the heart of what Iain truly cared about. "You were once a moss-trooper—quick to seize the shifting moment? Gauge the wind when you see Glencairn, then decide."

Nicholas sealed the last letter with a press of a signet ring on the hot wax and rose from his desk. "Guard these with your life, Iain

Johnstone." He handed the packet of letters to him. "The note from the King is carefully drafted and not all has been committed to paper. Let Glencairn know that His Majesty has taken note of his request for small fire pieces, firelocks and powder, as well as vessels supporting them on the coast. They are not, however, to act until Major General Middleton is sent to them. The King is firm on that."

Ah, another survivor from Worcester. "When will that be?"

Nicholas gave a nearly imperceptible shrug. "Middleton has been ill. We cannot endure the journey until he is sufficiently recovered."

Iain didn't reply; he had his answer. Let the great chess game begin. All the pieces would be set with urgency on the board, then left to grow moss until the King saw fit to play. He'd been through this before. "Aye, I'll let the earl know," he replied before tucking the packet in his coat.

"Have you sorted out your affairs?" Lewis asked. "You must be ready to board this night."

Iain opened his mouth to reply that he had, then reconsidered his answer. "Nay. There's still something I need."

"Allow me to guess. A fourth pass?" Lewis suggested.

The barrister used words like a dagger—a swift, sharp thrust straight into the gut. "Nay. A fiddle—I need a fiddle."

Whatever Lewis assumed Iain would ask, this clearly wasn't it. The man stared at him blankly. "I beg your pardon?"

"A violin, if you prefer. I'll be in your debt."

After a few moments of mulling, Lewis said, "I wouldn't know how to procure one before the ship sails."

"I've already found one." Iain gave him the street. "I need it before I leave for the harbour. 'Tis a parting gift."

Mairead minded the child while Elizabeth and her maid readied the evening meal, the last meal before Iain, Masterton and Killean left for the harbour. Outside, the sky turned a sapphire blue, and snow drifted lazily. She held the boy up to the window to show him the falling snowflakes while she kept an eye on the street below.

She was in a melancholy mood, made worse by not seeing Iain all day. She had hoped she'd have the opportunity to drink her long fill of him before he finally left. Disappointment would be her constant companion in the days and years to come. Might as well accustom herself to its acrid taste.

Little Thomas grew bored and squirmed in Mairead's arms. Just as she was lowering him to the ground, a movement below caught her eye—a body of men, cloaked and with hat brims lowered against the falling snow. Five in all. One drew her like a lodestone. She knew that walk, that confident stride.

"They're here," she called over her shoulder, feeling marvellously relieved. A few hours more, but she'd have those hours. No crying. No misery. Time enough for that later.

Boisterous voices sounded below, Hogendorp's being the loudest. The heavy tread of multiple boots pounded up the stairs. One by one the men filed in, but Mairead only had eyes for one. Iain shrugged off his cloak and shook out the snowflakes. Mairead was already there to take the garment from him to spread it by the fire to dry. His fingers lingered over hers, and she felt a frisson of energy. He smiled down at her with that cherished dimple. When she offered to take the oilskin bag he carried, he pulled it back with a shake of his head. "Later," he said with a wink.

The party settled at the table, and even Hogendorp's wife and her son joined them, the little boy carrying a jar of preserves. Dishes of buttered vegetables, roast fowl and poached fish were passed around, and their glasses were constantly filled with hippocras. Mairead's hunger proved to be shy, and she mostly toyed with her food and sipped sparingly of the sweet wine. Instead, she consumed the bittersweet moment, pressed beside Iain on the bench, revelling in his warmth and loathing the lantern clock that ticked cruelly on.

When the last of the cheese and nuts disappeared, Hogendorp leaned back and patted his rounded stomach. "Excellent, *Mevrouw* Hart. My compliments to you for this fine repast." And to Mairead he said, "Iain tells me you play the violin. A shame you didn't have the wherewithal to play for us on the *Zeelandia*. Play something for us now—something jaunty. I know how you Irish love your exquisite misery."

The request took Mairead by surprise. "I would, gladly, but I don't have an instrument."

Iain smiled and motioned to Killean. "Fetch us the sack, lad."

Killean returned with the oil-skin bag and with a grin passed it to Masterton, who then passed it to Hart, down the length of the table until it reached Iain. Mairead's bemusement turned into speechless wonder when Iain untied the drawstrings and pulled out of the bag a gleaming violin.

Oh! Mairead's breath caught in her throat, and her eyes widened, drinking in the sight of that glorious instrument. "How?" she choked, her gaze flying to Iain's pleased face. *"How?"* This, the only word she could squeak out.

"It's for you. I bargained with the very devil."

Surprise turned to wonder. With trembling hands, Mairead reached out and took the treasure from Iain. Her fingers skimmed over the silken body, caressing its contours with the devotion of a lover. She traced the delicate scrolled head and marvelled at the rosewood pegs. The wood still smelled of new varnish. Not one imperfection marred its surface.

His smile deepened, and he handed her a bow. "Play one last time for me, Mairead."

She blinked away the welling tears and lowered her head to hide her face. She made a few adjustments to the tuning, all the while giving herself a moment to compose herself. Mairead rose to her feet and stepped away from the table, bow poised over the strings.

The violin's tone ran deep and rich and glorious. Mairead started with an old melody, the first song she had ever learned to play, long ago in Galway. The tune had always been charming and lively, yet now a mature, sombre phrasing crept into the melody, transforming it into something new. The song eventually merged into another, tentative at first, like the first stirrings of love, then growing more assured.

The familiar tune of "The Gay Goshawk" filled the room. Mairead wasn't finished with the melody, it seemed, and it insisted on claiming her for its own. She leaned into the song and allowed the melody to carry her away.

Every note tugged at her heartstrings. She could feel Iain's voice in the violin's lower tones. Memories and images flitted through her mind and influenced the way her fingers released the notes. The longing for home was there, but underneath it a deeper longing infused every phrase. Iain framed against the sheaves of cane . . . Iain's profile carved against the darkness of the pond with the wind bending the trees behind him. Iain giving her that first, sudden smile. With every note, she replayed every emotion with loving precision.

When Mairead reached the end, she extended the bow slowly across the strings, drawing the final note out as long as possible. This would be the last song she would ever play for Iain Locharbaidh Johnstone.

Tears pricked her eyes, and she didn't fight against the sadness that washed over her. Mairead's gaze drifted to Iain, who watched her with an intensity that was both vulnerable and pained. Neither could look away.

Chapter 31

———◆———

Mairead waited on the pier, a distance apart, while Iain made his final preparations with the ship's captain, a sharp Frenchman who guaranteed secrecy. Lewis and Hart stood close beside him, occasionally adding comments, while Masterton and Killean appeared anxious to leave, alternatively shuffling and stamping their boots.

The snow had finally subsided, leaving the midnight sky a spray of icy stars. Mairead's breath puffed out as a cloud, and she burrowed deeper into her misery. Every second tore her apart. The moment when she and Iain would have to say their last farewells grew nigh. Would Mairead forget herself and sob in his arms, or would they part quickly with the efficiency of a blade to the heart?

She must not cry. Her tears must not be the last memory he had of her.

Sloshing water sucked and grabbed at the moorings, an underscore to the revelry drifting from the wharf-side taverns. On the pier, a lantern cast a thin yellow light, illuminating the lines of the ship. The sleekness of the vessel made it ideal for slipping in and out of the wild, rocky Scottish coastline or darting away from the larger English vessels patrolling the North Sea.

After a few more exchanges that ended with everyone nodding and shaking hands, Iain left the men and strode down the pier to join Mairead.

She held her breath. This was it. The end of their road. Iain stopped in front of her, less than an arm's length away. Shadows obscured his features, and Mairead couldn't read his expression.

The silence stretched between them until it became unbearable. Finally, Mairead spoke. "Everything is settled?" Her voice sounded strained even to her ears.

"Aye," he replied. "The tide is expected to go out at sunrise."

Mairead stared at the ground, gathering her thoughts. How could she say godspeed, joyful life and all the best? After everything they had been through together? The silence created a void between them, and Mairead rushed to fill it. "Mind Killean. Don't allow Masterton to sour his mind with the words of a crabby old man." She attempted a laugh, but it sounded hollow. "There is still a chance for Killean, to be sure."

"I'll do my best."

"And as for Masterton," she began, clearing her throat, "he has a better chance to weather his wife's storm if she learns of his return from him instead of through clacking tongues. Be sure to tell him that."

After a painful pause, he asked, "And what of me, Mairead? What would you have me know?"

Mairead was determined to keep to the light tone she affected, no matter what it took out of her. "Be safe, Locharbaidh. I know how reckless you can be, and try not to make too many enemies if you can."

Iain took a step closer, and Mairead itched to trace her fingers across his hard-edged jaw. She clenched her fists and kept them against her sides. "I don't know if I can do that, Mouse," he said. "The Southroners bring out the worst in me." His words sounded like a caress.

"Do your best," Mairead replied.

"As you wish." He stepped in and cupped her face between his hands, and her breath hitched in her throat. "Keep playing your fiddle," he whispered. She leaned into him and closed her eyes when he touched his forehead to hers. "You'll always be in my heart."

Mairead choked back a sob and struggled to push her tears aside. She tried to construct a tremulous smile, but it was too painful. "I'll not forget you, Iain." *Every song I play will be for you.*

Iain threaded his fingers through her own and brought them to his lips. Mairead closed her eyes and squeezed his hand.

"You should go," he said gruffly. "'Tis late. Hart is waiting to walk you back."

Mairead nodded, not trusting herself to speak. "Godspeed, Iain Locharbaidh Johnstone," she finally managed before she turned away. Every step was harder than the last, but she pushed on until she reached the end of the pier, where James Hart discreetly waited for her. To her relief, the Englishman didn't try to engage in conversation. He walked silently beside her as she kept her head down, allowing the curve of her hood to serve as a shield.

When they reached their lodgings, Mairead rushed up the creaking stairs to the second floor. Elizabeth waited for them in her night shift and a shawl. The woman had a quick, low conversation with her husband before he took his leave and withdrew into their chambers, leaving the two women alone.

Mairead retreated to the fireplace and sank into a wooden chair. Elizabeth slipped into the chair across from her.

"Can I do anything for you, my dear?"

She forced a wan smile. "You've been very kind. I . . . Please don't pay me any mind. I'll stay up a little longer, if I may."

Elizabeth canted her head and smiled gently. "If you prefer." She removed her woollen shawl and settled it around Mairead's cold shoulders. "If you need anything, do come fetch me. Don't be shy with the hour."

Mairead kept her head lowered and nodded, unable to voice her thanks. She heard the soft patter of Elizabeth's feet, then the scrape of a door shutting.

She gathered her knees to her chest and adjusted the shawl to fully cover herself. Thus cocooned, she watched the dying embers in the hearth glowing orange against the grey ash. The barest breath of air kept them simmering. She should get up and properly bank them, but she couldn't move a muscle, only stared hypnotically at the fire. One hour spun into two as she kept vigil with her memories.

Nearly a year since she had been pulled from her uncle's house. There had been a fire then, destroying her greatest treasure. That had been an innocent Mairead, who believed that the destruction of a varnished piece of wood was too great a tragedy to bear. With every trial, she thought she could not bear it, would surely snap like a dry twig, but against all odds, she had survived. *Only through Iain.* Mairead hugged her knees tighter to her chest.

Her mind wandered to the other night when he had held her and allowed her to cry her heart out in his arms. He had been singing to her in an undertone . . . a familiar song. It now occurred to her that it had been the words from "The Gay Goshawk."

Mairead's eyes widened. The voice. The deep baritone. Then she knew—should have realised from the beginning who had been singing in the hold, so long ago on the *Jane Marie*.

Iain.

It had been he who had given her hope when she thought she was going to die, had wanted to die. His voice, that solid, rich baritone, had tethered her to this world and given her the strength to survive, that day, and by his actions, every day thereafter.

All along, Iain had been her rock and her shore.

And now he was returning to his home, but what of her? Mairead's mettle had been tested, hardened in the fires of hell and back. Fear was slavery, and if she wasn't willing to seize her own

417

destiny, she should have remained in Barbados. Only Mairead O'Coneill could find her own way home.

Mairead unfolded her cramped frame and padded across the floor to the Harts' room. Don't be shy with the hour, Elizabeth had said, and Mairead hoped she meant it. Mairead rapped on the door. She heard a soft shuffling before Elizabeth opened the door, her eyes wide and searching.

"What's wrong?" she asked.

"Home," Mairead whispered. "I want to go home." Then again louder, "I *need* to go home."

Iain stood on deck waiting for the ship to set sail. Dawn was a distant hope on the horizon, and the tide was starting to turn. He leaned, elbows braced against the rail, staring at the rippling water below.

He imagined Mairead tucked under a quilt, still asleep at this hour. Soon the first morning rays would brighten the sky, and he imagined those same rays touching her sunburnt cheeks and scattered freckles. He'd never get that vibrant slip of a woman out of his head.

Iain was finally going home, yet a part of him would never return. That vital piece would remain with Mairead, forever and always. He had told Rupert that the thought of home had sustained him through all those months of bondage, but that wasn't entirely true. Mairead had.

He twisted around his finger a deep brown lock of Mairead's hair, marvelling at the silky texture. He had kept it when she cut it all off. With a sigh, he put it away in his pouch.

"*Lever l'ancre*," the ship's captain called out, then an answering, "*Oui, Capitaine.*"

Iain had heard enough launchings over the last several weeks, and each one held a measure of hope and excitement that he was headed in the right direction. Except now. Every other launching had Mairead standing beside him.

There was a commotion—there always seemed to be one, and each time a result of some complication—but Iain paid them no mind. The sailors sorted it out, for the ship started moving away from the pier.

Instead of facing the city, Iain focused on the warehouses and stalls that lined the harbour. To look back would be to search for a two-storied house in Lau Mazirellaan and the room with diamond-pane windows where Mairead still slept. To do so would inhumanely test his resolve. If he saw the houses slipping away, he might call the captain back and demand to be put ashore. And what would that serve? He needed to return to Scotland, now more of a duty than a heartrending need.

Iain leaned against the rail, and as he watched the ship slice through the waves, he started to hum the melody of "The Gay Goshawk" with the words filling his head. But he could no longer do the ballad justice now that he had heard Mairead play it. The song no longer had the power to soothe; it only made him think of the loss of his love and what he would never have.

He hung his head and closed his eyes. A faint scent of citrus drifted to him, fresh like the morning rains. He sensed a presence behind him before hearing the chorus of the song.

"An' what will be the love-tokens, that ye will send wi' me?"

Iain whirled around to find Mairead standing on the deck a few feet behind him. The ends of her hair lifted and feathered in the wind. Rosebud lips parted;, hazel eyes glowed more green than brown. He could only stare at her, entirely powerless to move, half believing that she was a water deity sprung from the harbour, that if he reached out to touch her, she'd dissolve into the mist. And yet here she was, flesh and blood, freckle by glorious freckle.

He didn't want to question it. He didn't ask the number of obvious questions that burst through his brain—how, why, what was she doing there? Instead, he answered, his voice thick in his throat, "Ye may tell my love I'll send her a kiss."

Mairead's smile became dazzling. "Iain Locharbaidh Johnstone," she said in a clear, singsong voice. "Slayer of sugarcanes; destroyer of hilltop guns; vanquisher of slavery's chains. Lover, loved . . . *my* love." Her gaze softened. "Iain Locharbaidh Johnstone is returning to the land of his fathers . . . with me." Then she closed the distance between them and tipped her head up to look him in the eye. "You're not the only one allowed to take on danger for a cause, and I've proven that I'm equal to the task."

"Mairead—"

She touched her fingers against his mouth to still his words. "You made me a promise, and a Johnstone always keeps their promise, is that not so?"

"Aye, I promised to take you back to Ireland—"

"Not entirely so," she said. "You promised to take me *home*." Her voice softened, and her glance melted him. "You're my home—my rock and my shore."

Iain caught his breath. An overwhelming rush of emotion surged through him. He cleared his throat. "I can't allow this—it's too dangerous, Mairead."

"We survived Barbados—hell on earth. How much worse could Scotland be?"

Iain threw back his head and laughed. "Point."

"Besides, we haven't finished arguing," she said. Now her eyes were large and searching. "Say you love me, Iain. You said it once—when you thought I wouldn't notice. Did you realise that?"

Iain's smile deepened. "I love you, Mouse."

Mairead's smile dazzled him. "Oh, you impossible man." And she pulled him down for a scorching kiss.

Chapter 32

---◆---

The ship anchored off the coast in a small inlet. Low grey clouds had dogged their journey as they sailed along the eastern coast of Scotland, providing Iain only tantalising glimpses of the land. He was eager to show Mairead a view of the land rising from the sea, but the shoreline remained ruggedly stubborn.

Water gently lapped against the prow of the boat as Iain, Mairead, Masterton and Killean made their way to shore. Fine mist steamed from the surface of the water. A hush had fallen in the inlet, broken only by the rhythmic sighing of the surf and the welcoming cry of a gull.

Mairead snuggled against Iain, and he drew her close, the top of her head tucked neatly under his chin. Iain drew a deep breath, filling his lungs with the bite of the cold air and the resinous scent of firs.

Iain savoured this moment. This was what he had been fighting for—the right to return, while not to the southern hills of his homeland, to Scotland nonetheless. He didn't know what the future would hold, but that wouldn't stop him from squeezing out every ounce of joy he could with Mairead. Live in the moment, and never glance back.

As they neared the shore, the clouds lifted and the mist thinned until the land materialised like a bride from her veil. Emerging in the distance, the hills rose dusted with snow. Thick woods skirted at their feet, alive with smoky hues of slate, brown and ochre. Iain heard Mairead's sharp intake of breath.

The oarsman beached the rowboat, and Iain leapt first out of the craft.

"My lady," he said to Mairead and held out his hand for her. Instead of lifting her down into the shallows, he scooped her into his arms and carried her ashore.

Laughing, she kicked and squealed. When they reached the pebbly shore, Iain lowered her to the ground. He linked his fingers through hers until both their hands were clasped. Lifting her hand to his mouth, he pressed a kiss upon her hand.

"We're home, Mairead Johnstone."

Author's Notes

---◆---

Following the last battle of the English Civil War at Worcester, approximately ten thousand Scottish soldiers had been taken prisoner and another three thousand killed. Those who were captured were held in various facilities across England, the majority being at Tothill Fields in Westminster.

Faced with the logistics of having to keep thousands of prisoners, Parliament fell back to the strategy they had employed a year earlier when they captured thousands of Scottish prisoners at Dunbar. Their solution was to transport them to the colonies in the West Indies and North America as indentured servants.

Approximately thirteen hundred Scottish prisoners were shipped from Tothill Fields to Barbados. A large number did not survive the gruelling eight-to-ten-week journey crammed in a hold, and those who did were sold to plantation owners for eight hundred pounds of sugar.

Although today Barbados is a popular vacation destination, in the seventeenth century, being "Barbadoed" was practically a death sentence. The Scots were ill-equipped to deal with the extreme heat and tropical diseases, and the labour-intensive sugarcane fields wore them further down. Those assigned to the fields would be working ten-hour days, six days a week.

We owe our understanding of life in Barbados and on a planation to Richard Ligon. He spent the years between 1647-50 in Barbados and was fascinated by every aspect of the island. He wrote about the day-to-day life of a "Christian servant" (as he referred to indentured servants), as well as all aspects of sugar cultivation, production and trade. Normally, the historical fiction writer needs to glean through various sources to build a world that reflects how people lived in the past, but all this is captured in exquisite detail by Ligon. If you're interested in the history of Barbados during this time, I encourage you to read Ligon's account, *A True & Exact History of the Island of Barbados*, which is available in the public domain.

There have been many discussions devoted to the differences between indentured servants and slaves, particularly as it pertains to those who were in Barbados. While indentured servants were often treated no better than slaves, there is an important legal distinction. A slave remained a slave, while the indentured servant had a defined term to their servitude (between five to seven years) and, in theory, had some rights under the law. That still didn't stop the plantation owners from extending their indentures arbitrarily based on perceived or actual slights, and it didn't spare the bondsman from severe punishments.

Escapes were common amongst both indentured servants and slaves. The extensive caves and the heavily wooded seventeenth century landscape offered both temporary and longer-term shelter. Indentured servants would often attempt to leave the island permanently, either as a stowaway or through trading their labour for passage. Not all succeeded. Sometimes the escapees found themselves sold to another plantation on another island.

It wasn't only Scottish POWs who were sent down to Barbados. The English had invaded Ireland to eradicate all Royalist support for King Charles II. In August 1652, after the remaining resistance crumbled, the English Commonwealth enacted the Act of Settlement, allowing for the wide-scale redistribution of Irish lands to

English supporters. Over the next several years, entire families would be dispossessed and forced to relocate to provinces in the west, such as Connaught. Those who did not go voluntarily found themselves transported to English colonies, the West Indies in particular. It has been estimated that over fifty thousand Irish were forcibly removed from Ireland.

Severed Knot is a work of historical fiction, and I've been as faithful as possible to the history, but it is first and foremost a story. As a result, certain minor liberties have been taken. Iain Johnstone is a fictional character, but I've made him the kinsman of Lord Johnstone, the Earl of Hartfell. Lord Johnstone was a Scottish nobleman who was a supporter of King Charles I. I've been interested in the history of this Border clan with their reiving history, and I trust they won't object to Iain sharing their heritage.

Under the category of historically accurate but requiring clarification, the modern version of the drink mobbie is different than the drink they referred to as mobbie in the seventeenth century. Ligon referred to it as a "drink made of potatoes" (likely sweet potatoes or yams), its strength being made stronger or "smaller" depending on the concentration used in its brewing. He likened it as just short of the strength of Rhenish wine.

For the principal towns in Barbados, I've opted to follow how they are referenced during the seventeenth century. Ligon refers to Bridgetown as "The Bridge" or occasionally "The Town". I wanted to keep the flavour of the time without creating confusion in the narrative, hence I've called it Bridge Town. Likewise, Speightstown was referred to in correspondences at that time as "Speight's Town".

In Ligon's time, plantation owners would go aboard a newly arrived ship to purchase their indentured servants. A decade later when the slave trade was in full swing, slaves and indentured servants were auctioned in the merchant's yard in Bridgetown. For *Severed Knot*, I've followed the later-day practice. With the volume of prisoners being shipped down after the war, it made more logistical sense to transact at a central location.

The attack on Antigua harbour by Prince Rupert is a historical event. On October 30, 1652, Rupert sent an advance strike force of fifty men, led by Captain Holmes, to disable the guns that protected Five Island Harbour, to allow his ship, the *Swallow,* along with a captured prize, to seize the harbour and the two English vessels anchored there. I have made free with these two English ships, re-imagining them as the fictional *Redemption* and *Zeelandia.* Prince Rupert of the Rhine is a fascinating historical figure, and my only regret was not being able to give him more page-time in *Severed Knot.* If you're interested in learning more about this man, I highly recommend the non-fiction biography *Prince Rupert: The Last Cavalier,* by Charles Spencer.

One final note on how quickly (or slowly) news travelled from England and the Continent to the West Indies. Although trade disputes were brewing between England and the Dutch since October 1651, the first Dutch-Anglo war finally broke out in July 1652. I have the news reaching Barbados a few months later, which is consistent with accounts of when Prince Rupert first learned of it. Even though he had been in the West Indies since the outbreak of war, the news only reached him in mid-October.

If you're interested in learning more about the history of this time, visit my website www.cryssabazos.com for articles and links to historical resources.

Thank you for reading *Severed Knot.* I hope you enjoyed the story as much as I enjoyed writing it.

Cryssa Bazos

Acknowledgments

———◆———

It takes a village to nurture a writer. I am deeply grateful for everyone who has been there for me, and especially for all the readers who have wanted more.

First and foremost, I'd like to thank my husband, Angelo, for being my foundation and for always believing in me. Without his unflagging support, none of this would be possible. He is my rock and my shore.

I'd also like to thank the members of my critique group, Gwen Tuinman, Andrew Varga, and Connie DiPietro for pushing me to do my best work. A warm thank you to Elizabeth St. John who kindly read progressive drafts of this novel. It's quite possible that Iain loves her more than he does me.

A special thank you to Ben Tuinman who provided the name of my Dutch captain and his ship. I grew very fond of Karel Hogendorp, and I expect that I won't see the last of him or the *Zeelandia*.

I'd also like to thank my dear friends Sharon Overend, Pat Ward, Denice Morris, and Lora Avgeris for their continued interest and support. A loving thank you to my aunts: Penelope Karkoulis, who transformed her balcony into a writing retreat, complete with trusty companion Luna, and Danae Marinakis, my biggest advocate.

A huge thank you to the lovely Jenny Quinlan, aka Jenny Q, of Historical Editorial who worked with me on *Severed Knot* from beginning to end, as both an editor and a cover designer. She understood my vision and, thanks to her collaboration, helped me deliver it.

I would also like to thank the Historical Novel Society and the 2018 New Novel Award for selecting *Severed Knot* for the long list. It was a distinctive honour to be included, and it gave me the burst of confidence that I needed to push to the end.

Last, but truly not least, a very special acknowledgment goes to Jay Stewart who passed away before his stories were complete. Jay was a member of our critique group and had a gift for storytelling and creating vibrant characters. He carried in his heart a deep love for Barbados, her people and history. In his honour, and with his permission, I adopted his main character, Killean Ross, and gave him a place in my story. For Jay, I brought Killean home.

About the author

––––◆––––

Cryssa Bazos is an award winning historical fiction author and 17th century enthusiast with a particular interest in the English Civil War. She is a member of the Historical Novel Society, the Romantic Novelist Association and is a co-editor and contributor of the English Historical Fiction Authors blog. Her debut novel, *Traitor's Knot*, is published by Endeavour Media. Traitor's Knot is the Medalist winner of the 2017 New Apple Award (historical fiction), a finalist for the 2018 EPIC eBook Awards (historical romance) and the RNA Joan Hessayon Award. Her second novel, *Severed Knot*, was long listed for the Historical Novel Society 2018 New Novel Award.

More from the author

Traitor's Knot

England 1650: Civil War has given way to an uneasy peace in the year since Parliament executed King Charles I.

Royalist officer James Hart refuses to accept the tyranny of the new government, and to raise funds for the restoration of the king's son, he takes to the road as a highwayman.

Elizabeth Seton has long been shunned for being a traitor's daughter. In the midst of the new order, she risks her life by sheltering fugitives from Parliament in a garrison town. But her attempts to rebuild her life are threatened, first by her own sense of injustice, then by falling in love with the dashing Hart.

The lovers' loyalty is tested through war, defeat and separation. James must fight his way back to the woman he loves, while Elizabeth will do anything to save him, even if it means sacrificing herself.

Traitor's Knot is a sweeping tale of love and conflicted loyalties set against the turmoil of the English Civil War.

Traitor's Knot is available through Amazon.

Printed in Great Britain
by Amazon